KADE

BOOK FOURTEEN OF
THE FALLEN WORLD

Christopher Woods

Blood Moon Press
Coinjock, NC

Chris Kennedy/Blood Moon Press
1097 Waterlily Rd.
Coinjock, NC 27923
http://chriskennedypublishing.com/

Publisher's Note: This is a work of fiction. Names, characters, places, and incidents are a product of the author's imagination. Locales and public names are sometimes used for atmospheric purposes. Any resemblance to actual people, living or dead, or to businesses, companies, events, institutions, or locales is completely coincidental.

Cover Design by Elartwyne Estole.

Ordering Information:
Quantity sales. Special discounts are available on quantity purchases by corporations, associations, and others. For details, contact the "Special Sales Department" at the address above.

Kade/Christopher Woods -- 1st ed.
ISBN: 978-1648551277

This Fallen World: Kade

Chapter One

I walked down the dreary street. Smoke hung in the air from the fires burning in the alleys. They led back into dark corners filled with the people less fortunate than those who resided in the buildings alongside.

Before the fall, those in the street would have been rounded up and hauled away in vehicles to be incarcerated. Now, twenty years later, you'd find a better grade of people living in the alleys than the ones inside the buildings. Hell, maybe it wasn't so different.

Those who had inhabited the city twenty years ago were pretty despicable. I know this because I was one of the bastards. How things change.

"Fresh fruit, mister?" a voice asked from my right.

I glanced toward the young girl with an apron full of apples, then pulled one of the apples from her apron. As I polished the apple on the lapel of my long coat, I listened for the telltale buzz from my rad marker. There was no buzz, so I handed the girl a coin.

"Wow," she said. "Is that an Old World coin?"

"They called 'em quarters," I answered. "Worth twenty scrip. Take that and hide it well. There's a grocery store over on K Street. He'll change it for you. He's good people."

She pulled a bag from her pocket and dropped the rest of the apples into it. She handed it to me.

"Mister, that's ten times the worth of the whole bunch," she said. "Thank you."

She slipped the quarter into a pocket and disappeared into the crowd.

I continued my trek down J Street. I couldn't spread too many of the coins I had found around too quickly. I had many more where that one had come from, but if word got out I was spending a lot of Old World coins, one of the Warlords would surely come down on me.

It didn't hurt to help the people around me when I could, though. Most of the good will I had around the city had come from similar acts. Those on the street didn't have much, and when I helped them, they remembered. There will be a time I'll need help, and there are quite a few people who will remember.

J Street crossed Third Avenue ahead of me, and my destination wasn't far down Third. There was a bar called the Strike Zone there. My contact said he had a man who wanted to meet me about a job. I tended to use the Strike Zone as a meeting place for potential customers.

I had helped the owner find his kidnapped wife eight years ago, and he kept a booth unoccupied for me to use at any time. Good will is a priceless commodity in a fallen world.

I came within view of the bar, and there were crowds of people waiting to enter. Some things never change. People search for escape from reality in any world, fallen or not.

The doorman nodded as I strode past the line of waiting patrons, some of which yelled in anger.

"Kade," he said as I reached him. "Welcome, as always. Your booth is clear, and there is a guest awaiting your arrival."

"Thanks, Sam," I said and walked into the noisy, smoke-filled room.

I made my way across the large room, full of dancing men and women. The pounding music was some sort of digital music created in the Old World. Several years back, I had found a stash of Old World music discs. I had traded most of the discs to Jared McKnight, the owner of the Strike Zone. I had kept a small collection of a style of music called blues. I liked the Old World blues music. Most of the rest had been dance music of some sort or another. Some digital, some of what they had called country, R&B, and hip-hop. I didn't care for most of those.

The Old World music had brought crowds of people into the Strike Zone, and Jared had been making money hand over fist. Then the local Warlord had stepped in and began taxing Jared to keep his bar open. Now, Jared made enough to get by, but not much more.

"Kade!" Jared's voice boomed across the room.

I looked to my right and saw Jared waving at me. He was pushing through the crowd toward me.

"Mathew Kade," he said with a huge smile. "A sight for sore eyes!"

"How are ya, Jared?" I asked.

"Could be better, but I'm still here."

"How's Jenny?"

"Pregnant."

"Really?" I asked with a smile. "Congratulations, my friend!"

"Thanks, Kade," he said. "It never woulda happened without you."

"I'm pretty sure I didn't have anything to do with that."

His laugh boomed across the room again.

"True enough," he said. "But you found her for me, Kade. I can never thank you enough for that. And now, I'm about to be a father."

"You deserve it, man," I said. "Take good care of 'em."

"Will do," he said. "I'll be by your table in a few. Had a little episode I had to deal with. Someone didn't like my reservation policy."

"I'll talk to ya then," I said and made my way to the conspicuously empty booth in the back.

As I slid into the booth, I could see two people taking an interest in me. One was an older gentleman in an old suit. The other was a young man with a perpetual snarl on his face.

I motioned to the older gentleman, and he made his way toward my booth.

"Mathew Kade," I said, with my hand outstretched. "I understand you have a job for me?"

"Yes, I do," he said. "My name is Cedric Hale. I need you to find my daughter. She disappeared three days ago, and I haven't been able to find a single clue as to where she has gone."

I motioned for him to have a seat.

"What made you search me out for this job?"

"I worked for a company called Obsidian," he said.

My eyes narrowed.

"I'm not here to let your secret out, Mr. Kade," he said. "I know what you were. I know what happened to you. It's amazing you were able to rebuild your psyche into something more than that of a drooling vegetable. Yet you did. You have the skills to find my daughter, no matter where she is."

"You know a lot about me, Hale," I said, "and I'm not very comfortable with that."

"When the end came, I know you were still in the imprinter, and it scrambled your brain," he said. "I also know you spent some time inside the Obsidian building, under treatment for serious mental illness. No one knows how you did it, Mr. Kade. Treatment did nothing and then, one day, you just stood up and became Mathew Kade.

"I'm not here to blackmail you or any such nonsense," he continued. "I just know what you were capable of before the Fall. If you have a fraction of that capability now, you can find my daughter."

A commotion on the floor caught my eye, and a bottle flew across the room. I came to my feet and caught the bottle in my left hand.

For just a second, I was someone else. The young man with the perpetual snarl was staring into the cold, dead eyes of someone entirely different from the man who had been sitting at the table. His eyes widened in fear, and he ran into the crowd.

After a moment, I sat back down.

Hale was smiling. "A fraction."

I stared at him in silence.

He placed a coin in front of me. I looked at it in surprise. It was a solid gold coin from the Old World. Probably worth ten thousand scrip now.

"This is a down payment," Hale said. "You find her, you get another. Return her to me unharmed, you get three."

"I'll see what I can do."

"Thank you, Agent," he said softly.

I nodded.

He passed me a folder, and I opened it and saw a picture of a pretty, young, red-haired woman. She appeared to be in her late teens or early twenties, and that could be bad. This fallen world is hard on young, beautiful people.

Warlords could swoop in with their troops and steal people at will. They were Warlords because they held the weapons or tech that gave them control over those around them.

There had been incidents for years. I had a great disdain for the term, Warlord. They were the ones who had found some advantage and abused it, for the most part.

There were a few good men, such as Wilderman, who held the reins of fourteen city blocks. He taxed his people, but he also provided true protection to those who lived in his domain.

Miles to the east, there was Joanna Kathrop. She held sixteen blocks and ruled with an iron fist. She had found a cache of weapons and provisions in her area several decades back. Her cadre of loyal soldiers backed her, and she had established her rule of that area.

There were others, both good and bad. Most of them were bad. They ran single and double blocks. The Warlord who controlled the area where the Strike Zone was located wasn't the worst, but he was far from the best.

I turned the page and found the sector where Hale and his daughter lived.

"You were under Yamato?" I asked.

"Yes," he said. "He took down the Bishop a decade ago."

"Yamato's always been fair," I said. "Did you take this to him?"

"He couldn't help me," Hale said. "She was traveling across the city."

"What the hell was she doin' travelin'?" I asked. "Was she in a Caravan?"

The Caravans were the only semi-safe way to travel the city. You paid for your ticket, and the Caravans paid a tax to run through the Zones.

"She was going to the new college, set up by Kathrop, in a small Caravan run by a man named Drekk. He claims she never showed up for the last leg of the trip."

"Drekk." I spat the word out. "I've heard of Drekk. If you want to travel anywhere, you have to use the accredited Caravans. You can't use people like Drekk."

His face fell. "We didn't know until it was too late. We aren't rich people, Mister Kade."

I looked down at the coin still in my hand, then looked back at him with one eyebrow raised.

"The life savings of both my family and the family of Seran Yoto, her fiancée."

"Poor would not be what I would call this, Hale," I said. "There are people in this room who won't see this much wealth in ten lifetimes. You dwell inside the Scraper. You have running water and electricity. Don't ever try to pass yourself off as poor. It's insulting."

He nodded.

"Who set up the Caravan?"

"I set it up through a man in the Scraper. His name is Denton. He owns a supply store on the bottom floor."

"Ok," I said. "That's where I'll need to start. I'll be there first thing in the morning."

"But the Caravans don't run at night…"

"Some people are safer to leave alone, Hale. When you get back to the Scraper, tomorrow, I'll have some answers for you."

"How will you cross three Zones tonight?"

"I'll walk, Hale," I said. "Corporate Agents can take care of themselves."

"You haven't been an Agent for twenty years."

"You're right, there," I said. "I'm something else, now. I'll see you tomorrow night at your Scraper."

I stood and walked away from the booth. Jared was beside the bar, talking to several suits.

"Yo, Jared," I said. "I'm on a job for a few days. Ya can fill the table if ya need to."

"Be careful, Matt," he said. "Last time, it took Jenny a week to patch you up."

"I'll try, buddy."

I had a feeling about this one. Things looked bad for Maddy Hale. Drekk wasn't known to be trustworthy.

Life can be dangerous in this Fallen World.

* * * * *

Chapter Two

I started walking back up the Avenue toward J Street. There, I turned toward the west. I took a pack of Nic-Stiks from my pocket and lit one up. Cigarettes had been outlawed nearly fifty years ago, but they had made a comeback after the Fall. I wasn't quite sure why I knew that.

As I passed a group huddled around a trash can of burning refuse, I took the bag of apples I was still carrying and handed one to each person. I took the others over to several people huddled against the wall.

"Rad-free," I said and pulled my rad marker from my pocket and held it up.

They all began eating what was probably the first fruit they had eaten in months. I nodded to them and continued west. I could travel that direction through one Zone, but I would have to bypass the next one by heading north. Anyone who set foot in Derris' Zone would wind up eaten. A south bypass was also out of the question. I imagined Blechley was still pissed at me after I broke his collarbone and killed three of his lieutenants last year.

My eyes roved across the street as I continued. Shadows darted along the left side. They thought I was an easy mark. My whole body was taut as I waited for the rush from behind. The shadows were the diversion, the true danger was from the rear.

I heard a slight scrape, and I dropped to the ground, three feet to the right, crouched. They hadn't adjusted, and they plowed through the spot where I had been.

"You get one warning," I said. I flipped my wrist, and my straight razor snapped open in my right hand. "Walk away or die."

My voice was calm, and I waited for a second. Then I stepped forward, toward the two men in the street. They turned and fled. Nine out of ten fights are avoided by the lack of fear someone senses in their prey. The straight razor was for the tenth.

A familiar voice came from the darkness. "One of these days, they're not gonna run, Kade."

"True enough, Wilson," I said. "What are you doin' out here?"

"The boss sent me to back you up."

"And why would Teresa do something like that?"

"She heard you were on the job and remembered the last time. She kinda likes you for some odd reason."

I chuckled. "It's my charming personalities."

"Probably," Wilson Poe answered. "Either way, I'm here to back you up. I can go with you or follow along behind, but I'm coming."

"May as well come with me," I said. "Keep me from talkin' to myselves."

Wilson walked out of the dark. He was six feet tall and built like a tank. I didn't foresee anyone wanting to tangle with Wilson. He didn't stand out at night because he wore black pants and a black sweater and his skin was almost as dark as his clothes.

"You could try to blend in with the night a little better," he said. "Who the hell wears a tan trench coat and walks the streets at night?"

"Not many people," I said. "This way, people know what they're about to get into."

"With one of the local Warlords pissed at you," he said, "maybe you should try *not* to stick out."

"What makes ya think Simon is still pissed at me?"

"You *did* break his collarbone."

"He's still alive."

"You made the man beg, Kade."

"No," I said. "He chose to beg. I didn't plan to kill him. He begged on his own."

"Somehow, I don't think he sees it that way, Kade."

"His boys shot me three times," I said. "I killed a lieutenant for each bullet. Now, why would I do that if I didn't plan on letting him live to learn from the lesson? He can't blame me for the begging."

Wilson chuckled. "I guess he should have studied a little Kade logic before he shot you."

"Exactly."

"You see the guy on the right?"

"Yep."

I flipped open the straight razor and started cleaning my nails with it as I passed under the streetlight. The form slid back into the shadows, silently.

"I really need to get me one of those," Wilson said.

"Very handy tool."

"No doubt," he said.

He tapped the two-handed sword across his back. It was enormous. "This tends to make them think before starting a ruckus."

"Not as useful in close quarters," I said.

"If they get in close quarters with me, they deserve what they get."

"Ya gotta point," I said. I had seen Wilson lift the side of a car before. If they got close to the man, he would break them in two...or three.

We were nearing the border of Derris' Zone.

"Gotta head north on Twelfth," I said. "Don't feel like takin' on Derris' bunch."

"One of these days, someone is going to have to do something about that place."

"True," I said. "I don't think I wanna take that on tonight, though."

"I don't want to either," he said. "When you decide to, make sure to let me know so I can go on a vacation. Somewhere far away."

"Shit no," I said. "That's at least a two-man operation."

"I would hesitate with two thousand men."

"Where's your sense of adventure?"

He shook his head. "I can't believe she likes you this much."

"She's always trying to help the 'special' ones. She's got too big of a heart. She loves puppies."

"We talking about the same woman?"

"I think so," I said. "Teresa Manora...beautiful...blonde...great big..."

He looked at me with the look he gives those that may be broken in half soon.

"Heart...I was gonna say heart. Where's your mind at, Wilson?"

"Sure, you were," he said. "Teresa Manora, Matron of the Society of the Sword. She has iron in her blood, steel in her bones. The Warlords tread lightly around her."

"Yeah, that's the one," I said, "and she loves puppies."

"How are you not dead?"

"Just lucky, I guess."

"You would have to be."

We made the turn up Twelfth Street. This would bring us into the Zone of Zane Palmer. He wasn't the nicest guy, but there were far worse. His guys were a bunch of punks, but most of them were held in check by Zane. One of his standing rules was, if one of his guys picked a fight and lost, he wasn't worth the money he was earning. He didn't tell them not to pick fights, just not to pick fights they would lose.

The only problem with such a rule was that a lot of punks had overinflated opinions of themselves. If we were lucky, there wouldn't be any incidents.

"Think we can get by Zane's guys without one of 'em being stupid?" Wilson asked.

"I doubt it," I said. "Ya know how they travel. In packs. Their stupidity feeds off each other's."

"A guy can hope," he said.

"Always expect the worst," I said. "You'll never be disappointed."

"That's a pretty crappy outlook on life, Kade."

"Rarely am I disappointed," I said. "Look to your three o'clock."

"Yeah, I see 'em," he said. "I was hoping for the best."

"Now, you're disappointed."

"Shut up."

"I'm not disappointed."

"Shut up."

We spread apart to give ourselves room to move. There's a time to try to talk your way out of a fight, and there's a time to just prepare and let things run their course. The one rule we had to follow was simple. They attack, we kill them. If we attack, the whole Zone becomes hostile.

There were only ten. I decided I wouldn't need to call up any reinforcements. I waited patiently as the crowd of punks swaggered across the open ground between us.

"Mathew Kade." The one in the lead stopped about ten feet from me.

"You know who I am," I said and looked past him. "And you only brought nine others?"

"I won't need no help for the likes of you, Kade."

"You really want to try by yourself?"

"I want that bounty all to myself," he said.

"Your funeral," I said. "Wilson, hold back unless anyone else decides to join in. I would hate for this idiot to have to share his bounty."

"You got it, Kade." He drew the huge sword from his back and stepped to the side.

"Go for it, boy," I said, my razor resting lightly in my right hand.

He lunged forward with a gleaming blade in his hand. I stepped by him in a flash, and he continued his lunge and landed face-first on the cracked cement. He tried to push himself to his hands and knees, but there was a wet splash as his intestines hit the concrete under him. There was a whimper, not from the dying punk, but one of the others facing me. I stood there with my head cocked to the side, as if I were listening to someone.

"Who would like to try to earn that bounty, next?" I asked. "Or would you like to try to earn a nine-way split...well...more like a four-way. I'll definitely get five of you. Of course, my friend will get the rest. So, it's really a lose-lose situation for you boys."

They turned and fled, leaving their erstwhile companion lying in his own intestines.

She's a cold bitch, this Fallen World.

* * * * *

Chapter Three

"**Y**ou didn't even get anything on your coat," Wilson said.

"I try not to," I said. "These are expensive. Hard to find."

"No doubt," he said. "No one else wears anything so useless. It has to get in the way with all the floppin' around your legs."

I just stared at him.

"Sorry," he said. "That must be one of those rules of yours. Kade's Rule, Number Twelve. Don't insult the useless coat that will probably get Kade killed at some point."

"I see how you wanna be," I said. "You're just jealous. You can't have one. They don't make 'em big enough to make a circus tent."

Wilson got very quiet.

"Pre-Fall nonsense," I said. "Sorry, I find I have random knowledge of the world before the Fall. Nobody wants to think about the Circus."

"There was a Circus before the Fall?"

"There were a lot of 'em," I said. "Not like this perverted version we have now. It was a place where people had a fun time, watching others do tricks and things. Did you know that clowns were even funny things back then?"

"My God," Wilson said.

We lost a lot when the Old World fell. Many of the things I have random memories of simply didn't exist anymore.

"You're young, Wilson," I said. "What? Twenty?"

"Twenty-three," he said. "I don't remember any of the world before the Fall. I was a baby when the Corporate Wars hit their final climax. The nukes took out so much of the world."

"There aren't many cities left," I said. "We got lucky, here. There's the Rad Zone to the north. If the nukes had hit fifty miles further south, there wouldn't be anything left here.

"Sometimes, I think it was for the best," I added. "The Corporate War had consumed everything in its path. I'm not sure they even knew what they were fightin' for anymore."

"How the hell do you know all this shit?" Wilson shook his head. "You're not that old."

"You'd be surprised how old I am," I said.

Wilson looked off to our left. "You see 'em?"

"Yeah," I said. "Only two of 'em."

"Some people are better off left alone," a voice said from the pair of shadows.

"Come on out," Wilson said, "and we'll talk about it."

"I'll keep my distance for a moment yet," the voice returned. "It has come to my attention that Kade is traveling tonight. I felt it would be easier to escort you through my territory than it would be to lose as many men as it would cost to collect a certain bounty."

"You must be Palmer," I said.

"Zane, if you please."

"Ok, Zane," I said. "I'm just passin' through. There's really no need for violence. Your boy back there was determined."

There was a sigh, and Zane stepped out into the light. "I hoped I would get here before any of my idiots."

"You sound disappointed," I said.

"Not this again," Wilson said.

Zane looked at us with one eyebrow raised.

"It's one of his stupid rules," Wilson said. "Expect the worst, and you'll never be disappointed."

Zane chuckled. "That is a sad outlook on life, Mister Kade."

"That's what I've been saying," Wilson said.

"Who, here, is disappointed?" I asked. "Not me."

Wilson sighed.

"You're welcome to join us, Zane," I said. "You can come along, down to Yamato's, if you want."

"I'll have to pass on that," Zane said. "Yamato is a little upset with me at the moment. Something of a romantic nature has occurred between my son and his daughter. These sorts of things tend to cause a little bad blood."

"Hopefully, you can work it out," Wilson said.

"Expect a full-scale war," I said. "You won't be disappointed by whatever ends you may reach."

"You travel with him willingly?" Zane asked Wilson.

"My boss ordered me to."

"That would explain it."

I shrugged and continued walking.

There was some activity around the Scraper as we came nearer to the center of Zane's Zone. It wasn't any of his men; it was merchants setting up stalls along the foot of the Scraper.

"Farmers comin' in tomorrow?" I asked.

"That they are," Zane said. "Should be a prosperous day for me. We've done well this month, and I should be able to buy extra stores this time."

For those in the Scraper, I was sure. Those on the street had to do the best they could. But the Farmers were a boon to the street dwellers, too. They sold to all and were protected by all.

If the Farmers quit coming, the city would starve. They kept their own militia and guarded their Caravans quite well. There was, occasionally, an idiot who would try a run at a Farmer Caravan. The roads would be littered with dead, and the Farmers would roll on through. Whatever Zone they were in when attacked would not be visited that month, and the neighboring Zones would be rationed to barely enough to get by.

It was in everybody's best interest to leave the Farmers be. Anyone caught messing with the Farmers would be dealt with, severely.

Eight years past, one of the Farmer's daughters had been kidnapped from the Caravan. The Caravan had stopped and sent word home. Half a day later, five hundred seasoned Farmer warriors had descended on the Zone. The search that ensued ended after they found her raped and murdered.

That was the only time I had ever worked for the Farmers. They had sent a representative and hired me to find out who had done the deed. During my investigation, I had found a pearl that belonged to her in a crack in the floor of the room of the head of the Warlord's Guard.

The Farmers had left with two heads on pikes. The heads of the guard and the Warlord's son. The Warlord was told he would be left alive to prevent any other transgressions against the Farmers. If he failed to prevent even a minor transgression, his head, and the heads of every member of his family, would join the son's.

No one messes with the Farmers.

The days when the Farmers are in a Zone are usually the most peaceful days a Zone ever sees.

"It's a good day when the Farmers come to the Zone," I said. "I think they're scheduled to come to our Zone next week."

"True," Wilson said. "Sure to be a very good week."

Truer than he might think. The Farmers were the only ones I could take a large amount of Old World coins to and sell them. They, as a rule, kept every transaction secret.

We continued onward to the west. We were nearing the boundary of Zane's territory.

"Can I ask a question?" he asked.

"You can ask."

He chuckled. "This bounty on your head. Is it true you killed three of his men and broke his collarbone?"

"Fairly close to true," I said.

"It sounds like there's more."

"He was looking for a Society kid," Wilson said. "He found where they were holding him. It was a couple of Blechley's lieutenants. When he went to retrieve the kid, he was shot three times by Blechley's men."

"He took the kid and hid him. Then he went to Blechley's Scraper. He cornered Blechley and killed three of his lieutenants, right in front of him. One for each bullet. Then he took a two-foot spike and hung Blechley from the wall of his throne room by the right shoulder, thus breaking the man's collarbone."

"Jesus, Kade," Zane said.

"Then he fetched the kid and returned him to our Zone."

"After being shot three times?"

"He's hard to kill."

"It would be easier if people would just do the right thing," I said.

"You have a better chance of Dynamo granting free power to your Zone."

"That would be something for the record books," Wilson said.

"True," I said. "Nothin' is free from Dynamo."

Dynamo was the guy who had gotten control of the old electric plants in the center of the city. His Zone supplied a great deal of the city's power. There were some Scrapers with windmills and solar cells, but they couldn't supply enough power to run a Scraper in comfort. So, every Warlord paid their tax to Dynamo. You could get by without his supplied power, but no one in the Scrapers wanted to give up the comforts of running water or climate control.

We reached the edge of Palmer's Zone. He turned to me. "Good luck, Kade. Watch your back; that bounty is a hundred K."

"He really wants me dead," I said.

"You should have killed him."

"If I'd killed him, he wouldn't have learned anything."

"Seems he didn't learn the right lesson from his last encounter with you," Zane said.

"He may need another lesson."

Zane shook his head and held his hand out. "Good meeting you, Kade."

I grasped his hand. "Same here, Zane. Take good care of your people, and you'll do well."

He nodded and strode into the darkness. Several shadows that had been tailing us converged on the track he had taken.

"I must be slipping," Wilson said. "I only saw two. There were four."

"Five," I said. "And they were good. Probably some of his lieutenants."

"Damn, I really am slipping."

"I barely caught on to the fifth one," I said. "She's slick."

"She?"

"Yeah," I said. "She smelled like roses."

"Damn it, man."

We headed back to the south on Seventeenth Avenue. From there, we would pick up J Street once more. J Street led straight to Yamato's Scraper.

"A hundred K is pretty high, Kade," Wilson said. "I wouldn't be surprised if we run into a lot of trouble over the next few days."

"You plan on workin' this whole case with me?"

"I wasn't until I heard about this bounty," he said. "I don't think the boss would appreciate it if I left and you got all killed and shit."

"I can take care of myself," I said. "But don't think, for a second, I don't appreciate the help. It certainly helps to have someone I trust at my back. The problem is, I don't know where this is goin' before it's over."

"Guess we'll just have to wait and see."

"We'll run into another bounty hunter before we reach the Scraper," I said.

"Plan for the worst?"

I scowled as a group of bounty hunters strode into the lighted street from the shadows ahead of us.

"Not disappointed."

"Shut up."

"Do we have to wait for them to attack?" Wilson asked.

"Hell no," I said. "That's Corso and his pack."

Corso was a well-known figure. He made a business of hunting those with bounties on their heads. He usually stayed out of the more respected Zones, but a hundred K must have been more temptation than he could stand. A pity.

"Good," Wilson said and pulled his massive sword from his back. "I was getting bored."

I thought about reinforcements but chose to handle this one myself. Who needed reinforcements when you had Wilson? I glided toward the group with my razor in my right hand.

I think they had planned some sort of threat session or something, because there were a lot of surprised faces when a six-foot-tall tank slammed into their midst, with four feet of sharpened steel, covering a six-foot arc in front of him.

They tried to scatter, but Wilson pulled his blade through an equally devastating backswing. Several tried to get behind him, and I glided by them. The first tripped as his hamstrings were severed. The other didn't have time to react before I was behind him, and my left hand snaked around his neck to pull his chin backward. The right made a lightning slice across his windpipe.

Properly slitting a throat is a learned skill. You cut too deep, your blade hits bone and dulls. Too shallow, and your victim isn't dead. I like to slide that little extra distance around the side and catch the carotid as well. My own version of the double tap.

I slipped away from my victim and ducked down. I slid my razor along the left side of the man I had hamstrung, just deep enough to slice about halfway through his kidney.

His screams told me he was out of this one.

Corso carried a pistol. It was an older weapon called a revolver. He was taking aim at me, so I moved. The shot went wide to my left, as I had gone right. I dove forward and down as the second bullet screamed over my head. I rolled and launched myself left this time, and his next shot was wide again. I felt the next one tug at the bottom of my coat just as I reached him. My blade sliced from his straddle, straight up to his sternum, as another shot whistled past my ear.

I snatched the gun with my left hand as I passed him on his right side, and his insides tumbled into the street. With a deft move of my left hand, I flipped the gun into a firing position and shot Corso's second-in-command right between her beautiful blue eyes.

Make your choices wisely. Consequences are deadly in this Fallen World.

* * * * *

Chapter Four

I dusted my coat off and looked, sadly, at the single hole near the hem along the bottom.

"You still don't have any blood on your coat," Wilson said.

"Yeah, but look at this," I said, with my finger poking through the hole.

"I think you'll be fine," he said. "You can hardly see it."

I sighed. "Maybe I should start a tab for Simon to pay when I go visit."

Wilson chuckled. "You are kidding, right?"

I stared at him.

He shook his head, and we resumed our trek. The screams of Corso's pack had become whimpers and moans by then. Soon, we had walked out of earshot of even those.

"I got blood all over me," Wilson said.

"Good thing you wear black," I said. "It takes a certain finesse to wear light colors. I'm pretty sure that thing can't be wielded with anywhere near the finesse it would take. Stick to black."

"Four people and not a drop of blood on the coat," he said with a shake of his head.

"If it wasn't for the rollin' on the ground, I'd get a white one."

"I don't doubt that."

"Looks like we made it to Yamato's," I said.

The huge Scraper we were nearing was bigger than any in our own Zone. "The Old World used to call them skyscrapers. Just another of those useless facts floating around in my noggin."

"I can see that," he said. "They are so tall, they scrape the sky."

"I think that was the idea," I said. "They date back to before the Corporate Wars. They used to house businesses in the old days. Then, later, they became the seats of power for the Corporations. Now, as it was then, the wealthy reside in the Scrapers. The poor do the best they can."

"How do you know all this shit?"

"Too many imprints, each with its own small pieces of knowledge," I muttered.

"Imprints?"

"Maybe I'll tell ya about it someday," I said. "There's some work needin' to be done here first."

"How 'bout you tell me what this case is?" he asked. "I seem to have been volunteered for a mission I know nothing about."

"Kidnapped girl, stolen from a Caravan. There's a shopkeeper here who set her up with Drekk."

"Drekk!" He spat the word out.

"I had pretty much the same reaction," I said. "First, I'm gonna find out if this shopkeeper is stupid or if he set up Hale to lose a daughter."

"Hold!" the guard just outside the main entrance to the Scraper said. "It's a little late for visitors."

I slipped a ten scrip into his hand as I shook hands with him.

"Just a little business to conduct," I said, "then we'll be on our way."

He nodded and motioned for us to proceed. This part was easy if you had a few scrip. Without them, I would have had to bring some form of proof I was working for Cedric Hale. Easier to just bribe your way in.

I held up a five scrip. "Can ya point me in the direction of a shop owned by a guy named Denton?"

"Sure thing," he said, and the scrip disappeared. "Straight to the back, last shop on the left. He's closed this late, but he lives in the shop. He may open up if you wake him."

"He'll open," I said. "Later, Guardsman."

"Keep out of trouble."

"You just spent a day's wages in the tunnels," Wilson said as we entered the Scraper. "Must be getting paid well for this one."

"I'm thinkin' Denton is gonna be more than happy to reimburse me," I said.

"Already convinced he's dirty?"

"Fairly certain," I said. "We both know how Drekk works."

"True enough," he said. "He usually stays away from the wealthier ones."

"Maybe he's trying to move up in the world," I said. "If so, he's just started swimming with the sharks. I don't think he knows what he's gettin' into."

"Probably true," he said. "What's a shark?"

"Top of the food chain in the ocean."

"Never seen an ocean," Wilson said. "Can you imagine travelin' that far in one trip?"

"There are people outside the city who do that kind of travelin'," I said. "Maybe someone can get the city under control so people can do that sort of thing again."

"No one can afford to bribe their way through that many Zones."

"What would ya think of a city where a person didn't have to use a Caravan and bribes to cross?"

"Good luck with that, Kade."

"Everybody's gotta have a goal, Wilson."

"Try to focus on one that you might be able to reach," he said. "I can name three reasons within a three-mile radius that you wouldn't reach that goal. And that's just the 'Big Three' reasons. There are hundreds of slightly lesser reasons after those."

"Yeah, I can think of a few, too."

"Derris."

I nodded.

"Blechley."

"Not as big a worry as some would make him," I said.

"Whatever," Wilson said. "But then there's the Circus."

"Yeah, that could be troublesome."

"Those are just the local 'Big Three' reasons," he said. "Shall I go on?"

"Nope," I said. "I know you love to hear yourself speak, but we're here."

"I have no idea what you're talking about."

The shop we were standing in front of looked like a General Goods store. I could see containers through the metal fence that undoubtedly held food supplies like flour or rice. There were various sorts of clothing, cooking utensils, and jars of spices. Overall, it appeared to be a fairly successful store. The shops inside the Scrapers were much different than the shanties and open shops around the outside.

I rattled the fence, loudly.

I heard grumbling from the back of the store, and a man came stumbling out of the dark, fumbling with a set of keys.

"It's late," he said.

I held a ten scrip where he could see it.

"We're leaving early tomorrow, and we need provisions," I said.

"Come in," he said, eying the scrip.

He unlocked the sliding metal gate and pushed it to the side far enough to let us in. It truly was a good thing Wilson wore black so the bloodstains on his clothing were hidden.

We stepped inside and followed Denton toward his counter.

"So, how many provisions do you need? Will this be a long trip and are you the only two traveling?"

I listened to the questions he asked. They could be innocent questions, or they could be questions meant to fish for enough information to set someone up for some sort of ambush. So far, they seemed innocent.

"We're traveling to the east. We need enough for two into Kathrop's Zone."

"Dangerous traveling to the east, my friend," he said. He pulled a map from under the desk and placed it on the counter. He pointed to the spot where Yamato's Zone was marked. "If you were to take this route, you could bypass several of the more dangerous Zones."

He traced a route east, then north around several Zones. Still, there was a possibility of innocence.

"Are you familiar with these Zones, my friend?" he asked as his finger followed a trail east.

"Can't say I've ever traveled those."

His finger backtracked just a tiny bit and turned south into Ramos Antilles' Zone. That was the clue I had been looking for. I've studied this city for nearly seventeen years, and I know the safest routes to almost anywhere. He was trying to send us right into the hands of someone who would almost certainly detain travelers and probably take anything of value from them.

"What can ya tell us about a possible Caravan?"

"There's a Caravan coming through Jaxom's Zone tomorrow about noon," he said. "If you're interested in that option, I can send word for him to meet you at a pre-chosen point so you can join them."

"How would you get a message to the man?"

"I have a shortwave radio," he said. "Most of the shops inside the Scrapers have ways to communicate."

"How much would this Caravan run?"

"His standard rate is forty scrip per Zone traveled. From Jaxom to Kathrop is eleven Zones. So, four hundred and forty scrip would take you through."

His price was too cheap. A Caravan wouldn't make much money at forty scrip per Zone. Normal rates for an accredited Caravan were a hundred scrip per Zone.

Everything was screaming the shopkeeper was crooked. He would get kickbacks from Antilles or kickbacks from his Caravan. The next question would make or break it for me.

"So, who's the Caravan Master? Maybe one of us knows him."

He smiled. If we weren't familiar with the area, we wouldn't know Drekk. "His name is Hodipis Drekk, and you won't find a finer Caravan Master in this corner of the city."

"Is that what you told Cedric Hale when you booked the trip for his seventeen-year-old daughter from here to Kathrop?"

"What...what?"

"The most important question you'll answer this night is the next one I ask."

Wilson stepped back to the gate and slid it closed.

"Just who do you think you are, coming into my establishment and...?"

His words were cut short as he saw, for an instant, the cold, dead eyes of an entirely different person staring at him.

"I've been hired to find the girl and bring her home," I said. "My name is Mathew Kade."

His face turned several shades whiter when I said my name.

"Oh, dear God," he whimpered. "What have I done?"

"That's exactly what we're about to find out," I said. "Tell me everything."

"He'll kill me."

I moved like lightning. I slammed his back into the wall behind him, and my left hand clenched around his throat. "Worry about me."

"I-I'll t-talk," he stuttered.

"Tell me."

"It's Drekk," he sputtered. "He pays me to send people to his Caravans. It's supposed to be a simple ransom."

"Kidnap and ransom?" I asked. "Then what are the demands? Hale received no demands."

"I-I don't know, Mister Kade," he sobbed. "He just sent word that the girl was gone."

"How many people have you betrayed, Denton?" I asked, my voice vibrating with anger. "How many lives destroyed? How much did he pay you to send a seventeen-year-old girl out into this perverted abomination of a city?"

His hands trembled as they withdrew a pouch of coins from his belt. "Take it. Please don't hurt me."

"Hurt you?" My voice rang in the room. "It won't hurt...long."

His scream never made it out of his mouth.

* * *

Hale arrived about mid-morning the next day and found Wilson and me sitting patiently on the steps leading up to the Scraper. He approached me warily.

"Looks like he expects the worst," Wilson said.

"He won't be disappointed."

"Have you found anything for me yet, Mister Kade?" Hale asked.

"I have some news," I said. "There was a plot to kidnap your daughter and demand a ransom for her return. Something must have gone wrong, considering you haven't had any demands. You haven't had any, have you?"

"No," he answered sadly. "Who was behind it?"

"Denton had a hand in it," I said. "The one behind it was Drekk. I'll be visiting him later today. When I have news, I'll bring it to you or send it with someone else."

"Please find her, Kade," he said. "She's all I have left."

"I will."

There was a commotion from the Scraper as several of Yamato's guards exited the front entrance. They had kept people from entering half the morning.

"What is the meaning of this?" Hale asked the guards.

"Found a shopkeeper this mornin', Mister Hale."

"He was hanged last night," the other guard said. "Wasn't a robbery, though. There were thirty coins scattered on the floor around him."

Hale looked at me with gratitude written across his face. Thirty coins for the betrayer. The consequences seemed proper.

Six hundred scrip is what he had been paid. Thirty coins from the Old World. He had sold a seventeen-year-old girl for seven dollars and fifty cents.

Life is cheap in this Fallen World.

* * * * *

Chapter Five

Wₑ walked north. Wilson was quiet. The case had become something else after the last night. He was there for Teresa to keep me from gettin' myself killed, sure. But he had looked straight into the eyes of that shopkeeper with me. We had witnessed justice being served, and both of us knew that justice was what we were truly after.

"Do ya think there's a chance the girl is still alive?" he asked.

"The truth is," I said, "there's not much chance of it. But we'll find her, or we'll find her body. Either way, I plan to set this right. You ok with that?"

"Damn straight, I am."

"Good," I said. "This might get ugly before we're through."

"You have no idea," he said. "I used Denton's shortwave last night. Reported to Teresa. She's called out the Knights and put them on alert. We drag this out in the open, and the Knights will be ready to do what is needed."

Knights of the Society of the Sword are some of the toughest bastards walking the city streets. You don't become a Knight easily. Wilson Poe is a Yeoman of the Society, and he's a walking army in his own right. There are thirty-five Knights. Most of the Society are Recruits, Yeomen, and Squires. The Knights travel the city, and they hate this sort of thing. But it's a big damn city, and there's a lot of it going on.

This had just gotten much bigger than Wilson Poe guarding my back.

"Well, what say we give the Knights a target then?"

"That, we should."

We headed north toward Jaxom's Zone. It was one Zone north of Zane's. At least, we would eat well, with the Farmers in Zane's area today.

The streets look completely different during the day. Some of the bravos still stood idle along the streets in various places. But there were regular folks as well. Travel through the Zones was always dangerous, but travel at night was unheard of for the regular inhabitants of this fallen city. I heard music ahead of us as we neared the Farmers' wagons.

They traveled with huge box wagons made of strong wood, banded in steel. The box wagons held almost anything that could be traded in the city or in the countryside around it.

There were entertainers, players of music, and even a wagon that opened into a stage for what used to be called theatre or plays. I'd sat and watched a play in our Zone three years earlier.

It had been a reenactment of the Fall. I had left halfway through the show. I had lived through the Fall, and I remembered so much from before. I didn't want to relive their reenactment of something that vaguely resembled what had truly occurred.

For a time, I had thought that, if they knew what had really happened, they would try to become something better than this mockery of the civilization that had been here before. Who was I kidding? Humans are some of the vilest creatures this world has ever spawned. Then I would meet that one person who gave me hope that all, truly, hadn't been lost, and that there might be a small chance that humanity deserved to survive.

Those, like Maddy Hale, who disappeared into the maw of this great creature spawned by the evil nature of humanity needed someone to stand up for them. I saw a part of this in the Society of the Sword. Teresa didn't strive to control all those around her. They flocked to her because she was a good leader. She cared about those who followed her. Technically, she was the Warlord of our Zone. Stiner was just the Warlord in name. What Teresa decided would be followed, or Stiner would be removed rather quickly.

He charged his tax and lived in his Scraper, but he would have rather rolled down the street over barbed wire than cross Teresa Manora.

I smelled something divine.

"What is that smell?" Wilson asked.

"My god," I said. "I think it's a taco."

"A taco?"

"You have to eat some," I said. "First time since the Fall I've smelled a taco."

"It smells different."

"Oh, that's because they are," I said as I saw the source of the wonderful smell.

Wilson followed me to the wagon. An old lady who had to be sixty worked over a wood-burning grill. There were taco shells in one rack and tortillas for burritos in another.

"You've made a man's dreams come true," I said to the woman as I reached the rough counter she had set up around the grill. "I haven't had tacos in decades."

"You don't look old enough to have lived long pre-Fall. Probably no more than ten years. You had tacos?"

"Little older than I look, Gran," I said. "Had tacos before the Wars really heated up."

She nodded. "Age is treating you well. What can I prepare for you?"

"I want four hard shells and whatever my large friend wants."

She turned her gaze to Wilson. "You, I would guess, have never had a taco."

"You'd be right," he said. "I'll try the same as he got."

She reached into the wagon and drew out some peppers I never thought I would see again.

"Jalapenos?" I asked.

"We grew our first crop this year from some seeds we traded for from the West Caravans."

The West Caravans traveled the route between the eastern coast and the western coast of the continent we lived on. It was a hell of a distance, and there were several Rad Zones in the middle of what used to be a great country. The nukes had been used to destroy the part of the country that produced most of the country's food. They had planned to cripple the Obsidian Corporation, which had gained control of that country.

The Caravans traveled far to the south to pass the Rad Zones and were the only connections we had with the other side of the fallen land.

"How would you like them topped?" she asked.

"Load 'em down," I said, my mouth watering.

"And you?" she asked Wilson.

"I really don't know," he said. "Same as his, I guess."

"Two scrip," she said.

I motioned Wilson back and slid another Old World coin across the counter, and she raised her eyebrows in surprise. It really wasn't common to use Old World coins. They weren't just lying around everywhere. Dealing with the Farmers was a good way to cash them in, though.

She started to make change, and I motioned for her to stop.

"I could use a little information, Gran."

"You ask, and I'll decide if the pay is enough."

"Nothing major," I said. "My friend and I are in a hurry to get to Jaxom's Zone, so we can't stay and really look around. I need to know if Grenwas is with you folks this year."

"Yes, he is," she said. "You'll find him around the Scraper about halfway down the street. I'm guessing you need weapons?"

"That, we do. You keep that, and good fortunes be on your day."

"That information is free, young man, but I have something that may interest you. What sort of weapons do you need?" she asked. "My son was lost to us in an accident this last year. He was of the Farmers' Guard. I intended to sell his weapons while in the city this week. If you are fond of the blade, the Farmers' Guard use only the best."

"Very fond of blades," I said. "It's not often quality weapons are available. I would love to see what you have."

She went to her wagon and pulled a chest from the corner. She laid it atop the counter and opened it. In a gleaming line were twelve beautiful throwing blades. They rested on a harness with scabbards for each blade.

"Now, that is beautiful," I said. "I was expecting a sword or dagger. These are magnificent. Price?"

"A hundred and fifty scrip," she said. "This coin is worth twenty. So, we knock that off…"

"No, that's yours," I said. "Here's the rest. Not often I find this quality. The only thing I've found of this high quality is my razor. It's made with Old World tech, and it's better grade metal than most anything I've seen. I think these may be Old World-forged, too."

I slid several Old World coins to her and took off my coat. After a few minutes of adjustments, the harness with twelve blades was over my shirt.

She saw the pistol I had taken from Corso in my waistband.

"He also had a holster that attached to the harness. It's under the cloth."

I lifted the cloth and found a worn leather holster that matched the harness. I attached it under my left arm. The pistol slid into the holster easily, and I pulled the thong over the hammer to hold it snugly in place.

"Nice," I said. "One stop shoppin'."

"Now, let me finish your tacos," the woman said and returned to stacking tacos.

"Never knew you to carry anything other than the razor, Kade."

"I got a feelin'," I said.

"That's a little ominous," he said.

"Yea, that's the feelin' I'm getting."

We left the woman's wagon with our hands full of tacos. I showed Wilson the proper way to eat a taco without losing most of it down the front of your chest. They were even better than I remembered. No industrialized ingredients; all Farm fresh. I was impressed, to say the least.

The harness felt different, but I would get used to it in short order. Now we had to find Grenwas. Then we would meet Drekk in Jaxom's or catch up to him if we missed the Caravan. Drekk had some explaining to do.

"We still need Grenwas?"

"Yeah," I said. "I need some bullets for this gun."

"Bullets?" he asked. "That's even more ominous. You never use guns."

"They're forever runnin' out of bullets," I said, "but it may be handy at some point. Worthless without bullets."

"True enough," he said. "Too bad we don't have a chapter here. We could get ammo there."

"That's just weird," I said. "It's the Society of the Sword, not the NRA."

"NRA?"

"Pre-Fall nonsense," I said. "Sorry, I get a little mixed up sometimes."

We rounded the corner as I finished my last taco. I could see Grenwas' wagon down the street. I also saw someone paying us a great deal more attention than I was comfortable with. The man turned and hurried into a building erected alongside the Scraper.

"Trouble soon," Wilson said. "Keep your eyes open."

"I saw him," I said. "He's a local, but it looks like he recognized us."

"Recognized you," he said. "No huge bounty on my head."

"You disappointed? I'm not. Expected as much."

"Shut up."

We reached Grenwas' wagon.

"Mathew Kade!" Grenwas exclaimed and shook my hand. "What can I do for you today?"

"Need some bullets for this," I said as I laid the revolver down on the counter he had erected around his wagon.

"Looks like a .44 caliber," he said and lifted it up to examine it. "Ruger was a good firearm in its day. Still holds up well."

"Got anything that'll fit it?"

"I sure do," he said. "I have a box of thirty cartridges that'll fit this. Five hundred scrip is the best I can do. High demand for these."

"I'll take 'em," I said.

Bullets are expensive. There's a booming business selling death in this Fallen World.

* * * * *

Chapter Six

We walked north toward Jaxom's Zone.

"Gonna be pushin' it to get there before Drekk passes through," Wilson said. "Might have to chase him down."

"True enough," I said. "That doesn't bother me as much as you might think. Better if we aren't right on top of the Scraper when we find him."

"Ya gotta point," he said. "Do ya even know how many guards he uses on his Caravan?"

"Probably twenty or so," I said. "Don't feel sorry for them. They work for Drekk, knowing full well what he's doin'."

"Wasn't feelin' sorry for them," he said. "Just wondering how we would split the number."

"We'll be fair," I said. "Half and half."

"I can live with that." He chuckled. "He's probably got guns."

"We'll jump off that bridge when we get there, but I expect many guns."

"Me too."

"Good, you may not be disappointed, then."

"Shut up."

I chuckled.

"Disappointment has a way of draggin' you down," I said. "You'll live longer if you don't have so many disappointments clutterin' up your mind."

"I hate you, old man."

I laughed. "I guess I'm lucky your boss likes me."

"Still tryin' to figure that one out," he muttered.

We turned left at the next corner. The huts and shanties looked even more dilapidated than the ones in Zane's territory. This was Polk's Zone, and he was a greedy bastard who bled his people dry to support his luxurious lifestyle. He was a pretty despicable guy. The problem for his people was that they couldn't leave and go to another Zone. They couldn't afford a Caravan and most local Zones wouldn't allow new settlers. They were trapped under the thumb of their greedy Warlord.

But he was the one with the guns, so what could they do?

The next Zone to the north was Jaxom's, but it was already after noon, and Drekk could already be there and gone.

"Nine o'clock," Wilson said.

"I see 'em," I answered.

Four guys were waiting in the shadow of Polk's Scraper.

"Looks like they're waitin' for someone," Wilson said.

"Definitely waitin' for us," I said.

"It could be a coincidence."

"What'd we just discuss about disappointment?"

He sighed as the men saw us and the one furthest away ran back into the Scraper.

"Now, you're disappointed."

He sighed again.

"Just keep goin'," I said. "When I give the word, we'll attack."

"Gotcha."

We continued down the street and passed the guys, acting like we didn't see them.

We were half a block past the lookouts when there was a commotion behind us, and Polk's guards poured out of the Scraper looking right and left.

"Shit," Wilson said.

"Could be worse," I answered.

More guys poured into the street from the side of the Scraper. There had to be thirty guards in the street. They saw us and pushed through the people in front of Polk's.

"Dammit!" Wilson exclaimed. "Don't say anything else."

"Run," I said.

We bolted.

"I hate running," Wilson said between breaths.

"Me too," I answered.

I heard gunfire as a bullet whistled past my ear.

"Idiots!" I muttered. "People packed in the streets ahead of us."

"I don't think they care who they shoot, as long as one of 'em is you."

"Rethinkin' that whole 'backin me up' thing yet?"

"Can't." His breaths were getting more pronounced. "More scared of her than them."

"Save it, Wilson," I said. "Just breathe. I have a plan."

"Oh shit," he panted.

I glanced back. They were falling further behind.

"Slow down a bit," I said, through my steady breathing. It pays to keep fit. Wilson was fit, but he was huge. Harder for him to keep running than it was for me.

"Thought we were trying to lose 'em," he gasped.

"One more block," I said, and we ran on.

Occasionally, I would hear the whine of a bullet and a gunshot. We crossed into Jaxom's Zone and neared his Scraper. The group didn't halt at the border. Seems Polk really wanted this bounty.

I didn't see a Caravan in the street in front of Jaxom's, but there were a lot of people there. This usually happened when a Caravan pulled out from one of the Scrapers. He couldn't be far. He would have gone south at the next street.

I rounded the corner with a yell. "Eureka!"

The Caravan was right around the corner. There were guards surrounding the six wagons, and I saw the familiar bulk of Hodipis Drekk right in the center.

I plowed through the surprised guards and grabbed Drekk at full speed. We tumbled over and behind the wagon to his left. Wilson was right behind me.

Thirty-two of Polk's men rounded the corner as we ducked down, and they opened fire. Twenty-eight Caravan guards ducked and located the gunmen.

Thunder rolled through the city streets as sixty guns opened fire.

I giggled and looked over at Drekk as he struggled to a sitting position.

"Hodipis!" I said. "How the hell are ya?"

"What is the meaning of this?!"

"Oh," I answered. "We have some things to discuss, you and I."

The gunfire had stopped, but the groans and screams could still be plainly heard. I peeked around the wagon for a second.

"Looks like three guys left out there," I said. "Sorry 'bout your guards, Drekk."

I stood up, and my hands blurred as I launched three knives, one after the other.

"Polk needs new guards, too."

Drekk struggled to his feet to see the carnage that had been wrought in the streets.

"What have you done, you bastard?"

I turned back to Drekk with that dead look in my eyes. "The question is, what have you done, Hodipis Drekk?"

He tried to back up, only to run into a wall named Wilson Poe.

"Maddy Hale."

His face paled.

"Tell me everything, Drekk," I said. "I've already seen Denton. I know his end of it."

"I d-don't know where she w-went."

"Where was she supposed to be? You wanted ransom but never followed up."

"Th-the d-damn Clowns…"

"You gave her to the Circus!?"

"N-no," he stammered. "I had a deal with the damn Clowns to hold her till the ransom got paid! We done it a lot of times. They said the guy who was to deliver her didn't show, and the girl is gone!"

I heard thumping from the wagon we were standing beside. Muffled yells sounded.

"Hold him," I said, and Wilson clamped down on Drekk's shoulder with a huge hand.

I moved to the back of the wagon and unlocked the door. I drew my gun from its holster and opened it. Inside were three women huddled in a corner. I said women, but two were little more than kids, fourteen or fifteen years old. All three were naked and bruised, and I didn't have to guess what had been happening to them. Something stirred inside me, a rage, but not just anger.

How had things come to this? A once-great civilization reduced to this.

"Stay in here for a second," I said. "I'll finish with Drekk, and we'll get you somewhere safe."

I walked around the wagon and shot Drekk in the head.

Wilson looked at me with one eyebrow raised.

"Look in the wagon," I said.

Jaxom's guards rounded the corner, and I walked out to meet them. Jaxom was among the guards.

"Mathew," he said, with a nod, "why are there over fifty bodies in my street?"

"Sorry about that, Jaxom," I said. "If it's any consolation, you have six Caravan wagons full of goods to move into your Scraper."

"That helps," he said, "but it's not really a good reason for why I have bodies littering my street."

"Short version," I said, "Drekk kidnapped the wrong girl. He has three more in his wagon who are gonna need treatment. I expect you to put them up until Teresa Manora gets here to collect them."

My words were a statement, not a question. He could see the fury stirring beneath my surface, and he didn't argue even for a second. He nodded.

"Everything else is yours."

"Generous," he said.

"I don't need a baggage train," I said. "You can use it here. I could use a couple boxes of .44s if you got any."

"I could scrape up a few," he said.

"I'll owe ya one."

Wilson walked up to Jaxom's guards. He pointed at three.

"Give me your coats."

Jaxom saw the look on Wilson's face. "Give 'em the coats."

Wilson walked back around the wagon. In a few moments, he returned with three forms huddled together. He walked up to Jaxom.

"Take care of these ladies. If anything happens to 'em, the Society will be back in force. You understand?"

"I wouldn't let anything happen to them, son," Jaxom said. "I'm not that idiot next door."

"I used the shortwave in the wagon to call Teresa," Wilson said. "A group of Knights will be here tonight to pick them up. The Society will take care of them."

"Understood, Knight," Jaxom said.

"I'm no Knight," Wilson said.

"You sound like one."

Wilson nodded and stepped back into his 'back up' position.

"You get me that ammo, and I'll be on my way," I said.

"Where to, if you don't mind my asking?"

"Polk just sent thirty-two men to kill me," I said. "I think I'll pay him a visit. Then I have to go see a Clown."

"Circus is an evil place, Mathew," he said. "I'd be careful in there."

I nodded.

Jaxom was one of the better Warlords. He was tough, but he was also merciful. He didn't hurt people unless they needed it. I had no doubt he would keep those girls safe until Teresa arrived.

Mercy is a rare commodity in this Fallen World.

* * * * *

Chapter Seven

"So," Wilson said. "We gonna have a talk with Polk?"

"Oh, yeah."

"Good," he said. "That was about ridiculous."

"Worked out pretty well though."

"True enough."

"I think he needs a lesson," I said as I retrieved my blades from the throats of three of his men. I spied the perfect thing. I picked up a two-foot-long piece of steel tubing one of his men had at his waist for a melee weapon.

"I see," Wilson said with a vicious smile.

I straightened up and turned toward Polk's Zone. Flipping the tubing from one end to the other, I strode down the center of the street. Wilson walked by my side, glaring at any who looked at us. People scattered as we walked by. It didn't take too long to reach Polk's Scraper.

I pushed through the doors of the Scraper and found myself facing seven men. I cocked my head to the side.

"Thirty-two tried. Give it your best shot," I said, "or get out of the way and clean up the mess when I'm done."

They were looking into the dead eyes of a killer as I spoke. They moved out of my path.

"Wilson," I said, "keep these guys company. I won't be long."

He nodded.

I entered the elevator and pushed the button for the top floor. Warlords always took the penthouse for their quarters when the

Scraper still had electricity. Polk was no different. I exited on the top floor and saw him standing across the room with his back to me. He was looking out the huge windows overlooking the city.

"Is he dead?" Polk asked.

"I'm not."

He spun around, eyes wide with surprise. "Why those useless…"

He snatched the pistol from the holster at his side and fired. But I wasn't there anymore. I dove forward and rolled to the right. Then I lunged forward again. He shot once more, and I felt a tug at my side as I dodged left. My side burned so I knew I was hit. It didn't matter; I was on top of him.

The pipe arced, and he screamed as the bones in his arm shattered. Then a backswing crushed his left knee. He screamed louder.

Something moved behind me, and I dodged to the right. My hand lashed out and snatched the arrow right before it would have planted itself in Polk's heart.

A form stepped from the shadows, staring at me in disbelief. It was a woman in a black leather outfit. She held a recurve bow in her left hand.

"Why did you do that?!" she almost screamed. "He deserves to die!"

"If you kill him, he won't learn anything."

Polk lay on the floor moaning.

"He killed my sister!"

I saw the rope looped around her shoulder, and an idea struck me.

"Then he should suffer for it," I said. "Give me your rope."

She approached slowly and handed me the rope.

I slammed the steel tube through Polk's shoulder and tied the rope to either end of the pipe. Polk screamed as I took the doubled end and tied it to his massive desk. Then I picked the screaming

Warlord up and slammed him through the window he had been staring out of. The glass shattered, and he went over the edge. The rope went tight, and I walked away.

As I left the elevator, Wilson turned. He saw the blood on my side.

"You gonna live?"

"It's just a graze."

I walked over to the seven men. "Who is Polk's second?" The third from the right nodded.

"You are gonna send a message to Teresa Manora. You're gonna request that she open a chapter of the Society right here in this Scraper. The rest of you can pull your boss back through his window, and you may even be able to keep him alive. Once that's done, you're on your own. I would suggest you take any advice Teresa's people give. Don't make me come back."

Wilson and I left Polk's Scraper and found the streets packed with the poor and downtrodden. Polk was rough on his people.

"This Zone will soon be under the protection of the Society of the Sword!" I raised my voice. "Teresa Manora is fair and just. She will help those in need and destroy those who would harm you. Your time under the heel of Kunley Polk is over."

I strode down the street, and the crowds parted for us.

"Guess she won't have a choice but to come in here now," Wilson said. "It's what she would want to do anyway."

"True."

"Stop when we get around the corner, and I'll take a look at that wound."

"Ok," I said. "Didn't want to show it to those folks."

We rounded the corner, and I sat on a stoop in front of a building. I shrugged my coat off and unbuckled the harness for the blades.

"Pretty deep," he said. "Needs stitches. We need to find a medic."

"I'll do it," a voice said from our left. It was the archer from Polk's quarters. "I was a medic in the Farmers' Guard."

I nodded, and she approached. She pulled a kit from her pack. She seemed competent as she threaded the curved needle. The wound burned like hell as she stitched it closed. Then she pulled some salve from the kit and rubbed it on the area. The salve cooled the burn immediately, and she wrapped a bandage around my abdomen to cover the wound.

"Pretty handy," Wilson said. "And who are you?"

"We met in Polk's office," I said. "We had conflicting ideas about how to deal with Polk. We compromised and threw him out a window, with a steel bar through his shoulder."

"I can always come back," she said, "and finish the job if I don't feel satisfied."

"Wilson Poe," he said with his hand outstretched. "How are ya?"

"Bella Trask," she said, grasping Wilson's hand.

"The Bella Trask?" he asked. "The one who cleared the way for Wilderman?"

"Yes."

"That was impressive work," I said.

"It was hard work," she said. "And I'm guessing you're Mathew Kade?"

"Most of the time," I said.

"You're the one who found the murderer of the Farmer's daughter?"

"True."

"They say you're bat shit crazy, over in Wilderman's Zone."

"Used to be," I said. "A little less so, now."

She nodded.

Wilderman was the head of the Zone where the Obsidian Corporation had its headquarters. When I left that place, I hadn't been in the greatest shape mentally. Several people had taken offense at some of the things I took with me, and it had been ugly. It had been seventeen years, and people still remembered me in Wilderman's.

"What sort of trouble are you into?" Bella asked.

"Kidnapped girl," I said. "Started with a shopkeeper. Sold her to a Caravan Master who had a deal with the Clowns to hold her until the ransom was paid."

"Had?"

"He can't make deals anymore," Wilson said. "Hard to do that with a bullet in your brain."

"I see," she said. "So, now the Circus?"

"I need to sleep before I deal with the Clowns," I said. "My place is not too far away. I'm on the edge of Stiner's."

"Probably a good idea," Wilson said. "We traveled all night last night. I can report to Teresa, as well."

"Then let's get to it," I said.

"If you can use another person, I will join you," Bella said.

"Clowns don't bother you?" Wilson asked.

"They are a disgrace."

"Yeah," he said, "but a damn scary bunch."

"Yes."

"You're welcome to join us if that's what you want," I said. "But this may get really ugly before it's done."

She nodded. "It's the least I can do after you removed the guards around Polk."

"So be it."

We walked south toward Stiner's.

In all honesty, I wasn't looking forward to a confrontation with the Clowns. Right after the Fall, the Circus sprang up. It was a place where you could buy anything your black heart desired. If you wanted to shoot another person, they would provide someone for the right amount of money. If you wanted to hunt someone down, they would provide a weapon. If you wanted to have sex with a child, they would provide one. Any twisted thing a person could think of could be bought at the Circus. It was a twisted abomination with occupants who should be in an asylum. And the Clowns were the guards. They were a fierce group of twisted bastards who would give the Knights a run for their money, one on one.

The problem was, there were about forty or fifty Knights of the Society of the Sword. There were close to two hundred and fifty Clowns. They followed a core group of thirty. Those thirty were some of the toughest bastards in this fallen city. Their numbers were why they hadn't been eliminated before.

I hated Clowns.

"Any plans on how to go about this?" Wilson asked.

"I'll do some thinkin' about it tonight, and we'll see in the morning," I said. "I'm thinkin' a straightforward approach would be best. We need information from the bastards. You can buy anything from the Clowns. If they refuse, well, that's when we have to get creative."

"From what is known in Wilderman's," Bella said, "the Clowns will respond to money."

"That's what I'm countin' on," I said.

We reached Stiner's without incident.

"I expected another attack before we got here," Wilson said.

"You're not disappointed at the outcome, are you?"

"Oh, my God, I'm startin' to think like you," he said. "Teresa should put a warning label on orders when they send us out to your general vicinity."

"Careful," I said, "you'll hurt my feeling."

"Feeling?" Bella asked. "You only have one?"

"Yep, and he's hurtin' it."

She shook her head.

We approached an Old World building.

"Used to call these banks in the Old World," I said.

"I'm familiar with the term," she said.

We pushed through a door that used to be glass and crossed a large room filled with rubble and trash.

"Nice place ya have here," Wilson said.

"This is the nice part," I said and opened a door on the left side of the room. Across the room was a huge, metal door. "This used to be the bank vault."

I worked the dials on the vault door and swung it open. The inside was pristine. I motioned my companions forward.

"Welcome to my home."

They passed me, then I entered and pulled the vault door closed. As the door clicked shut, lights turned on.

"You have electricity?"

"Made a deal with Stiner a long time ago. I run my place off his Scraper in return for mounting the solar system on his roof. It's mutually beneficial, so he had no problem."

On the other side of the Vault was a wooden door. I led them through it, and we descended a set of stairs that turned back and forth under the city. They ended at another door in a small hallway. We entered a huge room with concrete floors and walls. They were very old walls, except for two that filled huge, round holes at each end of the massive room.

"Is that an old subway car?" Bella asked.

In the center of the room was a luxury car from a train.

"I'd love to take credit for building this place, but it was mostly done before I found it. It belonged to Allen, the former Warlord. When Stiner took this Zone from him, he didn't know this place existed. So, I collapsed the tunnel from the Scraper to here and moved in. I did put the stairs in and make the new entrance in the Vault."

"Where's that door go?" Wilson asked.

He was pointing across the huge room to the reinforced metal door at the head of a set of concrete steps.

"Goes to the Tees," I said. "The tunnels that open on the sewer system."

"Why do ya ever leave this place?" he asked. "Climate control, electricity, I bet you even got runnin' water."

"Yep," I said. "Even a water heater."

"Oh my," Bella said. "Hot, running water?"

"The baths are that way." I pointed to the back corner where I had erected some of the partitions from an old place they used to call Chinatown. The material was a sort of paper stretched between frames of wood. I had found it interesting. The paper had crumbled, so I had replaced it with white fabric I found in an Old World hotel.

"Do you mind if I use them?" she asked. "I haven't had a hot bath in so long."

"Go ahead."

She headed to the back with her pack in hand.

"This place is amazing," Wilson said. "Wonder how many of these sorts of places are scattered around the city?"

"I've only found the one," I said. "Although I have found a lot of caches scattered around."

"Always wondered how you always have coin."

"Found a lot of that over the years."

I hung my coat over a fork of a coat rack I had found in an old building. Then I loosened the buckles and removed the knife harness. There was a lot of blood on my shirt and a jagged hole where the bullet had ripped it, so I threw it in a trash can by the door.

I entered the kitchen and opened the cooler. I pulled out a pot, carried it to the burners, and left the pot of stew sitting there to heat up.

"A good meal and a night's rest before we hit the Clowns."

"You expect a fight tomorrow?"

"You know what I expect."

"We're all gonna die while the Clowns dance around us naked?"

"That fits," I said. "I can't think of anything much worse."

"Humph."

"Indeed."

"That smells delicious," Wilson said. "What is it?"

"Stew."

"I smell carrots."

"Yep."

"Where the hell did you get carrots?"

"I have a small garden box on the roof," I said. "Bought some seeds from the Farmers last year. I sometimes can my own food instead of trading the jars back to the Farmers. It's something I enjoy when I'm not on a case."

"That's a handy skill."

"True," I said. "I don't like to be completely dependent on the Farmers. I'm slowly building my stores up."

"You think there'll be trouble with the Farmers?"

"At some point, there will be," I said. "They have too much power. It's just a matter of time 'til something breaks. You'd be smart to work toward the same independence."

"Teresa said something similar a few weeks ago."

"Have you ever met the Steadholder?"

"Nope."

"He's seventy years old," I said. "His rules are what the Farmers live by. How much longer do you think he'll live? When he goes, I don't like to think about the odds of another like him in charge."

"I see your point," he said. "What if they end up with a Blechley? Or a Polk?"

"Exactly."

"I think the odds are pretty good the next Steadholder will be much like this one," Bella said behind us. "I'm sure he is grooming his successor."

"That hasn't worked too well throughout history," I said. "Usually, the successor is corrupted by the fact that their rule was given to 'em."

"What history would that be?"

"Pre-Fall. Human history," I said. "You can hope for the best, if you want, but prepare for the worst."

"He believes in expecting the worst so he's never disappointed," Wilson said.

"That's a sad view of life, Mister Kade."

"That's what I said," Wilson added.

"And you live your life in disappointment," I said. "For instance, you thought you would be the next one to use the bath. And now you're disappointed."

I headed for the back to soak in the hot water.

There are a few moments of peace in this Fallen World.

* * * * *

Chapter Eight

I awoke refreshed. My bed was in the train car, and I heard Wilson snoring on the sofa outside the car. I shook my head and eased upright with a twinge of pain from the bullet wound in my side. It wasn't as bad as many of the wounds I'd taken in my life. There were scars all over my body from the various ways people had tried to kill me.

"Damn!" I heard Bella say from the door to the other half of the car. "You've been through the mill."

"Years of rough living," I said as I pulled a new shirt around my shoulders. "Could be worse."

"How's that?"

"Coulda killed me."

"I guess you have a point."

I pulled a pair of socks from a drawer and sat on the bed. I pulled the socks up and grabbed my boots.

"Where do you get all these things?" she asked. "That is an Old World set of drawers."

"Came with the place," I said. "Allen really made the place nice before Stiner killed him. I've added a few things, but mostly just useful things. I don't really care about the luxury. It was here when I got here, so I use it."

We exited the car. The snoring stopped, and Wilson sat up.

"That may have been the best night's sleep I've had in years," he said. "I see why Teresa likes you now."

"The bath would be enough," Bella said. "I'd have your babies just for that."

I laughed. "You're both welcome here anytime."

"Don't make promises like that," Bella said. "I'll never go back to Wilderman's."

"Teresa might get mad if you stayed here," Wilson said. "She's staked a claim on Kade. At least now, we know why."

"Who is Teresa?" she asked. "You've mentioned her several times."

"Teresa Manora."

"The Teresa Manora?" she asked. "Matron of the Society of the Sword?"

"That's her," Wilson said.

"I take it back then," she said. "No babies for you. I think I'll head back to Wilderman's after helping you. I'm not pissing off that woman, not even for the whole city."

"I can see that," Wilson said. "She ordered me to back him up, and I'm about to go face the Clowns rather than disobey her."

I chuckled.

"She likes puppies."

"Jesus, Kade," Wilson said. "I've seen her dogs. They're some sort of mutated breed. They're big as horses."

"She likes big puppies," I said with a shrug. "But they're puppies, nonetheless."

Bella laughed.

"What say we eat some more of that stew before we go?" Wilson asked. "What kind of meat was that? It was really good."

"You probably don't want to know," Bella said. "I've had rat before."

"That was rat?"

"Yep," I said.

He was silent for a second, "What the hell? It was the best rat I've ever eaten. Should I get it out of the cooler?"

I laughed. "Yeah. Let's eat well before we leave. We're all probably gonna die anyway."

"Aren't you just a ray of sunshine?" Wilson asked.

"Expect the worst…"

"Shut up."

"You're doomed to a life of disappointment, Wilson."

"That's ok," he said. "I think I can live with the disappointment. I'll keep my hopes, thank you very much. Now pass me some of that rat stew."

We left by the same route we had entered my house, and we once again headed west into the next Zone. It was run by a man named Devin. He pretty much kept to himself, but there were usually some cutthroats around his Zone at night. We were traveling during the day.

"Should be fairly easy crossing Devin's," Wilson said.

"Probably get ambushed."

"Keep those sorts of things to yourself, Kade," he said. "I don't need your negativity."

"Sure," I said. "But I just want ya prepared for what's about to happen."

"Ah, shit."

"Yep."

"Did we forget to tell you about the huge bounty on Kade's head, Bella?"

"I don't remember hearing anything about bounties," she said. "I'm assuming this group of bravos are here to collect?"

"That would be my guess."

The leader of the group of twenty stopped in front of the rest. "Mathew Kade!" he said. "I'm about to collect...Gack!"

"What was that?" I asked.

He gurgled. It's hard to speak with a knife sunk four inches into your throat.

He tumbled to the ground, and those around him stood there with their mouths hanging open.

"Hell with this!" I said, and I began snatching knives and throwing them. Eight men were down before any reacted. Arrows flew into several. Wilson had drawn his sword but decided to hang back as the missiles kept flying.

Three managed to flee down an alley.

I walked out to the moaning group and retrieved my knives, which I cleaned on their shirts and sheathed.

"Interesting conversation," Wilson said. "A little brief, don't ya think?"

"I'm tired of trying to talk these dumb asses out of tryin'," I said. "Gettin' rid of idiots helps strengthen the gene pool."

"So, why did I run through a Zone and a half yesterday?"

"They had guns."

"They weren't very accurate with 'em," he said.

"You're just mad cause you had to run."

"Well, yeah," he said. "What's that sort of thing gonna do to my reputation?"

"Not as much as sitting there with your thumb up your butt while we handled this bunch."

"I took care of most of Corso's bunch," he said. "You owed me one."

"That's how it is?"

"Boys, boys," Bella interrupted, "don't you think we should move along before we have to answer a bunch of questions?"

"Probably right," I said. "Come on, ya big baby. I'll try not to make ya run anymore."

He sniffed and sheathed his sword.

I laughed.

We continued after I stopped and retrieved a revolver from the leader.

"What are the odds?" I asked. "It's the same caliber as the other one. I could be a gunslinger."

"That's a pretty good name," Wilson said. "You make that one up?"

"Kids these days," I said. "Pre-Fall stuff."

"Figures."

I shoved the pistol into my waistband. Another might be handy.

We headed south as Devin's guards passed us, heading north in a hurry.

"Late to the party," Wilson said as we continued.

"Typical," I said.

"There is a great deal of chaos in the central city Zones," Bella said. "Wilderman keeps his Zone under control for the most part."

"They say Kathrop keeps hers under control, too," Wilson said.

"She does," I said. "Been there a few times. Difference between the local Zones and hers is like night and day. Stiner's is probably the only one that's safe to travel at night, locally. Kathrop's has a booming nightlife. There are some incidents, but she comes down on the culprits like a hammer."

"Maybe I should visit there sometime," Wilson said. "Would like to see a place where people walk around at night without bein' attacked by cutthroats and bravos."

"You should visit Wilderman's, then," Bella said. "He has much the same sort of control over his Zone. It doesn't have the party nightlife that Kathrop's has, but it's safe to travel, night or day."

"It would be an interesting place to visit," I said. "But you'd get bored in a week when no one picked a fight, and then you'd have to come home."

"Maybe I'd like to settle down."

"Wilson, people like us don't settle down," I said. "But maybe we can make a situation where others might be able to."

"That's what the Society stands for," he said. "It's one of the first things they teach us when we get there."

"Teresa is good people," I said. "She had a rough time after the Fall, but she's tryin' to make a difference. Maybe it's time for a difference."

"Comin' up on Franco's Zone," Wilson said. "He shouldn't be a problem. He spends most of the time hiding in his Scraper from the Circus freaks. I think he's just waitin' for the Circus Clowns to come and absorb his Zone."

"Heard about the last time the Circus expanded," Bella said. "They crucified anyone who objected to the merge."

They had lined the streets with crosses and stakes. Half had been crucified, and the others were impaled on the stakes. It's a horrible way to die, and it instilled a terror of the Clowns that does the work for them now.

"Figure the Circus will keep expanding 'til they meet something to stop 'em," I said. "They run into the Society if they expand north. I expect 'em to go south when they try to grow again."

The streets were quiet. Which, in a normal Zone would be ominous, but here, the day was quiet. The night was when all the freaks came out. Franco may have been the Warlord of the Zone, but it was in name only. His Zone was already run by the Circus. He just didn't realize it.

"You see that?" Wilson asked.

"Yeah."

At the corner of the Scraper stood a Clown, almost as big as Wilson. His face was painted a ghastly white with a huge red smile over his mouth. Once, this paint had been a sign of joy and fun. Now it instilled terror in those who looked upon it.

We strode past the Clown toward the Circus. His eyes followed our progress, and he pulled a two-way radio from his colorful shirt.

"They know we're here," I said. "At least, we won't have to hunt 'em down."

"I'm so relieved," Wilson said.

"Joy," Bella agreed.

"When we run into someone, Bella, stay as far back as you can. These guys are fast. If you shoot, shoot at one that's not lookin' at ya. If they see you shoot, they'll catch the arrow or bat it aside. They're that fast."

"Gotcha," she said.

"Wilson," I said, "if it comes down to a rumble, use the length of that blade. Don't let 'em in close."

"Right."

Clowns began to enter the street from the south. All of them were painted and wearing brightly colored clothes. The weapons didn't look bright or colorful. There were swords, clubs, massive hammers, and several guns amid the thirty-eight Clowns that arrayed themselves in front of us.

"Looks like we're a few Clowns short of the Circus." I giggled.

Who said you can't laugh a little in this Fallen World?

* * * * *

Chapter Nine

"Mathew Kade," one of the Clowns said and stepped forward.

"Blinky?" I asked. "Is that you?"

The Clown chuckled. "Most people start screaming when we talk to them. I think I like you."

"Oh, look," Wilson said. "You've made best friends with a Clown."

"You, I don't like."

"I'll try to contain my disappointment," he said.

"Told ya," I said. "Now you're disappointed again."

Wilson let out a long sigh.

"I've got questions to ask you, Clown," I said. "If your boy gets any closer behind us, he's gonna have a bad day."

A slight frown crossed his face, and a minute shake of his head stopped the large Clown we had seen on the way through from moving any closer.

"Nothing is free at the Circus."

"Then I'll swap question for question."

"We deal in scrip," the Clown said. "But there are some things I would like to know. Deal."

"Maddy Hale," I said. "What happened?"

He grimaced.

"I already know you have a deal with Drekk to hold his victims until ransom is paid. What happened to the girl?"

73

"She disappeared in transit from Golon to the Circus. We lost two of our agents in the process."

"She was never here?"

"Question for question."

I nodded.

"You worked for Obsidian. Rumor has it you were in the imprinter when the nukes dropped. Is this true?"

"Yes," I said. "She never made it to the Circus, so where did they disappear?"

"Their path would have been Simms, Overton, Jeffreys, Kort, Dozet, then here. Dozet never saw them, Simms did. They disappeared in Overton's, Jeffreys', or Kort's Zone. Is it true multiple imprints dropped in your head and drove you crazy?"

"Yes. How do you know what happened at Obsidian?"

The change in my questions set him back a little. He figured I'd ask more about the girl. I had enough information about that, but his knowledge of Obsidian bothered me.

"The majority of those you see here are imprinted. Corporate Guard."

"Are you trying to piss me off, Clown?" I asked in disgust. "How does a Corporate Guard become this…abomination?"

"I'm going to treat that as a single question," he said. "We're doing our job."

The job of a Corporate Guard is simple. Protect Corporate Heads. The ramifications of what the Clown had just told me were ominous. One or more Corporate Heads were behind the Circus.

"How many imprints did the machine dump in you? Are they accessible?"

"I'll also treat that as one question," I said. "And it is the last question. It dropped the database. Now, I'll give you a warning."

His eyes narrowed.

"You tell your bosses I said they are a disgrace. They were part of a civilized world; there's no excuse for becoming...this," I said. "Pray your path doesn't cross mine again; the next time I come to the Circus, I'll burn it down. In answer to the last question, yes."

He took an involuntary step backward. He knew a lot about the imprint database. Enough to be scared.

"You're gonna take that shit from this piece of..." said a voice from the left edge of the group of Clowns.

"Shut that idiot up, Funboy!"

Two Clowns closed on the outraged Clown. He snarled and grabbed his knife with amazing speed and hurled it.

I caught it and hurled it back. The two Clowns closing on the knife thrower caught his limp form as he sank backward with his own knife handle jutting from his right eye.

"You want to dance this dance?" I asked, staring out of the dead eyes of someone else. "We can dance right now."

"Back off, guys," the Clown said. "Kade and his companions are leaving."

"Smart choice, Clown," I said, with a smile that made the man flinch.

We turned east and walked away.

Kort was the closest Zone to where we were, so that's where we were going. We walked almost the length of the Zone before Wilson said a word.

"I've never seen anything like that, Kade," he said. "Clowns don't back down, ever. What the hell were you talkin about? Imprints, databases? Who the hell are you, Kade?"

"Old World shit, Wilson," I said. "I'm just a leftover from a dead civilization."

"What's an imprint?"

"Old World tech," I said. "There were worse things than Clowns back then."

"I still can't believe they backed down," he said. "I expected to die right there."

"See, you're not disappointed at the outcome," I said. "That's what I've been sayin' all along."

"See what I have to put up with?" he asked Bella. He was regaining his composure.

"You could leave," she suggested.

"Then Teresa would probably cut me up in tiny little pieces."

"I guess you're just doomed," she said.

"What excuse do you have?" he asked. "You can leave anytime."

"And lose the chance to use that enormous bathtub again? I think not."

"That *was* pretty nice," he said.

I chuckled and continued into the territory of a Warlord named Oliver Miz. He owned a single block with one Scraper. He was harmless. He spent his days fretting over which of his neighbors was coming to swallow his territory. Franco, Tully, Dozet, or Xeno.

"The first thing we have to do is spread out and ask questions in Kort's Zone," I said. "It would have been a small Caravan with closed wagons. The prisoner or prisoners would have been hidden from sight. May have been as small as one wagon and guards.

Shoulda asked what sort of group it was while questioning the Clowns."

"We could go back," Bella said.

"No, thank you," Wilson said.

"Probably not an option," I said. "I made a promise."

"Yea, I heard that," Bella said. "I've got matches."

"It's a blight on this city," Wilson said. "Which is saying a lot, as screwed up as this city is."

"The Circus' day will come," I said. "We have enough information to find out what happened. We just have to ask questions. And keep an eye out for more of Blechley's bounty hunters."

Miz's Zone was busier than Franco's. But there were no Clowns on the street so people weren't hiding wherever they could. The Clowns were known to be mean, twisted freaks. No one was safe when the Clowns were on the streets.

"No reason we should start askin' questions before Kort's Zone, is there?" Wilson asked. "Do you trust the Clowns' information?"

"Actually, I do," I said. "They lost men, so it would benefit them to learn where the threat is. And, for a bonus, they get to send us in first."

"I'm not sure I'm happy doin' the Clowns' work," he said.

"Me neither," I said. "But we're doin' my work, not the Clowns'. I wouldn't give one shit about their men if our girl weren't a victim, too. It would actually serve the bastards right to lose men when they do things like this."

We turned south and crossed into Dozet's Zone. There were still plenty of people out in the streets, but there were a lot more bravos leaning against walls or signposts.

"Keep your eyes open," I said. "More of the unsavory sort here."

"None of 'em want any of this," Wilson said. "I think the body count over the last few days has begun to trickle down."

"I see a lot of 'hell no' comments on their lips," Bella said. "Reading lips is one of those handy skills I picked up."

"That would be a handy skill," I said.

"It's useful."

"When we hit Kort's, we should split up. We need to cover most of the Zone, and it would be quicker if we split," Wilson said.

"I'll hit the Scraper," Bella said. "I spend a lot of time with that sort in Wilderman's."

"I'll take the bars," Wilson said.

"Alright," I said. "I'll work the street."

"Sounds good," Bella said.

I saw a fruit stand beside the Scraper and turned that way. I pulled a quarter from a pocket and smiled at the lady behind the counter. She saw the coin, and her eyes widened.

I normally don't deal with the vendors from the Scrapers. I'm not interested in giving money to those who already have it, but I needed bargaining power on the streets of Kort's Zone. The fruit would buy more good will than Old World coins.

I left with a fairly large sack of apples and pears. There were some plums and peaches in the mix as well. I guessed there was a small orchard on top of one or more of the buildings in Dozet's Zone.

We crossed into Kort's without incident.

"Meet back in two hours on the other side of the Zone," I said. "We should be able to find out if anything happened here by then."

"Sounds good," Bella said and headed straight for the nearest of the two Scrapers in Kort's.

Wilson nodded and headed down the street toward a ramshackle building built near the mouth of an alley.

I walked down the center of the street. After I passed the Scraper, I began walking near the right side. There was an old woman sitting near a stoop on one of the smaller buildings. She looked wary as I closed the distance between us.

I reached into my bag and pulled out an apple. I handed it to the woman.

"Hello, Gran," I said. "I need some information. I'm not from this area, and I wondered if you might know the best place to find out what's been goin' on around here."

She pulled a small blade from her side and sliced a small piece of apple. She ate the piece with a look of joy.

"You should talk to Rega," the woman said. "She sets up shop down the alley behind the next building. She hears more than any of us, considering the particular thing she sells."

I chuckled. "I'm guessin' it's something mostly men look for."

I saw her favoring the right side of her mouth as she chewed the apple. I reached back into the bag and pulled out a soft plum.

"Much obliged, Gran," I said and handed the softer fruit to her.

I stood up and walked onward, down the street. I may have gotten lucky. One of the most informed people in a Zone would be one who provides pleasure.

I rounded the corner and headed down the alley. A large building opened on the alley. It was six stories tall and by no means a Scraper. But the one who owned it wasn't considered poor, either. The door was flanked by two large individuals.

"I'd like to speak to Rega."

"She's not seein' anyone," the larger of the two rumbled.

"It's important," I said. "Ask her to see Mathew Kade."

I flashed an Old World coin, and the smaller giant's eyes widened.

"I said..."

The other interrupted him. "I'll check with her."

He turned and entered the door. I stared at the remaining guard, and he stared at me. I pulled an apple from my bag and began eating it. His eyes followed the apple.

"No fruit, lately?" I asked.

"Not 'til the Farmers come back through."

I threw him an apple. He looked at me suspiciously, and I shook my head. Generosity isn't a common thing. I had almost finished my apple before the other guard returned. He stopped and whispered something to his partner. A flash of disappointment crossed the partner's face, but he nodded. They both started into the street toward me.

The expression on my face hardened, and I set my bag down. They charged, and I stood up with a pistol in each hand. Two shots thundered in the alley, and a wound blossomed in the forehead of each man. The backs of their heads exploded onto the wall they had been standing in front of.

"Two more, Blechley," I muttered.

I set my bag of fruit behind a crate next to the corner of the building and loaded both pistols. One went in the holster and the other in my waistband. I drew my straight razor from its small pouch and stared at the door a moment.

Then I kicked it in. The door slammed inward, and I was through it in a flash. A man with a club was just inside, and I flashed by him. He toppled over as my razor crossed his abdomen. I ducked under the arms of the next guy and turned to pull his head back. I drew my razor across his throat.

I rolled forward as a sword flashed over my head. My razor flashed out once more. I sliced across the inside of the man's leg, severing the femoral artery. There had only been three guys in the hallway. Standing at the other end was a woman who had been quite beautiful in her younger years. She still had some of that beauty, but the life she led had been rough on it.

"Rega, I presume?"

She was staring in horror at the toppling bodies of her men. I stepped forward three steps and stopped. I closed my razor and placed it in its pouch. I cocked my head to the side as if I were listening to someone.

"I see," I said, and my hands flashed. The pistols came up, and I fired through the doors on each side of the hall as I stepped forward. A shot boomed from the left, but it hadn't been pointed at the door anymore.

The muzzle of the right pistol touched her chest and pushed her backward to the door behind her. She gasped as the barrel burned her flesh.

"Time for us to talk."

"Please don't kill me."

"Don't beg," I said. "If I was planning on killin' ya, you'd be dead."

"Anything…"

"I'm gonna ask you some questions; you're gonna answer 'em. Then I'm gonna hurt you for costing seven men their lives."

There was a look of sheer terror on her face. Terror is a high commodity in this Fallen World.

* * * * *

Chapter Ten

Bella and Wilson found me sitting on a stoop near the border of Kort's Zone and that of Moreau. No one goes into Moreau's Zone and comes back out. It's like some black hole that sucks in anyone who goes in. The only ones who do are the Farmers. They don't talk about Moreau's Zone.

"Found out where it happened," I said.

"Have anything to do with the gunshots I heard?" he asked.

"Maybe."

"Figures."

"I saw a local madam brought into the Scraper with a large piece of wood through her shoulder," Bella said. "Looked like a table leg."

"I don't know what you're talkin' about," I said, "but I learned that the Clowns were hit in Overton's."

"The shoulder, eh?" Wilson asked. "That sounds familiar."

I just looked at him.

"I'm just sayin'," he said.

"So...Overton's?" Bella asked.

"Yeah, he's a couple Zones to the north," I said. "He's a mean bastard. But he's not stupid enough to hit the Clowns. If it had been him, the Clowns would have already been in and killed everyone."

"That sounds about right," Wilson said.

"Then we need to go to Overton's and see if we can find out who hit the Clowns," Bella said.

"That's what I'm thinkin'," I said. "We need to go north through Jeffrey's Zone."

"Jeffrey," Wilson said with distaste. "He's a bastard. A slaver. The Society really doesn't like this guy, and he doesn't like us."

"Think we can make it through Jeffrey's without you pickin' a fight?" I asked.

"Yeah, but I don't know whether we can get through without him pickin' a fight."

"It's his funeral," I said. "He picks a fight, he'll deserve what he gets."

"I'm guessing it involves something broken and shoved through his shoulder," Bella said. "I'm detecting a pattern."

"Don't know what you're talkin' about."

"Yeah...sure."

We headed to the north. Jeffrey owned two Scrapers and a small plot that used to be a park. He grew a lot of his own food and didn't rely as heavily on the Farmers as others did. He also had an attitude. Plus his booming slave trade. He wasn't as severe a blight as the Circus or Derris, but he was, indeed, another blight on the city.

The city seemed to get a little darker and dirtier as we crossed into Jeffrey's. It was more of a psychological darkness. We didn't speak as we strode up the street toward the first of the Scrapers. It was the one Jeffrey lived in. The other housed his slave auction. People came there from around the city to buy and sell their slaves.

If the girl hadn't been held by the Clowns, Jeffrey would have been number one on my list of suspects. He would rather bathe in acid, though, than piss off the Clowns. They were some of his best customers. They needed a supply of people to feed through the grinder for the various twisted shows the Circus put on for the rich and depraved.

I still had a hard time seeing Corporate Guards as Clowns. How far the mighty had fallen. In the old days, Corporate Guard was the best job an Agent could get. Protect the Heads. They rarely traveled, so the Guards were home most of the time.

The Clowns' battle skills were much more easily explained by the fact that they were Guards. There weren't many who could match a Corporate Guard.

"There are a few, though," I muttered.

"What was that?" Wilson asked.

"Nothin'," I said. "Talkin' to myselves."

"This place disgusts me."

"The world would be better off without places such as this," Bella said.

"Very true," I said.

"So far, so good," Wilson said.

"We'll get hit."

"Damn, Kade," he said. "Just once, look on the bright side."

"That just ends in disappointment."

He let out a long sigh. It wasn't hard to figure out why. The busy street was becoming much less crowded as people began darting out of the way of the group of men that approached us. There were, easily, seventy-five men.

"Ah, shit," Wilson said.

"Disappointed?"

"Shut up."

The man in the lead approached us by himself.

"Mathew Kade, I presume?" he asked.

He was a tough-looking, dark-skinned man. Six feet tall and carrying several pistols.

"I'm guessin' you're Jeffrey," I said.

"True," he said. "The Clowns sent word you were heading in this direction."

"Guess they caught your interest with the bounty?"

"No," he said. "Oddly, the advice I got from the Clowns was to help you in any way I can. They also told me, under no circumstances, should I attack your party."

He fell in beside me as we walked north.

"Really?"

"If it had been just anyone telling me this, I wouldn't think much of it," he said. "But this came straight from a Clown, a high-ranking Clown. Clowns never preach caution, and I felt it would behoove me to listen when one does."

"That is a little surprising," I said. "What are your intentions?"

"I intend to escort you through my Zone to the next one," he said. "There should be no misunderstandings, this way."

"Did the Clowns tell you what I am investigating?"

"No, they didn't."

"They're probably embarrassed," I said. "Several days ago, a group of their agents was escorting a wagon with various captives toward the Circus. Someone hit that group. Everything disappeared. One of those captives is a girl I have been hired to find."

"I can see why they wouldn't advertise something like this."

"The thing is, Jeffrey," I said, with dead eyes staring into his, "if you had a hand in this, we're gonna have a conflict of interest. People don't tend to survive those conflicts."

"Number one," he said, "and I'm pretty sure you've already figured this out, I wouldn't hit a Clown's agent for all the scrip in the world. My guys are tough as leather, but the damn Clowns are monsters. Anything like that happened in my Zone, I would know. I keep apprised of the groups traveling my Zone."

"My information says it happened in Overton's," I said.

"That's not all that surprising," he said. "Overton isn't much. He sits in his Scraper while chaos reigns outside of it. I can tell you one thing."

"What's that?"

"This group traveled north through my Zone three days back. It never returned through my Zone. If it was taken in Overton, they traveled another direction from there."

I nodded. We were nearing the border into Overton's. He stopped, and his men waited.

"Good luck with your hunt, Mister Kade," he said. "I can't help wondering why a Clown would warn me about such a small group."

"They want to keep doin' business with you," I said. "They couldn't if you were dead."

"Very high opinion of yourself," he said. "That mildly offends me."

"That's good," I said. "If you're offended, you're still breathing."

I turned from the Warlord and walked into Overton's Zone.

"That was different," Wilson said. "First the Clowns, then Jeffrey. Who the hell are you, Kade?"

"Rumors abound in Wilderman's," Bella said. "I never thought I would actually be working with him."

"I'm just a leftover from a world that fell," I said.

My mind wandered back toward the past. The missions, the war, the death and destruction I had left in my wake.

"A world that needed to fall," I added. "We brought the Fall on ourselves. It's not a better world that we have now. Maybe, in time, it could be made into a better one if…"

Wilson slammed me sideways as I heard the thunder of a gun. His body rocked with the impact, but he kept pushing me to the edge of the street. His body rocked again as another shot hit him. Then we were under cover of the wall. I pulled him behind a wagon parked at the side of the street.

The shooter was on top of the building we were against.

"Son of a bitch," he cursed, "bastard got me."

"Looks like one in the leg, one in the side," I said. Something was beginning to boil inside me. I tore my coat from my shoulders and pushed it against the wound in his side. Bella rolled into the spot behind the wagon.

"Look after him," I said.

She nodded, and my eyes went cold and dead. I launched myself toward the wall and upward, my fingers grasping protrusions where you would think none could be found. I scaled the wall. I caught a windowsill and launched myself upward. I shot over the top and took three steps before the gunman even knew I was there. He spun around, and my right foot slammed into his chest like a piston. I caught his rifle as it flew from his hands and spun it around. I shot him three times before he hit the ground five stories below.

I wasted no time and went over the edge to reverse the path I had taken to the top. I dropped from windowsill to windowsill and landed lightly on the ground below. I reached Wilson.

"How is he?"

"The one in his side is rough. He's not going any further with us."

"Neither are you," I said. "I'll finish this. You get him to Stiner's and back to the Society. When I'm through, I'll meet you there."

"What about backup?"

"They better get more."

"They?"

"Yeah," I said. "They have no idea what's comin'. And when I'm done, I'm gonna have a word with Blechley."

I handed her a handful of coins. "Hire whoever you need to get him home."

"Home," he mumbled, "Teresa...kill me."

"Tell her I'll be along shortly, Wilson," I said. "You saved my life back there. You've done your job. Now, it's time for me to do mine."

I should have killed Blechley. For some people, mercy is wasted in this Fallen World.

* * * * *

Chapter Eleven

Rage was still boiling just below the surface as I watched Bella and the two guys she had hired to carry Wilson's stretcher leave to the west. Stiner's was the next Zone over, so she shouldn't have any trouble. I turned toward the east. Rega had said the Caravan was hijacked by some freelancers close to the border with Payne. I strode down the middle of the street and people sidestepped as I neared them.

I stopped as I neared the border. An old man sat on a stoop. He was carving a piece of stone, and there were quite a few chips around him, so I approached.

"Might you sell me some info?" I asked.

"Maybe."

"Ya been out here for a few days?"

"Been here for weeks."

"A wagon and some guys got hit here a few days ago."

"Saw what happened, I did."

I slipped a coin into his hand. "Tell me."

"Won't do ya no good," he said. "It was that cult, down south. Moreau, his name is. People go in there; they don't come back. If they do, its cause they workin' for him."

I nodded. "That's what I needed to know. Take another coin for your troubles and your silence."

He nodded as I slipped him another coin. Then I turned and walked into Payne's Zone. Moreau's was the Zone below Payne's. I'd never been into Moreau's for obvious reasons. It was unknown whether it was like Derris' or something else. It was rumored to be some sort of cult. If you went into Derris' you'd get eaten. It was unknown what happened in Moreau's if you didn't choose to join his cult. People just quit going into the Zone.

The skies were darkening from their normal burnt red to black; night was closing in. Perhaps that was a good thing. A little darkness might be just what was called for.

I stopped about halfway through Payne's when I saw a wagon with a fire and a grill. An old woman was grilling meat on skewers. I didn't bother asking what sort of meat it was. It didn't smell like pork, so it was safe to say it wasn't pork or human. That was good enough for me. I also saw some sort of bird on the grill.

"Too small to be chicken," I said, pointing at the bird. "What is it?"

"Pigeon," she said.

"I'll take that and one skewer of the mystery meat."

She laughed but pulled a skewer from the grill along with the pigeon.

"Two scrip," she said.

I slipped her two of the plastic chits that had ended up with the name "scrip" after the Fall. They were used to buy food from the Farmers and had become the currency of choice years ago. There had been one attempt to counterfeit the chits about ten years back in one of the Zones. That Zone was empty ten years later because the Farmers wouldn't supply that Zone again. Permanent ban. No one could move into the area for lack of supplies. Neighboring Zones couldn't supply the Zone, or they would have been banned as well and left to die.

Never pays to mess with the Farmers.

I took my meal over to an empty stoop and sat with my back to a wall. I would need to wait for about an hour to take advantage of the shadows as the sun set. Chewing on a piece of pigeon, I thought about what lay ahead. If the girl was in Moreau's, she had been indoctrinated into his cult or possibly disposed of. It depended on how long it would take to convert someone. There used to be ways to brainwash a person before the Fall, and I expected there were some who remembered the techniques.

Most of those techniques were pushed aside with the imprint tech. Obsidian Corporation had been the original developer of the tech, but it had spread to the rest of the world fairly quickly. Lots of money changed hands and, suddenly, the world had been a whole new place. Schools were replaced with imprint tech. Who would take the time to learn things, when they could have it imprinted straight into their minds?

Of course, things went sideways. The cost of imprinting was high, so the rich became the educated. The poor learned the hard way. It was discovered that a lot of the education programs weren't permanent. The joke was on them, I suppose. Many lost their imprinted knowledge. It seemed that Obsidian had sold faulty tech to most of the world. They, alone, held the permanent imprint system.

Oh, the glory days of Obsidian. This had begun the Corporate Wars. The Fall of the world followed as the nukes rained down. Obsidian versus the World. There were things I had done for Obsidian that made me sigh in relief as the nukes ripped great holes in our cities.

Damned if I hadn't survived it. Who would have thought?

The shadows were deep enough, so I stood and headed south toward Moreau's. I wouldn't have expected it, but I missed the banter between Wilson and me. Most of my life has been spent alone with the mess that rattles around in my head. Wilson had been a pleasant distraction. I found that I genuinely liked the man. His wounds weren't life threatening if Bella could get him to Teresa.

He shouldn't have pushed me out of the way. I could take the punishment much better than he could. Some of the alterations from before the Fall made me a lot tougher than most. But he had, and when this was finished, Blechley was going to learn a final lesson.

I reached the border and slipped into the shadows of the buildings to disappear. There were people in the streets, just like in Payne's Zone. But there was a tension in the air. You would think something like that couldn't be seen, but it's visible through something more than sight—intuition, perhaps. Using all the senses to passively read the world around you. I could feel a sense of desperation in the people who lived along these streets, where booths were set up to sell food or goods, just as in any other Zone.

I slid, silently, through the shadows toward the Scraper closest to the border. There were two, but this one was much larger. I stopped to survey the surroundings.

"You should leave," on older man said from the booth in front of me. His back was to me, and he never raised his head from the cookware he was cleaning. "Leave before the guard finds ya, boy."

"Can't," I said back, softly. "Have to find someone who disappeared into this place a few days ago."

"Ya can't help 'em, boy," he said. "Moreau's got 'em now."

"You saw 'em?"

"It's where any of the young go," he said. "I was too old for his tastes. I was told to sell these, and if I tried to run, they would kill my daughter. She's in the Scraper."

I was beginning to feel that rage building again.

"They come through the streets every so often with our family members, just to show us they live. I saw Frea two days ago. She saw me, but she showed no signs of recognition. She didn't know me."

I felt a hollowness in my stomach. Something was majorly wrong here. I looked around at the various people I could see. All were old. None were less than sixty. Where were the others?

"I still have to find her," I said.

"A girl?" he asked. "A red head?"

"Yeah."

"It's a pity. She was a beauty. They're hard on the beautiful. Ugly and you can still be a guard. The beautiful are for one thing inside the Scraper."

That hollow pit stayed in my stomach.

"They'll catch ya, son," he said. "But I'll wish ya good luck, anyway. Maybe ya can get her outta there."

"Thanks for the wishes," I said, the rage touching the surface. "But if they catch me, they'll wish they hadn't."

"I hope you're right, son," he said. He never lifted his head, and his eyes never left his work.

I slipped along in the shadows toward the Scraper. When I reached the side of the Scraper, I scaled the wall to the third floor, where I found a sliding window that wasn't locked. I was inside in seconds and found an empty room with a bed.

The door opened, and I backed into the shadows. The door closed, and a light came on. A pretty girl of about fourteen stood there looking at me. I was holding a throwing knife in each of my hands.

She didn't blink. I saw no fear, no surprise. Her eyes were filled with adoration.

"May I please you?" she asked as she slipped her loose white robe from her shoulders.

Something ugly twitched inside me. I had seen that look before. This wasn't brainwashing; it was much more sinister. I had seen this tear our world apart once. Moreau had an imprinter, and my mission had just become a great deal more than saving a single girl.

"No, thank you," I said.

Tears sprang into her eyes, and I shuddered in rage.

"I'm not pretty enough," she said.

"You're beautiful," I said and saw her tears slow. "And I would love for you to please me when I return. I must finish my job first. Wait for me here."

The smile changed her face to radiance, and I knew Moreau would suffer this day.

I had lived the imprints of thousands. This was worse than the rape of a body. This was a rape of the body, mind, and soul.

I walked openly out the door and down to the lobby where I knew there would be guards.

"Take me to your Warlord!" I yelled as I entered the lobby. "He can't just steal my wife and not face me!"

The guards closed on me, and I put up a token fight, bloodying a nose or two. If Moreau had recovered some of the lost imprint tech, something would have to be done. What better way to find it than to get an escort?

There are things that should never be recovered in this Fallen World.

* * * * *

Chapter Twelve

I was dragged to an elevator and pushed inside. Five guards joined me, and one pushed the button for the penthouse. Old World or new, they always wanted to be at the top.

"My wife..." I muttered.

"Shut up," one of the five commanded as he backhanded me.

I restrained myself. *Not yet.*

The elevator stopped, and I was pushed out of the small compartment into a lavish suite. They dragged me toward an extremely obese man who sat on a throne of sorts. It was a huge, padded chair.

"Who might this be?" he asked. I could see his jowls shake with the movement of his mouth.

"He claims to be searching for his wife."

Laughter rolled from the fat man.

"Then, by all means, let's reunite them!" he said. "What is her name?"

"It's Maddy," I said, "Maddy Hale."

He bellowed his laughter, again. "The new one? Oh. This is going to be wonderful!"

He pointed to one of the men. "Bring the new girl to me!"

The guard left and was gone for a few minutes. He returned, followed by Maddy Hale. She was in one of the white, flowing robes.

"Maddy!" I yelled.

"May I please you?" she asked me.

The fat man laughed.

"Come here, girl!"

She turned and almost ran to him.

"This is what is going to happen," he said, with an evil glint in his eyes. "First, we're going to strap you into this machine."

He pointed to a chair with straps that had a helmet hanging above it.

"Then your little darling, here, is going to service me right in front of you. Then she is going to service all twenty-five of my guards."

He waved his arms, indicating the twenty-five guards in the penthouse.

"Then we are going to turn on the machine, and you are going to come out of it with your only waking thought being to pleasure us. Then you will take your turn and service each and every one of us."

I decided it was the perfect time to call in the reinforcements.

My head sagged for a second, then I stood erect with the guards around me.

"No. This is what's going to happen. In ten seconds, I am going to break this man's arm. Then I'm going to incapacitate all your guards, from the right side of the room to the left. I'm not going to kill them because they are victims, just as much as she is. And when I'm done, I'll deal with you, Tubby."

"What the hell?!" he exclaimed. "Who are you!?"

"Just consider yourselves lucky," I said to the guard on my left. He was the one who had backhanded me. "Be happy he didn't send Gaunt. My name is William Childers, Obsidian Special Forces."

I snapped the arm of the man on my left. My stiffened fingers sank into the one on the right, and he toppled, trying to draw a breath. My elbow punched the side of the next one's neck hard enough to drop him into unconsciousness. I spun around and put stiffened fingers into pressure points on the other two that left them paralyzed. They toppled backward.

This had taken two and a half seconds. I spun again and launched myself forward toward the ten guards on the right who were just realizing something was happening. I had put down four more before the first gunshot boomed in the room.

I felt a tug at my leg but ignored it and ripped the gun from the hand of the man who had just shot me. I threw it, and it slammed into the throat of his partner. Then I dislocated both the man's arms as I twisted them backward with a pop.

I moved on to the next. His shot went wide as my foot sank into his solar plexus. He was done. The next three took stiffened fingers to pressure points.

I heard the guns and felt the tug of another hit in my side. I didn't slow down. I was among the ones on the left, and they would have trouble shooting me without hitting their friends. The guns still fired, and three of them fell from friendly fire. I felt the bullet go through my shoulder just before I throat-punched the last man.

I turned to Moreau, who cringed.

"Time for a change of regimes, fat man."

I dragged the blubbering Warlord from his throne and over to his own imprinter. I strapped him in and dropped the helmet down. A vacation printer. I felt a swell of relief as I saw what type of imprinter it was.

These had been used to give someone a month of being someone else. The imprint would fade. He'd been re-imprinting whenever the imprint started to run out. I flipped the switch on the side and Moreau's begging stopped. I raised the helmet.

"May I please you?" he asked.

I turned to the guards and retrieved my weapons, then I returned to Moreau. I unstrapped the former Warlord from the chair. There was a mark tattooed on his arm, so I drew my razor and cut it away.

He cried.

I walked to one of the guards I had paralyzed. I hit another pressure point and showed the guard the mark I held in my hand.

"Master?" he asked. "Orders?"

I pointed at Moreau. "Doctor his arm and chain him to the wall. His sole purpose is to pleasure every guard in the Scraper. He will do this every day. You will make sure it is done."

"Yes, sir."

I looked at Maddy Hale, who stood beside the throne with a blank stare.

"May I please you?" she asked as I approached. I showed her the mark.

"Master," she said, with complete adoration.

"Come with me," I said.

"Will I be pleasing you, Master?"

"Not yet," I said. "Soon."

I returned to the imprinter and removed several parts, including the limited database. I placed the parts in my pockets.

I led Maddy to the elevator, and we descended to the third floor where we returned to the room I had left the girl in.

"Master," she said, "May I please you?"

"Come with me," I said.

She followed along, and we descended to the lobby.

"Orders?" the first guard asked when he saw the mark I held out.

"Gather every guard in the Zone and report to the penthouse. Orders will be waiting."

Moreau was in for a hell of a month. All his men would deprogram before he would. They would retain the memories. He might survive that, he might not.

The girls followed me out of the Scraper. We walked north up the street. I stopped at a stand that sold cookware. The man looked up from his work. I handed him a flap of skin with a mark on it.

"Show this, and no one will interfere with you," I said. "Go find your daughter."

"I can never repay you, son," he said.

"Use that wisely," I said. "Stay away from the penthouse. A chapter of the Society of the Sword will be moving in here. Give that to the leader and go...or stay. This Zone is changing. May be worth watching."

"The imprinter?"

He was old enough to remember the imprinters.

"Destroyed."

"Who are you, son?"

"Mathew Kade."

"I'll remember it," he said and turned away. He almost ran toward the Scraper.

"Alright, girls, let's go."

"Will we be pleasing you?"

"Soon," I said.

We walked out of Moreau's Zone to the astonishment of those inside Payne's. No one approached. They stayed out of my way. It was the first time I had ever traveled at night that I didn't have to defend myself. We walked, unharmed, through Payne's, then Overton's, and on through Stiner's, to the warehouse that was the home of the Society.

The guard at the entrance recognized me immediately.

"Kade," he said. "You're bleeding."

"I'm ok," I said. "They're not."

He chuckled.

"I need you to take these two ladies to Teresa," I said. "I have some unfinished business to take care of.

"Protect them," I added. "Especially from themselves. You'll understand in a minute."

"Will do."

"Girls, go with him."

"Will we be pleasuring you?" they asked simultaneously.

"I see."

"Tell her it's imprint tech. It'll fade, but they'll need help when it does."

"I will."

"Wilson make it back?"

"Yeah," he said. "Too stubborn to die."

"True."

I nodded at the Squire and strode back into the night. There are more than blights in this broken place. Sometimes there are beacons in this Fallen World.

* * * * *

Epilogue

Simon Blechley awoke with a start. There was a wetness on his face. He reached out and turned on the lamp beside the immense canopy bed. He looked up and saw that the canopy was sagging and dripping something on his face.

He wiped his hand across his face, and it came away red. He started to scream just as the canopy split and the heads of all his lieutenants cascaded down over him.

His screech was cut short as a hand seized his throat.

"Hello there," a voice whispered to him. "I don't think we've been formally introduced."

"K-K-Kade?"

"Not today, Simon," the voice answered. "Stephen Gaunt, at your service. We have so much to talk about."

* * *

I walked across the floor to the vault I had built into the solid concrete of the platform. I turned the dials to open the vault door. I pulled the various pieces of the imprinter from my pockets and lay them on a shelf. Then I took the database from another pocket and placed it on a shelf with five others.

Some things never should have been created and never should be where people could get to them.

I left my vault and began to doctor my wounds. The quick healing from the alterations was a great boon to someone in my line of work.

Perhaps I would soak in the huge tub for a while.

* * *

K ade had been on her mind a lot lately.
SSWWSSSHHH
Too much for her comfort.
TTHHSSSSS

Kade. *How was he still alive?* Especially after the last days. And why did it matter to her? But it did, didn't it?

SSHHAAPP

The head of the practice maniq went flying as she twisted the katana blade at just the right moment. She didn't stop moving as the sword came back around and ended up in the scabbard at her side, without seeming to slow from the killing stroke. She loved the katana. It had been her mother's before the Fall and rested in a place of honor with its twin when not on her side or across her back. She placed it in the wooden wardrobe and closed the dark-grained door with a smile. For some reason, the thought of Kade gave her the same feeling as the thought of her mother. Well, not exactly the same, she thought with a wry grin.

"One of my weaknesses," she said quietly, "of which I have far too many."

A throat cleared across the room, and she came back to full realization of her surroundings and out of the heightened awareness of the fight. While in the practice session, she had felt and seen everything around her. She had felt Poe as he came up to the door and patiently stopped to wait for her to finish the bout. She had immediately dismissed him as a threat and continued to contend with the maniqs that attacked her from the floor and ceiling. Seven this time, a good workout coming right after the half hour of parkour training in full armor.

"What's up, Wilson?" she asked the big man. He was recovering from his wounds nicely.

"You have a visitor from the Tees, ma'am," Poe rumbled with head bowed.

The Tees was a tunnel system that ran beneath a large part of the city. After the bombings that led to the Fall, it had been blocked off. That was the story everyone believed. The Society of the Sword knew better. She had known about the system for several years and had dealt with the Mardins that inhabited the dark, damp labyrinth. She did an occasional favor for them and provided certain foodstuffs they had no access to, and they provided information and safe passage when needed—when it did not endanger their secrecy.

"Must be important for them to send an emissary above ground. Any idea what it's about?" She leapt effortlessly up from the sunken training area, plucking a damp towel from the rack on the way.

"No, ma'am. Only that it was of interest to you and that you would want the info immediately."

"Well, let's go see what's so important," Teresa Manora, matriarch and absolute leader of the Society of the Sword, said with a small smile. "Maybe they want a Chapterhouse opened."

"That's possible," he said. "Nothing would surprise me after Blechley's one remaining lieutenant came in asking for a Chapterhouse when he couldn't find all the pieces of his boss. But I think it's unlikely, since I don't think Kade has a beef with the Tees."

"Blechley deserved it," she said. "I swear, Kade's like a great big cat. He brings what he thinks are gifts to my doorstep."

"Sounds about right," he said. "We have four decent sized Zones to run, now. Kinda makes you wonder what will happen when he goes on another rampage."

"Who knows?" she answered as she approached the door to the meeting hall and motioned for Poe to enter. "Shall we?"

# # # # #

Broken City

Chapter One

I heard the mechanism begin to turn on the vault door, and I was moving. Not many people know the combination to my home, and I was going to be prepared if it wasn't one of those few.

I recognized the light step of Teresa and sat back down in the huge armchair the previous owner had graciously left for me. I slid the straight razor back into the pocket where it usually rested. I winced a little as I twisted and stretched the skin around the latest bullet wound.

Gettin' sloppy, boy, Childers chided me. *Need to exercise more.*

And the tacos? Stephen Gaunt's precise voice asked. *What were you thinking?*

"Quit squawkin'," I muttered. "Both of you."

Teresa Manora stepped through the door and looked at me with an eyebrow raised.

"Arguing with yourselves?"

"They're givin' me a hard time about getting shot again."

"I happen to agree with them," she said.

I'm not sure why Teresa has anything to do with me. I'm bat shit crazy, and she's probably one of the most powerful people in the central city Zones. Not to mention beautiful and one of the best users of the katana she carried I had ever seen.

Her blonde hair was pulled back in a ponytail so as not to impede her vision, and she wore black body armor that couldn't disguise the curves underneath. Her light step was silent as she glided across the floor toward me. Any noise she had made as she entered was for my benefit.

I stood back up, and she was in my arms, our lips connecting. We stayed like this for some time.

I took a deep breath as we parted and looked toward the train car in the center of the huge room.

"Unfortunately," she said after a long sigh, "I came with another purpose in mind. Although we might be able to get to that a little later."

"Promises, promises," I said. "So what, besides my charming personalities, has brought your lovely self to my humble abode?"

"Don't speak in Gaunt speak," she said. "It's disturbing."

I chuckled.

"The Mardins have sent an emissary to me," she said. "They have a problem and wanted my advice about how to handle it. I suggested they hire you for a job. I came to see if you were healthy enough to take on a case so soon after the mess with Moreau."

"It's possible," I said. "Depends on the job."

"Investigating a string of murders that run from one end of the city to the other."

"Gotta love a good, old-fashioned murder investigation."

"They are particularly vicious murders," she said. "If you want to take the case, I'll be sending a few Squires down to assist you."

"I almost got Poe killed last time," I said. "You sure you wanna send more?"

"Blechley almost got Poe killed," she said. "And I understand he's a bit torn up about it."

"True enough."

"If you're interested," she said, "the emissary is still at the Chapterhouse."

"Yeah," I said. "I think I am."

"Then get dressed and let's get this show on the road."

I chuckled and entered my train car. There were two large rooms inside. I had them both set up as bedrooms. They were lavish rooms since they were built before I took over the place. The former Warlord had built it before Stiner killed him and took his Scraper. Stiner hadn't known about the secret getaway, so I had taken it.

I took my shirt off and unbuttoned my pants. Teresa's hands slid around my waist.

"On second thought," she whispered in my ear, "I think they can wait a little while."

Our lips met again when I turned around, and we surrendered to the moment and tumbled onto the huge bed. We lost ourselves in each other for a time. Both of us have memories of terrible things we have done and terrible things done to us. But we could forget all of that for a while and just be together. Perhaps that's why she stayed with me. She had found someone who was even more broken than she was.

Afterward, we lay there looking at the ceiling.

"How the hell did you do that?" she asked.

"One of me is a very high-priced courtesan," I said. "She knows all the right spots."

"She?"

"Not all Agents were guys," I said. "I got the whole database."

"How many are there, really?"

"I don't know."

"Must be a hell of a thing."

"Not so much, anymore," I said. "The Kade persona pretty much took over. The rest took a back seat, and they all gain from life experiences as we go. It's a jumble sometimes, but we all get along well now. We've had seventeen years to get used to each other since the royal rumble in my head found a winner."

"So that's why you know how to do so many things," she said.

"Yep. If you need somethin', I got an app for that."

"App?"

"Never mind." I chuckled. "Old World humor."

"Figures."

"I think a bath would be nice before we go," I said. "Care to join me?"

"You didn't think I would come to your place and not use that enormous bathtub, did you?"

"You just use me for my appliances."

"My secret is out," she said and kissed me quickly.

She slid out of the bed and walked out of the train car. I thoroughly enjoyed watching her do that. I enjoyed the bath even more.

Despite the fall of civilization as we knew it, there are times when I realize it's ok to have a moment of joy in this Fallen World.

* * * * *

Chapter Two

I took a new shirt from the closet and a new trench coat. My last one had taken a lot of abuse. I had several because the one before that had been mostly destroyed as well.

A lady who traveled with the Farmers made them for me. Every couple of months, she would bring me a new set of clothing. She always tried not to charge me, but I would always insist. She was the mother of a young girl who had been raped and killed. I had found the person responsible for it.

Teresa came back into the bedroom, carrying the harness that held my weapons.

"You should use body armor," she said.

"Restricts my movement," I said.

"Yeah, yeah."

I slipped the harness over my shoulders and buckled the straps. I had added another holster to the harness to hold the second .44 I had picked up during the last case. There were some different guns in my vault, but the six shooters were good weapons. Ammo was hard to come by, so it paid not to have an automatic. By the time I had shot twelve times, they would be dead or close enough that I would need the blades. I had twelve throwing knives made of Old World metals and the ever present straight razor I had used for years.

I went to the cabinet and took several sacks down and put them in various pockets. I opened one.

"Jerky?" I asked and held the bag out to Teresa.

She pulled a couple of pieces of dried meat from the sack.

"Do I want to know what kind of meat it is?"

"Nope," I answered. "It's not human. That's all you really need to know."

She shrugged and tore a chunk off with her teeth.

"Not bad," she said, after chewing a moment. "Not too hard to chew, either."

"There's an old survivalist in here," I said, tapping my head.

"Survivalist?"

"Old World," I said. "We're all survivalists now. He knew how to make good jerky."

"You sure you're up for this?"

"I heal quickly."

"Poe's gonna be pissed that he gets left out of this one," she said.

"He'll get over it," I said. "I almost got him killed last time. He should be tryin' to stay away from me."

"He was doing his job, Kade."

"I should have killed Blechley the first time I dealt with him," I said. "Instead, there's a hundred or so people who died because of that damn bounty."

"You can't retrain humans to be human if you kill them all," she said. "You tried to give him a chance. That's something you should do. I'm not saying to let it go on and on, but a chance to be a human again should be there."

"You make my choice sound noble," I said. "It wasn't. I thought it would be fun to see what happened."

"That's what you tell yourself," she said. "I know better. I've seen who you are, Mathew Kade. Sure, you have all those people inside of you, but I've seen you walk the streets and give to the poor.

I've seen you help the helpless. You were paid to find Hap, not walk in and take on a whole Zone to free him. You did that because you couldn't let what was happening continue. The same with that girl, Maddy."

I snorted as I opened the vault door to leave my home.

"You still think you're that guy who worked for Obsidian Corporation," she said. "He did some terrible things for people who didn't deserve the service he gave. You may not see the changes in you yourself, but those of us who have watched you over the last ten years have seen them."

"Hmph."

"You keep telling yourself what you want."

We walked out of the old bank building. There were people in the streets. Some were operating small stands. Across from the bank was a shack where a hammer on metal sounded a rhythm as Soba plied his trade as a blacksmith. We had lost a great deal in the Fall. Factories used to do what Soba did and much more. Soba made several things. He used light metals to make bowls and plates and heavier metals to make tools and weapons.

I walked over and stepped into his shop.

"Kade!" he said when he saw me. "It is good to see you, my friend."

"How are ya, Soba?"

"Doing well, with the Farmers' contract you got for me," he said. "I never thought I would be making horseshoes."

"True," I said. "Not a lot of horses in the city."

"I am still amazed they gave me the contract when the have their own blacksmiths."

"I've seen their guys," I said. "They have three good blacksmiths. The youngest is nearly sixty years old. They use apprentices to do most of the work, now. You're lucky you spent the time before the Fall doing fairs and things. You've got ten times the experience of the apprentices, and you're better than at least one of their main guys. I wouldn't be surprised if you landed a lot more work from 'em in the future."

"You don't say?"

"You might even look into some apprentices, now, to be prepared."

"I don't have the scrip to hire apprentices, yet. Perhaps after this contract is filled, I can."

"I know some people with a little scrip," I said. "I've been talkin' to a few, and they would like to make a little investment. Would you be interested?"

"How big of a bite would they want of my business?" he asked. "I don't want to be stuck working for someone else, here. I built this forge."

"Ten percent," I said. "They'll provide the scrip to get your shop moving and to support apprentices and guards. They want a little input on the contracts. Not much, just suggestions. Ultimately, the business is all you. They may be able to steer some contracts your way."

"And you vouch for these people?" he asked. "If you trust them, I would be willing to do it. But only if you trust them."

"I trust 'em."

"Then my answer is yes, my friend."

I reached into my right coat pocket and pulled out a sack of coins. I extended it to a wide eyed blacksmith.

"You were that sure of my answer?" he asked. "They sent scrip with you?"

"This will get you started," I said. "I'll be your go between with these folks, and we'll talk more later. I have a case at the moment, and it's gonna take me out of the Zone for a bit."

"Jesus, Kade!" he said as he looked in the sack. "There's a lot of scrip, here."

"Just a start, Soba."

"I'll hire some guards, first, I think."

"I would suggest a couple of Squires from the Society."

He looked in the sack once more, "Yeah, I think so."

"Two will be on the way over in less than an hour," Teresa said behind me. She had been quiet throughout the whole conversation.

Soba's eyes widened even further when he saw her and realized who she was.

"Ma'am," he said, with a respectful nod.

"All right, Soba," I said. "I'm off, and you'll have guards very shortly. Keep that under wraps until they get here."

"That I will do, my friend."

"Tomorrow," Teresa said, "I would like to see you about a contract for a few weapons, if you have the time to meet me."

"At your convenience, ma'am."

"Perhaps early," she said. "So it won't interfere with your work day."

"Gladly, ma'am," he said. "I'll be here at sunup."

"Agreed."

We exited the shop of a very excited blacksmith.

"Investors?"

"Yep."

"I saw you take that sack of coins from your vault before we left."

"Hmph."

"Yeah, you're a bad guy. Keep telling yourself that."

"Yeah," I said. "How big is the weapons contract you're after?"

"We need some basic short swords for the novices to start with," she said. "Perhaps a hundred or so."

I chuckled.

"He'll have a heart attack," I said. "Break it to him gently. That's more weapons than he made last year."

"He's good, isn't he?"

"Oh, yeah," I said. "There're not many better. The Farmers have two blacksmiths, and Wilderman has one who's great. Soba is probably number four in the whole city on quality."

"If he's that good, there'll be more after that."

"He is."

"Then he'll do well."

We walked up the street toward the building that housed the Society of the Sword. It had been a large building of a modest ten stories, and it had covered a great deal of space. Teresa and her folks had built defenses around the building and had done a lot of remodeling inside. She had close to two hundred inhabitants who lived on the premises. Close to a hundred of them were novices who had come to learn how to defend themselves. Most of those were poor, but some were from wealthy families in the Scrapers. The Society had grown a great deal in the last five years. They hadn't opened other Chapterhouses until recently though.

People traveled to her compound to become part of the Society. If they passed her vetting process, she started their training. When a person graduated as a Knight of the Sword, they were one of the toughest fighters in our broken city. Knights traveled the city when they chose to, and they sought their own path after leaving the compound to start their life quest.

Teresa had taken a lot from the medieval history I had imparted on her. Knights and quests, things most people didn't know anything about from before the Fall and long in the past. She tried to form her Society with the best of those things and discard the worst.

Teresa would train almost anyone in basic skills to survive in this fallen world. Some would take the Oath of Allegiance to the Society and become Yeomen. They would train for a future as a Knight. The wealthy paid to have their children trained, and Teresa trained the less fortunate for other fare. Some would work in the compound as cooks, cleaners, and such.

"Ma'am." The sentry nodded toward Teresa with respect.

His eyes met mine, and he nodded toward me. "Kade."

"Michael," I said. "How's the wife?"

"She's the same as always," he said. "Crazy."

"They're all crazy," I said, with a grin.

"Some are crazier than others." He chuckled.

"True enough."

Teresa looked at me with one eyebrow raised.

"What?"

She shook her head and walked through the gate. I shrugged and followed. As we made our way toward the center of the building, we passed many of the inhabitants of the Chapterhouse. All looked at Teresa with the utmost respect. You didn't get that sort of respect unless you were something pretty special.

Considering the hell she had gone through right after the Fall, it was amazing she became the person she is today.

I saw a familiar face and stopped.

"Maddy," I said.

She had been walking down the hallway with her head bowed. She hardly ever looked into anyone's eyes.

She saw me, and the expression on her face went from sadness to wide-eyed joy. She ran straight to me.

"Kade!"

I hugged the girl who had been a captive of the Warlord, Moreau.

"How are you holdin' up, girl?" I asked.

"So much better, now."

She noticed Teresa and nodded to her. "Ma'am."

"I never got to thank you for what you did for me, Mister Kade," she said, turning back to me. "I only got free of the imprint a few days ago. The Matron has been helping me accept what happened and grow from it. She is an amazing person."

"I know," I said. "Have you seen your father?"

"He's coming tomorrow," she said. "I'm so scared about what he'll think of me."

"He'll think he's too happy to have you back to judge you for what you had no control over."

"I hope so," she said.

"Have you given thought to taking the training courses, here?"

"I have," she said. "If Dad is ok with it, I want the training. No one is going to make me a victim again."

I saw the smile on Teresa's face at the girl's words. She would make sure the girl knew enough to protect herself.

You're only a victim if you choose to be in this Fallen World.

* * * * *

Chapter Three

Teresa had a conference room where she met with future clients who wished to hire the Society for various jobs. I saw a pale man sitting in one of the chairs around the large, round table. He wore dark lenses over his eyes. I recognized the form of dress. I'd met some of the Mardins when I built the escape tunnel from my home. They lived in the Tees, the tunnel system underneath the city. Below them was the sewer, and they kept the system working in return for people from above staying out of their territory. Occasionally, they would hire some people from above to work in the Tees, but never very deep.

I nodded to the representative. "I understand you would like to hire me for a job?"

"You come very highly recommended, Mister Kade," he said. "I have been told you are a very good investigator."

"I've investigated a few murders over the years," I said. "Found a few items, recovered a few kidnappings. What can I do for you Mister...?"

"Fraans," he said. "There has been a series of deaths in the Tees. We are at a loss as to who is behind them. We would like to hire you to find the one responsible."

"To be clear, when I find this guy, do you want him alive to face charges?"

"We want the killings stopped," Fraans said. "If you bring him to us alive, we will charge and execute him. If you kill him, the killings stop. Either way is fine with us."

121

"What can you tell me about the murders?"

"They are particularly violent," he said. "I have pictures of the latest one."

"Pictures?" I asked. "It's been a while since I saw anyone who had a camera."

"You would be surprised by what is found underground in this city."

"Not really," I said. "I've seen some pretty odd things up here. The Tees having all sorts of things from the Old World doesn't surprise me at all."

Fraans nodded and lifted a briefcase from beside his chair and set it on the table. He opened it and pulled out a small stack of photos from the case and slid them across the table to me.

I winced when I saw the first one. There was blood everywhere. Pools and splatter. The body was that of a woman. She was pale like Fraans and, from what I could tell, not much older than Maddy Hale. I'd seen many cuts in my life and these weren't cuts. She had, literally, been ripped apart. The strength necessary to do the damage that had been done was staggering. This wasn't a normal killer. I would have thought it was a group if not for the next picture.

There were footprints in the blood. But it was just one set. I thumbed through the rest of the pictures.

"Ok," I said. "I'll take the job. Twenty-five thousand scrip. Payable when the job is done. I don't find him, you don't have to pay."

"Very high," he said. "But the part where we don't pay if you fail to find the killer is unusual. Most people want their scrip up front. What would happen if you did a job, and the client decided not to pay? The job would have been done already."

"Ask Blechley. He crossed me. Ask around."

He chuckled. "Just playing the devil's advocate, Mister Kade. I am well aware of recent events. And events that aren't so recent. The deal is more than fair. You will have full access to our territory during your investigation."

"I need a map of the Tees," I said. "I have a map of the city, but not the Tees."

"We will have an escort for you…"

"I don't intend to get lost down there if our escort disappears for any reason."

He nodded. "Understood. I wouldn't like to be lost above ground in unknown territory."

"Alright then," I said as I stood up. "You get the map, and I'll get my supplies ready."

He nodded. "Thank you, Mister Kade."

"Save that for when I find this guy."

Fraans stood and nodded toward Teresa. "Thanks once again, Matron."

"It is the least I can do." She stood and shook hands with the Mardin. "Your people helped a poor outsider when no others would. I haven't forgotten."

He nodded and left the room.

"That's where you hid after The General?" I asked.

"Yes."

"I wondered," I said. "Figured you'd tell me someday."

"It was a dark time," she said.

"I'd say so."

She stepped close, and our lips met.

"I'll go get Michael and Lindsey," she said as we separated. "I'm sending two Squires with you."

"That could be interesting," I said, with a chuckle.

"Shouldn't be boring." She laughed.

She walked out of the room, and I sat back down to look at the pictures again.

See the marks on the torso? The voice in my head belonged to Samuel Gladson, a former homicide detective. *Those are claw marks.*

"Some exotic weapon or somethin' much worse," I muttered.

I saw something like this before the Fall. Be careful.

I could see what he remembered in my head and suspected the detective was probably right. They hadn't caught the killer back then. The killings stopped when Gladson had gotten too close. If it was the same guy, this fallen world was the perfect hunting ground for him. There's no telling how many deaths he'd caused in the last twenty years after the Fall. The city was fractured into mini kingdoms, and someone could slip through the cracks much easier than in the Old World.

"What are the odds this is the same guy?" I muttered.

I'd say, pretty damn good.

I stood up and pushed the photos into an inside pocket. I left the room and headed down the hallway to the armory. I wanted some bullets for my pistols. The Society kept one hell of an arsenal.

As I turned a corner, I almost ran into a human wall.

"Wilson," I said. "How's the leg?"

"Getting better," he said. "I hear you're takin' on another case. The boss won't let me come."

He looked disappointed.

"You probably won't fit in the tunnels anyway."

"That's a nice new coat, there," he said. "Be a shame if somethin' happened to it."

I laughed. "Wish you could come, big guy. Instead, I get the Tanziks."

"Serves you right," he said, with a laugh.

"Expected as much," I said. "So, I'm not disappointed."

He laughed again. "Maybe I got that backward. Maybe it serves them right."

"I have no idea what you're talkin' about."

"Hmph."

"Got anything new in the armory?"

"Funny you should ask that," he said. "I have somethin' that will probably help in the Tees."

I followed as the big man turned and led the way to the armory. He wasn't limping as badly as I expected. Wilson was a healthy guy, and he had healed pretty fast from the shots.

We entered a room with weapons in every corner and in racks set up along the center. There were swords, axes, daggers, hammers, clubs, and a cabinet in the far left corner with guns displayed inside.

Wilson led the way to the cabinet and opened it. He pulled out an old automatic pistol with a long magazine. On the end of the barrel was a silencer. I hadn't seen one of those since the Fall. I didn't even have one in my vault. He handed me the pistol.

"Nice," I said.

"It's got a sixteen-shot magazine," he said. "It's a nine millimeter, and I have three boxes of rounds for it. All yours for the small price of your eternal soul."

"They don't call me a soulless bastard for nothin'."

"I thought I might be too late for that," he said.

"How about, if you give it to me, I won't tell your boss you're tryin' to sell her stuff?"

"Sounds fair."

"I think we have a deal." I removed a holster from the case that looked like it was made for the pistol. Looking closer, I saw the automatic's brand. It was a Sig Sauer, a very good Old World gun brand.

It took a few minutes to attach the holster to my harness, but it would be handy in the enclosed space of the Tees when I needed a gun. I added the boxes of shells to the pockets of my coat.

"Keep addin' weapons to that arsenal, and you won't be able to move," Wilson said.

"Probably right," I said as I twisted to test movement. "Better leave the other two here."

I removed the two .44s and the holsters from my harness. I twisted a bit, and it felt much smoother.

"I hate to admit it, but there is such a thing as too many weapons."

"I know how hard that was to admit," Wilson said. "Now, if you were a little bigger, you could carry that and a four-foot piece of steel on your back with little effect on performance."

"Yeah, but you're such a big target. You get shot more."

"You cut me deep, Kade."

"Did I hurt your feelings?"

"I'm devastated."

"I'll try to live with the guilt."

"Hmph."

I just stared.

"I see how it's gonna be," he said. "Got any ideas about these murders yet?"

"Yeah, I got a couple thoughts about them," I said. "But I need the map of the Tees before I can really tell anything for sure."

"Pretty brutal," he said. "Even for this screwed up world."

"Saw something like it before the Fall," I said. "They never caught the guy back then. There used to be some pretty horrible people. I know, 'cause I was one of 'em."

"I think you're too hard on yourself," he said.

"Got a lot to atone for."

"If you say so."

I heard voices in the hall outside the armory.

"Can't protect the boy from everything," a man's voice said.

"I'll damn well protect him if I want to," a woman's voice answered.

"You know what it's like out there."

"He's four years old!"

"Never too young to start learning," Michael said as he opened the armory door.

"Get this straight, Tanzik," Michael's wife, Lindsey, said. "There will not be a sword in that boy's hand until he's at least twelve."

"But…"

"That's all I'm saying on the subject."

Michael grunted.

Wilson looked at me and laughed.

"Shut up," I said.

He laughed again. "Good luck, buddy."

He turned and walked out the door.

"What do you think, Mathew?" the small woman asked. "Shouldn't a child get to be a child before we start hammering him with training?"

Michael Tanzik was about average in height and weight, being a couple inches less than six feet tall. Lindsey barely reached five feet. She had flaming red hair and the temperament to go with it.

"I thought that was the last you were goin' to say on the subject," he said.

"Is your name Mathew?"

"Nope."

"Then I was talking to someone else."

"I told you," he said as he looked at me. "She's crazy."

She pointedly ignored Michael and looked at me, waiting for an answer.

"Kids do learn quicker than adults…"

"So, now you're ganging up on me," she said. "I'll go get Teresa, and then we'll…"

"On second thought," I said, "I believe I should stay out of this one."

"Probably a wise choice," Michael said.

"Hmph," she said and turned away from us to look for ranged weapons.

"We're in tunnels," Michael said. "Cramped spaces."

"Shut your pie hole; I know what I'm doing."

"Only pie shuts my pie hole."

"My foot in your ass will shut it too," she said from across the room.

"You can't kick that high."

"You really don't want to find out, dear."

He chuckled and took a pair of short swords from a rack. They resembled gladii like the Romans used. I think one of my personalities was a history professor.

"These should do nicely in a confined space."

"Should," I said.

Lindsey had found a compact crossbow with a quiver full of bolts. She took them and moved down to a rack of blades. She picked a pair of long daggers. They were not much shorter than Michael's swords. They each donned sheaths and belts, then sheathed the blades.

"May want to stock up on travel food," I said. "No tellin' how long this is gonna take."

Lindsey nodded. "Maybe I can find some pie to shut his hole with."

"If you're lucky."

"Traitor," he said to me.

"Crazy is ok, buddy," I said. "But crazy with weapons…hell no."

"I see your point."

"I'm right here," she said.

"Wasn't there some kind of medication in the Old World for it?"

"It went pretty quick after the Fall when they couldn't make any more."

"I guess the supply got very limited after that," he said. "We just have to make allowances nowadays."

"I'm right here," she said again.

"Maybe we can find some sort of natural remedy," Michael said as he walked out of the armory with Lindsey.

I laughed as the door closed behind them. People will always be people, and some things haven't changed much in this Fallen World.

* * * * *

Chapter Four

Fraans returned after about three hours, and I met him again inside the conference room. He had brought a rolled up map with him.

"I need you to mark the places where all of the killings took place," I said as I rolled out the map.

He pointed to a spot on the map of tunnels.

"This was the first one," he said. "It was pretty gruesome, but death is common in the world we live in."

I marked a red "X" with a brush. "What I wouldn't give for a Sharpie."

"A Sharpie?"

"Old World stuff," I said.

We lost a lot of the little things that made life easier in the Fall. Now, we used things like stylus pens with ink bottles from the ancient days, or we used brushes and paint. If any markers or pens were left, they had dried up years ago.

Fraans looked at me strangely, then pointed to another spot on the map. "This is the second one we found, although it was an older killing. The room was off the beaten track and seldom visited because of the location."

I painted an "X" on that spot as well.

"This was the third one we found," he said, pointing to another room in the tunnels. "This is when we began to be alarmed. Death is common, but this was something else."

Another "X," and I was seeing something, or rather, Gladson was seeing something.

"Two others have been found since then," he said. "One here, and another here."

He pointed the spots out as he spoke, and I marked them with "Xs."

"We Mardins pride ourselves on being more civilized than the surface dwellers," he said. "It pains me to think one of our own is this brutal."

"All civilizations throughout history," I said, "have had their psychopaths. But I don't think this is one of yours. Look at the spacing of these murders."

I moved to our right and unrolled a map of my own. It was an Old World map of the city to which I had added boundary lines of the Zones I knew.

"The first was here," I said, pointing at the Zone above the first crime scene. "Then, here…here…here…and the last one, here."

"They're scattered all over the place," Fraans said.

"I think he is moving across the city. If you look at the Zones, you see the oldest murder happened in Krell. Krell is a semi-safe Zone. Then he moved up to Platis. If he had headed straight east, he would have been in Royles, and that's a no-go Zone. So, the choice was north or south. He lived in these Zones for a month or so, then moved on. Platis is pretty big, and the second murder was in the northmost part of the Zone. Then he turned east. The next three Zones to the east are pretty chaotic. So, he traveled through and set up in Morgan."

I pointed to the third murder, under Morgan's Zone.

"Now, Morgan is also a semi-safe Zone, so he stayed his month or so. Then he killed and headed south. North was out of the question. There are three Zones there that are perpetually at war. You enter one of those, and you're drafted and put into the meat grinder. You'd think a person could sneak off, but they shoot anyone who tries."

My finger traced south from Morgan's. "Gord is chaotic, so he continued south through Placer and then east to Trilla. He set up there for a month or so and killed this one."

I pointed at the fourth murder site.

"Here's where the monkey wrench gets thrown in my theory," I said. "The fifth is in Yarborough. It should have been in either Dunn or Gallis. Considering you have to go through Dunn to reach Yarborough, my guess is there may be a scene you haven't found yet. Or he killed up top that time. Either way, I need to go and see. If a murder happened there, we have a pattern. We can predict where he may strike next and intercept him."

There was a look of respect in Fraans' eyes. "We would never have put that together. Perhaps we need to take more notice of the surface."

"There's too much access to your territory for you not to take notice."

"We are aware of the surface," he said. "We walled off the tunnels under Derris' Zone just to your west. They are savages and cannibals."

"It will do your people a service if you cultivate the relationship you have with the Society. They're aware of the surface issues and can relay them to you. You have ways of traveling safely through the city that would benefit the Society. It would be a mutual benefit, and there is no one better suited to help you than Teresa's people. They may even work with your security."

"It has crossed our minds to do something like this," he said. "Years of hiding in the Tees, as you call them, has made us cautious."

"You've already got ties with her," I said. "Wouldn't be too large a step to go further."

"After this is through, I will bring it to the King's Advisors."

"I have to say, it's impressive that you guys have developed such a large territory. You work together, while the surface folks constantly fight among themselves."

"It wasn't like that in the beginning," he said. "It took ten hard years to unify the Tees. The result was a group of advisors, who used to be individual Zone leaders. They report to and advise the King, who carved his kingdom with a sword from the chaos that was."

"We could use a little of that up top."

"I understand you have already begun," he said. "I hear you have brought three Zones under the influence of the Society. This might worry the advisors and the King."

"It wasn't what I set out to do," I said. "The leaders attacked me, and I removed them. The Society can offer safety to the people in those Zones, so it made sense."

"Of course, it makes sense. It made sense fifteen years ago, when Grady O'Neal rose and assumed leadership of the Tee that belonged to Mardin. He built upon those original Mardins and spread out to eventually run most of the Tees under the city. There are still some he doesn't run. There are some that are walled off, barring any way of entering, such as Derris.

"The surface will be much harder to unite," he continued. "There are many more people on the surface than in the Tees. But consider the future if such a thing could be accomplished. Unite this broken city, and it will be a great start to uniting this fallen world."

"I'm no hero," I said. "I was just doing my job. I don't dream of uniting a city, just surviving it."

"I see," he said. "I wish you the best of luck in your endeavors, Mister Kade. Your guide should be here by now. You wish to go to Dunn?"

"Yeah," I said. "We need to check my theory before we proceed any further."

"Then I will take my leave, and Portus shall lead you anywhere you need to go in the Tees."

"I'll get this done as quickly as I can, Fraans," I said. "Hopefully, we can get to him before he kills again."

Fraans turned and left the conference room.

I looked at the maps for another minute, then rolled them up. We'd know soon enough if I was right. I heard the door open again, and a pale man of about five and a half feet walked in. He nodded at me.

"Portus, I'm guessin'?"

"Yes," he answered. "I am at your disposal."

"The first thing we need to do is go to Dunn."

"Not too complicated," he said. "We have to divert around the area under Derris."

"Fraans mentioned that Derris has been walled off," I said. "Let me get my escorts, and we'll get on our way."

"I will meet you in the basement," he said. "This lighting bothers me greatly."

"I imagine it does."

I followed the Mardin out of the conference room, and we went in separate directions. I made my way to the commons, the area in the center of the Chapterhouse that was open and used for training. That's where I would meet Michael and Lindsey.

"I'm not sayin' I want you to cook," I heard Michael say as I walked into the commons. "I just want you to learn how to cook a few things."

"What!?"

"There's surviving the Fall, and there's barely surviving the Fall."

"Just what do you mean by that?"

"If we could survive on what you know how to cook," he said, "it would barely be surviving."

"Why, you old bastard!" she said. "Maybe I won't cook anything anymore."

"We'd all be better off," he said. "Little Sammy is probably traumatized already."

"Sammy likes my cooking just fine!"

"Then why does he go over and eat at the Kord's all the time?"

"He's friends with the Kord girl."

"I'm just sayin'," he said. "The boy came home with a sack of leftovers yesterday. I caught him eatin' 'em in the back room."

"He said he wasn't hungry," she said. "Come to think of it, you weren't either."

"He brought a lot of stuff from the Kord's."

"You and he both…"

"Woman can cook a rat's ass and make it taste good."

"You son of a…"

"Hi guys!" I yelled. "Ready to go?"

Michael turned and walked toward me as Lindsey cursed under her breath.

"Sure thing," Michael said with a grin.

The two Squires followed me back into the building and down through the stairwells to the basement entrance to the Tees. Lindsey was still muttering under her breath as we followed Portus through the metal door and down into the dim light of the Tunnels.

"Guys, this is Portus," I said. "Portus, this is Michael and Lindsey Tanzik, Squires of the Society."

He nodded to the couple, who nodded back.

"We're headed to Dunn," I said. "We have to test a theory about the killings. If I'm right, we may be able to guess where he'll hit next and be waitin' for him."

"That would be nice," Lindsey said. "Catch him before he kills again."

"That's what I'm hopin' for," I said. "Let's take it slow through here, Portus. We need to let our eyes adjust before we do much travelin'."

"Understood," he said. "We'll go slowly until we pass by Derris. You should be ok long before we get that far. I can inspect the walls as we go. Scouts are required to check the walls anytime we are in this area."

"That's understandable," Michael said. "Derris' bunch are savages. They've been pushed back enough times on the surface to quit tryin' to break out of their Zone."

"One of these days, someone's gonna have to clean 'em out of there," I said. "Have to wait till Wilson gets better, though. I promised he could go, too."

"Better take more than just Wilson," Michael said, his eyebrow raised.

"They'll probably attack our Zone before then, anyway, since I promised he could help."

"Why would you think that?"

"Expect the worst," I said. "You'll never be disappointed."

"Poe told us about you," Lindsey said. "That's a pretty crappy outlook, Kade."

"I don't walk around disappointed."

"Yeah, he said that."

Both were looking around the area suspiciously.

"What?"

"He also said if you brought the subject up, something bad inevitably follows."

"I have no idea what you're talkin' about."

I heard running footsteps, and I grabbed my straight razor. A woman ran from the darkness ahead and saw Portus. She skidded to a halt.

"Scout! They've broken through!"

"What?!"

"They're in the Tunnels! E-Branch!"

"We don't have any forces over here!" he said. "Are the charges still good?"

"Yes, sir," she answered. "We have thirty people down beyond the charges!"

"There's nothing we can do," he said.

"There's somethin' we can do," I said. "We'll hold 'em long enough to get your people out of the area. Then we can blow the charges."

"You would do something like that for us? It is suicide."

"Poe's gonna be so mad," I said. "Get your people out."

I ran straight toward the faint sounds ahead of us. I slowed as we neared the sounds of metal clashing. I could see the metal boxes that held the explosive charges Portus had spoken of.

"You don't have to do this," I said to my companions.

"We are Squires," Michael said.

Then I heard the scream.

I launched myself down the tunnel system at the fastest speed my augmented body could attain.

I began laughing as I ran. There are worse things than savage cannibals in this Fallen World.

* * * * *

Chapter Five

I saw the branching tunnel the noise was coming from and rounded the corner. I took in the scene as I left the ground and rebounded from the wall to slow my speed. A group of pale Mardins fled toward me. The tunnels behind them were packed with half-naked, screaming savages with makeshift weapons.

I palmed the Sig and pulled the slide to load it in one smooth motion. The silencer absorbed most of the sound from the shots, but it was still far from silent.

I watched as head after head blossomed with the impact of the bullets.

The eighth shot hit the eighth head as Michael and Lindsey rounded the corner. Michael's hands blurred as his twin swords seemed to leap into his hands. He shot forward and leaped over the heads of the fleeing Mardins. He landed with his swords dancing around him. Lindsey was just seconds behind him, with her blades flashing.

Wilson Poe had been a Yeoman when he accompanied me on my last case, and he is a deadly fighter. A Squire is in another league altogether, and the savages hit an immoveable wall of steel. As one of the savages got too close to Lindsey, I shot it in the head. Seven more shots and seven more dead exhausted the magazine, and I dropped the Sig to the floor.

I stepped closer, and my hands blurred as I began throwing blades. The final blade sank into the throat of the last of the savages.

"Wow," Michael said. "He wasn't kidding."

"If you don't mind," Lindsey said to me, "let's not bring that up again."

"I'm not disappointed," I said. "Are you?"

She looked back at the heap of dead cannibals. "Not at this particular moment."

There were howls from deeper inside the tunnels, and I felt something I hadn't in a long time. It was the indignation the righteous feel at the sight of evil. I had been that evil in the world before the Fall. I still wasn't sure what I was in the fallen world. But I knew I would not let this blight upon our city take one more life this day.

I walked forward and let my coat slip off behind me. "If anything comes down this tunnel besides me, kill it."

"What?"

I launched myself forward and dove over the pile of bodies just as another horde of cannibals came screaming into the other end of the tunnel. I looked down for a second and slipped my razor into my hand. When I looked back up, someone else's smile was on my face.

"Oh, Mathew," Stephen Gaunt said breathily, "you take me to the most wonderful places."

I glided across the tunnel toward the screaming savages.

"Hello, my pretties."

They charged the spot where I had been. Three landed without moving. I had slit three throats with one swipe and rolled to the side. Then I was moving once more into the darkness.

"This won't hurt," I whispered in the ear of a barely human woman. "Long."

I slid my razor around her throat from behind as my left hand pulled her chin up. Then I was gone again. I reached out with my razor and a femoral artery was severed, a set of tendons sliced, a throat cut. The screams of rage became screams of pain. Then screams of terror.

"Don't run, my little darlings."

The Mardin security forces arrived in less than thirty minutes, which was a quick response, considering the distance they had covered. Michael and Lindsey hadn't come into the tunnel, even after the noise ended. I understood. Stephen Gaunt can be a bit...well...terrifying. But they were the first in when the security forces arrived. I think they expected me to be dead since I hadn't come out of the tunnel. I was standing in the center of the broken wall that had been keeping Derris' savages out of the Tees. The whole tunnel was littered with bodies.

"Jesus, Kade," Michael said.

Lindsey handed me my coat and the Sig.

"Thanks," I said.

"Would have been a shame to wear that in here," she said, looking at the mess. "Good choice."

"I thought so," I said. "Wilson already threatened to mess it up. Didn't want to give him the satisfaction of seein' it done."

The security forces were staring at us with wide eyes.

"Three of you did all this?" their leader asked.

"He did all this by himself," Michael said. "We helped with the bunch out there."

"One man did this?"

"That's debatable," I said.

"What do you mean?"

"Never mind," I said. "A little schizophrenic humor."

He looked at me in confusion.

"Just…never mind," I said. "You should have plenty of time to set charges and blast this tunnel without having to blow the other charges. They're not comin' back here anytime soon."

He nodded.

"Have you seen Portus? He's supposed to guide us to Dunn."

"He's standing by the charges, preparing to blow the tunnels if needed."

"We'll meet him there then."

I walked around the staring fighters and drew the Sig. I ejected the magazine and pulled one of the boxes of shells from my pocket. As we walked back along the path we had taken, I reloaded the magazine with sixteen bullets. The thing had already proven its worth.

"I'm definitely gonna see if Teresa will sell me this," I said. "I love it."

"I had a Sig before the Fall," Michael said. "Very nice gun. One of the best in its time."

"How old were you?" I asked.

"Twenty-two when the bombs fell. Had done a tour in OCAF," he said.

Obsidian Corporation Armed Forces was where I had begun, as well. But quite a few years earlier. They pulled most Agents from the armed forces. Some of the younger Agents had been pulled from other places. A few were even from prisons.

"I was three when it happened," Lindsey said. "Teresa found me when I was sixteen and pulled me out of a Zone in the east. They were about to do some evil things, and she walked in and destroyed the place with three Knights. Well…they're Knights, now. I don't think she had set up anything quite yet. I think it was the next year when she started the Society and moved into the Chapterhouse."

I had just moved into my new home under the bank when Teresa moved into Stiner's.

"Officers told us about Agents back then," Michael said. "They could be anyone, anywhere, and they were always on a mission."

"Teresa told us when we became Squires," Lindsey said. "You're at the top of the allies on the trusted list."

"What was the mission when the bombs fell?" Michael asked.

"Most of the Agents died, but the few who survived were stuck in the role they were playing at the end."

"I was in the imprinter," I said as we rounded the corner and saw an anxious Portus, standing under the explosives, with a torch ready to light the fuse. "It dumped the whole database into my noggin."

"Holy shit."

"Where are the fighters?" Portus asked.

"Guarding the breach," I said. "You won't be needin' to blow that."

I pointed at the metal-encased explosive charge. He pulled the torch away from the fuse.

"I think we can continue our mission, but you should check with your boys, first, just to be sure."

He nodded and sped down the tunnel toward the breach. I squatted down with my back against the wall. I pulled a sack of jerky from my coat.

"Jerky?" I held the bag out. Michael and Lindsey reached in and took a piece.

"This is what I'm talkin' about, woman," said Michael. "If you could learn to make this, our son wouldn't be trying to sneak out to eat at the Kords'."

"You just be careful, you old fart," she said. "I may use arsenic in the next dinner I make."

"Probably taste better," he muttered.

"What?!"

"Nothin'."

"I thought so."

"One of these days..." he muttered.

"Pow! Right in the kisser!" I added.

Lindsey looked at me with narrowed eyes.

"Sorry, Old World joke," I said and laughed. "Used to be a show on TV so long ago..."

I looked into confused eyes.

"Never mind."

We lost a great deal in the Fall.

"I can teach you how to make the jerky," I said as I started chewing on a piece.

"Don't you even start," she said.

"Just sayin'."

Anything more would be kicking a hornets' nest. Some things truly haven't changed in this Fallen World.

* * * * *

Chapter Six

We sat down and chewed on the jerky for a while in silence. Portus came back around the corner, his face paler than when he'd left.

"Is his face paler than before?" Lindsey asked.

"I wouldn't have thought that possible," Michael said, "but damned if it isn't."

"Y-you were correct, sir," Portus said. "We can proceed to Dunn."

"Lead on," I said.

I rose to my feet, wincing as the gunshots from Moreau's goons sent a surge of pain to my brain. During the fight, Gaunt had ignored the pain as adrenaline had filled me.

"You get injured?" Michael asked.

"Just a twinge from the gunshots I got a couple weeks ago."

"Teresa said you'd gone and gotten shot a couple times."

"Gettin' sloppy in my old age."

"Did you bust anything open?" Lindsey asked.

"Nah," I answered. "Just achy now. It'll go away soon enough."

"That's what you get for jumping into the middle of a mess like that," she said. "That's what we're here for."

"True, Kade," Michael said. "Teresa will kick both our asses if we let you get all messed up."

"I needed to let Gaunt out to play," I said. "He whines if I don't."

"Gaunt?" she asked.

"One of the personalities from the database?" Michael asked.

"Yeah."

"You can access them?"

"Most of 'em," I said. "The stronger personalities are the easiest to access. Some of the others are vague, but I can draw on their experience."

"That's the damnedest thing I've ever seen."

"Was a little rough for the first few years."

"I imagine so," Lindsey said.

We passed several people as we walked down the tunnels. A pale woman led four children in the opposite direction, and I paused to hand her a small pouch.

"Somethin' for the kids," I muttered and continued down the tunnel. I glanced back as we turned into a branch tunnel and saw her giving the kids pieces of jerky.

I kept referring to the map of the tunnels. I didn't look at the physical map; I looked at the one I had mostly memorized. I had studied the local tunnels closely while looking over the map. So far, it seemed to match what was in my head.

I didn't like being at the mercy of someone else when it came to where I was located. I'd explored the city to a great extent and knew where we were at the moment.

"I'd say we're under Devin," Michael said. "Possibly under Blechley."

"You mean Holden?" Lindsey asked.

"Well…yeah, now that you mention it," he said. "I heard Blechley came to a gruesome end. Know anything about that, Kade?"

"I have no idea what you're talkin' about."

"I heard something about finding him in many pieces," Lindsey said.

"Pinned to a wall," Michael said.

"With all of his parts arranged in alphabetical order," she added.

"He must have done something pretty bad for someone to do somethin' like that," I said.

"Must have," he said.

"Can't say I feel sorry for the bastard," Lindsey said. "Maybe he insulted his wife's cooking one too many times."

"I doubt it," Michael said. "From what I heard, he had excellent cooks."

"I bet you snuck over there and ate dinner a few times."

"Had to," Michael said. "There's only so many peanut butter sandwiches and noodles a man can eat."

"What?!"

"Damn the Farmers and their peanut butter. I hated it long before the Fall, and I almost forgave the ones who dropped the bombs when there was no more of the stuff."

"You ate it," she said.

"The Kords were over in Wilderman's…"

"You son of a…"

"So, Kade," Michael interrupted, "what was that jerky? It was spectacular."

"The key is in how you cut the meat. If you cut the sinew out and just leave the meat, it makes a tender jerky. Even if it's rat jerky. I have some pigeon jerky here, too. Wanna try it?"

I handed him another small sack. He pulled a piece from the sack and bit off a chunk. Lindsey reached in and took a piece.

"Damn. That's even better than the other one," she said.

He passed the sack back to me, and I nudged Portus. He turned and reached into the sack for a piece.

"Very good," he said as he chewed the meat.

We passed the sack around as we continued down the dim tunnels.

We heard running water ahead, and Portus rushed forward. We found a pipe with a strong leak around the next bend.

"Oh, this is not good," Portus said. "I have to report this. If you will remain here for a few moments, I will report and be right back."

"Can you report when we get to where we're going?" I asked.

"This is part of the Accords."

"Then go," I said. "We'll be here."

Portus took off at a dead run.

"Accords?"

"Yeah," I said. "The Accords were written up about ten years ago. It was an agreement between the Mardins and the Zones above. The Mardins would maintain the water and sewage under the city, and the Zones above would leave the Mardins alone. That's why some folks don't know who the Mardins are. And they take the Accords very seriously."

"I can see why it is important," Lindsey said. "If we lose the water up top, there would be utter chaos. No one would be safe. What little order we have would be gone in an instant."

"The city would consume itself," I said. "Many people don't know it, but we owe the Mardins as much as we owe the Farmers. Without the Farmers, the city would have self-destructed long ago. Same with the Mardins. I hate to say it, but we also owe Dynamo a great deal for keeping the electricity up and running."

"Yeah," Michael said. "He knows it, too. Although, of the three, the electric is the least important. Much of the city gets by without it. The Scrapers have electricity, and it's created an upper and a lower class."

"True," I said. "The Scrapers aren't nearly as nice without power."

"And Dynamo charges a tax for his services. The Mardins and the Farmers don't. They just want to be left alone."

"Worlds of difference between him and either of the others," I said. "We try to make our Zones self-sufficient, but, in all honesty, a city can never really be self-sufficient. We'll always be dependent on someone else."

"True," Michael said. "We've got our water towers and solar grids, but they would never support a whole Zone for an extended amount of time."

"And there's just not enough room to grow food for the whole city, which brings us back to the Farmers, the Mardins, and Dynamo."

I heard running feet, and Portus came back into view, followed by three other pale-skinned Mardins. He stopped in front of me.

"We can continue our journey, Mister Kade."

I nodded and followed him again toward the west. The pipes along the walls seemed more important than they had before. We take a great deal for granted in this Fallen World.

* * * * *

Chapter Seven

We continued west under the Zone of Jade, a woman who had been part of a criminal organization before the Fall. She had carved out her own little slice of the city almost immediately after the Fall and had held it, successfully, for twenty years.

Next to the west was Paris. This Zone had gone through no less than ten Warlords in the last twenty years. I expected Jade to get tired of the chaos and move in, but she never made any advances to expand her territory.

The tunnels angled to the southwest for a while and crossed under The Saint's Zone. He called himself Saint, but he was far from a Saint. He was a cold-hearted mercenary. He had trained soldiers under his command and had expanded three times since the Fall. Perhaps he was the reason Jade had left Paris' Zone alone. It was a sort of buffer Zone between her and The Saint.

We would almost reach Wilderman's before arriving at Dunn. The tunnels all looked close to the same, and I could see getting lost in them very easily. My eye was drawn to the pipes running along the tunnels.

"A lot of patched pipes down here," I said, motioning toward a six-inch pipe with a clamp around it. "No one knows how close to the edge we really are."

"I've seen at least ten of those clamps since we left that leak," Michael said.

"We are ever vigilant, my friends," Portus said. "We live by the Accords."

"I know of the Accords," I said, "but I never really understood how important that one agreement is."

"The life of this city is flowing through these pipes." He touched one of the pipes, almost reverently. "We protect this life with our own."

I nodded to the man.

"We have reached the edge of Dunn," he said. "This area is less populated than some of the others, due to a breach in the tunnels into the sewer below."

I could smell the difference as we neared our destination.

"I need you to organize a detailed search of the area," I said. "If he hit down here, we need to find the scene. I'll go up and see if he hit up top. According to his pattern, there should be a body in this Zone."

"The search is already underway," Portus said. "We started as soon as you established a pattern."

"Good," I said. "Where's the nearest surface access?"

"Right this way."

We heard the commotion before we started to climb the ladder. Running feet and several yells.

"May not need to go up to Dunn, after all," Michael said. "Sounds like someone found something."

A pale-skinned man ran around the corner and skidded to a halt before Portus.

"We've found it, sir," the man said.

"Lead the way, Sarto."

We followed Sarto deeper into the tunnels. Several twists and turns later, we stood before a door. The stench of the sewer was almost unbearable, but my nose detected more than just the sewer. It was a familiar smell to Gladson.

Decomp, he said in my mind.

"It's in this room," Sarto said. "We didn't go in after we opened the door. It was pretty obvious this was what you are looking for."

"Alright," I said. "I'm goin' in to examine the scene. You guys wait for me to get a good look before comin' in."

I twisted the lever and pushed the door open. The smell of the decomposing body was stronger. Stepping into the room was like stepping into the past life of a homicide detective. Gladson had entered many rooms like this one.

The torso was in the center of the room in two pieces. I snarled as I saw the blood splattered in several directions. The arms had been ripped off and slung into a corner. You could tell by the blood patterns that the victim, a pale-skinned man, had been alive when they were ripped off. The blood pattern was similar for one leg. The victim had died after the leg. The other leg had been torn off, as well, but the blood spray was different.

Not many of his victims lived through their legs being torn off, said Gladson in my head. *Never understood how they were kept still between acts, though.*

"Some sort of drug, maybe," I muttered.

The rest of what had been done to the body occurred after death. The torso had been disemboweled, and the spine had been broken, leaving two halves of the torso. The head had been twisted off and spiked to the wall, directly in front of the door opening, so it would be the first thing anyone saw when the body was found.

It would have taken enormous strength to do something like this. Possibly an Agent? But what sort of Agent would do this? Gaunt is a psycho, but would he do this?

Not randomly, Gaunt's voice echoed in my head. *I could do this, but it would be for the shock factor, not just for the kill.*

"This guy isn't an Agent with any of the personalities in the database," I muttered, "which probably means he's not an Agent. Unless a Clown was ordered to do it."

"What's that leave?" I asked myself. "Cyborg?"

Most of the Cyborgs were gone now. Their technology was so hard to maintain, they died shortly after the Fall.

I stooped low and looked closely at the abdomen. It looked like an animal had torn it open.

What if it was a Geno Freak? Gladson asked in my head.

"They died out years before the Fall," I muttered.

The Geno Freaks were a fad that had swept through the youth about ten years before the war. They would do illegal gene splicing with animal DNA to give themselves cats' eyes, foxes' ears, and a multitude of other traits. It was illegal because it didn't work. Sure, you got the eyes or ears or fur-covered body, but you also received a lifespan of about four years. Needless to say, Geno Freaks were a short-lived fad.

"There aren't many humans with the strength to do what's been done here," I said. "Whatever it is, it's gonna be a handful when we catch it."

"Alright, guys," I raised my voice. "You can clean it up. I have all I'm gonna get here."

Michael and Lindsey were the first to enter the blood-soaked room.

"Damn," he muttered.

"This is pretty gruesome," she said. "Hard to believe one person did it. Only one set of prints in the blood, though."

"A damn big set of prints," he said.

"Yeah," I said. "This guy is big. Probably as big as Wilson Poe."

"That's big," she said.

"Stronger than anyone has any right to be," Michael said, looking at the body. "Ripped the arms and legs off with his hands. Those aren't cuts."

"Agreed," I said. "Let's let these guys clean up. We need to head back east. This proves my pattern is correct. There are three possibilities for the next attack. All three are stable Zones near Yarborough."

"You have figured out where we can possibly catch him before he kills again?" Portus asked.

"Yeah," I said. "I needed to prove my pattern to be sure."

We exited the room and let the rest of the Mardins in to clean up.

"Where shall we begin?" Portus asked.

I squatted down and pulled the maps from my coat. Spreading them both on the floor, I pointed at Yarborough.

"From here, he could go two Zones to the north and stop in Morris. Or he could go straight east to Trew. But, if he's studied the Zones any, I'd guess he went three Zones south to Plagis."

"Why Plagis?" Lindsey asked. "Both of the others are closer."

"The next few moves would answer that," Michael said, pointing at the map. "If he goes to Trew, there aren't any other stable Zones on that path for about six Zones. If he chooses Morris, his next move is pretty easy. He'd go to Hiller. But after Hiller, he'd have to cross the warzone."

"I can see the problem with that one," she said. "No one wants to cross the warzone."

Three Zones were in a perpetual state of war with each other. There were about twelve other Zones that were always in a state of war near these three. It wasn't a very safe place to cross. Some days, you could cross the area without incident, others, you could end up among a hundred or so warriors battling in the streets. It was a good place to avoid.

"So, Plagis would be the smartest place for him to set up," Michael said. "That's if the man has prior knowledge of the area. He may just be traveling till he hits a stable place."

"The path he's already taken says he has some prior knowledge," I said. "He's avoided a couple of bad routes by going the way he's going. He's planning his moves well ahead. This city is the perfect hunting ground for someone like him. All the different Warlords and Zones. If he knew how well the Mardins were connected, he never would have picked them as victims. He thinks in upper Zones."

"I think you're right," Lindsey said.

"We know a little about the guy," I said. "He's a loner. He doesn't associate with others; they're just prey to him. If he were social, he'd be someplace like the Circus, where he could do this sort of thing for clients. They do some twisted shit in places like that."

"Makes sense," Michael said. "He's not one of the rich, or he'd just buy slaves and do his thing where he lived."

"He's a wanderer," I said. "He may take jobs as a warrior for the Warlords, but he doesn't stay very long. A month's pay would keep him fed, and then he'd move on to the next. No one would turn down someone with his strength if he requested work as a fighter."

"He's also a coward," Lindsey said.

"How's that?" Michael asked.

"If not, he'd have joined one of the Warlords in the warzone. He could kill as he pleases and get paid for it."

"Might have a point there," I said. "Too much chance of gettin' killed by some lucky shot during one of their skirmishes."

"He's a psychopath," Michael said. "He gets his jollies from killing the helpless."

"The drugging of his victims backs that," I said.

"Drugging?"

"If you noticed the blood patterns, they show a distinct lack of struggle from the victim. I think he drugs 'em in some way."

"I'm really not liking this guy," Michael said. "I'm thinking I'm gonna enjoy killing the bastard."

"Just remember the strength this guy has," I said. "It's not completely human."

"What? Like a Cyborg?"

"Cyborg, Agent, Geno Freak," I said. "There's something more to this guy than just bein' a twisted bastard."

"Geno Freak?" Michael asked. "Doubtful. They died out years before the Fall. Cyborgs are gone. Are Agents that strong?"

He looked at me with eyebrows raised.

"Yep," I said. "But none of the templates in the database fit this guy."

"An Agent from another Corporation?"

"Obsidian was the undeniable victor of the wars," I said. "But it's possible an Agent of one of the others survived. The problem is this guy was killin' folks years before the Fall." I tapped the side of my head. "I got a detective up here who was after him a long time ago. He's seen this before. The whole scene. This guy was killin' people and leavin' 'em just like the victim in that room back there. It was close to twenty-five years ago. If this guy was an Agent from the other side, he would have been doin' Corporate business during the war. Not killin' civilians."

"Twenty-five years ago would put him in range of the Geno Freak theory," Michael said. "But, surely, he wouldn't still be around now, would he?"

"It's possible one survived, but what would he have to be spliced with to live this long?"

"Maybe some sort of lizard," Michael said. "Some lizards can live long lives."

"That makes sense," I said. "Either way, he's gonna be a handful when we find him. He's strong enough to be a danger, but if he's a Geno Freak, he's probably got the speed to go with it, and there's no tellin' what else. We need to be careful."

"No doubt."

"Regardless, we need to head for Plagis," I said, pointing at the spot on the tunnel map. "Portus, we need to get here."

"Yes, sir," he answered.

"And I'd increase forces in these two areas, as well," Michael added. "If we're right, he'll hit under Plagis. If not, it is highly likely he'll hit one of these two."

"I will contact the patrol and let them know as soon as we get to a point where we have comm systems."

"Good," I said. "Let's get movin'."

Portus started back up the tunnel we had come down to get here, and we fell in line behind him.

If I had been an Agent back then instead of just a cop, Gladson said in my head, *I'd have found this guy.*

"Maybe," I muttered.

"What?" Michael asked behind me.

"Nothin'," I answered. "Just talkin' to myselves."

He chuckled.

Agents only had one personality at a time, Childers said. *It may not have helped to be an Agent when you pursued the guy back then.*

True, Gladson admitted.

Many of the personalities in my head had just been regular people. Every Agent came from somewhere. Somewhere out there was a body that belonged to a former homicide detective who became an Agent. His body could be dead or stuck somewhere as whatever it was programmed to be when the bombs fell. It could be a damn Clown, for all I knew. It could even be Samuel Gladson, survivor of the Fall. His most current program would still be in the database. Any number of people could be out there that are in my head, as well.

It worried me that there could be another Stephen Gaunt.

I'm mildly offended, Gaunt's voice said. *But I often worry about the same thing.*

I giggled.

"Did he just giggle?" Lindsey asked.

"I believe so."

"I have no idea what you're talkin' about," I said.

"Must be an interesting conversation going on in there," she said.

"Sounds that way."

Sometimes a little crazy is all you need to keep sane in this Fallen World.

* * * * *

Chapter Eight

"What's that sound?" Lindsey asked.

I had noticed a clanking sound coming from in front of us. There was a noticeable movement of air around us, too.

"We are nearing one of the ventilation stations," Portus said. "It is shorter to cut through the area than to go around."

We rounded a corner and found a large room with immense fan blades suspended far up in the shafts in the ceiling. I could see the huge electric motors above the fans. They were disconnected from the fan assemblies.

"Motors burned out?" I asked.

"About five years ago," he answered. "They are driven by the belts under the motors now. We have five shifts that work the fans. Ten people per fan on each five hour shift."

"Hard job," Michael said.

"Yes," Portus said. "But it is probably the most important job in the Tees. There are twenty of these ventilation stations in our territory. All but one are manually operated, now. One still has power, but it is expected to fail at any moment."

"I can see the importance," I said. "Without the air flow, no one can survive down here."

"There are already people on the lists waiting to be hired as others finish their service," he said. "Every Mardin will serve at the Vents at some point in their lives. I did my service when I reached my eighteenth year. It was an honor to serve my people in such an important task. Most of us do our Vent service when we reach adulthood. Afterward, we are considered Citizens and have the right to live in the Tees."

"Makes sense to me," I said.

"There are three services," Portus said. "In a Mardin's life, he or she will perform these three services. Each brings the Citizen to a higher level in the citizenry."

"My guess is the Vents and Water are two of them," I said.

"That they are," Portus said. "The Sewer is the third. It is the hardest of the three services to do. But a Citizen can never be eligible to vote for or become an Advisor unless they have done all three. It is also the one we have to hire outsiders to help with. Some Mardins are happy without the right to vote. All are required to serve in one to stay in the Tees. Two gives them the right to be a patroller. Three grants them full citizenship."

"I like that setup, for some reason," I said. "To lead, you must walk through the shit of a city."

"The Accords leave us responsible for the water pipes and the sewer flow," Portus said. "That is why they are requirements to become full Citizens. The Vents are what keep us alive."

"And the power?"

"Dynamo needs water, too," Portus chuckled. "We did not come away from the Accords with nothing, Mr. Kade."

I laughed.

"I guess you guys can deal with the Farmers in any sector over your territory, too," Lindsey said.

"Most of them, though we deal mostly while the Farmers are in Wilderman or Kathrop," he said. "Of course, it seems there is a growing area in the center of the city that is becoming safer and safer."

"Hmm," Michael said. "I wonder why?"

"I have no idea what you're talkin' about."

"Doesn't surprise me," Lindsey said.

"Are the Farmers anywhere near where we're headed?" I asked.

"They are around the Kathrop area over the next week," Portus said.

"That's a shame," I said. "There was a wagon with tacos the last time I saw 'em."

"I haven't had a decent taco in over twenty years," Michael said.

"What the hell is a taco?" Lindsey asked.

"Kids today," Michael said and shook his head.

"Who are you calling a kid, you old bastard?"

"Someone who's never had a damn taco."

"I bet I could make a taco," she muttered.

"Oh my God, woman!" Michael snorted. "You can't even boil water."

"Bite me, you damn fossil!"

I was trying not to, but I may have giggled again.

"You shut up, you giggling bastard!"

She stomped past me and fell in behind Portus.

"Sad part is," I said, tapping the side of my head, "there's all these people up here, and none of 'em know how to make a damn tortilla."

"Why didn't you ask the Farmer?"

"Cause I'm a dumb ass."

We turned south into a larger tunnel. There were steel tracks in the center where the subways used to run. A noise was coming from ahead of us.

"Please move to the side," Portus said. "Cart is coming through."

The noise approached our position, and soon, I saw a large cart with a load of dirt and rocks. The sides of the cart had handles protruding. Each had a Mardin behind it. They pushed the cart past us, then Portus returned to the center of the tunnel.

"We are excavating a collapsed tunnel that used to lead to the central hub of the railways."

"Surprised all the rails haven't been pulled up for the steel," I said.

"We use the rails," he said. "There are a lot of unused tunnels with rails that will never be used."

"You could pull in a good amount of scrip with that steel," I said. "Perhaps, you might put in a word to the bosses about the idea. I know a blacksmith who could use a good source of strong steel."

"That might interest the King," Portus said.

"Just let me know, and I'll put you in touch with Soba," I said. "He is really just gettin' started with larger orders, but the man is good."

"I will relay this to Gevik, my superior."

"Good."

"There's a noticeable lack of sewer smell down here, excepting the area under Dunn," Michael said. "It kind of surprised me."

"The sewers are ventilated by completely different systems than our tunnels. It is a common mistake for surface dwellers to think we live in the sewers."

"You're right about the rumors," Michael said.

"It does serve to keep fewer surface dwellers from trying to explore our territory."

"More light than I had expected," Lindsey said. "For that I am grateful."

"There's very little lighting here, Mrs. Tanzik," Portus said. "Your eyes are adapting to the darkness and finding more residual light than before."

"I just thought it was brighter, here."

"I was thinking the same thing," Michael said. "I think he's right, though. We probably are getting better at seeing in the dark."

I smiled behind the two. They actually agreed with each other every so often.

"We'll be near the southern edge of our territory when we turn east," Portus said. "We will have to be careful; we have incursions from the southern territories pretty frequently. Most of the Patrol spends its time on the borders of our territory, but numerous Patrols have been pulled to cover the three areas you designated."

"It figures," I said.

"Don't you even say it," Lindsey warned.

"What are you talkin' about?"

"Expect the worst, and you're never disappointed."

"Damn, woman!" Michael exclaimed, and his hand hovered near the sword on his left side. "Now, you've already said it."

"It doesn't matter if one of us says it," she said. "It just matters if he says it."

I heard noises from the southern tunnels, and I smiled at her.

"Doesn't it?" she asked nervously.

I chuckled.

"You're shitting me! What was that sound?"

"It sounds like someone is having a spot of fun, ahead," I said with Gaunt's precise voice.

"Son of a bitch..." she muttered as Portus turned toward us in alarm.

I nodded toward the man. "We'll lend a hand, Portus. Follow as you can."

I drew the Sig with my right hand, and the straight razor with my left. Launching myself forward with my enhanced speed, I quickly left the three behind. The tunnel curved, and I could hear the clash of weapons and the grunts of fighters just ahead.

I rounded the bend and took in the sight ahead of me. There were eight Mardins in two staggered lines of four. In front of them was a tunnel full of pale-skinned attackers. They wielded swords, much like the Mardins did, but there was no organization to their ranks, which was why the Mardins had held their ground so far— their formation supported one another.

I took aim and fired the Sig. One of the attackers in the front line lurched as a small dot appeared in his forehead, and the back of his head blossomed with the exit of the bullet. One of the defenders took a blade in his side and staggered backward. The man to his left in the staggered formation stepped forward and took his place.

The Sig coughed, and the action slid again, as the second of the attackers toppled backward with a spray of blood from the back of his head. The Sig spouted fire twice more, and two more of the lead attackers were slammed backward.

Then a form shot by me at full speed. Michael, with a sword in each hand, had launched himself over the heads of the Mardins and landed in the opening I had just created. His swords blurred, and blood sprayed in several directions. Lindsey shot past me, aiming for the left wall where the line had been weakest. She bounded over the Mardin and hit the wall with both feet. Her blade flashed as she rebounded behind the attacker in front of the Mardin, and he staggered as his spine was severed just below the spot where it joined his skull. Lindsey began to weave in and out of the startled attackers, and bodies slumped to the floor.

The two of them took center in the Mardins' formation, and the surprised Mardins stepped forward and resumed the staggered formation around the two Squires. Before our arrival, the line had been pushed backward several times. Now they stepped forward.

I shot two more times, and two more fell. They were on the right side of the tunnel, so I switched to the left and fired two more times. One fell, but the other moved just in time to survive…for about a second. I fired a second round and obtained the expected blossom from his head.

Getting sloppy, old man.

"Hush," I said and shot a woman on the right side of the tunnel.

The lines stepped forward again, and I could see two forms in the back of the attacking mob. I fired four times, and those two forms toppled. Two shots apiece just to be sure. Five more forms slumped along the front lines as Michael and Lindsey stepped forward again, flanked by the two Mardins.

They broke as someone screamed from the back, "Silas is dead!"

The mob seemed to vanish as they dropped their weapons and ran. Two of them kept their weapons, so I shot them in the backs of their heads. I would have let them go if they had dropped them.

"You shot those two in the back," one of the Mardins accused.

I popped the magazine from the Sig. Calmly, I began reloading the magazine with new rounds from the box in my coat.

"They should have dropped their weapons," Lindsey said. "We don't let them live to fight another day. At least, not with the same weapons."

The Mardin started to say something else, until he looked into her cold, pitiless eyes. He turned and joined his Patrol around a wounded fighter.

"Lardes," one of them said to the man. "You can make it. We'll get you to the Medics."

"You have to guard the Tees," he said. "You can't leave the Tees unguarded."

"But you'll die!"

"Do your duty, Patroller!"

"We'll take him in," I said as Portus rounded the bend.

The Patroller looked at me with doubt.

"You heard him," Portus said. "I am a Scout. I will show them the way. Get us the stretcher."

The Mardin nodded and ran back the way we had come. He returned with a medical stretcher. It was from before the Fall. It looked like a rescue board from a helicopter. They eased the Patroller onto the stretcher, and Portus took one end. Michael sheathed his blades and took the other.

"We thank you," the Mardin said.

I nodded and followed Lindsey behind the two carrying the stretcher.

"Lesson learned," Lindsey said as she tried to get the blood off her shirt.

"Don't even talk about it," Michael said.

"You should wear black," I said. "Then you can't see the blood."

"Black, hell," she said, "I'll wear red if we ever go anywhere else with you."

"Shoulda talked to Poe."

"Why?"

"He wore black."

I smelled alcohol.

"We're close," I said. "Smell the alcohol and vinegar?"

"Yeah."

"They're a couple of cleaners that are easy to make."

"I use alcohol at home if I can keep the fossil from drinking it."

"You'd have a lot less trouble keepin' him out of vinegar."

She laughed.

We turned down a side passage, and the smell got stronger. There was a brighter light source ahead which blasted my eyes when we hit the chamber ahead of us. I narrowed my lids to keep the light dim.

"What is this?"

"One of the Patrollers was injured in a battle with Silas' forces," Portus answered. Two big Mardins closed and took the stretcher from Portus and Michael.

"You can wait in the outer tunnels," the doctor said.

"We are on a mission and will not be waiting," Portus said. "Please report to the Patrol about this man when you are done."

The doctor nodded. She looked to be about fifty or so. She must have finished her medical degree right before the Fall; it hung behind a desk on the left wall of the room. The Mardins had been extremely lucky to get a true doctor to staff their infirmary. People knowledgeable in the medical field were scarce in this Fallen World.

* * * * *

Chapter Nine

We exited the infirmary and turned to the east.

"We keep infirmaries close to all the trouble spots so we can get our men to them quickly," Portus said. "We have seven facilities set up. All the staff has trained under Doctor Killian, the head of our medic program."

"I'm guessin' that was Killian back there?" Michael asked.

"Yes. She was a licensed surgeon when the bombs fell, and she took cover in the tunnels with a small group of soldiers. With them was a man named Clyde Mardin. He set up the immediate area around them to hold off attackers and established the original Zone in our territory."

"What happened to him?" Lindsey asked.

"He became ill and turned to a young soldier named Grady O'Neal to keep his people safe. O'Neal is the man who united the territory we call Mardin by both force of arms and diplomacy. They say no one can match him in battle, but I'm not so certain of that anymore."

He was looking askance at me. If he only knew. Grady O'Neal was a familiar name to me. He was a soldier and a hero in the War. He was the one who took the Rift. The Rift had been a strip of urban hell. It was an evil piece of civilization and home to a group of terrorists who had been responsible for thousands of civilian deaths.

Obsidian had sent an Agent with the forces that went into the Rift. His name was Grady O'Neal. Apparently, he'd made a home for himself after the Fall. His was a personality I couldn't find much of after the dust up in my noggin. I knew he was there, but he was just a shadow in my mind. A lot of the personalities in there were like that. I could access memories, but not much more.

The man was probably on par with William Childers, my Special Forces persona. Probably not anywhere near Gaunt, the Corporate Assassin.

"It would've taken a strong man to do what he's done down here," I said. "He's done good things for the city, and he's in no danger from me."

Portus nodded.

"How much farther is it to Plagis?" Lindsey asked.

"It isn't too far now," Portus said. "Then we must wait until the man attempts to strike."

"If he hasn't already," Michael said. "Seems like it's been about a month since the last one."

"True," I said. "Let's hope he hasn't already killed again. We'd have to wait another month to catch him in the act. We might find him up top, but there's no guarantee."

"We'll find him above ground if we have to," Michael said. "It'll be harder without the support of the Mardins, but we'll do what needs to be done."

"No doubt," I said.

Running footsteps sounded in the tunnels ahead of us. A few minutes later, a form came into view. It was a Patroller.

"We found him!" the man yelled. "We have him cornered in Tunnel Seven. There's no way out of there except through our forces."

"How many forces?" I asked quickly.

"Fourteen Patrollers, sir."

"It's not enough," I said. "Catch up as quickly as you can."

I shot forward. They shouldn't have cornered him. It would be ugly. I consulted the map in my head. There were two paths to the area where they had him. I turned left at the next branch.

I was moving so fast, I had to rebound off the wall and back to the floor as I turned. They were wrong about exits from Tunnel Seven, according to the map. There was an entrance to the sewers down in the back of Seven. They were blocking him from the surface. I doubted they had even thought of the sewer. Maybe he wouldn't find it.

I heard screams ahead of me and drew the Sig. I turned another corner and found the tunnel ahead of me coated in blood. There were Patrollers, torn and broken, littering the tunnel. More screams came from closer, and I ran past the dead men.

I rounded another bend with the Sig extended and ready to fire. A shadow flickered on my right, and I turned toward it with the Sig. Something slammed into me like a battering ram, and the pistol flew from my hand. Huge hands seized my wrists and pulled outward.

He loomed in front of me and grunted in surprise as I pulled back in with my arms. My foot lashed forward and connected. The huge man staggered and lost his hold on my wrists. I had kicked hard enough to push myself backward from the Geno Freak.

It was pretty obvious that's what he was. There were scales on his clawed hands, and I could see yellow eyes staring at me.

"Geno Freak," I said.

"Don't call me that!" the huge man roared and charged again.

I dodged to the left, and my hand shot out to hit a pressure point. It wasn't there. His hand grasped my wrist and yanked me toward him. With a violent twist, he tossed me through the air, and I slammed into a tunnel wall.

"What are you?" he rumbled as I regained my feet.

I was starting to get mad. "I'm the guy who's gonna kill you."

We charged one another. His clawed right hand swept toward my side, and I twisted out of its path. My fist slammed into his throat. It felt like I had punched a wall when it hit the corded muscle of his neck.

We circled back around for another pass. He didn't seem to have the same weaknesses as a regular person. That throat punch would have crushed a man's neck. He charged forward, and I let his arms encircle me so I could get close enough to grab hold of him. I realized my mistake almost immediately. His jaws spread wide, and fangs pivoted from the roof of his mouth. His jaws clamped on my shoulder. I felt the fire as he injected venom through his fangs.

This must be the poison he had used on his victims. And I had just been dosed.

I grabbed him around his ribs and squeezed with all of my enhanced strength. I heard a crack as ribs broke inside the Geno Freak. His jaws released me as he screamed. I twisted around and threw him across the tunnel so he could have a turn at being slammed into a wall.

He staggered to his feet. Instead of coming at me again, he ran out of the tunnel toward the exit to the surface. I launched myself forward and fell on my face as the venom took effect on the left side of my body.

Two forms shot into tunnel.

"Damn, Kade," Michael said.

Lindsey helped me as I was struggling to regain my feet. I could feel my enhanced system burning away the paralytic. I was shaking as my body poured adrenaline into my blood stream.

"That hurt." My voice was raspy.

"What the hell happened?"

"Definitely a Geno Freak," I said as the two of them supported me.

Portus and the Patroller ran in from the darkness.

"Dear God!" Portus gasped.

There were several surviving Patrollers in the tunnel. Most were severely injured. One of them was looking at me, with open fear in his gaze. He'd seen the short fight between me and the Freak.

"W-what are y-you?"

"A guy who just got his ass kicked," I said. "Just like you."

He shook his head but didn't press the issue. We heard more footsteps, then Patrollers came into sight. They began helping the wounded, who were whispering and casting sidelong glances at me.

"Looks like the rest of this is gonna be done on the surface," I said. "Now, we pursue him up top."

Michael nodded.

I staggered forward as I burned through the paralytic that still filled my blood.

"We can't let up on him, or we'll lose him," I said. "We need to get movin'."

"You're not moving anywhere very fast," Lindsey said.

"It'll burn off," I said. "Let's go."

We moved slowly down the tunnel toward the nearest exit to the surface. Portus came up behind us.

"What will you do now?"

"We're gonna find this guy and kill him," I said. "He's not gonna stop killin' folks, and it's gonna take people like us to stop him. Tell your boss we'll finish the job."

"I will," he said. "You scared some of our men back there. What did you do?"

"Like I told your boy, I got my ass kicked," I answered. "Not gonna happen the next time. I know about that little trick now."

"Good luck to you, Mathew Kade," he said. "And good luck to you as well, Mr. and Mrs. Tanzik."

"By the looks of things, we'll need all the luck we can get," Michael said. "I need you to do me a favor. Contact Teresa and tell her where we are and what the situation is. We may need the Society to keep its eyes peeled for this guy."

"It will be done."

"Thank you."

The steel door to the surface hung open from the hurried exit of the Freak. I limped through the opening, followed by two worried Squires. A fire was burning inside me as I thought about the monster we were pursuing. He was a relic leftover from a time best forgotten. I am one of those relics from the Old World. It was fitting one relic would be used to destroy another.

The cool temperature was refreshing, and I was glad it was nighttime after our prolonged stay in the dark. It would give us time to let our vision return to normal as daylight came.

Unfortunately, the night was the time when the predators plagued this broken city. In the mood I was in, it was unfortunate for them.

I heard groans in the distance. "This way."

I limped toward the east. We hadn't gone far before I smelled the metallic scent of blood. Three forms were lying in the street. Only one was alive, and he was in bad shape. His arms had been twisted so hard they were nearly unattached. He was bleeding profusely and had moments to live.

"Which way did it go?" I asked when he saw me.

His head turned, weakly, to the east.

"There's nothing I can do for you," I said.

"I know," he gasped. Then he was gone.

"He'll be joining you soon," I muttered.

"He's gone over the edge," Michael said. "There's no telling what he'll do now."

"He'll kill anyone who gets in his way," I said. "He's hurt pretty bad. I crushed a few ribs."

"We have to find him as quickly as we can," Lindsey said. "There will be innocents in the streets come daylight."

I limped toward the east. My stride was getting stronger as my body worked on the venom. The bullet wound from my last case hurt, and I was pretty sure I had reinjured it in the fight with the Freak. The bite wounds in my left shoulder burned, and I knew I could use some medical attention. But there was no time.

"We catch him tonight," I said.

We covered about half the block before shadows moved from the darkness.

"What have we here?" A blocky, shaven-headed man said from the front of a group of about fifteen thugs. "Aren't you a pretty thing?"

"Thank you," I said, "but I'm not really interested."

"You have one chance to leave this street alive," the bald man said, glaring at me. "Her."

"You don't," I said.

"Don't what?"

"Have that chance."

My hand blurred, and one of the twelve blades on my harness sank into his throat. He gurgled and toppled backward.

"Now, you all have one chance to leave this street alive."

Michael's and Lindsey's blades rasped as they drew them. I slid my razor from its sheath.

There were still fifteen thugs, and their numbers made them brave. They started to move closer.

"Ah, to hell with it," I said and drew the Sig. I didn't pause as I fired four shots. The front three men went down, and I stepped forward, firing three more times. Three more fell, and the rest stopped approaching. I shot two more while they thought about it, and the rest fled. I stepped forward and pulled my blade from the leader's neck.

"Don't have time for this," I muttered and popped the magazine from the pistol.

We walked down the street to the east as I thumbed cartridges into the magazine. More shadows came from the darkness and closed on the fallen men. I glanced back as I walked and saw men and women removing various articles of clothing.

We increased our pace as the venom burned away. The guys he'd killed had been fresh. He wasn't far ahead of us.

"Why is he going east?" Michael asked.

"Was the direction he'd been plannin' on," I said. "He's hurt and runnin' on instinct."

"And he's killing anything in his path," Lindsey added.

"We need to catch him."

I heard screams ahead and tried to speed up. It didn't work.

"Go," I said. "Be careful. He's a damn handful."

Michael and Lindsey sprinted forward, and I stumped along after them. The venom was stubbornly slowing me down. I rounded a corner and saw the Freak run into a Scraper. The Squires were right behind him. I felt a little more of the venom burn away, and I sped up. I shot through the door and stopped to listen. The sound of running feet came from the stairway.

"Figures," I muttered.

Following the noise, I climbed five stories. The sounds of a fight were coming from down the hall to my right. The door slammed open in front of me, and it seemed as if time slowed down. I took in the scene ahead of me.

Michael had sliced the Freak on his left and had been slammed across the hall against the wall. I was familiar with that and knew it hurt. Lindsey closed from the right and sank a blade into the Freak's leathery hide. He grabbed her, and his mouth began to open wide.

Michael bounced back and pounded his fist with the metal gauntlet into the Freak's mouth, behind his fangs. His other gauntlet slammed into the front, and the Freak screamed as his fangs shattered.

He dropped Lindsey and punched Michael in the chest. Michael flew across the hall and hit the wall again with a thud.

Squires are tough, but the two of them were outmatched by the Freak's speed and strength. They'd done more than fourteen Mardin Patrollers could, but it wasn't enough. There's a skill taught to Special Forces. They can push their adrenal glands to maximum with sheer will. It's dangerous and only used as a final measure. About thirty percent of the time, it ends in the death of the soldier. An Agent is a little tougher but doing so could still kill them.

I willed the gland to full output.

All the pain disappeared as my body jerked. The venom was like an afterthought. I launched myself down the hallway.

The Freak took another cut at Lindsey, then slapped her aside. He held her down with one huge hand and raised the other to rip his claws across her body. As his hand descended, I hit him at full speed.

An Agent's strength comes from the enhancement of his or her muscles and bones. They are higher in density than those of a normal person. This makes Agents heavier than their size would suggest. I would, if I were a normal person, weigh about one hundred and ninety pounds or so. With the density of my muscle and bone, I weighed about twice that.

After impact, we both slammed into the windows at the end of the hall and smashed through the shattering glass.

"Kade!" I heard Lindsey's voice behind us.

The Freak clawed my back, but I planted my knees in his chest. Just before we hit, I jumped upward with all my strength. The force of the jump added to his impact and took away from mine. I landed on his chest and felt the satisfying crunch as it collapsed under me. I also felt my left leg break. The adrenaline faded, and my racing heart almost redlined.

I drew the Sig and placed it under his chin. After pulling the trigger three times, just to be sure, I rolled off him.

I reached over and patted the dead man's shoulder. "Thank you. You broke my fall, nicely."

Darkness began to settle across my vision as I saw Michael and Lindsey running toward me. The darkness didn't bother me with the two of them there.

It's nice to have friends in this Fallen World.

* * * * *

Chapter Ten

I awoke in a bright room that looked distinctly familiar. I was in the infirmary we had taken the injured Mardin to. Or one that looked the same.

"That's gonna leave a mark," I muttered.

"That it will, Mister Kade." I didn't recognize the voice. I turned my head to look at the speaker.

He was short and stocky, but I recognized the sort of man he was. The way he held himself. He looked as if he was ready to erupt in violence at any moment. Special Forces.

"You must be Grady."

"That would be correct," he said. "It seems I have a lot to thank you for."

"Just doin' my job."

"Maybe so, as you killed the man who has been killing my people for some time," he said. "But you also stopped two attacks on my people that would have been quite devastating. The second time, you even killed the man they called Lord Silas and his second in command, Yelvin. This single act has done my people a great service and paved the way to expanding our territory. Silas was a tyrant and a slaver. His second was just as bad. I have sent an offer to the third in line, who is a much more reasonable person."

"Buildin' empires?"

"No," he said. "I'm uniting a city. Well, an undercity. The unification will benefit the surface as well as our people. The Accords will extend through the southern Zones of the city, almost to the Boroughs. There will be running water and working sewers throughout a large part of those Zones where we've only had sporadic success."

"Could do a lot worse than Mardins," I said.

"It could be a great boon to your quest to unite the city above as well," he said.

"I'm not on a quest," I said.

"Call it what you want, Agent. In the last two months, there has been a change on the surface. The area around you seems to be coming together under the influence of the Society of the Sword. Rumors abound about why this is occurring. Certain Warlords have been removed and replaced with a Chapterhouse."

"I'm just doing the jobs I'm paid to do."

"I can see the way things are heading on the surface. It was becoming more and more violent. This quest that isn't a quest is a thing that could bring us back to a civilized place in this broken world."

"Like I said, I'm just doin' the job I get paid to do."

He nodded, with a slight smile. "Speaking of pay, yours is in the bag on the table. We thank you for finding the killer."

I nodded.

"I understand you have a blacksmith who would be interested in a source of good steel. I will contact this man and possibly work out some arrangements. I could use several things a blacksmith can provide, and he is much closer than the Farmers."

"Soba is good," I said. "He'll be as good as the Farmers, given the chance."

"I will also be talking to Teresa Manora about a closer relationship with her Society. I feel it will be a power to be reckoned with in the future."

"You can benefit from each other," I said.

"I believe you're right."

"I need to be on my way," I said. "Thanks for the medical."

"No. I thank you for the job you've done and the extra help you provided my Patrollers. I must be on my way, as well. I must meet the messenger I sent to the south. We will know shortly if my offer is accepted."

He shook my hand and turned to leave.

"Grady," I said. He looked back at me. "Remember the Rift? The world up there is much worse than the Rift ever got. It could stand some of what was done back then."

"It was a long time ago in another world," he said. "I keep my people safe down here, Kade. But there might be a time when I can help in your quest."

"Ain't on a damn quest," I muttered. He smiled and walked out of the infirmary.

Two other forms came from the shadows.

"Don't even think about it," Lindsey said.

"You don't wanna know how to make it?"

"Just leave him alone about it."

"The kid might stay home more…"

"Don't even go there, you old fart!"

"How you holding up, there, Kade?" Michael changed the subject.

"I'll live," I said.

"Killian said you had a broken leg and four broken ribs, and your gunshot wounds from before reopened. Along with the bite the Geno Freak hit you with, you have four cuts from his claws on your back. She stitched those up nicely."

"Yeah, I think I'll take a break."

"You need to," Lindsey said. "How did you survive that fall?"

"The Freak used his body to break my fall."

"Was awful nice of him," Michael said.

"I thought so."

"Ready to get outta here?"

"Definitely," I said. "Where's my coat?"

"Don't worry about that," Lindsey said. "Doctor Killian won't let you up, yet, so we're wheeling you out with one of her chairs."

"Let's get to it, then," I said. "If I'm gonna lay around, it's gonna be in my big, comfortable bed."

"Our orders are to bring you to the Chapterhouse," Michael said. "I don't think Teresa wants to leave you alone yet. Right now, you're not as scary as she is, so we'll follow her orders."

Michael strode across the room to fetch the wheelchair.

"I love that old bastard," Lindsey said. "And he's right. She's much more terrifying than you."

I guess there are scarier things than a schizophrenic Corporate Agent in this Fallen World.

* * * * *

Epilogue

"Kade," Wilson Poe yelled from the front room of Teresa Manora's quarters.

"Come on in," I said.

"Teresa requested you join her in the conference room."

"Sure thing."

"Want me to wheel you there?"

"I guess," I grumbled. If she saw me out of the chair, I'd never hear the end of it.

He pushed my chair out of the office where I had been spending most of my time.

"Still won't let you go home?"

"Nope."

"You could sneak out."

"You think I would ever hear the end of that?"

"Probably not," he said as he pushed the door open and pulled my chair through.

"Probably has another job for me," I said. "I like some time between jobs to heal up. At this rate, I'll be a quadriplegic before the year is out."

He laughed and kept pushing me to my doom.

He pulled the door open and pushed me into a conference room where nine people sat around the table. I knew all nine of the men in question, one way or another.

Zane stood and pulled my chair up to the table as Poe stepped back through the door with a grin. I looked around the room at eight of the Warlords from the general vicinity, including Stiner, the Warlord of our Zone. Zane, Jaxom, Devin, Yamato, and Stiner were

Warlords who had been in place for some time. Holden, the replacement for Blechley, and Safro, the replacement for Polk, were new to their jobs.

I chuckled as I saw the final member of this group. I had first met him in the street of Moreau. He'd warned me to leave. I'd last seen him when I gave him the skin with the mark on it to control those under the influence of the imprinter.

"Moving up in the world?"

"I kept the mark and took over for a while to make it easier on the folks in Moreau," he said. "As the folks came off the imprinter, they recognized that I had treated them well and stayed. They made me the Warlord by election. I couldn't say no when they asked."

"Understandable," I said with a grin.

"The name's Kalib," he said.

"We requested that you be here for a reason," Jaxom said.

"We all came together to create something today," Yamato said. "An alliance of sorts. We are signing contracts to place our Zones under the control of one person."

"Hell no…"

"Teresa Manora," Zane said.

"Thank God," I said. "You scared the crap out of me for a second."

Jaxom chuckled. "All of us have agreed to this alliance, with one stipulation. It is hard to give such a degree of trust, and we will only sign if this contract will be enforced by someone who is strong enough to remove anyone who breaks it. No one doubts that you could be that enforcer."

"We want your signature on the contract and your word that you will enforce it if necessary," Yamato said.

I find I can still be surprised in this Fallen World.

# # # # #

Enforcer

Chapter One

I walked down the well-lit street and looked around with a smile on my face. It was two hours after dusk, and people were walking around. Not thugs or killers. Real people.

I stopped and looked at the building to the right of the square. It had been a little over seventeen years since I left that place behind me.

What had happened inside was jumbled in my head, but I remembered some of it. The guy who had taken care of me for the first six months was prominent in my mind. The doctors who had taken over, less so. The various methods they had used to "fix" me caused them a lot of pain and misery when I left. They didn't leave at all. I had left the place in quite a mess.

The people in Wilderman still remembered what I had done to the men who tried to dissect me. Their shock treatments hadn't brought me out of my vegetative state. They had grown tired of helping me and had strapped me to a table where they planned to take me apart. I had settled the royal rumble that had been going on inside my noggin and decided not to let them.

The building was still dark and empty seventeen years later. I'm sure some brave souls had gone in and looted the place, but the building was still unoccupied.

"The people in this Zone have long memories," I muttered. "They'll probably come after me with torches and pitchforks."

A girl who sat on a stoop looked up at me as I walked by, talking to myselves. Even a prosperous Zone like Wilderman separated its rich and poor. The girl looked to be about eleven and wore a dress of multiple-colored fabrics. Whoever had made it had used whatever material they could find. She held a basket that contained small figurines.

"What have you got there?" I asked.

"My momma makes them from some of the stones I collect." She pulled one of the figurines from the basket. "This one is Thomas Wilderman."

I looked closely at the stone figure. "Do you mind if I look at the others?"

"Sure, mister." She smiled and held the basket out for me to see.

I reached in and pulled out a female figurine.

"That one is Bella Trask, Hero of Wilderman."

"Doesn't look much like her." I saw the disappointment in the girl's face, so I turned the figurine sideways. "Ah, there she is. Your momma must have seen her from the side."

Her face lit up.

Softie. I chuckled at Childers' comment in my head.

"You've met the Bella Trask?"

"Yes, I have," I said. "She helped me and a friend with a job way over in Stiner."

"Is she amazing?"

"You wouldn't believe how amazing she is."

"Yes, I would."

I pulled out another figure.

"That one is the Beast," she said in a hushed tone. "Momma said he came from that building over there. She said he killed every one of the people inside and escaped into the city. It was a long time ago, before I was born."

"He looks quite scary," I said.

"He was one of the scariest things ever."

"And this one?"

"That one is Teresa Manora, Matron of the Society of the Sword. She's said to be very pretty. Momma has never seen her, but she has talked to many who have met her, so she did the best she could."

"Pretty close," I said.

"You've met her, too?" The little girl's amazement was something I hadn't seen in years. It reminded me of my days as a child, comparing comics and baseball cards, before everything went completely off the rails.

"Yes, I have."

"Oh, my momma would love to meet you!"

Another of the figures made me grin, "And this one?"

"That is the man who conquered the Beast. His name is Mathew Kade. He has a coat just like yours!"

"Yep. I really like his coat, so I got one too."

"He's the toughest man in the whole city." She added in a low voice, "They say he even killed some Warlords."

"Really?"

"That's what Momma said."

"How much for the whole basket?"

"The whole thing? All of them?"

"Yep."

"Momma said they are ten scrip each."

"That's, what? Ten figures? A hundred scrip?"

Her eyes were wide.

"Are you going to be safe with that much scrip?"

"Yes, sir." She nodded. "Nobody wants to anger the Peacekeepers."

"Alright, then," I said. I handed the girl the chits. "Put those in your pocket just to be safe."

She counted the scrip, then quickly pocketed it.

"Momma will be so happy, mister."

"Good. She does fine work."

She pulled the figurines from the basket and handed them to me. I slipped them into various pockets.

"Here's a little extra in case you want to slip over to that stand and get one of those sticky buns." I slipped her an extra ten scrip.

She inhaled excitedly, and the smile that crossed her face let me know my generosity had been worthwhile.

"Thank you!"

I nodded as she turned and ran for the stand. It had to have been hard for her to sit there, trying to sell the figurines, with the glorious smell of cinnamon and sugar permeating the air.

Don't even think about it, Childers said.

"Boy, those smell delicious."

You'll get fat and get us all killed.

Almost makes me long for a bullet wound, I thought.

I could hear Stephen Gaunt chuckling.

"Quit your whinin'," I grumbled and continued down the street. "I'll stay away from the damn things. But if I see a taco stand, all bets are off."

Bloody tacos will be the death of us, Childers said.

"You know you love 'em, Bill."

Dear God, man. It is William. Not Bill or Will. William.

"Alright Willy," I said. "Let's go find out why Wilderman sent for us."

With a final look at the Obsidian building where I had spent a great deal of time before the Fall and the three years after, I continued down the street full of people and vendors who would never be set up this late in most places. All the streetlights worked, which was damned unusual for anywhere in this broken city.

I walked three more blocks that were pretty much the same as the first block I had passed coming into Wilderman. There were more red-uniformed Peacekeepers in the outer edges of the Zone, but I was seeing fewer as I headed toward the huge Scraper Thomas Wilderman called home.

The main entrance to the Scraper had been impressive before the world went down the crapper, and I had to stop and admire the ornate statuary. What impressed me more than anything was that they were still there. Wilderman's people had done good work, cleaning and restoring the statues.

Most folks wouldn't know what they were. The griffin, a mythological beast from the Old World, combined the body of a lion with the head and wings of an eagle. The statues had been there for decades before the Fall.

"First time in Wilderman?" one of the guards asked. He wore the red of the Peacekeepers.

"Nope, but it's been a while." I shook my head. "These used to be in worse shape."

"Yeah," the young Peacekeeper said. "Mister Wilderman had them cleaned up a couple years back."

"I'm suitably impressed with the Zone." I gestured back the way I came. "If you see people out this late in most places, they're trying to kill you."

"Is it really as bad as they say out there?"

"In most places, it is," I replied. "There are some good folks in some of the Zones. Many have never traveled out of the Zone they were born in."

"I've never left this Zone," he said.

"Place like this," I said, "there's no need to leave it."

"I was going to go out and see the world, but my father convinced me to join the Peacekeepers. Maybe I'll go after my five years are up."

"Your time in the Peacekeepers should help when you do go out there," I said. "It's a rough place, and you need to know how to fight if you plan to travel. You need to learn about each Zone before going into it. Stepping into the wrong one can get you killed."

"I'll do that, Mister..." He looked at me with a questioning expression.

"Kade, Mathew Kade."

"Oh." He looked surprised. "We were expecting you later this week. The next Caravan is still two days out."

"I don't use Caravans."

"Then it must not be as bad as they say."

"It is," I said. "But some people are better left alone. I usually travel through Zones where they know that. Others find out the hard way."

"Anyway, Mister Wilderman is in the Great Hall, Mister Kade. Go straight through the entrance and cross to the double doors. The guards there will tell him you're here."

I looked back at the people on the streets.

I guess, if there are Zones like this, there may be some hope, after all, for this Fallen World.

* * * * *

Chapter Two

"You must be Kade," the big man said as I entered the Great Hall.

He was over six feet tall and dressed in a nice, Old World suit.

"Wilderman," I answered, with a nod. "Gotta say, my curiosity was piqued when I got the message you wanted to see me. Last time I was here, this Zone was a lot smaller."

"True." He nodded. "And there was a whole building full of dead people."

"If it helps, they were pretty bad people."

"Were they?"

"Bad enough. Wanted to cut into my brain and see what it looked like. I didn't like the idea."

"And the stories began about the 'Beast' who came out of that place."

"I don't take offense." I shrugged. "Fella who walked out of that place was pretty beastly. What I'm curious about is why you asked me to come back. Frankly, I expected you to try to arrest me. Then things would have gotten ugly."

"Why did you come if that's what you expected?"

"Expect the worst. You'll never be disappointed."

He stared at me for a moment then started laughing. "That's what I've been telling these bastards for years."

I looked at the small man to Wilderman's left. He shrugged and nodded. "He has."

"I'm rarely disappointed," Wilderman said.

"Same here," I returned.

"This is going much better than I expected," he said. "And I'm not disappointed. I don't want to arrest you, if that makes you feel any better. I'd like to hire you for a job. I heard you've been pretty busy lately. I'm hearing about a nice little chunk of this city that's going through some changes."

"That's the Society," I said. "They're trying to clean things up a bit."

"I heard it began with you. As a matter of fact, I spoke with the Matron recently. She said something about a certain fellow who keeps dropping presents on her doorstep. A Zone run by a madman is suddenly under new management and requesting a Chapterhouse. A couple of others lost their Warlords and would also like Chapter-houses. I even heard about a new alliance forming in those Zones and several surrounding them."

"I just did my job," I said. "Shit happens."

"She said something similar. Things seem to happen around you. When I talked to her, she suggested you for the job I have in mind."

"What kind of job?" I asked.

"I need someone to escort a valuable person across the Zones to Kathrop. She has the College, and my daughter wants to attend."

"What about a Caravan?"

"The problem with Caravans is the time they take to cross. They move slowly, and they stop throughout the city," he said. "Mister Kade, I have enemies. You don't build something like this without enemies."

"Makes sense," I said. "But there's safety in numbers."

"I have numerous enemies."

"Alright." I nodded. "Pretty long trip. Probably take two days unless you want us to travel nights. But doing so would put your daughter in more danger."

"A Caravan would keep her in the streets for nearly a week. Two days is much better. No need to travel nights if you have a safe place to stay."

"I do."

"Then you'll take the job?"

"Depends," I said.

"I assume you're talking about pay?"

"Guy's gotta make a living."

"Escort and bodyguard duty," he said. "Five thousand seem fair to you?"

"I can deal with that." I nodded. "When do you want us to move out?"

"I wasn't planning on her leaving for another two days."

"Okay," I said. "I want to look around anyway. Haven't been here in a while."

"I'll have a room prepared for you."

"No need," I said. "I'll stay down the road a piece. I had a nice room last time I was here."

I could see he wasn't pleased but, when he looked into the dead eyes of someone else, he decided not to say anything.

Instead, he nodded.

"I'll be here bright and early."

I turned and strode out of the large meeting room filled with people.

Trap? One of the many voices asked.

"Not sure who it's for," I muttered. "If it's me, he'll need more men."

I expect the trap is for someone else, Mathew, Childers said. *Perhaps one of those gents in that room.*

"I expect so," I said.

"What, sir?" The same young guard I spoke to earlier asked as I walked by.

"Nothin'," I answered. "Just talkin' to myselves."

"Umm…"

"Don't worry about it, kid."

I grinned and walked on past the young Redcoat. My head was probably the best place I knew for decent conversation in this Fallen World.

* * * * *

Chapter Three

The dark building looked much the same as it had seventeen years earlier. I remembered bits and pieces of what happened here. I remembered the pain more than anything. But there was a time before that when someone had helped me. I couldn't thank him at the time, but he kept me alive.

Then the "doctors" arrived. I shook my head and pushed those memories aside. They'd paid for their sins with their lives. One day, I hoped to meet the other guy, though. He was an Agent. It had taken an Agent to restrain me when the madness came over me.

"Stands to reason he'll still be around, somewhere," I muttered.

Perhaps we will meet him someday, Childers said. *I would love to thank him.*

"Me too."

There was a great deal of pain after he turned us over to them, another voice added.

"All of us felt that, David," I answered as I pushed open a large double door leading to the facility behind the Atrium. "If I had stepped forward more quickly, we might not have had to live through that."

If we had not lived through that, you might never have pulled yourself back together, Mathew, Doctor Amanda Fender said.

"Don't hear much from you, Doc," I said.

Your profession is very hard for me, Mathew. And the company you keep is dubious, at best.

"This whole damn world is hard for you, Doc."

It is. But I will be there for you when you need me, Mathew.

Her consciousness faded into the background.

Death troubles her, Childers said. *She is too gentle for a world like this.*

I tapped the side of my head. "Several folks, up here, are too gentle for this place. Luckily, there are a few who aren't."

"Very true, Mathew." I had dropped into a completely different voice as Gaunt spoke.

"You know I look crazy carrying on one-sided conversations. When I start answering, it goes to a whole new level."

I heard Stephen laughing in my head.

"Laugh it up, Chuckles," I muttered. "Doc's probably right. Seems like you guys who are closest to the top are dubious characters."

"She must be referring to William," Stephen said.

"Not me, I'm sure," Childers returned.

"Great," I mumbled. "Now it's a three-sided conversation."

Do you actually plan to sleep here? David Rasting asked. *There are a lot of bad memories in this place.*

"Why not?" I shrugged. "He killed everyone who hurt us back then."

He certainly did, Childers said.

I reached into a pocket and pulled something from it.

Oh, dear, David said. *You're going to do that here?*

"It's Tuesday."

I'm not sure why you bother, my friend, Childers said.

"He's one of us, too." I shrugged and sat down near a lamp with a good bulb I had found. I plugged the lamp into a battery pack I pulled from another pocket. "This has been one of the handiest things."

He is dangerous, Gaunt said.

"That's kind of funny, coming from you."

Nevertheless.

"He's not so bad," I said and opened the book and started reading aloud.

I will never quite understand you, Mathew.

"It's part of my charm, Stephen." I shrugged and started reading again. "Do you like green eggs and ham? I do not like them, Sam-I-Am."

Something moved around a bit in my head. Something we kept in a cage.

There are some things that should never be released. Not even in this Fallen World.

* * * * *

Chapter Four

"**M**ister Kade." Wilderman nodded. "How has your stay been?"

"Fine," I said. "Relatively peaceful. No one has tried to kill me yet."

"Yet?"

"The day's still young."

He smiled and beckoned to a girl who was standing nearby.

"This is Melody."

"Miss," I said, with a nod.

"She is packed and ready to go whenever you are," he said.

"Grab your pack, and let's go," I said.

"Yes, sir."

"Be careful with my girl," Wilderman said.

"No one will touch her, Wilderman." I gave him the cold, dead stare of someone else. His eye twitched a little.

Melody picked up her pack and slung it across her back. She raised the hood on her poncho.

I smiled a little as I turned toward the door.

"Stay behind me for the first bit," I said. "When we step out of the Zone, move up to my left."

"Yes, sir."

We walked straight down the street and past the checkpoint into Wilderman's Zone.

As soon as we were out of hearing distance of the checkpoint, I motioned for her to step up.

"Did she leave yesterday, or will she be leaving today?"

The girl was silent for a moment.

"He said you weren't stupid," she said. "She left yesterday with a group of traders who aren't really traders. We are a decoy."

"How did they get you to put your life on the line?"

"I love her."

"Makes sense," I said. "People do stupid shit for love."

"Sir?"

"I expect we'll get hit before we get through the first Zone. When that happens, do exactly as I say, and you may live through it. No sense dying for love if you don't have to."

She nodded.

"Always watch your surroundings and always take note of any nearby cover. When the shooting starts, dive for that cover."

"Yes, sir."

"They'll likely wait until we get out of sight of the checkpoint, so any moment now."

Fifth floor, third window.

"Yeah, I see it."

"What?"

"Just talking to myselves. Get ready to run for that corner on the left."

I saw her eyes widen. I'm not sure she really understood what she was getting into when she volunteered to be the decoy.

"When I say run, run like your life depends on it. Get behind that corner and drop to the ground."

Fastest route or safest? Stephen asked.

I glanced to the left side of the street. "Fastest. Third floor, fourth window on the left."

"Run for cover." I nudged the girl. She sprang forward, and I shot to the right. I reached the wall of the building on the right before she had covered five feet.

Jumping upward, I caught a ledge and threw myself up to the next one. The guy across the street fired, and the glass in a window below me shattered. I was already twenty feet above it. A gun boomed right above me, but the shot went wide because I was pushing it. Then I was in the room with the gun, and the woman who had fired flew out the window, screaming.

I turned, raised my rifle, and shot the man staring up at me from the third floor.

Glancing down, I could see five men running toward the alley where the girl was hidden, and I calmly shot four of them, emptying the rifle's magazine. Then I went through the window, dropped down a story, and caught a ledge with my left hand. It was just a matter of moments before I landed on the ground and threw the rifle.

It made an odd noise that reminded me of a propeller as it spun. It slammed into the back of the fifth man with enough force to send him hurtling down the alley.

I heard a squeak from the girl as the dead man flew past her.

"How long have you been in Wilderman?" I asked as she peeked up at me with wide eyes and a pale face.

"B-Born t-there."

I shook my head. "Only problem with a Zone like Wilderman is the lack of danger. If you don't learn to fight, you're just another victim in this Fallen World."

* * * * *

Chapter Five

I'm pretty sure they expected better results from their hit team, so I figured we would be able to cover a Zone or two without any more trouble.

"Let's move," I said. "Walk on my left."

"Yes, sir."

She fell in beside me, and I glanced at her out of the corner of my eye. I could see her hands shaking.

"Fear is good," I said. "It will help keep you sharp. Can you use a weapon?"

She shook her head with a sharp jerk. The girl was terrified.

"Damn, Wilderman," I muttered.

I could take her down to the Tees and get the Mardins to let me run her across the Zones, but I suspected the real daughter was being escorted through there. Being the decoy meant we needed to stay visible.

"What?" she asked.

"It would have been so much simpler if he had let me escort his real daughter. This bait and switch shit just complicates things. It's hard to keep someone alive when I can't use the stealth routes. Decoys are expendable. Sucks for the decoy."

"Stealth routes?"

"Yeah. But they're not an option for us."

My eyes narrowed as a familiar form slipped out of an alley. She stopped at the edge of the street and beckoned to us.

"Hi, Honey," I said with a grin. "Fancy meetin' you here. What the hell have you gotten me into?"

Teresa Manora gave me a crooked smile. "I planned to catch you before you left Wilderman, but you took off at dawn. Missed you."

I followed her into the alley, with the girl in tow.

"Hello, Tamara," she said. "It was brave of you to volunteer for something like this. Whether her father agrees or not, Melody does not think you are expendable. She wants you to join her. I brought someone else to stroll through the Zones with him."

She pointed at me. "Traveling with this one is not for the faint of heart. I have it on good authority there is a pretty sizable group of people in Jankida's Zone who wish to hurt Thomas by capturing or killing his daughter."

"Do tell," I said in someone else's voice.

Tamara looked at me oddly, but Teresa just shook her head. "Stephen, you will probably enjoy what I have in mind."

Another form slipped from the back of the alley to join us.

I chuckled. "Whoever is in Jankida is in for a rude awakening. How the hell are you, Fenris?"

The small woman shrugged. "Good as can be expected, considering I haven't slept in two days, trying to get here in time for this."

"I guess they'll be in for an even ruder awakening than I thought." I laughed. "Fenris is bad. Fenris with a lack of sleep, damn!"

Judy Fenris grinned. She wore the same poncho as Tamara.

"I think this just got interesting," I said.

Judy Fenris was a full Knight of the Society and a walking disaster for anyone who came after us.

"The Mardins will escort Melody's party under the streets while you two take a pleasant stroll."

"And you?"

"I have business with Wilderman. I'll be along in a few days."

"Looking forward to it." I grinned.

"I bet, you lecherous old bastard."

"I resemble that remark," I said.

Fenris snorted.

I placed a hand on Tamara's shoulder. "Go with her; she'll see you safely to your girl."

She nodded.

"She'd be better off going to Stiner and getting a different education," I muttered as she followed Teresa back into the alley.

"Both of them," Fenris said. "Neither has any weapons training."

"Wilderman's a dumbass."

"Agreed." She turned toward the street. "Shall we? I think we have an appointment with a crowd of idiots in Jankida."

"That, we do." I grinned and followed the Knight.

There is no shortage of idiots in this Fallen World.

* * * * *

Chapter Six

"Walk alongside," I said. "We'll try to stick to the same patterns."

"Gotcha," Fenris answered.

"What have you been up to for the last few years, Fen?"

"Trying to set up a Chapter out on the east end." She kept her head down so no one could see her face. "Hard sell out there. There are some pretty vile Zones on the coast."

"I was out there about seven years ago, for a few days, but not long enough to get a real feel for the area," I said.

"Slavers work on the coast, bringing in new people for the Flesh Peddlers. There's a whole pipeline of slaves coming in from there. Some end up at the Circus."

"One of these days, something has to be done about those bastards," I said. "But I know my limitations; it's going to take more than me to get the job done."

"When the time comes, the Knights will be with you. You know that."

"There are at least thirty Clowns who are Corporate Agents. Knights are bad asses, but Agents are on a whole other level. Knights can match or beat the other Clowns, but that core group is going to take Agents. We don't have the manpower to take 'em out yet. I'm good for several, but I can't take out thirty at once."

"Jesus, Kade," she said. "They're Agents?"

"Yep." I nodded. "And you don't have to call me Jesus when we're alone."

"She told me I would probably stab you before we're done. I didn't believe her. I'm starting to see her point."

"You wouldn't stab little, old me, would you? After calling me Jesus and everything?"

"Yep."

"Why I always get to work with the crazy ones is beyond me," I muttered.

"No one else will work with you."

"You might have a point." I shrugged. "Hasn't worked out all that well for the last few. Poe got shot, and Michael and Lindsey had some bones broken."

"Poe wanted to come out for this one, but he wouldn't fit in the cloak."

"It would take ten of them to cover the big bastard. Besides, we might have to run, and he hates running."

She chuckled. "I wasn't planning on running."

"Might need to, to keep our cover. The longer they think you are Melody Wilderman, the better. We'll probably end up running all the way to Kathrop."

"Why would I do that?"

"Expect the worst, so you're never disappointed."

"I'll hope for the best and live with my disappointment, thank you," she said. "It builds character."

"I have plenty of characters," I said. "Don't need to build any more."

"Hmm."

"What?"

"Just trying to see what she sees in you."

"I keep telling people. It's my charming personalities."

"I heard something about a huge bathtub."

"It could be that too," I said as we reached the boundary of Zemmich, the Zone in which we had been hit.

"I think that first hit was just to feel us out," I said. "I'm not sure they're really aware of what they're dealing with."

"They have a little better idea now," she said.

"Not really," I replied. "They saw a little of what I can do, but you are still a wild card."

"What's that?"

"Christ, you've never played poker?"

"No. And you don't have to call me Christ when we're alone."

"Touché." I grinned. "Poker is a game of chance played with a deck of cards."

"What are the rules?"

I sighed. "Never mind. I'll show you next time we're both in Stiner."

She shrugged. "I hear that's where the bathtub is."

"Nobody cares about anything except the damn bathtub," I muttered.

"What?"

"Nothing."

"So, what's the play when we get to Jankida?"

"I reckon we'll kill a bunch of folks that need killing."

"That's a given," she said. "Do you want me to keep my cover?"

"As long as you can."

She sighed. "Defenseless girl."

"Cheer up." I smiled. "They'll probably send a couple hundred seasoned killers. You'll have to fight through the majority because I'll get shot right at the beginning."

She sighed and shook her head.

"What?" I shrugged. "Low expectations lead to pleasant surprises."

"That's just another way of saying the same thing, Kade."

"Damn Wilderman stole my other line."

Fenris shook her head. "Sometimes, it's ok to feel good about things."

"Nope. As soon as that happens, everything goes down the crapper."

"Those fellows up ahead look like they're up to no good."

"You were starting to feel good about things," I said.

"Oh, shut up!"

"Right down the crapper. Probably get blood on my new coat."

"Maybe they're waiting for someone else. They don't look like much of a hit squad."

"Just your average idiots," I muttered.

"Give us the girl," the leader of the pack of ten men said when we got close enough. "Give us the girl, and you can walk away."

"I wish we didn't have to keep this stupid cover," I muttered. "I could just give you to them."

She chuckled.

"I guess you'll have to run for cover when this starts."

"I think I'll keep her," I said. "But I'm going to warn you. If I get blood on my coat, I'm gonna be pissed."

All but one rushed forward. He drew his pistol and fired it at me. I wasn't where he was aiming when the bullet passed through, but I did feel a tug at the very bottom of my coat.

"Son of a bitch!" My hand blurred as I pulled a throwing knife from its sheath and buried it in his throat.

"That's just as bad as getting blood on it! I already have one at home with a damn bullet hole in it!"

I continued throwing blades as the group got closer and smaller. A single person reached me. I slapped the blade from his hand.

"Gack!" was all he managed as I gripped his throat and lifted him off the ground.

"Do you see this?" I asked, pointing toward the tear in the bottom of my coat.

"Gurk!"

"A man of few words. It seems you have a lesson to learn, which means I can't kill you, or you won't learn it. Just know, this is going to hurt me just as much as it hurts you. Well, actually, it's going to hurt you a lot worse."

I dragged him over to one of his partners.

"This looks good." I picked up a piece of old, galvanized pipe the guy had used as a club.

Sometimes learning is painful in this Fallen World.

* * * * *

Chapter Seven

"**D**id you have to leave him hanging there?"

"No," I answered. "Could have killed him."

"I thought that spike through the shoulder bit was reserved for Warlords who piss you off."

"Nope, it's for people who cost other people their lives through sheer stupidity." I shrugged. "If I kill them, they won't learn anything."

"That's true, but you may end up with another Blechley."

"That guy is no Blechley," I said. "But if he does anything like Blechley did, he'll learn the next lesson."

"And that is?"

"Blechley could tell you."

"I heard that Blechley's organs were nailed to a wall in alphabetical order."

That was a beautiful arrangement, if I do say so, Stephen said.

"Lesson learned."

"I guess so," she said.

"I can't believe I've got a hole in my coat."

"Seems like it would be a common thing in your line of work," she said. "Who wears one of those?"

"Says the girl in a poncho."

"And it's coming off as soon as possible. Stupid cover." She muttered the last two words.

I chuckled.

"It's forever getting in the way. That's what makes me wonder why you wear that useless coat."

"I honestly don't know." I shrugged. I tapped the side of my head. "No one up here really has a preference for it. Maybe I really liked the coat before all this crap."

"Maybe?"

"I don't remember much from before except bits and pieces."

"Before the Fall?"

"Before the imprinter," I said. "I remember more about being an Agent than I do about the time before."

"How do imprinters work?"

"They drop a personality and skill package into an Agent's body. That's who you are until the mission is complete. Most of the Agents who survived the Fall are living the lives they were given for their last mission."

"So, you don't know if that's your original body?"

"I know it's not."

"You sound pretty certain."

"I do remember some things," I said. "The original Mathew Kade was killed during a robbery. I threw the guy who killed him through a window."

"The more I get to know you, the more confused I become." She shook her head. "You, Mathew Kade, threw a guy out of a window after he killed Mathew Kade?"

"Yep."

"Weird."

"I thought so."

"I guess it was pretty satisfying, though, to kill the guy who killed you."

"It was. I really liked Kade. I wish I could remember more about him. I was close to ninety when I joined the program, and I remember very few of those years."

"That's awful," she said.

"The upside is I have memories from quite a few of the imprints that were dumped in my noggin. Now, I'm the guy who drinks and knows things." I chuckled.

She turned to me with a raised eyebrow.

"Just a reference to an old television series. There was a dwarf who drank and knew...never mind."

Fenris was probably thirty, so she would only have a child's memory of the world before the Fall.

I smelled food cooking.

"That smells interesting," I said. "Smells like actual beef."

We were crossing into Fogel. Then I heard the music.

"The Farmers? I didn't know they were coming to Fogel today."

"Didn't you come in this way?" she asked.

"No, I was north of Wilderman when I got the message. At the new Gorman Chapterhouse."

"I didn't know Gorman had gotten a Chapterhouse."

"They didn't either. They pissed off a Knight."

"Never a smart thing to do." She shook her head. "Who was it?"

"Hargrave."

"She shoot them all?"

"Becca wouldn't shoot them all, would she? How do you set up a Chapterhouse if you kill all the people?" I asked.

"You have a point. She probably didn't have enough ammo to kill everyone."

"I don't know. I've never seen Becca run out of ammo. I didn't get to ask her. She was already gone by the time I got there. Teresa just wanted me to make an appearance to show support. Who knew this Enforcer gig would mean I'd have to do that?"

"I heard about that. You're a cop." She laughed.

"Nope you're a cop. Teresa's Chief Gordon." I grinned. "I'm Batman."

She laughed. "I understood that reference."

Perhaps all is not lost in this Fallen World.

* * * * *

Chapter Eight

A delightful smell came from a wagon close to the Scraper.

"Those ribs smell divine," I said as we stopped at the fold-out counter on the side of the wagon. There were three women behind the counter who were obviously sisters. They all looked alike with their black hair, brown eyes, and Native American bone structure. The only difference was their age.

"Ladies," I said in greeting.

"Good day, sir," the oldest of the three answered. "The ribs are just about finished. Teira would probably hit me with something if I took them off the grill early."

"How much longer?"

"Less than a half hour."

"That'll be fine," I said. "We'll look around a bit. Always like to see what you folks are offering. Changes from Zone to Zone."

"You aren't from Fogel?"

"Nope, we're traveling through. I'm from Stiner."

"I didn't see a Caravan," she said.

"Just the two of us."

"There's no way I would travel this city with a single companion," she said. "Unless it was one of the Pratt brothers. Anyone foolish enough to attack one of them deserves whatever happens."

"Isn't that the Steadholder's last name?"

"Yes, it is. He has two sons, Zee and Jimmy. Zee is the Commander of the Farmers' Guard and Jimmy is…well he's just Jimmy. No one wants trouble with Jimmy."

"I know it's none of my business, but what are they like? I worry about what will happen after the Steadholder is gone. I know he's getting on up there in years."

"Zee is next in line for the position. He doesn't want it, but he really doesn't have a choice."

"Have to play the hand you're dealt."

"This is true. There may be another, though, if she is ready by then. Zee's daughter, Allie, could take the position. But only if Kendrick makes it another ten years or so. She's not ready yet, but another decade, and she'll make a fine Steadholder. I have no doubt Zee would be happy to pass on that position."

"Frankly, I'm surprised you're this free with information," Fenris said.

"Part of each vendor's job is to help assuage the fear of the city folk. The Farmers are here, and will be, for the foreseeable future. Lord knows we don't want the city to sink back to where it was when I was a girl. I wouldn't wish that on us."

"This city is still a pretty awful place," Fenris said. "But you're right. I would hate to see it fall back to those days."

"You said you're from Stiner?" she asked.

"Yep."

"I haven't been there yet, but I am looking forward to the opportunity. I would dearly love to meet the Matron of the Society of the Sword. Have you met her?"

"A few times." I chuckled.

"A few?" Fenris asked, shaking her head.

I shrugged.

"I think she would be very interesting," the vendor said. "I have great respect for anyone who can do what she has. I think a person who instills that much loyalty in her people would be worth knowing."

"She's a pretty amazing woman," I said.

"Listen to me jabbering on like an old woman," she said. "Go enjoy the wagons and come back in a little while for the ribs."

I nodded, and we walked toward another cluster of wagons.

"You could have told her who you were. It was pretty obvious she didn't know. Most folks know you two are an item."

"Then she would have clammed up, and I enjoy watching people talk about her. She inspires them, and I can see it every time they mention her. I scare them."

Sometimes anonymity is a good thing in this Fallen World.

* * * * *

Chapter Nine

The ribs were delicious, and the barbecue was perfect. I placed the bones inside the paper wrapper and gave them back to the woman. She smiled.

Fenris looked at me with a raised eyebrow.

"Dog," I said.

"Makes sense." She turned to the vendor. "What breed?"

"We have several breeds," she answered. "My favorite is the Shepherd. He is always the first to greet us when we get home."

"German?"

"Australian."

"Very smart animals," Fenris said. "We don't see many dogs in the city. I've only seen two. If they were not kept in, they would be in a stew pot fairly quickly."

"We have many dogs. The early days were not as rough on the Farms as they were in the city. Some years, we contemplated eating the dogs, but now there is plenty of food, so we can keep them as pets."

"Still, there are quite a few places in the city where there's not enough."

She nodded. "We try to keep the city supplied. Sometimes, we cannot. The Farm Caravans roll all year 'round, but some Zones are not as welcoming as others. Some are harder on the poor than others. The system in place is the best that could be developed at the time, but some of us feel it could have been better."

I chuckled.

"What?" Fenris asked.

"If you knew how many times that's been said, you'd laugh too."

She shook her head and looked back at the vendor. "I was here, in the city, before the Accords. It's easy to say things should have been done differently, but I saw people I grew up with commit murder, rape, and cannibalism. I saw streets filled with the dead and gutters running red with blood. I was twelve when we fled the city. I lost three brothers and a sister in that escape. We were captured by a newly self-proclaimed Warlord. I watched as the Accords were signed. I saw the changes first-hand. I'm not sure there was any other way to bring about a semblance of peace to the city."

"Perhaps you're right," the vendor said. "Sometimes, I wish there was more we could do. The Accords keep everything at this level. There are times I wish we could push harder for what was here before the bombs. That is why I wish to meet the Matron. She is doing things I wish we could do. Our sources say she has united more than ten Zones in the last year. She is even known to be in a relationship with Mathew Kade…"

Her eyes narrowed as she glanced at my long coat. "Oh, my…"

Fenris laughed.

"What?" I asked.

"I am guessing that under that coat is a leather harness from the Farms holding some throwing knives made of Old World steel and a straight razor that has been talked about in more Zones than you'd think possible."

"What makes you think that?"

"I know Marigold, and I should have placed that coat as soon as I saw it. You're probably wearing a pair of her pants and a shirt, as well."

"I guess my secret is out," I said.

I heard a gunshot in the distance, and I became someone else for a split second.

"Oh, my…"

I looked back toward the vendor.

"That would explain a lot," she said. "For a moment, I was looking at someone much like Jimmy Pratt. You're an Agent?"

I looked more closely at the woman. "You're saying Pratt is an Agent?"

"I am. And I would wager you are too, Mister Kade."

I frowned. "And Zee Pratt? If Jimmy is an Agent, I would expect him to be in charge of the Farmers' Guard."

She shook her head. "Zee is something else. He doesn't talk about it. There is a lot of talk about what you are doing, though, Mister Kade."

"So much for anonymity," I muttered.

"If you wanted to be anonymous, you shouldn't have worn that stupid coat," Fenris said.

I started to say something, but arguing with a woman is futile in any world, fallen or not.

* * * * *

Chapter Ten

We were a single Zone away from Jankida.

"You see that?" Fenris asked.

"Yep." I watched the window from the corner of my eye. "He ducked inside as soon as he saw us. I'm guessing he's a lookout."

"I would love to grab him and find out what's waiting."

"I would too. Sucks being bait."

"It'll suck more when they attack," she said. "I have to play helpless."

"You get to be a damsel in distress," I said.

She looked at me in a way I should have been worried about.

"I haven't been a damsel in distress since I was thirteen and followed Teresa out of that hell hole."

"I wondered who else had come out of the General's Compound. You were one of them."

"I said, back there, that we were caught by a Warlord."

"The General was bad news. I've heard some of the stories about the Compound." I turned my head toward her. "That was before I got a handle on all this."

I touched my pointer finger to my forehead.

"Teresa doesn't talk much about what you've got going on up there."

"Lot of folks up here," I said. "Some are whole, some are just wisps of memories. They give me a whole reservoir of skills to pull from. And then, there are some things that should never be spoken about."

Truer than many would believe, Childers said.

I would almost take offense at that, Stephen returned. *Except I know it is the truth.*

I chuckled.

"What?" Fenris asked.

"Talking to myselves," I said.

She shook her head. "They got any idea what to expect when we hit Jankida?"

"If they plan to snatch you, they'll send a lot of guys, hoping to swamp me."

"How long do you want me to play the damsel in distress?"

"Until they get close enough to you."

"How close is enough?"

"You be the judge of that," I said. "We want to draw as many of them as we can in close, so they can't get away. After this, they'll know we're not the ones they're after. I'm hoping we can kill enough of them to make that knowledge useless."

She nodded. "Let's get ready, then."

There was a suspicious lack of foot traffic in the street. Alleys overflowed with bodies.

"Looks like you were right."

"Head for the cover of that stoop."

"Gotcha."

"Alrighty, then. Stephen?"

My whole demeanor changed in front of her, and she looked a bit startled at the grin on Gaunt's face.

"That's not disturbing," she muttered as she turned and ran for the stoop.

"Hello, my lovelies!" he said as he moved faster than anyone had a right to move. I was ten paces closer to the incoming horde in less than a moment.

"I have something special for you," he taunted them. Then I was among the horde.

They had been warned I was dangerous, but they really had no idea what they had gotten themselves into. I held a throwing blade in each hand and flowed through them like water. I wasn't really interested in killing them as much as disabling them.

I severed a hamstring. I sliced a femoral artery. Someone raised a gun, and I rocketed a blade across the street where it sank into her throat. I grabbed another blade. Where I moved, bodies fell, and yells became screams of pain. Soon, the street was filled with screams of terror.

I felt a tug at my left side and threw a blade that embedded in the eye socket of another gun wielder.

"Don't run," I whispered into the ear of a man who tried to flee. "You haven't seen the fun part."

I grabbed the man by the back of his leather garb and turned him toward the crowd that had almost reached Fenris.

"Almost time for the surprise!" Gaunt's voice was more excited than I had heard in some time.

"Watch!" he barked as the man tried to squirm.

The poncho split along the front, and Fenris drew two short swords. They were a little smaller than the gladius Michael had used, but they were shaped much the same way, with both the blade's edges sharpened.

The group closest to her never realized she wasn't the helpless girl they expected as her swords began to dance. A Yeoman is a bad ass, a Squire, even more so. But a Knight is a wonder to watch. Especially doing what they are best suited for in this Fallen World.

* * * * *

Chapter Eleven

The street was littered with bodies, and the metallic smell of blood filled the air. Fenris slid her blades along the shirt of one of the dead to wipe away the blood. Her arms were coated to the shoulder, and her black armor dripped.

"How the hell did you do that and keep your stupid coat so clean, even though you got shot?"

"It's a gift," I said. I looked down at my side, still holding the man up by the scruff of his neck. He was crying.

Tossing him to the side, I looked up toward the skyscraper that housed the Warlord, Mortimer Jankida.

"This didn't happen without his support," Fenris said.

"Perhaps it's time for a lesson," I said.

"I've heard about some of your lessons," she said. "Our cover is blown. We may as well head back to Stiner."

"Agreed, but only after I go see Mortimer."

"I'm guessing a new Chapterhouse is about to be requested?"

"Could be," I said and reached down to pick up a four-foot-long piece of rebar. "Ah, this is perfect."

She chuckled and followed me into the Scraper.

"Oh, Morty?" Gaunt's voice echoed in the open lobby. "Where are you, Morty? I think it's time we had a bit of chat!"

Some lessons are harder than others in this Fallen World.

# # # # #

The Bastion

Chapter One

I slipped into the alley and ducked under a small overhang to block the rain that had been falling steadily.

"Good for the garden," I muttered.

Less worry about Lucy's garden and more about the task at hand, William Childers chided me. *Four ruffians ahead.*

"I see 'em," I muttered to the OSF Operator.

Obsidian Special Forces had been Childers' cover when he was loaded into an Agent. The Agent program was long gone, but there were remnants still wandering the city. Remnants like me. Nanite-enhanced men and women, some with psychopathic tendencies. Others who would have been called sociopaths. Then there was me, the schizophrenic. I got the whole enchilada. Now, Childers was all mine, along with all the others inside my noggin.

I paused, remembering the lab where I finally managed to come out of the squirrel cage in my head. All the imprints that had dropped into my head were fighting for control and I, most certainly, would have died without the Agent who kept me alive for the first six months. Then, the doctors who showed up kept me alive for the rest of that time. Their way was much more unpleasant as they tried to figure out how to get the database back out of my head intact.

They'd finally given up and were just experimenting to see what reactions they could get with different stimuli. I remembered them all. The shock treatments were the worst. They were trying to bring personalities to the surface. They succeeded, but the one who came to the front was a monster. His name was Luca Stiglioni, and it took a long time to get him back under control. The fight to regain control brought me, Mathew Kade, to the surface, and I had been the one in charge for the last seventeen years.

In those seventeen years, I had seen the city brought out of that savagery into a better age. It was still a savage place, but it was multitudes better than the city I awoke to. My attention returned to the four guys standing near the door I had been searching for.

"They picked a bad time to park themselves there."

They may work for the one we came for, Childers said.

"Could be." I shrugged and stepped out into the rain. Broken glass crunched underfoot as I strode down the narrow alley. Perhaps twenty feet separated the old brick apartment buildings, and the stench of something decomposing was barely discernable. "They'll regret it if they do."

"What do we have here?" the one I had pegged as the leader asked. He stepped forward. "What you doing in my street?"

"I need to go in the door you're blocking. Move aside, and this doesn't have to get ugly."

"Boss don't want nobody to come in there."

"You work for the guy inside the building?"

"I do. What's it to ya?"

"Do you know what he does?" I asked.

"Do you?" he returned.

"I'm pretty sure I have it figured out. He won't be doing it anymore after tonight."

"You came for the boss?" He looked past me. "And you came alone? You not very smart."

I smiled. "Ugly it is, I guess."

"Damn right it's…gak!"

"What was that last bit?" I asked.

He gurgled and toppled over with a knife protruding from his throat.

"What the—" the next closest of the group of four started, before collapsing with another of my throwing knives sticking out of his eye.

The third had seen how quickly his partners had dropped and tried to turn and head for the door they had been guarding. I threw a final blade which sank into his neck just below the skull. Number four was already in close, swinging an old, hardwood baseball bat.

He swung for my head and I caught the bat with my left hand. His eyes bulged in surprise just before I slapped him across the face with the augmented strength of a Corporate Agent. There was an audible crack as his head spun to face the opposite direction.

That may be the first time I have seen that particular strike, Childers said.

"Seems like I remember it from somewhere," I said. "But I was a woman when I did it. Which is a little bit weird because I was still Mathew Kade."

If you could remember everything, you would have some very interesting stories to tell, he said.

"I wish I could," I answered as I retrieved my knives.

The one that had severed the spine was a little more difficult to pull out as it was wedged between bones. I pulled a little harder and quickly stepped back to avoid the splash of blood when the skin ripped. It was a short burst of blood, but I didn't want it on my coat.

Before Childers could comment, I said, "It's my last one. It already has a bullet hole in it."

I opened the door the four thugs had been guarding. The place used to be an apartment building. This area of the city had less Scrapers and more of these sorts of structures. Eight-to-ten story brick and stone buildings with numerous small housing units inside.

Somewhere in my cluttered mind I thought of low income housing. Maybe this had been used for that originally. Now, it was something else altogether. The man I had been looking for over the last few days would be inside. I doubted if Lorianne Waldon would still be alive, but I would find her or her body before closing this particular case.

The scuffle outside had made very little noise, so I slipped inside and moved away from the door.

My left eye twitched as I took in what I could see. The large atrium of the building was all that was left, and it was filled with things that would make a medieval torturer blush. Across the room was a single man with his back to me. I could see a girl strapped to a table in front of him. They seemed to be the only ones in the place. He was holding a serrated tool in his right hand and lowering it toward her.

I was across the room in a flash, and I seized the man by the back of the apron-like garment he wore. I threw him across the room, and he slammed into the exterior concrete wall.

He hit hard and dropped limply to the floor.

I looked at the girl who was gagged and strapped down, with her limbs pulled painfully tight in a spread-eagle position, on the table. I severed the bonds on her left side with my straight razor, then I circled the table to cut the other side.

"You're going to be okay now," I told her.

Then I heard the man groan from where he had landed on the floor.

I could see her shake when he made a noise.

"He won't be hurting you anymore," I said. "What's your name?"

"L...Lori," she stammered.

"You're Waldon?"

She nodded, but her eyes flooded with terror. "C...can't go back there..."

My eyes narrowed, "We'll talk about that in a moment."

I turned to the man who was slowly staggering to his feet and rumored to be a former surgeon and a cannibal. "Doctor Gharik, I presume?"

"Who the hell are you?" he asked as he pulled a large knife from the sheath at his side. "I'm going to eat your heart."

He charged me, and I met him halfway. I slapped the blade from his hand, and he screamed as his wrist broke. He dropped to the floor and grabbed the broken wrist with his other hand.

His scream was high pitched and cut off abruptly as my left hand settled on his neck to lift him from the floor.

"Just...doing...job."

His gasp was barely audible, but I could make it out.

"Who pays for something like that?" I growled.

"Father," he gasped.

I dropped him. "Her father?"

"Yes," he groaned, holding the broken wrist.

"Tell me about it," I said.

"You'll let me live?"

"No. I'll let you die quick instead of by inches," I said. "Either way you die today."

He looked at all the torture devices and shivered. "She ran away, and her father paid me to make her suffer for it before she died. He gave me a list of things I was to do, and she was to know exactly why it was all happening."

I dragged the doctor to one of his own devices.

He struggled. "You said you would make it quick."

"I lied."

I hit him once to stop his struggling, then strapped him into the device and flipped the switch.

The doctor was screaming as I led the girl from the chamber of horrors she had spent the last day and a half in.

She cringed as we passed the four dead thugs outside the door, and I wished I could bring them back so I could kill them again.

Sometimes, I wished the bombs had taken this city when they took the world. It had once been called Philadelphia. Before the Corporate Wars. Before the bombs. All that was left was the skeleton of a huge city and the evil that seemed to thrive in it. Warlords ruling city blocks, ruling because they had the most guns or they were strongest. Most ruled with fear but, occasionally, there was someone better. I thought of Teresa Manora and her Society of the Sword. They still give me hope that there is something worth saving in this Fallen World.

* * * * *

Chapter Two

I looked down at the sleeping Warlord. His face was cruel, even as he slept. The two naked girls beside the man made my eye twitch. They were several years younger than the girl I had just rescued from the doctor, and she had been fourteen.

I lowered the wooden bat I had brought back with me and tapped lightly on the corner of the bedpost. The man stirred. One of the girls' eyes popped open, and she cringed away from me.

I motioned toward the door with my head. She slipped out of the bed and circled around to pull her sister from the other side. I lowered the bat onto the chest of Gregori Waldon. His eyes opened wide, and he tried to sit up. I kept pressure on the bat so he couldn't budge.

"What is this?" His eyes landed on me as I smiled down at him. "Kade?"

But it wasn't Mathew Kade standing over the struggling Warlord.

"Hello, Gregori, Mathew is not in today. My name is Stephen Gaunt. There are things we must talk about."

Stephen Gaunt was a Corporate Assassin, one of the most feared of the personalities that reside in my head. He has unmatched fighting skills and a love for his job that is quite terrifying.

"I have fifty men within shouting distance. Give me a reason to—"

"You *had* fifty men. Now, you *may* have two children within shouting distance. After what you did to them, I strongly doubt they will be inclined to help you."

"You'll never make it out of this Zone alive," he snarled.

"I will certainly get further than you will with that shattered knee."

His eyes widened. "What?"

I lifted the bat from his chest and slammed it down. Stephen Gaunt chuckled while the rest of us watched from inside my head.

* * *

"I thought I might find you here," a voice said as I rounded the corner.

A large black man leaned against the wall, with a sword resting point down in front of him. He was over six feet tall and three feet wide at the shoulders. The sword was a huge, two-hander that was four feet long.

"Hey, Poe." I grinned. "How the hell are you?"

"Was doin' just fine until Teresa sent me a message to come get you." He pushed off the wall and joined me, walking east. "Ran into a girl who looked pretty rough in the Tees. She was being escorted by a couple of Mardins. Once she told me what happened, I figured I better head this way. Is this gonna be one of those Zones that'll have a Chapterhouse for the Society in the near future?"

The Mardins were the people who lived in the Tees, the tunnels below the city. They kept the water flowing and the sewers working for a large part of the city.

"Maybe," I said, with a short chuckle. "She might think about adding another one. The Warlord seems to have lost his daughter. He's a little broken up about it."

"I'm not sure I want to know."

"Probably not." I grinned. "Wouldn't hurt to send word to Teresa, though. Place needs new leadership."

"No warning this time?"

Several Warlords had been removed over the last year. I typically gave them a warning first. The Society of the Sword opened Chapterhouses in each of the Zones, and they now kept the peace.

"He didn't deserve a warning."

"That bad, huh?" Poe asked.

"Yeah," I said. "Two more girls are on their way to Teresa. Dropped down in the Tees and snagged another Mardin."

"They're gonna get tired of being delivery boys."

"They don't mind, not after that dustup with Derris' savages." I looked toward the big man. "So, what does my lovely lady have in mind for me next?"

"There was a request from a Zone east of here. They sent a message with the Mardins about some cult of savages that were massing to attack them. You know how she is when something like this goes down."

"Yeah," I said. "She's not fond of savage cults."

"And this place is supposed to be something pretty special," he said. "Not sure what it is, but I figure we'll find out when we get there. Two Squires are already on their way, Rowland and Green. Several Knights have been notified, but they're too far out to do any good. And then there's us."

"Three Squires are an army in their own right," I said. "And conflatulations, by the way, on your promotion to Squire."

"I'm pretty sure that's not the right word."

"Sure, it is."

"I can't believe I'm doin' this again. But when Teresa says go, you go. I can't just say no; she might cut me up into little pieces."

"It's not so bad." I patted his huge arm and turned to the east. "Just think about all the savage cultists."

The big man sighed and strode beside me toward the beleaguered Zone.

"What's the name of the Zone?" I asked.

"They called it the Bastion."

"Intriguing," Gaunt said aloud.

"Indeed," I answered.

"You know, it was disturbing when you had those conversations in your head. It's even worse when you do it out loud. You gonna be doin' that the whole time?"

"Maybe."

He sighed again.

"You gonna be doin' that the whole time?"

"Probably," he said.

I chuckled and glanced toward the big man. I had enjoyed his company on our last venture until a sniper had shot him. He'd pushed me aside, out of the line of fire. I had been distracted for a moment, and the big man had taken two bullets for me. Luckily, we had been close to Society headquarters, and he had gotten medical attention in time. He didn't have the healing capability of an Agent, and I owed him.

We all do, Childers said. *That first shot would have been a head shot. Even an Agent doesn't walk away from that.*

"True enough," I muttered.

Some debts are more important than others in this Fallen World.

* * * * *

Chapter Three

"That group is eyeballin' us," Poe said.

I pushed my coat back to bring the Sig Sauer in my shoulder holster into view. The two punks in front of the others lost their swagger when they looked into the cold, dead eyes of a different person than the one they had initially picked out as their mark.

"Why would they even think of attacking someone as big as a house?" I asked as the bravos turned to retreat into an alley.

"I wonder that all the time. Worse, they take one look at you and crap their pants." Poe sounded puzzled. "Maybe I need to start carrying something to get their attention."

"You could always walk around with a necklace of skulls or something."

"Then everyone would run, not just the bravos, and I couldn't stop at the vendors along the streets. I think that might be a little too much."

"Could be." I shrugged. "So, do you know anything about this Bastion?"

"Not much," he answered. "I think Martin discovered them some time back. She's one of the Knights Teresa would have normally sent over here since she likes to stay in this part of the city. She's doing some work down south, though."

"Lori?" I asked.

"Yeah, that's her."

"I met her once while I was stuck at the Chapterhouse in Stiner," I said.

"Stuck?" he asked. "Weren't you recovering from that thing with the Geno Freak?"

"Yep. Teresa wouldn't let me go home."

"You had three broken ribs and a broken leg, and you reopened the bullet wounds from that other case." He shook his head. "You can't blame her for that."

"I guess," I said. "At least, I didn't get wounded on the job for Wilderman."

"Fenris said you got shot," he said.

"It was just a scratch," I said. "Can't even call that a wound."

"Probably because you spent the majority of the time watching her cutting that bunch into squishy little pieces."

"What?"

"That's what she said, man." He shrugged. "Sounds about right, though. I remember that time up in Yamato's Zone."

"I distinctly remember killing several of Corso's thugs, along with Corso and his second."

"Yeah, four. I was left with nine. I think I'll take *her* word for it. She is a Knight, after all. They take oaths and shit."

"Have you ever watched that woman fight?"

"Can't say I have," he answered.

"It's glorious, it's magnificent, it's—"

"You just stood there and watched, didn't you?"

"Well, for a while. I'd already killed a bunch of them," I said.

"She said you left another Warlord hanging from a wall with a piece of steel through his shoulder."

"He let close to sixty thugs attack us in his street in broad daylight. He was lucky I didn't just throw him out the window of his Scraper."

"Sounds like he might have deserved a warning."

I pulled my coat around and stuck my finger through the hole left in it by the bullet that had grazed my side. "Do you see this? This is the last one I have until I see the Farmers again."

"You pinned him to a wall with rebar because they put a hole in your coat?"

"Of course not. He was in on the attack. A lot of those guys were his men. I left him pinned to a wall with rebar for sending his men to kidnap an innocent girl and kill me in the process."

His left eyebrow was raised when I looked toward him.

"I broke his arm for the hole in my coat."

He shook his head.

"What?"

"That damn coat," he said. "One day, it's gonna trip you up when you try one of those crazy Agent moves. I just hope I'm there to see it."

"You're just mad because they don't make them in your size."

"Whatever."

"I could see if Marigold will make you one," I said.

"I don't want one of those useless coats."

"She probably wouldn't charge more than double price for the extra material."

"Look how it flops around," he said. "One day, you're gonna trip over it and, just like that, you're all dead and shit."

"I can ask when I order my next batch."

"I don't need one of those damn coats. If I wore somethin' that stupid, I'd be dead in a week."

I shrugged as we continued walking down the street. The smell of humanity permeated the air, and the vendor stalls along both sides of the street reminded me of something that hovered just out of reach of my fractured memories.

Fair, one of the voices deep inside my head said.

I nodded.

He sighed. "Do you think she could make one in black?"

Wonders never cease in this Fallen World.

* * * * *

Chapter Four

The sound of fighting ahead barely reached my ears.

"What is it?" Poe asked. He couldn't hear it, but he could see me pause as I listened.

"How much farther to the Bastion?"

"Next Zone."

"Shit," I said. "There's fighting."

He scowled. "Go. I'll be there as quick as I can."

I nodded and launched myself forward. The speed an Agent can attain is much more than Poe would have been able to make. The Zone we were in was pretty barren, but you could tell a lot by the upkeep of the streets. Many had clean streets and vendor stalls for the Caravans as they passed through. This one was shabby and dirty. Still, there was no smell of feces in the street as there was in some of them. The Mardins kept the sewers running, and I have great respect for their dedication.

The sound of fighting was closer, and I slipped my straight razor into my left hand and pulled the nine millimeter from the shoulder holster with my right. It used to have a silencer, but they have a limited lifespan, and I had used it enough to make it more of a hindrance than a help.

I rounded the corner and found the street filled with a lot of armed thugs assaulting a wall of stacked cars. The wall of cars looked like it had been there for years. It spanned the whole street between two buildings that had been reinforced with steel plate.

"Bastion," I muttered.

The defenses looked pretty formidable, and it would take a lot of people to get through them.

But there was a mob of fifty or sixty people in the street brandishing weapons. I could only see about ten stationed along the top of the wall. Not enough defenders to stop this mob if the mob went at it hard.

The fighting was centered, not on the wall of cars, but on a small group of armored forms who had been caught outside the walls. They were surrounded, and the mob would soon overwhelm them.

"That's your cue, Stephen," I muttered and receded into the back of my mind as Stephen Gaunt, the Corporate Assassin, took the lead. He holstered the Sig Sauer and looked at the razor in his right hand.

"Oh, Mathew, I think you've done it again," I said in his voice. "You bring me to the loveliest places. But that is a lot of throats to cut."

He slipped the razor back into its pouch and drew one of the sturdier knives.

"This should do nicely."

I would say that I charged into the group, but Stephen doesn't charge. He flowed through the crowd like water, and people began to fall. I severed a femoral artery, then flowed past and snaked my arm around a neck to pull the chin up, and the blade flashed. Then I was gone again. One after another fell before they even realized I was there.

Then there was a roar from behind me as Poe rounded the corner with his four-foot-long blade swinging in a deadly arc. People tumbled backward, several in multiple pieces. He swung the sword back in an arc that was just as deadly as the first.

Poe is a big man, and he is all muscle. When he hits something, it moves, and he was cutting a swath through the crowd. Another form dropped from one of the buildings to our left. She'd been descending along a fire escape when we hit the crowd.

Peggey Rowland, one of the Society Squires, landed lightly, drawing the rapier from her side. The sword danced around, and those near her died.

I ducked as a club arced through the spot where my head had been, and I grasped the front of the wielder's shirt. I threw him into several of his cohorts with enough force to send four sprawling on the ground. Then my blade flashed several times, and the squirming pile was still.

"Don't worry," Gaunt whispered in an ear as I reached around with the blade. "It will be over soon."

Once again, I was moving through the crowded street, and screams of rage and hate became screams of fear. There's something terrifying in witnessing a man giggling as he dances through a throng of people, leaving only the dying or already dead in his wake.

But Stephen Gaunt is a terrifying sort of guy. Typically, they don't stay terrified long.

I ended up looking into the eyes of Peggey Rowland as both of us reached the same person in the much less crowded street. The majority of those who were left were fleeing.

"Hello, luv," Gaunt said.

Peggey looked a bit confused, and I stepped forward from the backseat in my head.

"Sorry," I said and smacked the man who was screaming something I assumed was a battle cry. His head tilted at an odd angle, and he fell sideways.

"Hi, Peggey." I grinned. "How's it going?"

She was shaking her head. "You should be covered in blood. How did you not get any more than that on your coat?"

"More than what?" I asked and looked down at the right hem she was pointing at. "Dammit!"

There was a red splotch about the size of a closed fist.

Peggey had blood dripping from her armor, and I glanced over to our left to look at Poe. He was covered with it.

"Last damn coat," I muttered.

I heard the group of defenders who had been cut off from the Bastion approaching and turned around and saw the leader taking off her helm.

My mouth dropped open. "Brandy?"

I had memories in my head of this woman. Someone deep inside the pile of people in my head was doing the mental equivalent of jumping up and down and waving their arms. The barrage of memories was fast, but it was detailed. I remembered this woman as a baby, a child, a youth, and an adult. The personality that was hailing me was her father.

"Do I know you?" Brandy Bolgeo asked with narrowed eyes.

I scratched my head. "I know you...kind of."

"I thank you for your timely appearance," she said. "But *I* don't know *you*. Either way, we need to get inside."

She waved to the men atop the wall, and one of them yelled into the interior, "Jonny! Open the gate!"

One of the metal panels that guarded the building on our right pushed outward. A fellow in coveralls, with a pair of short swords in scabbards on his back, looked out the door.

"You still with us, Boss?"

"Thanks to these folks," Brandy answered.

I can't believe she's still alive, Tim Bolgeo said in my head. He had been pretty far down in the depths of my mind for a long time.

Brandy kept looking at me, trying to place who I was.

"I guess I need to tell you a little story," I said. "It's about your father."

She scowled. "My father is dead. The people he spent years working for sent him on one of those damned missions and dropped the bombs right on top of him."

I could see the depth of her rage at Obsidian, who more than deserved it. That rage was a common thing to see in this Fallen World.

* * * * *

Chapter Five

We were less than ten feet inside the door when she turned to me. "Now, tell me about my father."

It was an order, not a request. There was an iron will in her that filled me with a father's pride. Bolgeo was just under the surface now, and I could feel his emotions.

"Okay," I said. "You know what he did?"

"He was an Agent."

"That makes things easier to explain. Are you familiar with how Agents did their thing? The imprints?"

"Dad told me how it worked," she said with a shrug. "I know, it was supposed to be classified."

"Nothing's classified now." I pointed a thumb back toward the door we had come in. "Not much point in that anymore."

"That's true."

"If you know about the imprints, this is easier still. When an Agent goes out needing a specialty personality, their personality is uploaded to the database. Then it's downloaded back into the body when it returns. There was a copy of your father in the database."

"What's that have to do with this?"

"Everything." I tapped my temple with a forefinger. "When the bombs dropped, I was in the imprinter. Something shorted out, and it downloaded the whole database into my noggin."

"And Dad is in there?"

"That's how I recognized you. Some of the imprints are more accessible than others, and your father was pretty deep inside until I saw you. Now, he's right under the surface. I'm going to step back and give you two a couple of minutes."

"This is a little too much to take in. I believe I have heard enough." She turned to walk away.

My head dropped for a moment, and someone else was looking out of my eyes when my head raised.

"Brandy Marie Louise Elizabeth Bolgeo," Tim admonished.

Brandy paused in mid stride.

She turned back to face me as Tim looked around. "Swimbo? Is she here?"

I could see the acronym in his mind and chuckled inside. SWMBO (She Who Must Be Obeyed).

When Tim said that word, though, Brandy's eyes widened, and her mouth dropped open. Up until that very moment, she had not believed.

"D...Dad?" she stammered.

He stepped forward and wrapped his arms around her armored form. "I'm sorry I left you, girl. Wish I had stayed home when they called."

I felt tears running down my cheeks.

"I'm sorry, Mom didn't make it, Dad."

I could feel the well of sorrow as Tim thought of his wife, Linda.

He sighed. "I guess you're Swimbo, now, not Swimbo, Jr."

"No one's called me that in twenty years, Dad."

"Well, they should."

"They're coming back for a run at the walls!" one of the guys on the wall yelled.

She grimaced. "Seems like our reunion is going to be short lived. Those bastards mean to kill us all."

"Then, what say we kill them first?" Tim Bolgeo said and turned to the two Squires. "Let's join the ranks on the walls."

"One of your Squires is on the front wall," Brandy said to me. "Should we join him?"

Tim glanced around. "They hitting more than one wall?"

"They're hitting all four," she said. "There are hundreds of them."

"Which one gets hit the hardest?"

"Front."

"How many fighters here?"

"A hundred and twenty people, about half of which are decent fighters. The others will fight, but they're not really fighters."

He scanned the area and made a decision. "One Squire on each of those walls, and I'll take the front wall."

He glanced up at the front wall and recognized the Squire. "Joe! Take the right wall!"

"Got it!" he yelled back.

Tim jumped from where he stood to the top of the wall of cars where they had welded a parapet for the defenders to stand on.

He heard Brandy giving orders. "Jonny! On the right! Hillbilly, join him."

She was motioning to an armored form in the group who had come in with us.

"Got it, Swimbo."

She stared at him, and Tim grinned down at them from the wall.

"I got it, Boss." He held his hands up.

He was chuckling as he took off toward the right wall.

Tim turned around to look over the wall of cars at the horde of people coming down the street toward the Bastion.

That's a lot of damn people, I said.

"It certainly is," Tim answered.

"What?" one of the defenders asked.

"Just talkin' to myselves."

He looked confused, but shook his head and turned back toward the oncoming horde.

"We have contact!" someone yelled from the right wall.

"They're in the back, too!" Poe yelled as he climbed the wall.

The whole defended area was about five hundred feet by five hundred feet, and there was very little inside the walls.

"What the hell are we defending?" Tim asked.

"The Bastion is underground, Dad. It's the Bastion of Literacy. We've been collecting every book we can find in the city and preserving them. We're going to need that knowledge in the future."

Tim grinned. "That's my girl."

It explained a great deal about the setup of the defensive walls. It was like the way the Mardins under the city had walled off the area under Derris' Zone to keep the savages in check. This was the same in reverse.

"You affiliated with the Mardins?"

"We know some of them, but we aren't part of their society. We have our own setup."

"We can discuss it in a little while," he said. "Let's welcome our guests."

"Ready the pots!" she yelled.

There were about eight big cauldrons steaming along the parapet. They sat on racks with fires burning under them.

"Oil?" Tim asked.

"Boiling water and flour," she answered. "Sticks to them like glue."

The horde reached the wall and started climbing the cars. She waited for a few moments before yelling. "Pots!"

The cauldrons were pushed over, and the white liquid fell onto the mass of bodies. Battle cries changed to screams as the boiling concoction clung to them. They began falling backward onto the others where the paste-like substance spread.

There was a vicious smile on her face. "Read that in a book, you assholes!"

"Ready weapons!" Brandy ordered.

Tim chuckled and drew the Sig from his shoulder holster. He waited until the flour and water had gotten on as many as it looked like it was going to. Then he raised the pistol.

Others on the wall raised their rifles and pistols as well.

"Target the ones who aren't already injured!"

I felt the great swell of pride that coursed through Tim as he watched his daughter.

"Open fire!"

Tim pulled the trigger, and the man he was aiming at toppled with a bullet in his brain. He calmly shifted his aim, and another head blossomed. This one was female.

Sometimes, a person needs to be an equal opportunity killer in this Fallen World.

* * * * *

Chapter Six

"Here's where it gets nasty," Brandy said as several of her people placed their rifles on the ground at their feet. "We're out of ammo."

She drew the gladius from the sheath at her side. "Now, we get bloody."

Tim shot the last round from the Sig, and I muttered, "Going to have to get more mags from the Farmers."

He released the mag and started rapidly feeding cartridges into it.

"Dammit, man," Brandy said as she saw the speed at which he was filling it.

"Lots of practice," he said as the last one slid into place.

The savages hadn't reached the edge of the wall yet, so he leaned over and began firing down into them. Sixteen shots and twelve dead.

A little sloppy, Childers said.

"Give me a break," Tim said. "It's been twenty years."

"What?" Brandy asked, looking toward him.

"Nothing," he said.

When the first head popped over the wall, Brandy took it off with the sword.

Good execution, Childers said.

Quite good, Gaunt agreed.

Those two agreeing hardly ever happened, and it was worthy of notice.

Use the strength, I said.

He nodded and stepped close to the edge to punch the first savage who topped the wall in our area. The head jerked back at an odd angle.

The savages kept coming, and they died as they topped the wall.

Then the wave slackened, and we heard a thump as something hit the building between the front and right walls.

"Shit! They crashed a truck into Building A!" someone yelled. "They're inside!"

Tim leapt from the wall into the courtyard just as the savages poured from the building.

"More your area, Mathew," Tim said, and he let me step forward inside my mind.

I grabbed my blade and charged toward the screaming savages. I glanced left and saw a huge form slam into them as well. Two others dropped from the walls and took up positions on the right and left of Wilson Poe. Peggey's rapier flashed and Joe Green's twin swords blurred. The savages who reached them encountered a wall of steel. It channeled them in my direction.

If you don't mind, Mathew?

I grinned.

"What have we here?" Stephen Gaunt said as I let him out. "You've brought me playthings."

I glided forward under Stephen's control and slipped under the swinging club of the first attacker. My blade flashed, and the man dropped the club and clutched his abdomen where his intestines were trying to drop from the gash I had left. He toppled forward, but I was already ten feet away, severing an Achilles tendon. Then I sliced a femoral artery.

I slipped up behind a woman and pulled her chin up with my left hand as my right flashed across her throat.

"This won't hurt...much," I whispered in her ear. Then I was gone again into the crowd.

"Blow the charges!" I heard Brandy order.

I saw someone in the very center of the courtyard throw a lever, but nothing happened.

"Something's wrong, ma'am!"

"Son of a..."

I saw two more forms drop from the right wall. One was the guy she had called Hillbilly and the other she had called Jonny.

They slipped into the building.

"What are they...?" I heard from the wall above me.

CRUMPT...CRUMPT.

Debris exploded from the opening the savages were pouring from and I heard screams. Then the whole building shuddered.

"Shit!" Poe yelled. "Back up!"

The Squires ran away from the building as it collapsed on top of more than a hundred savages and a couple of damned brave men. The debris cloud exploded outward, and I went into it after the surviving attackers. All the rest of them heard were screams and, maybe, laughter.

Stephen enjoys his job a bit more than is comfortable for most folks. Most think Stephen is crazy, but there's a need for his brand of crazy in this Fallen World.

* * * * *

Chapter Seven

As the debris began to settle, we could see the corner of the Bastion's Building A. It was a pile of rubble that would be almost impossible to navigate.

Brandy moved up beside me. "Those magnificent, crazy bastards. They set the charges off manually."

I looked toward her and saw the pain on her face.

"Looks like they're coming back for the walls!"

She grimaced, and I could feel the fury growing inside Tim Bolgeo.

Can't go out there while we're needed on the wall, he said.

"I know," I muttered and jumped and landed on the wall again. "We leave the wall, and they get in, and everyone dies."

I pulled the Sig and refilled the mag as I watched them come down the street. As soon as I slammed the mag back into the pistol, I racked it and emptied it into the front of the approaching savages. Fourteen bodies were trampled by the others.

I refilled the mag again and unloaded it with similar result, then the horde started back up the wall.

I moved back a step and over to the center of the wall so I could go whichever direction I needed.

"You want this?" I asked Tim.

You're doing better than I was, he answered. *Been gone for too long.*

I nodded and shot forward as one of the savages topped the wall between two of the defenders. My foot slammed into his chest with a crunch, and the body flew backward over his allies' heads. He landed twenty feet away from the wall on top of a screaming woman.

One of the defenders staggered back as a blade sank into his neck in the spot where the armor met the helm. I jumped twenty feet and landed where he had been, then hit a woman, who had just topped the wall, with an open hand that sent her sailing backward.

"Karen! Medic!" Brandy yelled. Several people scrambled from the center of the defended area. They ran up the stairs and pulled the wounded figure down toward the ground.

She stepped into the spot beside me. "I have this position."

I nodded and stepped back so I could watch for any that got through. One got particularly close to Brandy, so I sank one of the twelve blades I wore into his right eye.

Almost every one of the defenders had taken damage as the sun began to drop behind the buildings to our west, but the horde had not broken through. Then they fell back.

Everyone atop the wall was breathing heavily. Swords hung from exhausted hands, and the bodies were piled halfway up the outside of the wall.

I watched the savages retreat into the growing darkness with a grim smile as Tim stepped forward again.

"They've sworn for years they would storm our walls," Brandy said. "They would have, without you and the Society."

"They almost had us until those two blew that building."

"Hillbilly always swore he'd go out blowing himself up," she said. "I didn't think he would actually do it. His name was Scott Tackett, but we always called him Hillbilly because he came from West Virginia."

She shook her head. "And damn if Jonny Minion didn't do the same. It took two to blow the charges that took the building down. Neither of them hesitated."

"Brave men," Tim said.

"Ma'am," the medic yelled. "We lost Ken."

"Damn," she muttered and turned to the tired men on the walls. "I have to check on things."

"Ma'am." The closest of the men nodded.

"They're regrouping," Tim said. "Would be a good time to see to the wounded. I'll watch the wall."

"They won't be back 'til morning," Brandy said. "Phobes don't fight at night."

"Phobes?"

"They hate books, they're bibliophobes."

Tim grunted.

"We'll get some rest and see to the wounded," she said. "Then we'll get ready to do it again tomorrow."

"I don't think there will be any fighting tomorrow," Tim said as he looked out into the darkness. "They've made a fatal error."

"What?" She looked at him in confusion. "What error?"

"I don't have to be on this wall any longer," he said.

My head dropped a fraction, and her eyes widened when she saw the transformation. My features became those of someone else. It was the same face, but every feature had shifted. As my head raised, my mouth curled up in a wide smile.

"Dad?"

"Not at the moment, luv," I said in Gaunt's breathy voice. "Stephen Gaunt at your service. Your father has requested my assistance. He is good at what he does, as are Mathew and William. But I am the best at what I do. And, oh, the things I am going to do."

She swallowed.

I removed the long coat and held it out to her. "Please be a dear and hold this for me. Mathew would be so upset if I wore it where I am going. Phobes, you say? I wonder if they are afraid of the dark. If they are not, already, they will be. Perhaps it is time for a lesson."

I leapt over the parapet rail and landed on the pile of bodies. Another jump took me out past the pile, where I faded into the night.

I stopped, and I heard voices from the wall. I recognized Poe's voice. "Did he just give you the coat?"

"Yes. He said Mathew would be upset if he wore it where he was going."

"Looks like someone is going to have a bad night, ma'am. Did he say his name?"

"Stephen Gaunt," she answered.

"Did someone say Stephen Gaunt?" Joe Green asked.

"Yep," Poe said.

"If it was any other day, I would feel sorry for those poor bastards. But today? Serves them right."

"He's only one man."

"Not really," Poe said. "I agree with Joe. I'd pity the idiots out there if they hadn't just spent the day trying their best to kill us. As it is, screw 'em."

I grinned and slipped out into the night, toward the Phobes, as they set up their camps.

There are more dangerous things than savage, book-burning cultists in this Fallen World.

* * * * *

Chapter Eight

I sat, patiently, on the edge of the campsite, watching the sleeping Phobe. His eyes opened, and he sat up.

"Hello, sleepy head," Gaunt said. "We've been waiting for you."

The man looked to his right and left, with growing horror. There had been thirty-two people arrayed around the fire. Now there were thirty-one obvious corpses. Obvious because their heads had been severed and placed atop their prone bodies. All of them were facing him.

He screamed and leapt to his feet to run, but I was next to him faster than any human should have been able to be.

"No, no, we have things to discuss."

I grabbed the man by his neck and dragged him from the camp. He whimpered.

I hit him with my stiffened fingers so quickly, he didn't even see my hand move, and I placed him in the single open spot among fifteen living, but unmoving, people, sitting in neat rows of four.

"Now, the lesson begins," Stephen said.

He turned and walked to a spot where all sixteen of them could see him. "Throughout history, people have destroyed cultures and left ruin. Some of them even burned all records of the defeated, but there is an inherent folly in doing so. You wished to destroy the books these folks have spent so many years collecting. They wish to preserve what knowledge they can, and you want to destroy it. The folly of such a goal is quite obvious if you only look at it. If you destroy all knowledge of the past, you are doomed to repeat it. Herein is the lesson."

He pointed to them. "I chose to keep one of you for every fifty I killed. If I had removed all of you, who would tell the following generations of your folly? As it is, this job falls to you. In about half an hour, the first of you I brought to this place will regain the use of his, pardon me, her limbs. When the rest of you join her, you will go back to your people and tell them of the horrible fate that awaits them if they ever return. Because, if they do, I will also return. And if I do, I will not be as forgiving as I have been this night."

I stood up and walked toward the Bastion, leaving sixteen horrified Phobes behind.

* * *

Karen Boyd looked up as I entered the warehouse-size Library in the pre-war underground bunker. She was a medic who had spent the last few days patching up the wounded. I could feel the wonder that filled Tim as I gazed at the many shelves of books. I couldn't help feeling some of that wonder as well. The monumental task of gathering them was not lost on me. I'd dug and scavenged all through this city.

"Mister Kade," she said. "We can't thank you enough for what you did. If there's anything we can do, please let us know."

Oh, my, Stephen said in my head as he looked at a stack of books.

"Might I trouble you for a few of those?" he asked. "I know someone who would dearly love to read them."

Softie, I said.

"I'm sure we can spare a few."

I nodded and continued toward the person I had come to the Library to meet. I stepped back and let Tim take the lead.

"You're leaving again," she said.

"I would love nothing more than to stay here," he said. He tapped the side of his head. "Mathew has started something we've all been needing. He's walking a path of redemption. All of us did some pretty awful things to people who didn't deserve them. He wonders what drives him so hard sometimes. He did things he's not proud of, but he isn't the only one in here. That drive comes from the sins of a thousand souls. Or however many of us there are in here. We have a responsibility to the Society and a bunch of Warlords who want to bring civilization back to this broken city. I know Tim Bolgeo died twenty years ago in Los Angeles, but I'm still here. I will always be here. If you don't mind, I would like to stop by and visit from time to time."

There were tears in her eyes as she wrapped her arms around him. "You're welcome here anytime, Dad."

She gave me an extra squeeze. "And all the rest of you."

She stepped back. "There's a big dinner tonight, and I expect you to be there. You can't go until everyone gets to thank you."

I nodded.

"I'm going to go get things underway," she said and walked out of the library.

I picked up the first book Karen had laid on the table and sat down. "It is Tuesday."

If you don't mind?

"Of course," I said. He was the last one I would expect to ask. Perhaps the time with us had changed even *him*.

Stephen opened the book. "One fish, two fish, red fish, blue fish...."

There was a sort of movement in the cage inside my mind as Luca happily listened to the words.

* * *

I watched as Brandy raised her glass in the air. The room fell into silence.

"Before we take part in this wonderful dinner Connie and Charmalee have prepared for us, I would like to raise a glass. To fallen comrades," she said.

"Fallen comrades," I answered along with the others, feeling the pride Tim felt in his daughter. Joe sat on my left and Poe on the right. Peggey was down about halfway on the other side of the huge table where she had been talking to several of the people she had met on her previous encounter with the Bastion.

"To Ken Roy," Brandy said.

A tall man at the far end of the huge table stood. "I met Ken as we fought together to escape a Warlord named the General fourteen years ago. We found our way here after meeting several of the Explorers. He never regretted joining the Bastion, and he died protecting her."

"Ken Roy," Brandy nodded.

"To Jonny Minion," she said, and another stood.

"Jonny came to us several years ago. We never knew his last name; he just took the name of Minion. He was driving a big truck that surprised us all. There weren't many vehicles still in use in the city. He had a trailer full of canned vegetables we all enjoyed, and he stayed after he met us. He was a kind soul and selfless all the way till the end. He loved this place, he loved the people, and he loved arguing with Hillbilly."

"Jonny Minion!"

"To Hillbilly…Scott Tackett," she said. "He showed up one day, shot and near death. After he recovered, he started working with Gabe in the forge. Used to be a diesel mechanic before the Fall, which explained why he and Jonny always argued. No truck driver is ever going to get along with a diesel mechanic."

There were chuckles around the room.

"The two of them were arguing on top of the wall," Joe added. "Counting how many of the Phobes they had killed."

I remembered an old movie with an elf and a dwarf and smiled.

The names and stories continued, and I listened to each one as the defenders talked about their friends who had fallen.

"Tomorrow, we will have to go out and clean up the bodies and burn them," Brandy said. "But, tonight, we celebrate a victory that wouldn't have happened without the aid of our new friends. So, eat, drink, and be merry! For tomorrow, we all may…work our asses off!"

I watched the people of the Bastion as they cheered, and I realized, once again, there were things worth saving in this Fallen World.

# # # # #

Warlord

Chapter One

I sat atop a rundown Scraper and looked down at the city that had been known as Philadelphia. No one called it that anymore. It had become part of the huge urban sprawl that had been Obsidian. Then it had become the urban wreckage I looked at today. The bombs had taken most of the east coast and left a ruin of the old Philadelphia where I made my home.

Our home. I chuckled as Stephen Gaunt's voice echoed inside my head.

"True enough," I muttered. "I guess there's no reason to perch on top of a building like Batman."

I actually understood that reference, William Childers said.

"Sadly, I can remember something like that, but I can't remember the stuff I should know about my past."

I haven't heard you talk about that issue much, Mathew. The voice in my head was female.

"Hey, Doc."

Would you like to talk about it?

"Tryin' to head shrink me, Doc?"

It's what I do Mathew, she said. *What else is a psychologist supposed to do in a place like this? Our situation is completely unprecedented. Even when we were in a world of imprints and Agents.*

"I would have been a head case then," I said. "Just like I'm a head case now."

I'm pretty sure they couldn't have used an imprinter to pull us out of your head once the whole database was loaded into it. Frankly, I don't understand how we are able to survive. It was thought impossible for something like this to happen, she said.

"I have little pieces of memories about someplace else I was, maybe, a mayor…or something like it." I shook my head. "I even remember being there with some of you guys. I remember meeting Gaunt in a garden…"

If only you could remember all of it, Childers said.

"Yep, it would be nice to remember who I was before I became an Agent. Or even remember all the time I was an Agent. There are so many fragments that seem like they would be interesting, but I can't remember enough to really see them."

Perhaps, if you hadn't kept all of us… Angela Richards, my resident psychologist let the comment drop.

"What would give me the right to purge any of you? This isn't my body either. Every one of us has the right to live in it."

"You are a much better man than many of us," Gaunt said aloud. "I'm fairly certain things would not be the same if one of us had become the dominant personality. Seventeen years ago, I wouldn't have given a second thought to purging this mind of everyone but me."

And you would now? Childers asked.

I have grown quite fond of our little family, William, he answered. *It would pain me to do it now. Perhaps I have gotten soft.*

Perhaps we all have, Childers said.

"It's not a bad thing," I said as I stood and slipped back from the edge of the roof toward the access. "What say we go inside and get this job done so Lucy can work on the garden tomorrow?"

She does like the garden, Angela said.

"We all like the food she produces," I said.

Much better for us than those blasted tacos you are so enamored with, Gaunt said.

"Leave my tacos alone," I said and entered the door.

The Warlords always live at the top of the Scrapers. They think the top is the safest place. Not from someone who can scale the outside of an immense building, though. I only had one floor of the Warlord's people to deal with if I came in from the top.

"Alright, Stephen," I muttered, turning control over to the former Corporate Assassin.

"Thank you, Mathew."

I slipped through the shadowy hall like a ghost. Stephen is a master at what he does. He can move in ways most people can't even imagine, and his imprint is one of the few originals that makes full use of an Agent's body. It wasn't that I couldn't fully use the body, but Gaunt had the imprinted training, along with the skills, to be a master assassin. Whereas I would have had to concentrate to do what he did, he did it out of habit.

There was a guard at the far end of the hall. I'm fairly certain he wasn't supposed to be sitting in the chair with his head lolled back, snoring lightly. It was a mistake he would never get to acknowledge.

I could feel the aversion from Angela.

It's bloody work, I said. *He works for a guy who buys pretty little boys and girls for his perverse pleasure.*

It doesn't mean I have to like it, she said.

"Ah, but I do," muttered Gaunt.

I pushed the door inward and slipped into the room.

Something was wrong. Instead of the sleeping Warlord I expected, I found him standing in the center of the room. Several naked women were huddled near the wall.

"Kade, I presume," he said in a deep voice. I had a flashback to a movie in the depths of my mind about a giant black man who had been in prison for a murder he hadn't committed.

Only I knew this giant had murdered plenty.

"I've been waiting for you," he said. "Right now, forty of my toughest men are on their way up those stairs. But they aren't who you have to worry about." His hand flashed, and I caught the handle of the knife he had thrown.

"Which imprint are you?" I asked with a savage grin. "I can let you talk it out with yourself."

"What are you yammering about? I'm no Agent. All natural here, baby. Teledyne's finest."

I could hear running footsteps coming from the stairwell.

His other hand flashed, and I caught the second knife.

"Oh my, I haven't had a Specialist in ages," I said in Gaunt's voice. "They're so much fun."

"Shit!" I said in my own voice.

"What the hell is the matter with you?" The giant Specialist looked confused.

"He just realized the gravity of the situation," I said in Gaunt's voice. "I am going to get blood on his coat. Alas, sacrifices must be made in this Fallen World."

* * * * *

Chapter Two

Hart, the Warlord in question, charged forward with another blade in his right hand. He was incredibly fast, but Gaunt really is the best at what he does. I slipped to my left and sliced the muscle along the back of the arm holding the knife, using one of the blades he had thrown at me.

Hart grunted, and the arm fell in toward his body.

"Quick little bastard."

I looked at the blade. "This is very nice. Do you mind if I keep it?"

"I'll be taking it from your corpse, Agent." The big man moved his already-healing right arm. "You got no idea what you're messing with."

"Enhanced healing nanites," Gaunt said. "Those are lovely."

I glanced past the Specialist and saw the door at the end of the hall bang open. Guards erupted into the hallway. Then I looked down at my coat and saw several small splotches of blood on the sleeve. I shrugged and sighed.

Hart grinned and charged again.

I dodged to my right and sank the other blade to the hilt in the Warlord's left ear. I turned back to look at the big man as he swept by me and toppled face first to the floor.

"You were saying?" I asked. I smiled at the women, who were staring with wide eyes at the former Warlord, and grasped both sides of his head. "Get behind the bed."

The men were about halfway down the hall when Hart's head rolled to the leader's feet.

"Perhaps you should have stayed just a bit closer to your boss, my good fellows."

A second later, I was in the hallway and moving fast. The first knife Hart had thrown at me was a wonderful blade, and I used it to sever arteries and tendons as Gaunt danced between the men in the hallway.

Angela had receded into the back of my mind so she wouldn't have to watch. The hallway was too small to worry about blood, and Gaunt had already gotten Hart's blood on the sleeve of my coat.

"If I'd known you were gonna mess it up three days after leaving the Bastion, I would have let you keep it on when you went to talk with the Phobes."

"Shush, Mathew. This is a thing of beauty. Don't ruin the moment."

"Psycho."

"Yes. Isn't it glorious?" Gaunt has way too much fun in situations like this.

The fight down the hallway was short and brutal. The last ten or so men started firing weapons at me since it was pretty obvious that those who got close to me were faring badly. I dropped and rolled to the side and rose with a pistol. I only had one magazine left, but it held sixteen shots. More than enough to clear the rest of the hallway.

One of their shots had grazed my side, but the bleeding was already slowing because of the healing nanites.

"I would like to have some of those healing nanites," I said as Stephen stepped back from the forefront.

They would be very nice, Childers said. *I would say you were getting sloppy, Stephen, but I doubt I could have dodged ten shooters in such a small area.*

"Gonna have to agree," I said. "Very well done, Stephen."

Probably would have gone better if you would lay off the tacos, Mathew.

"I told you to leave my tacos out of it."

I could feel their amusement.

"May as well head down the stairs and let everyone know the place is under new management."

By the time I reached the ground floor, I was not alone. There was a line of children, teens, and adults, who had been freed from the rooms they were being held in, following me. There was more than one dead guard along the way as well. After seeing the faces of the prisoners at the sight of the guards, I didn't spare any. Outside, in the street, were the forms of the erstwhile captors, lying where they had fallen from almost every floor of the Scraper.

My left eye was twitching as I watched the line of women and children I had freed exit the Scraper. If I could have brought Hart back, I would have killed him again. Some monsters have no business living in any world, whether a Fallen World or not.

* * * * *

Chapter Three

The streets of Hart were filled with people who looked worn out. An air of doom seemed to lay heavily on their shoulders. These were people who had been under the thumb of someone they couldn't do anything about, even if they had wanted to. They looked about as defeated as any I had seen in this city.

I raised the wrapped bundle I had carried down the stairs. I figured they wouldn't take my word, so I tossed the Specialist's head into the street right in front of them.

"Hart is dead," I said. I pointed at the crumpled forms who had fallen from the Scraper as I descended. "Most of his lieutenants are lying in the street where they landed. You have a chance to make something better of this place. Representatives of the Society of the Sword will be here in a few days. If you are smart, you'll listen to what they have to say. Teresa Manora is good people."

"What about us?" a young girl, perhaps fifteen, asked. She had been one of the captives. "I don't have anyone in this city except my sister who was taken at the same time I was."

"Where are you from?"

"My family was living on an island down south until pirates raided us. My sister and I were kept because...well, I guess you can figure that out after seeing what was inside."

"I would suggest the Society. They can help you learn to protect yourself. Where's your sister?"

"I don't know. We were sold to different buyers at the water-front. I, for one, don't think I can stay here. Many of us are from different places and know very little about this city."

"Then I will make sure you make it safely to the Society," I said. "It's several Zones to the west of here."

"Thank you. I thought all the people in this awful place were animals."

"Not all of us," I said. "There are some good people left here, but it's hard to find them among the awfulness. We're trying to do better over to the west."

"Thank you again," she said and turned to the others. "This man is going to take us to a safe place if we want to go."

I hadn't really planned on escorting them, but it was on my way home. The job at the Bastion had been interesting, but I wanted some down time.

Well deserved, Tim Bolgeo said. *Thank you for letting me spend the time with my daughter.*

"Family is important, Timmy," I said.

The girl turned back to me. "What?"

"Nothin'. Just talkin' to myselves."

She shook her head and went back to directing the other former slaves.

She is a natural leader, Angela said.

"She'll do well with Teresa," I muttered. "And speaking of Teresa, I guess I should send her a warning."

I touched the girl's shoulder, and she tensed. "If I was gonna hurt you, I would have already done it."

She took a deep breath. "I'm still up there in my head." She pointed back at the Scraper with a thumb.

I nodded. "Understandable. I'm going to drop down to the Tees and send a message to Teresa. She needs to know I'm bringing fifty-three people to her."

The girl looked scared.

"I'm not leavin'," I said. "You can come with me if you want to, but you seem to be the person they need right now."

She looked back at the others, all of whom were looking to her for direction. "How did that happen? I'm fifteen years old. Who looks to a fifteen-year-old for leadership?"

"Teresa wasn't much older when she started the Society."

"They told us stories about her at night. They needed to give us hope."

"Who?"

"The older slaves. They weren't as appealing to the animals as we were, so they worked as cleaners and cooks. They told us that one day she cut off the head of the man who held her captive for three years. She was fifteen years old."

"She did," I said. "He was called the General, and he was a bastard. She left his head mounted on one of his bedposts and escaped with a small group of people. I met one of them recently in a place called the Bastion. The others stayed with her and, later, became Knights of the Sword."

"They say she learned to fight from a master swordsman and founded the Society to help the innocent."

I chuckled.

"What?"

"Not exactly a master swordsman."

"Then who was he?"

"He was an old Corporate Agent with too many voices in his damned head." I turned toward the nearest entrance to the Tees. "I'll be back in a few. Get your people ready to make the trip."

I stopped and pointed at a man wearing a red armband that resembled those of the guards I had thrown out of the Scraper. "Gather food and enough clothing for these folks to wear. Not this thin see-through shit, either. They are not to be bothered by anyone, or you can join your friends. If you're wearing that red armband when I get back, I just might feed it to you."

He swallowed and glanced toward one of the crumpled forms who had impacted the pavement. "Y…yes, sir."

I walked toward the Tees, shaking my head. What people will do with no one to keep them in check makes my skin crawl. I understood some of the reasons behind these people. The Specialist, Teledyne's version of an Agent, was someone who could easily dominate. No one with the ability to stop him lived here. I had no doubt some of the Knights who had disappeared over the years had done so here, in Hart, or the Zone that used to be called Hart.

I opened the door centered in an otherwise blank brick wall under one of the buildings and stepped inside.

"Hello, Mister Kade."

"Portus," I said, "it's almost like you were waiting for me."

Portus was the Mardin who had led us through the Tees during one of the cases I was involved in last year.

"Perhaps we have discovered that a Mardin should be available in any Zone you are active in, sir. We do watch topside to keep apprised of any violence."

"Really?"

He laughed. "Actually, pure chance had me here. When bodies began falling from the Scraper, I thought I should investigate. There aren't many people who have your flair for the dramatic. The Farmers used to, but they haven't let Zee and Jimmy back into the city for some time."

"I heard a little about them from a vendor some time back. The Steadholder's sons?"

"Yes," Portus said. "They were a force to be reckoned with until the Accords were signed, forbidding them to return to the city. Zee's daughter runs one of the major Caravans into the city now."

"I've met a couple of the Caravan Masters," I said. "Not sure if I met her."

"She just began her term as a Master recently. Allie Pratt is much like her father. She brooks no nonsense. Do not provoke the Pratts."

"I don't plan to," I said. "Who did she replace as a Master? It wasn't that old bastard, Kalet, was it?"

He chuckled. "No, Kalet will run his Caravan until he dies of old age. No one has been able to kill him, but many have tried. It was Reynard."

"Reynard?" I asked. "I thought he was happy where he was."

"They said something about a new posting that was much sought after."

"He's good people," I said. "Glad he got a promotion."

"Agreed," he said. "But I seriously doubt you came into the Tees to talk about the Farmers. What can we do for you?"

"I need a message relayed to Teresa. I just freed fifty-three women and children from Hart and will be bringing them to her."

"I will send it on the shortwave."

"Thanks, Portus."

"Thank you, Mister Kade. Without you, we would have been quickly overrun by Derris' savages last year."

"One of these days, I need to have a discussion with Derris."

"His people have stayed out of the Tees since their confrontation with you and the two Squires."

"Speaking of Squires, you might also tell Teresa that Hart is in need of new management."

He chuckled again. "I assumed as much when the bodies began falling from the sky."

Some days, the rain isn't the worst thing falling from the sky in this Fallen World.

* * * * *

Chapter Four

I stopped just past the corner of the building and watched as a fifteen-year-old girl wrangled fifty people into a group. She was handing each one a small package of food from the supply the guard was carrying along behind her. His red armband was gone, and he was following any order the girl was giving.

"Natural leader, indeed."

Reminds me of another young woman, Angela said. *A certain woman you took in and trained.*

"She has some of the qualities," I said. "Teresa will make a good Knight out of her."

Perhaps we could find her sister for her, Childers said.

"It's not out of the question," I said. "We get them to the Society, then we can put out some feelers."

Looks like they are as ready as they are ever going to be, Gaunt said. *Some of those chaps look like they might want to try our patience.*

He was right. Several of the men were talking among themselves. Occasionally, one of the men looked hungrily in the direction of the girl and her charges.

I slipped around the corner, rounded a building, and stepped out of the shadows directly behind the man who seemed to be the ringleader. I tapped the knife I had planted in Hart's brain lightly against the side of his neck, just a fraction of an inch from his jugular.

He froze.

"If you were to try what you're thinking about, I would let a friend of mine skin you alive. These people have been through enough. You will turn to your right and start walking. If you stop before you are completely out of this Zone, your head will join your former Warlord's. Do you understand?"

He swallowed and nodded.

"Good. Now walk." I looked at the four who had been talking with the man. "That is your only warning. If you're still standing here in five minutes, well, you can figure out from the condition of Hart's guards what will happen to you. These people are off limits."

They scattered. They wanted no part of the man who had killed their leader and tossed most of his thugs out of the windows of his Scraper.

Should have killed them, Gaunt said.

"If we kill them, they won't learn anything."

I could hear Gaunt chuckling in my head.

As the thugs fled down the alley, I stepped back into the square in front of the Scraper where the girl was gathering her people.

"I wasn't sure you would come back," she said.

"Understandable," I said. "This place hasn't done much to instill trust, has it?"

"You've done more in an hour than anyone has done in the two years I have been away from the island."

"There are good people left," I said. "Not as many as there should be, but more than what you might expect. There are probably some right here, in this street, who have been afraid to step forward. A guy like Hart is enhanced and would be hard to take down without special skills."

"But you did," she said. "Mister…?"

"Kade," I said. "Mathew Kade. Most of the time, anyway."

"I'm Lynx," she said. "Lynn Xavier. My sister and I called each other Lynx and Jynx. Her name is Jennifer. She started calling herself Jynx after the accident."

"Accident?" My eyes narrowed.

"She lost an arm and a leg when the boat crashed. Dad was an engineer before the world went crazy, and mom was a surgeon. Between the two, they saved her."

"This is crazy," I said. "Teresa has an assistant named Jynx. You say she lost an arm and a leg? Did they build cybernetic prosthetics?"

"What?" She was staring at me with her mouth hanging open. "Yes! They built her an arm and a leg! Is she already there?"

"I doubt there is more than one girl named Jynx with cybernetic prosthetics in the city. I am fairly certain she's already at the Society. I haven't talked to her much. I got her some parts to tune up the leg some time back."

"That has to be her!" The girl was bouncing with excitement. I was amazed she could be as exuberant as she was after the time she had spent in the Scraper. Perhaps it was why her people followed her lead when they were freed. What she had gone through hadn't destroyed her as it had many.

Her excitement was contagious. I grinned. Sometimes, there is a ray of sunshine in the dark, even in this Fallen World.

* * * * *

Chapter Five

The Zone to the west of Hart was called Gord. The Warlord held his territory through the help of some ex-military types he had pulled together after the fall. He had been in charge of his territory for all the years since. Anyone who had been around for that length of time was there for a reason. Gord wasn't as bad as some, but his men were standing in the street as my group of refugees entered the Zone.

"I understand there was a ruckus next door," the leader of the guards said as I approached.

I motioned to Lynx to hold back. "Not particularly happy with the notion of slavery. Seems like this area is a little better than most. But there was this blight to an otherwise decent area."

"Hart," the man said. "The man's an Agent. Not much we can do with him except stay out of his Zone. The guy before him was a little better to deal with."

"The next guy should be a little better," I said.

"He's gone?"

"Yep."

"Who the hell are you?"

"I'm the guy who removed Hart from his position. I intend to take these folks west to Stiner. They've been treated pretty rough by Hart and his men. They'll be taken care of there. You gonna have a problem with us crossing through here?"

"You took out Hart and his men by yourself, and you're heading to Stiner. My guess is you're Mathew Kade. I'd rather wrap myself in razor wire and roll down the street than cause you any problems. My boys will provide you with an escort through our Zone just to be on the safe side. Some people are idiots, and I'd rather make sure none of them interfere."

"That would be greatly appreciated…?" I let the statement trail off into a question.

"Avery Foiler," he said. "I'm Gord's head of security. I'm very familiar with what an Agent can do, and I understand you are one of the best."

"Maybe," I said. "It's hard to say."

"I'd rather go with it and offer you any help I can."

"Thank you, Foiler. I'm sure these folks have seen enough violence to last them a while."

"Undoubtedly."

I motioned for Lynx to bring her people forward. "If you don't mind, I would like to get underway."

"Do you mind if I walk along with you?"

"Not at all," I said. I looked at Lynx. "Lynx, this is Avery Foiler. He's decided he is going to escort us through this Zone so there won't be any trouble."

"Thank you, Mister Foiler." She went over to help one of the kids that followed.

"She's pretty young."

"Hart was a right bastard," I said.

"He was that," Foiler said. "Saw him take apart a whole squad of men about five years ago. We've stayed out of his Zone since then. I had my suspicions about what was going on, but what could we do?"

"It's not my place to say, but a sniper shot to the brain would have ended it."

"And if the sniper missed, he'd have signed the death warrant for a whole Zone. You know what an Agent can do."

"You're right. He deserved an Agent. And he got a bunch."

"What?"

"Inside joke," I said. "Sometimes, I wish all of the enhanced had died with the Corporations."

"That would include you, Mister Kade."

"Yep."

"I see."

"World would be a better place without the nanites, the genetic mutations, and the damned imprint tech. Teledyne, Obsidian...they were two sides of the same coin."

"Agreed. I worked for Obsidian, but they weren't any better than Teledyne. Ran into a squad of Teledyne guys just before the end and took them prisoner. They were just guys like us, and the time we spent guarding them was more of an eye opener than any other part of the war. Guess you didn't spend much time talking to anyone else. Agents always seemed to be on a mission."

"You'd be surprised how many."

"Really? I didn't think they let you guys out unless you were on a mission."

"They kept more than the Agent programs in the database," I said.

"That makes sense," he said. "Guess you got one of those."

"You could say that."

"We're getting close to Fandi," he said. "I sent word ahead. You should be clear for the next two Zones, and the Farmers are in Jeffrey, so there shouldn't be any trouble. Just leaves a few Zones between them and Jeffrey."

"Normally, I would go around Jeffrey but, with the Farmers there, I agree. He shouldn't cause trouble. Antilles and Payne shouldn't be too bad. They know me. Thanks for sending word. It was good to meet you, Foiler."

"Good to actually meet you, too, Kade. My boss might be interested in this thing you've got going with the Society and a certain group of Warlords. If you think your people might have an interest, I can talk to him and see what we can work out."

"There would definitely be interest," I said. "And there will be a Society presence right next door in the near future."

"I'm glad." He slowed his pace as we neared the boundary of his Zone. "Be nice to see some stability in that area."

I nodded as he raised his hand, and the guards dropped back from the flanks of our group.

"He seems to be a lot better than the guys who worked for Hart," Lynx said as she walked over.

I saw how she kept a wary eye on the man as he walked away. She was a strong girl, but I knew she had been treated badly by most of the men she had met in the last year. How badly, I might never know, and I'm not sure I wanted to. Most of those who had been behind the mistreatment had taken a dive from various floors of the Scraper.

We walked down the street toward the Scraper Seamus Fandi held. He was somewhat new to his position since Darvis had crossed someone he shouldn't have. You didn't try to screw over the Circus. I heard three Clowns had walked into Darvis and had left the Zone freshly renamed Fandi. Kelly Darvis has never been seen again that I am aware of.

Gaunt chuckled inside my head. *It doesn't pay to make that kind of enemy.*

"True."

"What?" Lynx asked.

"Nothin, just talking to myselves."

"You are a strange man, Mister Kade."

"It's not like we haven't heard that before," I said, with a grin.

"We?"

"A little schizophrenic humor." I laughed. "There is a good side to my situation. I may be a schizophrenic, but I'll always have each other."

She shook her head and walked silently beside me as I chuckled.

That was rather horrid, Mathew, Gaunt said.

"It wasn't that bad," I muttered.

Lynx glanced at me sideways, with a raised eyebrow.

"Hmpf," I grunted.

Everyone seems to be a critic in this Fallen World.

* * * * *

Chapter Six

"I thought there would be more people here," Lynx said. "I haven't been out of the Scraper in close to a year, but there were more people around when they brought me in from the waterfront."

"Waterfront is the other direction," I said. "But I think Fandi took Foiler's warning to heart."

"Does he have that much power?" she asked. "I admit, I don't know a lot about the city."

A man who wore makeshift armor darted into an alley, muttering, "It's him..."

"Or is it you they're afraid of?"

"Maybe."

"I think it is," she said. "I saw you throw men around as if they weighed nothing."

"They deserved what they got," I said. "You can't deny that."

"Considering where you found me," she said, "I don't deny it at all."

I remained silent.

"I just wonder who you are," she said. "You showed up like some hero of old."

"I'm no hero," I said.

"Then why did you do it? You had no reason to save us. Even if you had reason to kill Hart, you had no reason to save us. No reason to be leading us through several Zones where we would have been taken as soon as we crossed into them. That hungry look I see on those men over there is one I know quite well. If you aren't a hero, you would have left us behind and gone about your business. We would be back there in a Scraper serving someone else. Maybe someone that isn't as bad as Hart was, but there is always someone."

"Pretty young to be that cynical," I said.

"From the moment my parents were slaughtered, all I have seen is one evil person after another. There weren't any good among them. The only good people I found were those who were being held in that Scraper, just like me. Then you arrived like one of the old Greek heroes my father used to tell me about. Whether you want me to or not, I see you as a hero, just like these people who are following us do."

Never been called a bloody hero, Mathew. She doesn't know me very well.

I chuckled. *More of a hero than you think, Stephen. We all saw your moment back at the Bastion. Unexpected, but welcome.*

Momentary lapse, I assure you, he said.

I could hear the others snickering in my mind.

Have your fun, Gaunt said.

I chuckled again and walked onward through Fandi's Zone. The street was fairly clean, which spoke well of Fandi on some level. Many of the Zones throughout the city were piled with refuse. It was kept to a certain level, though, or the Farmers would bypass the Zone. Even the savages throughout the city were on their best behavior when the Farmers came through.

The next Zone was Rollins, and the people there were preparing for the arrival of the Farmers. They were three Zones away, in Jeffrey, but they would be in Rollins in the next few days. The Farmers tended to stay in a Zone for a day and then move to the next. In the early days, they ran through many Zones each day, but they were working to save a city.

Sometimes, I wondered if it had been worth it. There were days I wanted to walk away and leave the city behind. Then I would think about Teresa and the Society trying to make a difference and know that I couldn't leave. I owed too much for the things I had done.

"Oh...Hello," I said as my eyes were drawn to a vendor on the left side of the street. "I haven't seen that in a long time."

"What?" Lynx asked.

"That's denim." I approached the vendor who was a woman of about fifty years or so. "I haven't seen that in some time."

"You like what you see?" the lady asked with an accent I'd heard somewhere before.

Romanian, Angela said.

"I do. If you have some of those pants in my size, I'd like to buy some."

"You look like about a thirty-four-inch waist."

"Yes, and a thirty-two inseam."

"I have four pairs that would fit you, sir."

"I'll take them."

"You didn't ask for the price," she said.

"I think this will cover it." I laid a coin on her table that she quickly covered with her hand.

"Not many of these around," she said. "Amazing what you can buy with a silver dollar. I remember when you could buy a drink with it. Now, there are places where you could buy a person for this coin. I don't have enough scrip to give you the necessary change."

"The coin is yours." I pointed to the pants. "Consider it an order for some more if you still have access to denim. I would like ten more pairs. Have them delivered to the Society in Stiner. If you agree to the delivery, I'll add another coin."

"Placing a lot of trust in a stranger," she said.

"I know where to find you if you don't follow through," I said, and she recoiled just a little as she detected the change in my demeanor.

"Not many would cross you," she said. "The coat, the blades, and I believe there is a certain straight razor in one of your pockets. You are known, Mister Kade. There are stories of Warlords who fear your coming. Conveniently, our own brave Warlord, Rollins, is up in his tower with the majority of his men. I like thinking of him up there, quaking in his boots, as Mathew Kade walks down his street. Your pants will arrive within two weeks, Mister Kade."

I smiled and drew another coin from my pocket and placed it near her hand where she could easily cover it.

"If you would step around here, I will get a few measurements, and I can make them to fit you precisely. I was a tailor before the fall and managed to acquire the denim from the Farmers this year."

"That would be great," I said. "What other sorts of fabric do you have? You see, I need a new coat. This one is taking a beating."

"Perhaps a darker color?"

"Dark colors make me look pale. Better stick with light."

"As you wish." She smiled. "It takes all kinds to make a world, Mister Kade."

I nodded. "Even in this Fallen World."

* * * * *

Chapter Seven

A ntilles' Zone was much like Rollins'. People were preparing for the Farmers to come their way.

"Who are the Farmers?" Lynx asked.

"I don't hear that question very often," I said.

"I never saw them when they came through Hart," she said. "We were always locked in our rooms when they came through. They were the only people I ever saw who frightened Hart."

"They're a force no one wants to be on the wrong side of," I said. "Pretty sure they are the reason this city survived right after the Fall, not that it deserved to."

"What did they do? Hart forbade us to even speak about them. There were whispers, but most of us were terrified of him."

"When the bombs fell, farms to our west banded together and sent Caravans of food into the city. They brought some order with them, and they were well on the way to dragging this place back into the light. Then something happened, and they changed. I'm not sure what it was, but I have my suspicions after I met some Clowns last year. The Accords were signed, and the Farmers became merchants instead of benefactors."

"Clowns? I love the books my mother gave me about them."

"These Clowns are different. You definitely don't want to contemplate ending up at the Circus."

"I like the tigers."

"You've never seen a circus like this. Those you saw in books were shows to entertain children. This one is a twisted perversion of the old ones. Anything a twisted soul wants to see or do can be found at the Circus. The Clowns are the guards."

"That's horrible," she said. "Why do you let them continue?"

"I'm tough, girl. I've never hesitated to face anything this shitty city has thrown at me, but I need help to take down the Circus."

"They are that strong? I thought Hart was the strongest person I had ever seen. But Lydia said you killed him so fast, she barely saw you move. I saw you throw men, who weighed hundreds of pounds, as if they were toys."

"They are," I said, looking to the southwest. "One day, I may have to do something about them, but how is the question."

"You'll do it," she said matter-of-factly.

I shook my head and continued walking down the street. None of the bravos who normally loitered along the sidewalks were there. Apparently, Antilles didn't want to provoke anyone. Most of the Zones around the area knew the Society and wouldn't provoke Teresa for all the scrip in the city.

"Do you really think the girl you know is my sister?"

"Odds are really good. Jynx is not a common name, and cybernetics are very rare. Most of them don't work anymore."

"Jynx had a catch in her leg," she said.

"It's her, girl. That catch got fixed using the part I got for her from my guy in Dana's Zone."

"I can't wait to see her again," Lynx said, looking west. "I hope she's been treated better than I was. I'm not sure she could have…"

The statement trailed off.

"I think she's been at the Society for about eight months," I said.

I was thinking about what had been done to this girl and wishing I could kill Hart and his thugs again. This was the first job I had done that hadn't coincided with a case I had been hired to do or asked to do by Teresa.

Perhaps you can see what you've been doing, now, Tim Bolgeo said. *I think our path to redemption demands that we do something.*

"Nothing out of you for years," I muttered. "Now you're preaching redemption."

I could feel Bolgeo laughing inside my head.

"What?" Lynx asked.

"Nothing," I answered. I tapped the side of my head. "Voices are getting restless."

You gave me back my daughter, Bolgeo said. *Now, you're stuck with me. I do know some useful tidbits about defensive tactics.*

"Do you really have voices in your head?"

"Yep. Some of them yap a lot."

"I've read some of my mom's books. Schizophrenia is serious."

"That's what the doc says." I tapped my head again.

"Doc?"

"She's a psychologist."

"So, I guess you could say you're already in therapy," she said and grinned. "That's one of the first steps in the book."

I chuckled. "I guess you could say that."

Her smile was infectious. How did someone live in Hell for two years and come out smiling?

She is refusing to be a victim, Angela said. *She will face her demons on her own terms, Mathew. Once she is somewhere safe where she can do so. She is a strong one. Reminds me of Teresa.*

"Yep," I muttered as we crossed into Payne's Zone.

Jonas Payne and a large group of his guards were waiting a short distance inside his Zone.

"Payne." I nodded at him. "We have a problem here?"

"Absolutely not," he said. "I heard you had a problem with Randall Hart and ended it in a rather permanent fashion. No, I do not have any problem with you or your little band of refugees. I came out to meet you and warn you about what happened in Overton yesterday. Last year, a group of representatives of the Circus were robbed and killed."

"I remember a little bit about that." I chuckled.

"I figured you would," he said. "Yesterday, three Clowns walked into Overton. When they left, there wasn't a single person alive in the Zone."

"Damn," I said. "None?"

"Every man, woman, and child."

"There were a lot of people there who had no choice, Jonas."

"I know. That's why I'm here. I don't know about you, but I'm scared. The only thing I can think to do is look for allies. If you will give Manora a message for me, I'd like to talk about this consortium you, Teresa, and the others are building around here."

"I can do that," I said. "There are rules, and they are enforced. I know you skirt the edge on many of them. You need to keep that in mind if you want to move forward. Jeffrey won't like it. He makes his scrip as a slaver, and I understand many of his Caravans come through here."

"I understand the price of admission. He can find another route."

"Then I'll relay the message with my endorsement. Something has to change in this city. These are the first steps."

"Agreed."

"I'll go through Jeffrey's Zone and bypass Overton's by using Xeno's. Somehow, I don't think these folks need to see what the Clowns left there."

"I wish I hadn't seen it. Manora is there with her folks, cleaning up the mess."

"I'll go back after I get these folks to the Society in Stiner."

"I was about to go back to Overton's to talk to Manora, but I think it might be better if it came from you. I'll send men to help her clean out the area."

"That will say more about your intentions than any amount of talk," I said. "Would show more if you go with them. Talk to her. I'll add my endorsement when I get there. Not that it will make a difference in her decision. Teresa does what she thinks is right whether I say anything or not."

"Then I'll go, too."

"I think it's be a better approach."

"Thank you, Mister Kade."

"A few more like you, Jonas, and we may actually make a difference in this Fallen World."

* * * * *

Chapter Eight

We heard the noise from the streets ahead long before we could see the wagons. The Farmers were lined up along the street throughout Jeffrey's Zone.

"These are the Farmers?" Lynx asked when she saw the colorful canopies.

"Yep," I said. "If you've never met them, it's a sight to see."

A woman was close behind us, and I recognized her as one of the women from Hart's chambers.

"I saw them years ago," she said. "Before I was..."

There was still a haunted look in her eyes. It was hard to think about what they had been through when I talked to Lynx.

"The Society is a safe place," I said. "You won't have to worry about that sort of thing anymore...?"

"Lydia," she said. "Lydia Savrill."

"Teresa can show you how to fight, Lydia."

"Like you?"

"I'm a little different. I've been enhanced like Hart was. We don't have the technology to do that anymore, and that's not a bad thing. But being a full Knight of the Society is about as close as you can come."

"How long does it take to become a Knight?"

"It takes years to reach Knighthood," I said. "Some never reach that skill level, but the strength of the Society isn't her Knights. They are like family. If you attack one of them, you attack them all. They will come from all corners of this city if the call goes out."

"They sound too good to be true."

"In a city like this, that doesn't surprise me. It's not hard to sound too good to be true."

"If there was a way to just leave this city…" she said, wistfully.

"There is," I said. "We're about to walk through a Zone full of a way out of the city. The Farmers are always willing to hire workers. Farming requires a lot of work, and they have a lot of farmland."

"They would let us go with them?"

"The only way to know is to ask them. We'll take our time through here." I was watching Lynx getting further ahead of us, looking at the wagons with a wonder I wouldn't have expected from someone who had been through what she had the last couple of years.

"You like the girl."

"She reminded me of a friend when I first met her."

"She is one of the pretty ones, so they limited the places they left scars."

My eye twitched.

"They were not gentle people, Mister Kade."

"They are now."

She smiled for the first time since I saw her in the penthouse. "Yes…yes, they are."

We followed Lynx down the row of wagons. She was looking into each one as she passed, but she wouldn't spend much time at any. She had no scrip, but she wanted to see everything.

"She kept me going when I wanted to end it," Lydia said. "She was the only brightness in our dreary lives. Every time she came back to the cells, she would wipe away the tears and lie down. When she woke, it was like the sun rising in our dark rooms."

"Teresa was like that when she came out of that place on the waterfront. I was in a dark place, and she walked into my camp like the morning sun. She didn't speak much about what she had been through, but she came out the other side forged into something different."

"The Matron?"

"Yes."

"Everyone knows the story of the Matron. She cut off the General's head and left it impaled on his bedpost and escaped with her friends. Then she found a master swordsman who trained her to be the greatest fighter ever..."

Her words trailed off as she looked at me and my smile.

"She found you, didn't she?"

"Yeah," I said. "She saved me from myself, and I taught her some things about the swords she carried. Don't know about that master swordsman thing though."

"I saw what you did with a small blade, Mister Kade."

I shrugged. "I don't use a sword very often, but there's a time for it, and it pays to know how to use one."

"Who would I speak to about joining these Farmers, Mister Kade?"

"It's Mathew," I said and turned toward a stall.

The guy working it raised his head in acknowledgement. "What can I do for you?"

"Looking for the Master. Is this one under Kalet?"

"Nope, this is the first run for Allie," he said, pointing toward a woman who held the reins of a massive, black horse.

"Thanks."

He nodded.

I strode over to the woman. She was tall and fit, with black hair. When she looked up at my approach, I noticed her striking, silver eyes.

The horse stepped toward me.

"Now, Shank," she said and patted his chest. "Back up."

The horse snorted.

"I know," she said and stepped between me and the horse.

"He looks like a handful."

"He's overprotective, but I would trust him with my life. He sees you like I do. You walk like my uncle. Enhanced can hide it, but not to those who know what to look for."

"I heard some things a little while back about your uncle. If he is who I think he is, I owe him my life."

"Uncle Jimmy has saved a lot of people."

"I don't doubt it." I motioned toward the refugees. "I have some people who would love to leave this place behind. I was wondering if—"

I spun and grabbed my blade in both hands as a commotion interrupted my question. A pale man was sprinting straight toward me.

I stepped toward him, and he skidded to a halt in front of me.

"Mister Kade! Derris hit a group of our people and dragged them into his Zone! They were meeting with Manora's people! I have to find the Matron!"

"Slow down. When?"

"It's been an hour and a half, sir."

"How many people were taken?"

"Four Mardins and the Matron's assistant, the girl with the prosthetic."

"What?"

"The novice was setting up a meeting for the Matron," he said. "They dragged all five of them into Derris' Zone! We don't have the forces to go in after them, sir."

I heard a sob behind me and turned. Lynx had dropped to her knees.

My whole body was trembling with rage when I turned back around to face Pratt. I pulled a handful of coins and held them out to her. "I need you to guarantee their safety. I'll pay whatever it takes."

She looked at the sobbing girl and said, "They'll be safe. What are you going to do?"

"I'm going after them." I pointed toward one of her guards, who wore two short swords on his back. "I need those."

"Not selling my—"

"Give him the swords, Allen," Pratt said. "I'll get you another set when we get home."

Allen unbuckled the harness. I removed my coat and slung the harness over my shoulders. "Teresa is in Overton's. Can you send a runner to tell her what is happening?"

"Absolutely."

I turned and laid my coat across Lynx's shoulders. "If she's alive, I'll bring her back. You understand?"

She looked up with tear-filled eyes that made my chest hurt and nodded. I turned toward the street that led to the west into Xeno.

The world seemed to slow as I leapt forward into a sprint. An Agent can attain speeds a normal person only dreams of, and I was running at my enhanced body's highest output.

"Guards! Mount up!" Allie Pratt yelled as I turned the corner.

All I could see was the face of a despairing girl, and fury filled me. Not just my own fury. Everyone in my head had been affected by her brightness. I was feeling the fury of a thousand souls, and there's not many things that drive a person like rage in this Fallen World.

* * * * *

Chapter Nine

*S**he could be alive,* Angela said.

Not likely, Gaunt said. *Derris' people have never been much more than savages.*

I growled as I leapt a pavilion along the street entering Xeno's Zone. I turned north and poured on the speed again and dodged several people who didn't have time to notice me before I passed them.

Have to find out, Bolgeo said. *This could break that girl. All she went through just to have this happen. It could.*

"Not if I can help it," I said between breaths.

Moments later, I turned left inside Stiner and charged straight toward Derris' Zone. The Society headquarters flew by on my right, and I heard yells from the guards at the front gate.

I ran past the old bank building I called home and drew the twin swords.

"Derris!"

My voice echoed from the buildings. The streets ahead of me were already full of his people. They were unclean and wore whatever they could find as armor or clothing. Some didn't bother with clothing at all. But they all carried weapons, and they all charged into the street to meet me.

My swords were moving faster than the eye could see, and body parts sailed through the air. I wasn't using anything but brute force to slice through them. There is a beautiful dance that can be done with a sword that is filled with grace and skill. I didn't do that. I charged straight into the crowd of screaming savages. All that were left in my wake were dead or dying. My rage seemed bottomless as I thought of a girl's tears.

I found one of the Mardins, still alive, near the largest Scraper in the Zone.

"Jynx?" I asked the woman. "The Matron's assistant?"

She looked back at the street full of dead, and her face became even paler than it already was. "Th…they dragged her inside there."

She was pointing at the Scraper, and I was moving again. There was nothing living that could hurt her behind me. I heard the noises, chanting of some sort, coming from inside the Scraper.

The door was made of steel, but I kicked it completely off its hinges, and it slammed to the floor inside. I was met by three men who screamed and charged right into my swords. I kicked one in the chest with a pleasant crunch as the other two fell, headless, to the floor. I heard the chanting getting louder behind a pair of double doors that led to some sort of auditorium. I slammed a shoulder into the doors. They exploded inward. Inside were fifty or so of the savages. At the front of the room was a stage, and on the stage, I saw a large man holding a small girl by her arm. Her other arm was held near his side. He had torn the cybernetic arm from her shoulder with his bare hands.

He tossed the screaming girl to the side, pulled a piece from the arm, and placed it in a spot on his wrist.

Then he turned toward me. His eyes glowed red, and I recognized him for what he was.

"War Borg," I said.

"Are you the one making such a racket out there?" Derris asked in a deep voice that didn't sound completely human. "What are you? Agent? Specialist?"

"I'm the guy who's gonna kill you," I said.

"We'll see," he said and glanced at the girl in the corner. "I'll be back in a minute darlin'. You got somethin' else I want, but I gotta kill me a little Agent first."

Over where Jynx was struggling to her feet, there was a pile of prosthetics and cybernetics.

"I thought the cyborgs had stopped working over the years," I said. "How long have you been harvesting them for parts?"

"Since the beginning," he said and looked at the group of followers between him and me. "Kill him."

"Alright then," I said. "Let's see what you got, you bag of bolts."

Fifty savages and JalCom's answer to the Agent program charged toward me. I grinned and met them halfway.

* * *

I staggered as I tried to climb one of the steps in the auditorium. I felt someone slip in under my arm on the right side. My right eye was swollen shut, and I could feel the nanites already working. My stomach felt like a hollow pit.

"You're heavy, Mister Kade," Jynx said.

"Thanks, girl," I grunted.

"You just saved my life," she said. "The least I can do is help you up the steps. I don't know how you survived that. I've never seen anything like that before."

"I'd like to say I haven't either, but..."

I looked down at the object I carried under my left arm. "How 'bout you?"

"Are you really talking to that?"

I chuckled and grunted. "That hurts."

As she helped me step over the door, I heard a yell and saw someone running toward us with a large axe. Then an arrow was protruding from his chest. He tumbled and landed on his face.

I chuckled again and almost fell.

With my left eye I could see a group of people approaching. Teresa was in the lead, but the person beside her held the bow loaded with an arrow, ready to fly.

"Lynx!?" I almost fell as Jynx was suddenly gone.

She was running toward her sister. I staggered again and smiled a red-toothed grin. I could still taste the blood in my mouth. Then Teresa was there and caught me before I could fall.

"What did they do to you?" she asked.

"I'm okay," I muttered. "They're not."

I grinned again and swayed drunkenly.

"Dammit, Kade."

She helped me step forward. "You know you're not bringing that home, right?"

"Really?"

"Really," she said. "Drop the head."

I sighed, and it hurt.

Derris' head thudded as it landed in the street.

"I guess you just can't get a head in this Fallen World."

Teresa snorted.

* * * * *

Chapter Ten

"I thought you were supposed to let me help," Wilson Poe said from the door of the infirmary.

"You were too slow, buddy."

"I hadn't even been back from the Bastion for a day when someone at the gate said they saw you running toward Derris like a bat out of hell."

"Had things to do, people to kill," I said. "If you can call that bunch people."

"We spent the day clearing out the stragglers. Can I ask you a question?"

"Sure."

"Why did you pick who you did to be the Warlord of that Zone?"

"She'll do better than you think."

"How do you expect a fifteen-year-old girl to hold it?"

"If anyone has a problem with her, they can deal with me."

"Okay." He shrugged. "I was just curious."

"Did you guys gather all the cybernetics?"

"Yeah," he said. "What do you want us to do with them?"

"I know a guy over in Dana who can put Jynx's arm back together. He owes me a favor."

"That makes sense."

"I thought it did."

"Yeah. Your choices are just a bit suspect. Seems like you spend a lot of time in the infirmary."

"A lot of my decisions are suspect, but that one? Nope. That one is solid. Have you met the girl?"

He laughed. "Yes, I did, and I know why you did it. I would have made the same choice in your shoes."

"Keep your big feet out of my shoes."

Poe laughed and walked back out the door.

Teresa stepped in, and her smile lit up the room like the morning sun.

Some things are worth fighting for in this Fallen World.

# # # # #

Kade: Origin

Part One

I awoke with a start.

"Damn this decrepit old bladder," I muttered as I dragged myself out of bed.

"Be a little quieter," Ringold said from the other bed. "Tryin' to sleep here."

"Shut up, you old fart," I grunted as I pushed the walker toward the bathroom.

My whole body hurt these days, and I couldn't seem to nail down which part hurt the most. The burning in my groin was almost unbearable, but I made it to the bathroom in time.

"Heh, heh," I laughed. "I beat you this time, you bastard."

"Victory!" Ringold yelled from the room.

I pushed the walker back out of the bathroom. "Damn straight."

"Celebrate the victories, Kade." He chuckled. "They're a lot scarcer as you go. Maybe you'll get lucky and kick the bucket before you have to call a nurse every time you need to go."

"Nope." I shook my head. "They'll have to wipe my ass and sponge bathe me for decades before I get to die."

"That's no way to think, Kade."

"Probably won't even send in that pretty redhead. It'll be Carl."

Carl was the size of a Packer's linebacker and wore the face of a serial killer. He was one of my orderlies.

"Damn, Kade."

"Expect the worst, and you'll never be disappointed," I said, then winced as my hip felt like a knife had been jammed into it.

"Damn Dellik Unified and their damn booby traps," I said.

"Hip gettin' you again, old man?"

He'd pried that from me one day while we waited for the nurses to come change the beds, and we got to sit outside for a couple of hours. We were just running a normal Patrol in Atlanta when one of their IEDs had gotten my squad. I had been lucky enough to be on the other side of Corporal Jayden. He took the brunt of the shrapnel, but I still got a chunk right through my hip. More frag took me in the knee, effectively removing one Mathew Kade from service. I got shipped back up north to the Reach, which was part of Virginia.

I remembered when we had been a country of states. Many people still called it such, but those of us who served knew better. A lot had changed in my ninety years. Now, we were a land of Corporate Territories. Oh, the states were still there, but the dividing lines within this country had become more fluid with the nature of the Corporations, and the Corporations never had enough. They were always participating in a hostile takeover somewhere. Obsidian had become a juggernaut in the Corporate World, and when they settled into any semblance of peace, another would make a play for Obsidian Territory. Then the war would begin again. Dellik Unified had been a rough one, better than six years long.

I had been taken out of that conflict by that IED in the second year. Now, Dellik was just a memory, a bad memory for many vets, but a memory, nonetheless. Years ago, I had seen the news vids about JalCom making advances from the Midwest Territories into Obsidian. I had known it wouldn't take long before someone else made a play for the east.

That conflict still hadn't reached a conclusion, but I figured Obsidian had a few tricks left.

"Hey, Ring?"

"What?"

"Look out that window."

"Oh, that's a thing of beauty."

We were looking at a pretty, yellow, convertible Corvette. Looked like it was from the twentieth century.

"Let's go steal it," I said.

"Alright."

He climbed out of bed, and we pushed our walkers out the door and down the hallway to the side exit. I ran a card across the scanner.

"Whose card did you swipe?"

"Carl's."

"You lifted that big bastard's card?"

"What's he gonna do? Beat up a ninety-year-old geezer?"

"He might." Ringold chuckled.

"He'll have to catch me first."

"Dammit, Kade," he grumbled. "I'm outrunning you. It's not going to be a hard job for Carl to catch you."

"Yeah, but when you passed me, I slipped the card in your pocket." I laughed. "Run, you old fart!"

"Dammit!"

We rounded the corner beside the Corvette only to see a pretty blonde slip into the driver's seat. The car started, and she pulled away from the curb in our direction. She smiled widely and waved as she passed.

"I reckon that smile was worth the walk out here," he said.

"I'm gonna agree with you, there, Ring."

"Just what are you two doing out here?" a voice said behind us.

We both turned and found Savannah Garvey standing behind us with her hands on her pretty hips.

"You were going to steal that car, weren't you?"

"Of course not," I said. "What sort of fella do you take me for?"

"We all remember the incident last May, Mister Kade."

"What?" I asked. "What happened in May?"

"You can't tell me you forgot what you two old reprobates did."

"I do well to remember my name if it ain't used pretty regular," I said.

"Who are you?" Ringold asked.

She laughed. "They said that if you stole another car, they'd put you in jail."

"Somehow, I don't think they'll jail a ninety-year-old man," I said. "We were gonna bring it back. I just wanted to feel the wind in my hair."

"What hair?" Ringold asked.

"I have a couple left."

"Maybe in your ears," he said.

"Wind still blows through them."

"You only made it ten miles," Savannah said.

"But it was a fast ten miles," I said, with a grin.

"We would have gotten farther, but he had to stop and pee." Ringold laughed.

She smiled and shook her head. "Now, are you going to give me any trouble going back inside?"

"No, ma'am," Ringold said. "But only if you'll walk in front of us. I'll follow you anywhere you want to go."

She looked at him with one eyebrow raised. "Hmm."

She turned and walked toward the door we had exited. I swear she put a little more sway into her hips just for Ring.

"I'd like to bite that butt, develop lock jaw, and be dragged to death," he said.

"Die happy, I reckon."

"Yes, sir. Very happy."

She turned to us as we neared the door and stretched out her hand.

"The card?"

"I don't have a card," I said. "Door was open."

"Here it is, darlin'.'"

I shook my head as Ring held out the card I had slipped into his pocket.

"Brave man," she said, looking at the name on the card.

"Wasn't me," he said. "It was that idiot."

"Not all that surprising." She grinned. "I'll try to slip it back to Carl without him knowing."

"He better not mess with Kade," Ringold said. "War hero and all that. Liable to get kicked in the shins."

"I'm done with all that since I took the arrow to the knee."

"An arrow, Mister Kade?"

"Well, an arrowhead. Those DU bastards put the damnedest things in their explosive devices. This one had an arrowhead in it with all the other crap. Hit me right in the knee."

* * *

"You have a visitor, Mister Kade." Carl's deep voice came from behind me. "Don't you step too close to me, either, you thieving old fart. I'd like to keep my access card today."

"I have no idea what you're talking about," I said. "Who is the visitor? I ain't had a visitor since Elena passed. Her family finally decide I was someone again? If it's that cousin of hers, Tom, I don't want to see him. He tried to say I'm unfit and take all the money I have left."

"None of her folks, Mister Kade."

"Well, now, I'm curious."

"Some fella from Corporate."

"They're pissed about the car?"

"No, I mean Corporate with all caps, Obsidian Corporation."

"Curiouser and curiouser."

"Do I send him in?"

"I reckon so, since they're the ones paying for my stay."

"He'll meet you in Meeting Room Three, Mister Kade."

"That's the one across the building?"

"Yep."

"Asshole," I said.

"Don't be pickin' my pockets, Mister Kade."

I chuckled. "Guess I had that coming."

"You need the exercise, anyway, old man," Ringold said from the other side of the room. "You're gettin' flabby."

"Look who's talking, you fat bastard."

He laughed as I pushed my walker out into the hall behind Carl.

It took some time, and I scowled at the big man's back. But I probably deserved it. After crossing the whole facility, Carl opened the door to Meeting Room Three.

I slapped his shoulder as I went by and said, "Sorry about the card."

He chuckled and walked away as I stepped into the room.

A man stood across the room, staring out the window. I glanced past the guy, and my eyes opened in surprise. The car parked outside was spectacular. It was an old Camaro from way back in the sixties. The nineteen sixties. I hadn't seen one of those aside from pictures. It was a deep, candy apple red.

I pushed my walker over to stand beside the man and stare out at the car.

"That's a piece of art," I said.

"That it is," he answered and turned to me. "I'm Nathaniel Bern, OAS." His hand stretched out, and I grasped it. It was soft, and his grip seemed weak. But it could just be that he was being careful of an old geezer.

"OAS, huh?" I commented. "You're not a grunt. I'd have to say a spook or an egghead."

He laughed. "I'm more of the latter, Mister Kade. Although I'd have to claim both."

"Well," I said, "I have to wonder what a spooky egghead wants with me. Been out for decades. And I'd make it good if I were you. It's almost lunch time, and they have pudding. Obsidian Armed Services doesn't make a habit of calling on old men."

"Not much for small talk, Mister Kade?"

"Too old for it. Comes a time when you're old enough that every minute is important. There's not as many of them left. So, Bern, let's get right to it. Today is banana, and I love banana pudding."

"Then I'll get right to it," he said and motioned to a seat at the table.

I sat down with a sigh. My hip was throbbing.

"You were a damn fine NCO sometime back, and I understand you pulled twenty years in the Service before injuries retired you."

"Yeah, that about sums it up."

"In all that time, I'm sure you heard about the Agent program."

"Yeah, I did. Crazy bastards. All sorts of mods to the body. I thought about going that route, but they told me I wasn't quite the right sort of person they were looking for. I guess they wanted a bit more moral ambiguity."

"That is one of the prerequisites for the program."

"Sociopaths."

"It is true."

"I'm pretty sure you don't want a ninety-year-old Agent, so I have to wonder what you do want."

"You're right and wrong, Mister Kade. We do want a ninety-year-old to join the program, mostly."

"Mostly? If you're going to take parts, try this blasted hip and knee."

He smiled. "Let me tell you a story."

I sighed and settled back into the chair. I had to admit, my curiosity was piqued.

"Ten years ago, a project began to build what we call an imprinter. We can, literally, imprint memories into a living mind. Tests began with mice. We ran ten mice through a maze and used the imprinter to download the memories of all the mice. Then we imprinted these memories into an eleventh mouse who went straight through the maze without a single mistaken turn. The early tests were a great success, and we have now successfully imprinted people. We've transferred complete memories from one person to another. We've even begun to build skill packages. They aren't quite as successful. It seems skill packages don't take if the person has no skill at all in the area. We can't give a fisherman unparalleled skill in martial arts. But we can take that fisherman and give him a Marine Biology imprint, and he'll retain the majority of it."

"That's impressive,"

"It is, Mister Kade."

"You want a lab rat," I said.

"In a manner of speaking." He nodded. "We want to make Agents. We want to build imprints we can use in Agents."

"Unlimited skills for sociopaths," I snorted. "I'm filled with anticipation when I think about something like that. Wait a minute, maybe that's something else...anxiety, distress? Are you frigging crazy?"

"This is why we need you, Mister Kade. We don't want to build sociopaths. We want to build complete personalities to fit any situation. We want them to have the skill set to do whatever job needs to be done, and most of all, we need to be able to return the originals back to their bodies after the job is done."

"And what's that got to do with me?"

"Mister Kade, you have decades of experience. You've done things in those ninety years that would allow almost any personality to be built around it. Mister Kade, we want your mind."

"You gotta be kidding me. I'm going to get some pudding."

"Just hear me out." He held out a placating hand.

I eased back into the seat.

"What I'm offering you is immortality. I'm not talking about removing your brain. Let me tell you about the next step we took in the program."

"Go ahead."

"We started building personalities, but none of them were anything more than surface constructs. The mind is much too complicated to build from nothing. We were almost to the point of shutting the endeavor down and proceeding with the Education Imprint Program. A couple of us developed a theory, and it has proven itself, up to a point. Several volunteers had their minds uploaded to the databanks. We used those minds as templates for the personalities. I say, up to a point…because they all went insane," he admitted. "First the minds and then the templates."

"That fills me with all sorts of anticipation…nope, nope. Anxiety again."

"The problem, Mister Kade, is that all of the volunteers were young and healthy and couldn't take the loss of their bodies. In theory."

"So, you want to copy the mind of some old goat who is tired of his body."

"Not just that, sir." He frowned. "I have seen both your medical files and your psyche eval. I know what you've been told, and I know what you've let them see of your mental state. I'm pretty sure no one has seen what your mental state truly is, except you."

I grunted. I guess the secret wasn't really a secret.

"I know that your body is failing. And worse, it is just a matter of time until it starts to affect your mind."

"Yeah, those moments I told you about are all that more precious, now."

"I can imagine." He scooted his chair back and stood up, facing the window. "Will you, at least, come and look at the program?"

"I'll tell you what I'll do," I said. "I'm going to go eat some pudding. Then, if you'll help me do something, I'll go with you and look this thing over."

"What can I help with?"

"You help me steal that car."

He looked at the car with a grin, "Done."

"And one more thing," I said.

"What's that?"

"Drop this off at the front desk."

I pulled Carl's wallet from the pocket of my robe and placed it on the table.

Bern raised his left eyebrow.

"Made me walk all the way across the place." I shrugged.

He chuckled. "Done."

It was almost half an hour later when I eased into the driver's seat of the Camaro. I grunted as I reached under the seat, looking for a spare key. Always check before trying to hotwire a car. A lot of folks just throw the keys under the seat, out of sight. Something jingled, and I raised my head and saw Bern holding a set of keys.

My eyes narrowed. "Your car?"

"No, sir, Mister Kade, yours. It would be a shame to damage the steering column."

"No doubt," I said and took the offered keys.

The engine rumbled with power, and I smiled. Immortality? Hmmm.

* * *

"This place looks well-guarded," I said as the Camaro rumbled into the drive of a military compound.

"It is," Bern returned. "The guards don't even know what they're guarding."

"There's plenty of them." I pointed to our left. "Looks like seven posts on the left, four on the right. Then the two guys in the shack."

"Pretty good, Mister Kade. There are six on the right."

"Damn these old eyes," I muttered.

"Pretty good for an old man, Mister Kade," he said. "Stop at the gate."

I stopped at the gatehouse and watched the two guards approach the car from either side.

"Doctor Bern," the guy on the left nodded. "Who is this?"

"If you'll look on the orders in the shack, you'll see I am expected with company."

He grinned. "I did, Doc. Didn't really expect someone so…"

"Old." I chuckled.

"Yeah," he said. "Most of the folks coming in here are a bit more spry."

"I used to be, Sarge."

He smiled as I commented on his rank. "You served?"

"Back when the DU was causing a ruckus. Took some shrapnel to the hip back in forty-two."

"Those were rough years, sir," he said.

"Don't call me sir, I worked for a living."

"You're still around after all that," he said. "I'll stick with sir."

"Guess I'll live with it as long as you don't start thinking I was a lieutenant or something."

"Staff?"

"Gunny," I answered.

"Maybe I should salute." He grinned.

"Been civilian for a long time," I said with a laugh. "I don't think they'll let me re-enlist."

He smiled and waved us through.

"You've been re-enlisted since we left the vets home," Bern said.

"I'll be damned," I said. "Obsidian must be pretty desperate if they're re-enlisting ninety-year-old gunnery sergeants."

"This is the Hail Mary, Mister Kade," he returned. "If this doesn't work, we're back to enlisting sociopaths. I, for one, would like to change that."

"I guess we'll see," I said.

"You're on board?"

"Really, what have I got to lose?" I shrugged as he motioned toward a parking spot near the smallest of the clustered buildings on the base. "Six weeks of hell as my mind begins to go?"

"The report says you have a year and a half before the effects are seen in your mind."

"It says six weeks to a year and a half."

"You may have more time…"

"Expect the worst, Doc. You'll never be disappointed."

"That's a pretty bad outlook, Mister Kade."

"I am almost never disappointed, Doc. Disappointment will eat at your soul."

He chuckled. "Alright, then."

I brushed my hand across the top of the magnificent car as we headed toward the door to the small building. My walker kept us moving at a pretty slow pace.

"Welcome," Bern said as he motioned me inside.

There were three checkpoints along the hallway that made its way around the perimeter of the building before ending at an elevator. The walls were reinforced steel with the standard concrete on the exterior that hid what was inside.

"Hard place to get into."

"It needs to be," he said. "This is the future. What we do here could end the wars. Not the war. The wars."

"You have a lot of faith in this system of yours."

"There's nothing wrong with the system. The hardware is flawless, Mister Kade." He tapped his head. "It's the wetware that seems to be the problem."

"Good luck," I said, pointing at my own head. "The noodle you're about to try hasn't ever been considered flawless."

"I think you may surprise yourself," he said.

"Whatever."

I stopped and leaned on my walker. This was the farthest I had walked in some time.

Bern pushed a button, and the elevator opened. Inside was a pretty redhead with a wheelchair.

"Oh, my stars and garters, that's the most beautiful thing I've seen in years," I said and sat down in the chair. "You're not too bad either, miss."

She chuckled. "I thought you might appreciate getting off your feet, Mister Kade."

"I most certainly do." I turned to Bern. "Let's get this show on the road, Doc."

"Just like that?" he asked. "You're all in?"

"Hell, Doc, I was all in the second we got in the car," I said. "Like I said before, what have I got to lose?"

* * *

There was nothing. I would have smiled, but there wasn't a mouth for me to use. I could understand why the others had gone nuts. But there was one huge difference, the pain was gone. I hadn't even realized how much there was until it was gone.

Perceiving something in the distance, or what seemed like a distance, I moved toward it. It was disconcerting as the light that had seemed so far away a moment ago was right there. It was a door.

I walked through the bright white opening into a room. It wasn't an impressive room, just a simple, round room with a table and two chairs. Walking toward the table, I realized I had a body in this room. There were none of the normal inputs you would have, though, except the visual. The virtual body moved with the same mental commands as the real body. It seemed to follow the same rules.

"Mister Kade?"

The voice came from everywhere and was just a bit disturbing.

"I'm here, Doc."

"Unexpected, but a good sign."

"Unexpected?"

"I hadn't connected you to the room yet," he said. "How did you find it?"

"Saw a light and moved toward it," I said. "Then walked through the door into this…round room."

"Interesting," he said. "Can you remember everything?"

"I think so," I answered. "How would I know if I don't remember something?"

"True," he said. "Let's go through a few questions."

"Sure."

"What is the most important memory you can think of?"

"That's easy enough," I answered. "Elena."

"And what memory is that?"

"Doc, that's a whole lot of memories. Thirty-two years of them."

"Good."

"How about more recent memories?" he asked. "Do you remember stealing a car?"

"Which time?"

"We'll discount the last one since it was my car and was more of a gift."

"There were a couple of times, even without that one. I stole my first car after Elena died. I used the 'Vette I stole to take her ashes to the ocean. She loved this spot out there where we used to go, and I spread her ashes there on the beach. When I came back, I left a bit of money and a note on the seat of the car. No one figured out who took the car for six hours. I was in better shape then." I chuckled. "They noticed the last one within thirty minutes. I blame Ring. He was with me that time, so I might as well blame him."

"Well, it certainly seems to have worked correctly, Mister Kade."

"I like the pain being gone, Doc," I said. "Hadn't realized there was so much of it until it was gone. But it's real dark in here."

"I have some programs I made for the others to make it seem more hospitable. Programs much like this room."

"Good."

"There are a few things I would like to do differently with this trial that I didn't do with the others. This has to work, or our program is over, so I will be giving you administrative access to the programs. This is as much an experiment as the rest of it, but the fact that you found the room without being tethered bodes well for the interface."

"Okay, Doc," I said. "Let's do it."

"I am inputting a program called Environ. It is a building program that you can use to build an environment around you like this room. It's a rather large program because of the number of available aspects. What I don't know is how the interface will work for you since you are inside the system. Your access keyword is HJDRFETY. You may change that after you access the program. I'm going to leave you to examine it for a bit."

"Alright, Doc."

I said the key aloud, and a console materialized on one side of the room.

"That was easy enough," I muttered and walked over to the console.

"Enjoy the program, Mister Kade."

"Thanks, Doc."

I searched through the console commands to find the settings and found the access key. With a few commands, I changed the key to something I could easily remember, then I signed out. The console disappeared.

I walked out of the meeting room into the dark, moving away from the bright door.

"Who dat? Who dere?"

The console appeared in front of me again. Then I really dug into the different landscapes.

* * *

"You appear to have been busy, Mister Kade." The Doc's voice came from everywhere again.

"It's kind of fun," I said.

"The gardens are quite splendid."

"Elena loved flowers. She would have loved building something like this."

"It is beautiful. I was planning to leave you alone for a pre-determined amount of time, but we have a small problem."

"What is it?"

"You seem to have disappeared."

"I'm right here."

"No, the other you. He got a little upset when I told him we were going to download his mind so we could update your consciousness inside the machine. I let him be for a little while to calm down and came back to find him gone."

"It must be getting worse," I said. "He knows I'm free of the pain, now. He doesn't want to send his pain to me."

"I thought as much, but it might be needed to continue the experiment. We did this with the others, and it made them worse. They began to miss their bodies much more."

"Doc, I don't miss it, and bombarding me with memories of more pain isn't going to make me want to go back. Let me think a minute, and I'll help you find him."

"Thank you, Mister Kade."

"Call me Mathew, Doc."

"One more thing, Mathew," he said. "He stole a gun."

"Shit."

* * *

"He did, indeed, go where you said he would," Doc said. "We were too late to stop him."

"He's gone, then."

I wasn't sure how I felt about what my old self had done. I had only spoken with him once since I had been downloaded into the machine. I'm pretty sure Doc was unaware of the conversation we'd had. He was beginning to lose some of his memories. Our worst fear had started. The cancer had moved into his brain. We had known it would come at some point, but we both hoped it would kill him before it took that. Most people with this form of cancer die well before it reaches the brain.

"How did he do it?"

"I expected him to commit suicide, Mathew," he said. "Even after you told me he would not. He went down into the city and found one of the worst sections of town. There, he interrupted a robbery and shot three men before a fourth managed to shoot him. He lived long enough to shoot the fourth, who is now recovering in a hospital on Grave Street."

"Tough old bastard," I said.

"Yes, he was. But now we have no backup if your program doesn't work."

"We didn't have one in him either, Doc. The cancer was into his brain."

"He never said anything about that."

"He told me he was losing memories of our past, Doc."

"Then you expected something like this?"

"Actually, I didn't. This place has changed the way I think more than I would like to admit. I can look back and see where I would have expected it, but time in here has changed me."

"You have been inside longer than any of the other volunteers, Mathew. You feel no longing for the physical world?"

"Not so much, Doc."

"The next experiment will be the one that tells us whether we will succeed or not."

"And what's that?"

"You are going outside for a bit, Mathew. Time to stretch your legs."

"Alright."

I was…familiar with the theory of being downloaded into a body. It was pretty anticlimactic when it actually happened.

"When are we doing it?"

"It's done, Mathew," he said. "The part where we see if the experiment is a success will be when we upload the copy back into the machine, and the two merge."

"That could be interesting."

"Indeed. Here we go. I will speak again with you after you assimilate."

"Okay, Doc. Let me have it."

The memory was as vivid as the memory of building the latest construct in the machine. It was as if I had lived them both, and in a way, I guess I had.

* * *

My eyes opened. I felt them this time, and the sensations of the body I had been missing inside the machine. There was only a little pain, but the sensations seemed odd to me. I raised my head and looked down.

"Doc?" My voice was much higher pitched, but very soft. A voice I would have enjoyed listening to, once upon a time. "Why do I have boobs?"

I heard a giggle from my left and turned my head and saw the red-haired nurse who had met us at the top of the elevator.

"You've changed your hair," I said. "Close to a foot longer."

"It has been some time since you last saw me, Mister Kade."

I looked back down at my chest. "I guess it's Miss Kade."

She laughed again. "At least you're a good sport about it. Doctor Bern insists that the first body one of you is placed into is of the opposite sex. It gets the shock over with."

"One of you?"

"The others who came before you. Some of them handled the transition tolerably well. Some, not so much."

"It's just a body," I said and sat up. I twisted to the side and let my legs hang off the bed. The wall was mirrored, and my eyebrows arched. "An extremely attractive body, certainly."

"Sometimes, the Agent can't be a male."

"I got no problem with that," I said and slipped off the bed and dropped a little before my feet touched the floor. "Where is the person who came out of this body?"

"There was no one inside the body, Mister Kade."

"Now, I'm curious."

"Extreme cases in the prison system are sentenced to death. Our mode of execution is much different than it used to be. Instead of killing them, they are sent to us, where we wipe thier mind. The body is an empty shell. Then we use the bodies for Agents. It's a relatively new system since we have had little success with the 'wetware' up to this point. We have high hopes for you, Mister Kade."

"Alright."

The door opened, and Bern entered.

"How are you holding up, Mathew?"

"May as well call me Mattie for the time being, Doc."

"You are handling it well," he said.

"These," I patted my chest, "are going to be a distraction. They seem to get in the way."

I twisted and moved my arms, which kept connecting in unfamiliar places.

Red laughed again. "Welcome to womanhood, Mister Kade."

"You may as well call me Mattie, too. At least as long as I'm in this body. Mathew when I'm not. Mister Kade is...was a crotchety old man."

"I can do that."

"Alright, Doc," I said as I turned to Bern. "What's next?"

"I have a job for you, Mathe...Mattie. One you just might be glad to take care of. It is somewhat of a personal matter. I want you to remove someone."

I was silent for a moment. I'd killed many men in my time as an OAS trooper. This seemed different.

"Kill someone," I corrected. "Don't mince words, Doc. Own it."

"Yes," Bern said. "I want you to kill the man who killed Mathew Kade."

I watched Bern, closely. He was angry.

"That, I can do," I said. "You guys were closer than I thought."

"He was my friend," he said. "It needs to look like an accident."

"I can do that, too."

"Good. You have all the tools necessary for the job in that Agent's body. I would suggest you go to the gym and see what you are capable of before you leave the facility. You will find that you are much stronger, faster, and more durable. You also have many skills you are unaware of. If you think about it, you may remember many years of training."

"What training?"

My mouth dropped open as sixty years of skills and training dumped directly into my memory bank.

"Holy shit," I muttered.

"That training."

"Damn, Doc.

"That is how the imprinter works, Mathew. If you have a grounding in any given field, it can be instantly added to your skill set. You have had many years with an affinity for violence. Now, you have many years of training to accompany it. Some of it will not last, but some of it will be ingrained into you after this."

"Okay, Doc. I'll hit the gym and then go take care of business."

"Thank you, Mathew."

I nodded to him and turned to Red. "I never caught your name, but can you show me to the gym, and tell me where I can get some clothes?"

"It's Regina," she answered. "And you can follow me. I'll take you to a dressing room first."

I followed Regina out of the room where I had awakened. It felt a little weird walking down the hall naked. Even weirder to walk down the hall as a naked woman. There were subtle differences in my gait. More movement in the hips than I was accustomed to.

I laughed.

"What is it?" Regina turned to me.

"Walking feels a bit weird." I grinned. "Things move a little different."

She laughed and opened a door. "Step on the scale," she said, then put her hand out to stop me. "But first, tell me how much you think you weigh."

"How am I supposed to know?"

She cocked her head to the side. "Really?"

"I figure about a hundred and twenty at the most. This body has good musculature which weighs in heavier than it looks."

She smiled. "Now, step on the scale."

"What the hell? How do I weigh two hundred and forty pounds?"

"The bones and muscles are denser than a normal person's. Increased strength and durability. You'll find that you can do things you never would have thought possible."

She pointed toward a locker with the number four stenciled on the front. "The clothes in number four will fit you."

I opened the locker and pulled a lacey pair of underwear from the top of the pile. I paused, looking at them, as it sank in where I was.

"You're thinking naughty thoughts."

"Just give me thirty minutes," I said.

She laughed and shook her head. "Men."

I chuckled and pulled the panties on.

"That's weird," I said as the thong slid into place.

"I take it you never wore a thong?"

"Yeah, for some reason they wouldn't let us wear 'em at the Vets'."

Next, I pulled on a pair of thin, stretchy pants.

"May as well go naked," I muttered.

They were really comfortable though.

Glancing to the side, I caught my reflection in the mirror. "Yep, thirty minutes."

Regina laughed again.

I took the top from the locker and pulled it on. It was a sort of sports bra-type thing.

"That helps keep the damn things under control," I said and moved my arms around without as much interference.

"The gym is through here," she said, with a grin.

I followed her through another door into a large room with lots of exercise equipment and a wide open space in the center. Glancing up, I could see the ceiling about thirty feet above us.

"The first thing I want you to do is jump straight up," she said.

"Okay." I shrugged and jumped.

I gasped as I realized I had jumped higher than the top of the door behind us.

"Damn."

"That was what you could do with what you expected. Now, I want you to jump all the way to the ceiling."

"Really?"

"Absolutely."

I squatted a lot further and really pushed off. The ceiling approached pretty quickly, and I raised my hands to stop myself from hitting it with my head. Then, I was falling back down. I remembered my training from the OAS and let my legs bend to absorb the shock.

There wasn't as much as I expected though; the body was made to handle things like that.

"Son of a bitch," I muttered.

"Now, let's go lift some weights."

* * *

"This is different," I said as I relived the memories of slipping into the hospital.

I'd gone out a window and climbed up the side of the building to bypass the guards outside the room of Delmar Maples. He looked up as I slid his window open and dropped into his room.

"Who are you?"

"You killed someone very close to me, Mister Maples."

His eyes widened as I dragged him from the bed he was lying in. His mouth opened, and I clamped my hand over it.

I held him in front of the open window. "What do you see out there? A world of victims? You shot three people and an old man who walked into a bank. The old man was my friend."

I removed my hand from his mouth.

"That old bastard killed three of us."

"Yes," I said. "That glorious, old bastard did. And now, he's going to kill the last one."

I gave him a small push, and he staggered forward, out the window.

I left the window open and climbed back out. After a few short jumps, I was on the roof and walking calmly toward the roof access door.

* * *

"They said he jumped out the window instead of facing the courts," I said to Bern as my reverie into the past faded.

"Yes, they did," he said. "They closed the case the next day. Not even much of an investigation."

"That seems to have worked out well," I said.

"Yes," he agreed. "I'm curious why it took you so long to return after the mission."

"A gentleman never tells."

I heard a giggle from the speaker. Apparently, Regina was also on the other side of the conversation.

"It seems I need to build a new training ground in here to keep these new skills," I said. "Give me a holler when you need me again, Doc."

* * *

I spent many hours using the fighting techniques that had been imprinted in the previous body, but many of them still slipped away. Not all of them, but some faded. I had hoped to keep them all.

I sat in the garden and read a book from the unlimited library in the computer system.

"Mathew!"

Doc Bern's voice was frantic.

"We are under attack!"

"Get me a body," I said.

"It is underway," he said. "There won't be time to acclimate. You must get into action immediately!"

"Gotcha."

I waited for something to happen, but there was nothing. Then I realized what was happening. They'd downloaded a copy, just like before. I would just have to wait until he returned.

It seemed like a long time as I paced around the gardens.

"Nothing you can do about it, old man," I muttered to myself. Or maybe it was just a thought. It was pretty much the same thing in the machine.

Then everything went dark for a moment.

"That doesn't bode well," I said.

Then there were memories flooding my awareness. I staggered and dropped to the ground in front of the roses I had planted for Elena.

Everything was jumbled and almost impossible to follow. I was here, but I was there, and at another place. After the memories stopped flooding in, I sat in front of the roses and tried to make sense of what was happening. Then I realized what they had done. I had been downloaded into six different bodies at the same time, and all the memories were clamoring to be first.

"That's enough!" my voice, or thought, rang out across the gardens, and the memories were pushed aside. "One at a time."

I sifted through six different versions of me as they took up the defense of the facility. After a bit, I settled on the one that had awakened as Number One.

* * *

I awoke before they could pull me from the imprinter. It was a cylindrical device that encircled the body like an old MRI machine or tanning bed...I sat up as the straps holding me to the platform tore.

"Situation, Doc."

"A large force of JalCom troops are flooding into the base, Mathew," he said. "I don't know how they found us."

"How many?"

"Hundreds!"

"Safe to say, they found out what's happening here."

"We can't let this fall into their hands, Mathew."

"Load me into all the remaining Agent bodies, Doc," I said as I strode from the chamber toward the locker room. I went straight to the number one locker and pulled clothes on quickly. I saw something in the back of the locker.

"What do I tell them?" Doc's voice came through the comm in my ear. He was still in the control room.

"Tell them to kill anyone that ain't us, Doc."

I pulled the object from the locker and flipped the straight razor open with a smile.

The closest place I would find a gun was the armory. This would do until then.

"How long until the others are ready?"

"Number two is downloading."

"Alright. I'm heading for the armory," I said. "Tell him to grab what he can and join me there."

I was at the door in an instant.

"Damn, these Agent bodies are fast," I muttered and sprinted down the hall toward the ramp that circled the facility.

I saw a group of our guys crouching behind the first checkpoint.

"Hi, guys!" I yelled as I leapt over them and kept running.

Someone in a tan camo uniform rounded the corner and met with a straight razor across his throat. I caught his body in one hand

and drew the holstered sidearm on his right. The strap had been over it, but I ripped it from his side without much problem.

His body slid to the floor, and I looked around the corner. Three more followed the guy I had killed, about halfway down the hall. I launched myself forward, careened off the far wall, and opened fire with the stolen pistol. Two of them went down before the last got off a shot. I was already halfway down the hall toward him and bouncing like a pinball from side to side. There was a tug at my leg, but I was already too close for him to do anything except die, as my fist folded around the closed razor, and I slammed into his chest like a pile driver.

There was an audible crunch, and he flew backward.

"Damn!" I mused at the strength behind that blow.

"Doc, tell your guys at Checkpoint One to start moving forward as I clear these out."

"Okay, Mathew. Two is on the way."

"Almost to the armory."

I dropped and peeked around the next corner and saw another group of JCs between me and the armory access.

"Alright, then," I said as another form approached behind me.

I glanced back and saw Agent Two coming up the hall with something that looked like a prosthetic leg gripped in his hand.

I looked at him with one eyebrow arched.

"What?" he asked.

"Nothin'."

"What are you waitin' for then, old man?"

He sprinted around the corner faster than any human has the right to move, and I followed right behind him. He slammed into the group of four like a football player and started laying them out with the leg.

I shot one who looked like he was going to raise his rifle.

"Heh, heh," Two giggled.

"Sometimes, I have to wonder about myself," I said as I moved past the grinning idiot.

The JCs had killed the four OAS troopers guarding Checkpoint Two on the far side of the armory access. Glancing back, I saw the guys I had passed earlier coming up the hall behind us. I motioned to the other checkpoint.

"Hold them while we get armed."

"Yes, sir."

Two and I grabbed vests and slid them on. I buckled up and saw him stick the foot through an adjustable loop.

"You're keeping that?"

"Of course," he said and cinched the loop to hold the leg along his left side.

The vest had pockets for pistol and rifle magazines; I filled them all. I had holstered a pistol and slung a rifle when I turned around and saw Two cramming grenades anywhere he could put them.

"What?" He shrugged.

"I'll take a few of those."

We left the armory just in time to see one of our guys go down from fire on the other side of the checkpoint.

I pulled the pin and tossed one of the grenades down the hall.

The explosion was deafening in the closed area, and my ears began to ring, but I followed the grenade into the hallway, firing my rifle into the group of JCs. They were disoriented by the grenade blast, and I made short work of them. The ringing in my ears was already easing. Regina had said the bodies healed very quickly.

We were nearing the open area at the front of the building, and I knew there would be a lot of JCs in there.

"I'll take the left," I said to Two. "You take the right."

"Gotcha."

"I'll take the middle," a woman's voice said as Four ran past with nothing on but a savage smile. She was carrying two kukri knives and hadn't bothered with a gun.

"They'll all be watching her," I said and charged out of the hallway behind the naked Agent. I shot the first two on the left, while they were still distracted, and ejected the mag and slammed another back in its place. I glanced to the right and saw Two slam his rifle through the chest of a JC.

"That's not how you're supposed to use that!" I yelled as my mag ran out again.

Two looked like he was giggling again.

"Shit," I muttered and did the same thing as the JCs got too close.

I didn't even reach for another weapon; I just grabbed the first JC I could. I pulled him in close with my arm around his neck, and I squeezed and ripped his head completely from his shoulders.

"Maybe she had the right idea all along," I said and threw the head into the face of another. Then I was right in among them.

When my fists connected, bones broke and organs ruptured. There were a lot of screams. Three exited the hall and started shooting from the edge of the room. Every shot meant another dead JC, and soon, the room was completely empty except for the cooling bodies and pooling blood.

"When we head outside, everyone has to keep moving. Only way they're going to stop us is from a distance." I pointed toward the doors that had been blown open.

"Gotcha."

The three answers came as one, and it was just a little creepy since I knew they were all me.

"Distraction time," Four said.

"Go for it," I said.

She grinned and charged out the door with her bloody knives.

"I'd say I was in love, if it weren't me," Two said as he followed her.

"Nothing wrong with that," I said as I went through the door. "I love me."

* * *

It was dark outside, and we moved faster than any of the JCs were expecting. It was the very definition of a target-rich environment, but it only took a moment for them to track us. I felt a fire in my side that seemed to fade into the background as I reached the first soldier. I had seen Four jerk once as she crossed the clearing, and Two had been hit as well.

But then we were among them. My pistol was empty, and I left it embedded in the throat of a woman with beautiful blue eyes.

"Sorry about that," I muttered. Unfortunately, I had one of those old-fashioned attitudes that demanded respect for those of the opposite sex. Fortunately, when they are trying to kill me, I can work through my issues fairly quickly.

The next one was a young man, barely old enough to shave. It was depressing but had to be done. Then Four was thrown through the air.

She impacted the ground and was back on her feet in an instant. I saw where she was looking, and it wasn't pretty. The man was huge, with grotesque bulges for musculature. He had to be some sort of experiment by the JCs to offset the Agents. It would stand to reason that, if they had such a thing, it would be deployed for this.

"Two!"

He looked in our direction and saw the Behemoth. I couldn't think of a better descriptor.

The Behemoth charged Four, and I moved in her direction on an intercept course. There was nothing graceful about my charge through the few remaining JCs. I kicked or punched with the force of a pile driver. Two was also on an intercept course.

"Come on, big boy!" Four yelled and moved forward to meet him.

Then the whole back of the Behemoth's head exploded as Five fired the Barrett from the rooftop.

The giant took three steps forward before toppling.

A bullet whizzed past my ear, and my attention returned to the fight.

"They probably brought ten of those," I muttered as I plowed back into the rest of the JCs.

"They brought two," Five said over the comm as the Barret boomed again.

Why didn't I think of sniping from the roof? I guess maybe I had if you looked at it the right way.

I chuckled as my open hand contacted the side of a JC's head, spinning it all the way around with a crack.

Four paused beside me.

"Sometimes, I worry about myself," she said, shaking her head at my apparent amusement.

"I'm not the one running around out here naked," I said.

"Yes, you are," she argued.

I shrugged. "I guess I am."

She laughed and moved off to our right, toward the next group of soldiers. They had sent close to five hundred men and women to take the facility, along with two Behemoths. They would have rolled right over the thirty-two men and women guarding the place, if not for the six of me.

The four of me on the ground were wounded.

I had taken one to the leg and side as well as several stabs in my arms.

Two had been shot once in the arm and stabbed in the side.

Three had been firing from the entrance to the building, but he had still managed to take a bullet in the shoulder.

Four had been shot, stabbed, and hit by the Behemoth, which had left a massive welt on her left side.

Five was on the roof with the Barrett, and Six was protecting Doc Bern and Regina.

All the JCs were dead.

* * *

"They'll have a Plan B, Doc."

"What do you mean?"

"If the attack fails, they'll have a contingency

plan," Two said.

"We do too," Bern said. "We'll move to the northern lab. No one knows about it."

"Then we have to hurry," I said.

"How did they find us?" Bern asked.

The sound of the gun was deafening in the closed space, and my pistol was in my hand without conscious thought. Five bullets and a kukri knife slammed into the OAS traitor who shot Bern.

"Shit!" I cursed.

Regina had caught the Doc, who lay in her lap with blood spreading across his chest.

"They've killed me, Gina," he gasped, looking up at her.

"Not yet, they haven't!"

I grabbed Bern and dragged him to the imprinter.

"What are you doing?" Regina screamed.

"Not me," I said and pointed at her. "You are going to upload him into the database."

"I can't do that!" She shook her head. "He'll go insane!"

"Or he'll die," Four said.

I pushed him into the imprinter. "Do it now, Regina."

She ran to the console and initiated the machine. "It will take ten minutes. Can he last that long?"

"We'll just have to see," I said and began digging in her purse. "You have any pads?"

"Pads?"

"Gonna tape him up so he doesn't bleed out in the next ten minutes."

"I got it, One," Five said. "You guys patch yourselves up."

He pointed at Four. "And you put some damn clothes on. I've got a reputation to uphold."

She nodded and headed to the locker room.

I nodded to him and turned to the other OAS men. "Prep a truck to move to the north lab, like the doc said. Then you are to report back to your headquarters and tell them what happened here.

"Won't you need us for defense?" Sergeant Malcolm asked.

"We'll be defense until we get there and make contact."

"Yes, sir."

Two was trying to patch one of the wounds on his own back.

"Let me help you with that," I said, grabbing the pad and duct tape. "Three, go help Four get patched up. She had several wounds I know she can't reach."

He grinned.

"Pervert."

"I happen to know you've…"

"Piss off," I said.

I had almost gotten Two taped up when Regina's hand landed on my shoulder. "It's done. He's gone."

I placed my hands on her shoulders. "It had to be done, girl. It's his only chance to survive."

"I know, but I hate to think that I condemned him to insanity."

"Doc may be made of sterner stuff than that," I said. "At least, he's not in there alone."

"He will be until I can get the database back up and running in Philly."

"Then we had best get a move on. Get it packed up, and we'll plant the charges."

"Charges?"

"We can't leave all this tech behind," I said and pointed at the imprinters.

She shook her head. "You're right, Mister Kade."

"It's Mathew," I said. "Now get me and the Doc all packed up while the rest of myselves get ready to move out. We'll be going north with every damn thing in that armory."

I could tell she was close to the edge, but she had guts. She took a deep breath and straightened her slumped shoulders. Then, she nodded to me and returned to the computers.

"Let's go load some guns in the truck," I said to Two.

"Damn straight."

* * *

"You know, I almost terminated this copy of my-self when you put me into that Agent body. Hard to believe it's been close to a year."

Bern moved his knight toward my bishop.

"Kind of glad you didn't, Doc."

"Surprisingly, I'm rather glad you talked me out of it," he said.

"You'd miss all of this," I said, motioning toward the surrounding greenery in the virtual garden.

"The periodic updates from the version of myself outside help keep me straight."

"They've been good for me, too," I said. "I still have all of the memories from them and those from myself. As a matter of fact, there should be a new upload soon from that last copy the other you downloaded. He said he was going to try something new. Didn't elaborate much past that. Have you had an update recently?"

"No, I haven't."

"Oh, well." I shrugged. "I guess we'll find out together."

I glanced to my right and saw another form walking toward us through the garden.

"That's odd," I said, pointing at the new inhabitant.

He looked up and saw me, and I recognized those eyes. They were mine.

"That's not the way one of these normally goes," I said.

"Indeed," Doc agreed.

"Hello Mathew," the newcomer said with a precise voice unlike any I would use. "My name is Stephen. These roses are absolutely delightful."

He looked over his shoulder, and I could see dozens of additional people coming. They all looked different, but they all had my eyes.

"Oh, yeah," he said. "I forgot to mention it. I'm not alone."

Things can get complicated in this Fallen World.

* * * * *

Part Two

I opened my eyes.

"You're looking good, Red," I said and paused as I heard my voice. "And…I'm a woman again."

Gina chuckled. "At least you're young again. I don't have that luxury."

The last ten years had been good to her, but she had still aged. There was a touch of gray where her hair was beginning to turn.

"I don't think I qualify as young at the ripe old age of a hundred and twelve years."

She handed me a mirror. "You're aging well, Mathew."

I looked into the mirror into vibrant green eyes and Asian features. "Where do you find these bodies? I look like a schoolgirl."

"Miss Chu has been an Agent donor for six years, Matt. She signed up at age twenty-one. You know the nanites don't let you age quickly."

"Maybe I'm just getting old," I said. "She looks like she's twelve."

"I thought you old geezers liked the young ones."

"I like them around forty-five, with red hair. Nurse's outfit is optional."

She shook her head. "You have hit on me almost every time you load up, Mathew. Be careful. One day I might take you up on it."

She brushed a hand across my cheek. "And you wouldn't want that time to be when you're a teenage girl."

I grinned.

"You're incorrigible, Mathew Kade."

"Just part of my charm, girl." I rose from the imprinter. "What's the job?"

"We have a heated conflict near Headquarters, and they have requested an Agent to end it."

"Ah. Just need an old soldier."

"I figured you would like the time out. I suppose I could have called up Childers. But, frankly, I like it when I can talk to you. Do you know you're the only one who comes out of the machine with any memory of the time inside?"

"What about the Doc?"

"Well, I guess you're one of two, then. But I don't get to talk to him anymore. Not since they moved him upstairs."

"Is that why he hasn't been uploaded in a while?" I asked. "He's been wondering when they'll do a refresh."

"I'm not sure they'll upload him again."

"That's a little disappointing. These uploads are what keep us sane in there. If they stop, I don't know what the repercussions will be."

"Maybe when the war with JalCom is wrapped up."

"They have to be close to folding," I said.

"There are rumors. I think this latest attack is their Hail Mary."

"We'll see," I said. "I guess I should get some clothes. Perhaps when it's done, we can—"

"Go do your thing, Mathew."

I chuckled and strode up the ramp toward the locker room and armory. The time gave me a chance to adapt to the body I was using.

It didn't take me long, I'd been using all sorts of Agent bodies for over a decade. There weren't many I couldn't adapt to pretty quickly.

I glanced up at the cameras. "That's new."

I kept moving and entered the locker room. There were twenty lockers, and all of them were empty except the one labeled "Chu."

"Looks like we're pretty busy," I said.

I opened the locker with a thumbprint. Inside were a set of BDUs.

I slid the underwear on and snapped the bra with more experience than one would have thought. They had loaded me in every type of body imaginable over the years. Being a female was nothing new.

The clothes went on in quick order, and I pulled the boots from the locker and sat to pull them on.

I glanced over and saw another woman enter the locker room.

"Gloria," I said as I finished lacing my boot. "How bad is it?"

"We have the transport ready, Matt."

"I'll grab some weapons, and I'll be there ASAP."

"You still have a half hour of adaptive time before we leave."

"Don't need it," I said. "Been a girl before."

"But—"

"I'll adapt on the transport."

"Roger that."

I stood and followed the soldier to the armory where I donned the body armor and weapons of the trade. I pulled two extra combat knives from the rack and attached them to my harness.

Chu's body was strong, but not as strong as it could have been if she had been a large man. But she would be fast, and speed meant more than strength in the middle of large number of people. Her size would also make her a smaller target.

I wasn't dissatisfied with what I had to work with; I just needed to plan accordingly.

Slipping the two knives into sheaths, I turned to Gloria Dans. "Let's do this. You can give me a SitRep on the transport."

She nodded.

* * *

"Really getting tired of seeing this," I said.

"It seems to be getting worse," Gloria said.

"It always does near the end. Most of what's left are the fanatics. The regulars have left the company by this point. The DU was the same. The last days featured some of the most brutal fighting."

"You were in the DU?" she asked. "I thought the Agent program started after that war."

"It did. I was a regular grunt back then."

"That was seventy years ago."

"That it was, Major."

She nodded.

I looked at the display. "This will do."

"We're still pretty high, ma'am," the pilot said.

"Don't worry about it," I said and winked at Gloria. "Meet you at the extraction point, Major."

"What the—"

The pilot hadn't expected me to jump out of the craft. We were only fifty feet above the tops of the buildings. Not too difficult for an Agent. I landed with suitable flair, the prerequisite knee and fist hitting the ground.

"Not sure if that is necessary *every* single time," Dans said over the comm.

"Of course it is," I said.

She chuckled. "Of course it is."

I grinned at the flyer as it cruised into the darkness. Gloria had sent me out on more missions than most of the other handlers at our hub. We weren't the closest hub to this particular action, but it seemed that JalCom was turning up the heat as far as they could before they went down. It was obvious they were done, but some of the company heads would rather destroy everything than let Obsidian win. I never understood this mindset. All it did was get more of their people killed. I remembered a country before the Corporations that would have fought to the last breath, but Corporations were different. Most of their people had already left their employ, but there was a core of fanatical forces that would fight until told by their "Kings" to stop.

And those "Kings" were going to fight to the end. Or their people would. When there was no one between them and the warriors of Obsidian, they would surrender. They wouldn't die for their cause like they expected their most loyal forces to. We'd all be better off if they would load up our boy, Gaunt, and just remove the Heads.

Or I would gladly do the job. Almost any of the imprints would be happy to do it.

Obsidian wouldn't allow that. After all the pawns were dead, the Kings and Queens would be absorbed into the great corporate machine. Meanwhile, their soldiers died.

I remembered the time before the Corporations were in charge. I got to watch the greatest country in the world collapse around me and become something else as I grew up.

But we are what we are, and the price I paid for the chance at immortality was to serve one of them. So, I did the jobs and watched as the best of those Corporations slowly fell into the same pattern as the others. Obsidian used to be something to be proud of. It had slipped into the gray area between good and bad a long time ago. I felt like I was seeing more and more of the darkness lately.

"Maybe ending this war will give us time to get some of it back," I said as I looked over the edge of the building I had landed on.

I shook my head, dropped over that edge, and caught a ledge about thirty feet down, then dropped another thirty or so to grab another ledge. Many of the new Agents were more hesitant about doing the incredible things they were capable of.

I had been doing them for over a decade and didn't think twice about dropping over the edge of a sixty-story building. Each drop took me that much closer to the ground, and I landed lightly.

I accessed the visor of my helmet and located a sizeable group of our people who were pinned down.

"That's my first target," I murmured and launched forward down the street, dodging people running the other way.

There were always innocent people involved these days. JalCom didn't care about collateral damage anymore, and I wasn't sure Obsidian did either. The soldiers still cared, and they tried to mitigate the damage as well as they could. That was part of the reason they were pinned down at the moment. They had to keep the JalCom forces engaged while the civilians escaped the warzone.

"Allied reinforcements incoming."

Gloria was informing the Obsidians I was coming.

"How many should I expect, ma'am?"

"One."

"One, ma'am?"

"One is all you will need."

"Oh shit," I heard, as he still had the button pushed. "Agent inbound! Look sharp!"

I heard part of that in stereo because my hearing picked it up from just ahead.

"Ally, incoming!" I yelled.

"Incoming!"

I leapt over a car and walked into a position where fifteen soldiers crouched behind the crumbled walls of a fallen building.

I crouched beside the sergeant. "My sources say there are close to two hundred JCs closing. Keep a sharp eye out. I'll handle them. If any make it past me, shoot them."

"Yes, ma'am."

I nodded.

"Two hundred is a lot, ma'am. Are you sure?"

I grinned. "Don't worry, Sarge, I got this."

He was still looking doubtful as I drew two combat knives and jumped straight up twenty feet to clear the ragged wall between them and the approaching forces.

The helmet HUD showed a concentrated group of red dots, and I charged out of the darkness into their midst. Blades flashed, men and women screamed, and I left a trail of blood behind me as I entered the night, once more, on a direct course with another cluster of red dots.

Three JalCom soldiers made it past my assault, and I heard the gunfire as they ran into our boys. It took me less then fifteen minutes to slaughter two hundred and sixteen of them. I found myself hesitating at several points, but the dead behind the JalCom forces changed my mind. There were soldiers lying in the streets, but that was to be expected. What caused me to withdraw any pity I felt for the JCs was the family of five lying in the ally where they had been hiding.

The JCs had shown no mercy, so I served them their own treatment. If I hadn't seen the three that made it past me killed, I would have pursued them and seen to it myself.

I crouched atop a building and watched the Obsidian soldiers leave their position and follow my trail of death as the sun lightened the horizon.

The final days were always the worst.

I turned and crossed the rooftop, then jumped to another, quickly making my way to the medical center where the transport would be waiting.

I slipped inside the door, and the pilot gasped. I was covered in blood.

He looked at me with wide eyes, several times as the transport lifted off. He stopped looking when I grinned. It had to be a little disconcerting to see the Cheshire Cat grin on my blood-soaked face.

"Please, stop that, Mathew," Gloria said. "I don't want to have to bring in a new pilot."

"What? What'd I do?"

"And can you make sure you clean up well before giving the body back to Chu. You left blood in Denny's hair. He freaked out just a little. Chu is a sweet girl and doesn't need the trauma."

"What the hell is she doing in the Agent program?"

"Body donor, only. Blanks are getting rare."

"Is there something going on I need to know about?"

"No, sir. You just broke the back of JalCom's final action, though," she said with her head cocked to the side.

I heard a couple of the words from the report. There was no context, but I wasn't sure I needed any context to know what was happening. I had heard the phrase, "west coast" and another word that put a scowl on my face. "Teledyne."

* * *

"Shit," I said as the latest upload merged with my consciousness.

"That doesn't sound very good," Nathaniel Bern said.

"You got that right, Doc."

"What's going on?"

I was sitting across from him in the diner I had added to the little, virtual city I had built inside the data bank where they kept us.

"JalCom is down for the count, but I don't think we're going to get a break anytime soon. I heard some talk about Teledyne when I was returning from this one."

"That's not good," he said. "Teledyne has some impressive nanotech. Their Specialists are every bit as powerful as Obsidian's Agents."

"If they're really about to go toe-to-toe with a giant like Teledyne, it'll get bloody."

"I don't know if they truly understand how bad this could get," Bern said. "Teledyne's tech is every bit as advanced as Obsidian's.

The only true advantage Obsidian has is the Agent imprint program."

"That's a pretty strong advantage."

"True."

"Have you spoken with Stephen lately?" I asked.

"I haven't." Bern looked around. "That man makes me nervous."

"You don't know the half of it," I said. "He said the latest upload was interesting. They took imprints of over forty martial artists and combined the knowledge base into one skill package which they uploaded into him."

"That sounds a great deal like one of the projects I was working on," he said.

"I think that may be why the Doc out there is up on the top floor. Gina says she hasn't seen him in quite a while."

"It has been a long time since I was uploaded back into the database."

I nodded and remained quiet for a minute, drinking my virtual coffee. "So, how much do you know about Teledyne? I doubt they're going to let me retire anytime soon if they've already kicked that bear."

"They're big. As big as Obsidian. They got their nanite breakthrough at the same time as Obsidian, thanks to a double agent with way too many doubles before the agent. I'm still uncertain what happened there. He was the guy sent in to procure an astounding new technology. When everything shook out, he had given it to both Companies, and he became the first to be augmented with them. Not sure which company was behind that, or if he had it done in the facility before leaving, but he became persona non grata with both."

"Damn, that took some nerve. Not a lot of sense, but a whole pile of nerve."

"It did."

"So, their nanites are just as advanced as ours."

"They may be ahead of us, a little, with the nanotech. But they can't do what we can with the imprints. That's all thanks to you, my friend."

"Me?"

"You gave us a steady template to build from. With that template, we've made imprints that survive in different bodies all the time. Before my outside self stopped being uploaded, they were changing things in the other databases."

"What sort of things?"

"They did away with the whole world inside the machine. This is the only one that is left. If they do away with the world here, they would have to remove you."

"What's that mean for the imprints? Would they start going crazy again?"

"No," he said. "They are stable imprints, and they aren't conscious of the time in the machine like we are."

"Damn," I said.

"Even all of these imprints inside the construct are different." He motioned to the various people walking by the picture window. "These are like us in that they absorb what the uploads know when they are uploaded, but they aren't part of the download. The download comes from the file, and that file has no memory of the interactions between the ones inside the construct."

"That's way too complicated. I distinctly remember that I remember the machine while I'm out there."

"That's because you're an Admin. Your file is always your file."

"Yep, complicated. How did the others get that way?"

Bern cocked his head to the side a little. "Really? You don't know?"

"What?"

"When I set you up with the Admin codes, you did this as you built the construct."

"Umm."

"Yeah." He shrugged. "You're the one who did this."

"But you have Admin codes too."

"I don't have codes that allow me to do what you do. I have codes so I can access a lot of systems from the computer, though."

"But you remember your time in the machine, don't you?"

"I do have limited Admin access so, yes, I do remember."

"How do you have less access than I do when you gave it to me in the first place?"

"It's how everything was set up. There was a limited time when you uploaded me to the system, and some of the access I gave you wasn't there for me. I have a feeling they'll never give me that sort of access again."

"Well, I'll be damned."

* * *

I crouched on top of the hotel, looking over the edge at the approaching motorcade. The body I rode was a beast. He was six feet, three inches tall, and his dense musculature brought him in at close to four hundred pounds.

I had done the prerequisite testing that told me what the limitations of the body would be. This one would hit like a truck.

"Sadly," I said, quietly, as I raised the rifle. "I won't be punching anything."

Just as my scope settled on the driver of the second car, I caught a blur of motion in my peripheral vision. I kicked back from the raised edge of the building, and a knife that would have sunk into my neck impaled my right bicep.

I rolled backward and back to my feet.

"You're faster than I expected," the small redhead that stood where I had been crouched said.

She was, perhaps, five feet three inches tall, with flaming red hair that was tied back. She was well built, and I was sure those looks had distracted many a man long enough for her next attack to reach them.

She covered the distance between us in a split second, but I struck before she expected it. My left hand slapped her aside, and she tumbled across the roof.

Then I reached up to my right arm and pulled the combat knife from my biceps. Over half the blade had sunk in, which said something about the force she had used to strike.

"Girl, I don't want to kill you, and you don't want to be dead. I suggest you leave me to my job."

"Can't let you kill the boss man," she said.

"Wasn't planning to," I said. "But now that you've interfered, the parameters have changed. A message was to be sent. Now, you made me miss that message. If your boss makes it to the meeting he is going to attend, there's nothing I can do to prevent it."

"That's only if you survive long enough to do anything," she said and charged forward again.

The blade was aimed at my groin, but I twisted just enough to take the hit to my thigh. She wasn't so lucky. As her blade sank into the dense muscle, my hands settled alongside her head.

With a savage twist, I sent her headless body tumbling away from me.

"Damn it," I mumbled as I dropped the head, pulled the knife from my leg, and returned to the edge of the roof.

The motorcade was gone, and now, I would have to kill a lot of people.

I looked back at the girl. She had been as strong as I was when I was a female Agent. Bern was right. These Specialists would be a whole new level of bad for us.

I shook my head and turned away from the corpse. "I guess it's time to clean up the mess."

I looked down at the red splatter that covered the front of my coat. "Guess this one is ruined." I shrugged. "Only gets worse from here."

* * *

"Did you stop the meeting?" Gloria Dans asked. She sat behind a large, mahogany desk. Her office had very few decorations, which surprised me a little. Most of them had an I Love Me wall.

"Didn't manage to stop it, so I had to go to Plan B."

"That's unfortunate," she said. "Will we need a cleaning crew?"

I pointed to the blood covering the clothes I wore.

"Yeah, I guess that's a dumb question." She shook her head. "I thought you were supposed to cripple the motorcade so they missed the meeting."

"Ran into one of those Specialists," I said. "They're gonna be a problem."

"We have more Agents than they have Specialists," she said.

"That may be true. But it's gonna get bloody."

"If it was easy, we'd just let the officers do it."

"Uh, Major?"

"What?"

"Last time I checked, you are an officer."

"Doesn't make it any less true."

I laughed. "True enough."

I turned away from the major and headed toward the showers. "You know where to find me when you need me."

"Actually, we have another mission for you before you upload," she said.

"That's unusual," I said, halting at the door. "What is it?"

"Simple bodyguard assignment. One of the VIPs is in town and wants some muscle in her vanguard."

"Don't they have any Corporate Guards with them?"

"Most of the Agents in the area are busy," she said. "I could download one to the body you're in and send him, but I thought you might like the job. Should be easy work. You can have the rest of the week in the body to stretch your legs. The Head needs you for two days; her guys will arrive by then. You're on your own for the rest of the week. Have fun."

"Now, *that*, is what I like to hear. I could use some free time."

"I thought you might appreciate that."

"Thanks, Gloria," I said. "You're not too bad for an officer."

"Don't worry, I'll find some way to re-instill your lack of faith in the officer corps."

I chuckled, and she slid a piece of paper across the desk.

"Take one of the limos and report to this address to pick up Rosalyn. Clean all the blood off Garik's body. Chu found a piece of an ear in her hair. At least, we think it was part of an ear."

"Did you see how much hair she had? How's someone supposed to clean all that? I washed it three times."

"Very carefully," she answered. "Maybe you should be a little cleaner. Stop getting blood everywhere."

"Alright, already. I'll go wash up pretty boy, here," I said with a grin.

"You left that ear on purpose," she said.

"I don't know what you're talking about." I shrugged.

"I told you, Chu is a nice girl."

"Maybe she needs to know what she's being used for," I said.

"Well, that's not really your call to make, Mathew. Sometimes, I forget you're not like the other imprints. Then you do something like this." Her expression had grown serious. "I don't think we should see that particular mistake again."

I shrugged again and left her office. I probably shouldn't have left it, but I *did* feel the girl needed to know what she was into. Everyone involved in the Agent donor plan needed to know what they were allowing Obsidian to do with their bodies. She was right about the imprints. They all came with set parameters. They followed orders without hesitation. Good little soldiers, one and all. They weren't allowed to do that with me. I was still the old curmudgeon they had uploaded so many years ago. Of course, they could violate the contract we had signed, and I had no doubt they would if I lost my usefulness.

But I would do what I thought was right in circumstances where I could. They put up with the little things like that because I closed missions where others failed. I remained useful. And I had a friend or two in the program.

As I took a shower and watched the red circling the drain, I wondered when this had become so common that I could pick up a piece of an ear and bury it in my hair. Sometime in the last twelve years, I had lost something.

It was possible they had already broken my contract and taken that part of me that would have felt disgust at what I did. But I didn't think so. I was pretty sure I had done so much over that twelve years that I was growing immune to the effects. Nine times out of ten, there were multiple copies of me out at the same time. Plus, there was the *me* in the machine. In my years since joining the Agent Program, I had actually lived close to sixty years in accumulated time from the various versions of me. That was a lot of killing, and it would certainly explain some of the way I felt.

I had spent sixty years fighting JalCom in a ten year war. Perhaps that was why I was so disappointed when the thing with Teledyne started up without a single day of peacetime. If not for the peace I had created inside the machine with the construct, I would have been lost a long time ago.

* * *

I pulled the limo into the reserved spot at the front of the Westgate. It was owned by Obsidian, and incoming VIPs would land atop the massive building instead of using standard vehicles. From there they would be driven wherever they desired.

I got to be the driver this time.

"Lucky me," I said as I got out of the driver's seat and walked toward the front door.

A couple of guards stepped out the door.

"You the local guy?" the one on the left asked.

"Yeah, I'm Matt."

"Derick." The speaker pointed at himself and then used his thumb to indicate the other guy. "Leroy."

"It's Will, asshole."

Derick chuckled.

"Will, Leroy…Whatever. He's a new guy," Derick said. "How am I supposed to remember?"

Will made a rude gesture at the other Agent.

"New guys," I said, with a shrug. "What're you gonna do?"

"I know. Right?"

"I'm not that new," Will said. "Just new to you."

"Keep telling yourself that, kid," I said.

"Really?" He held his hands out and shook his head. "Been an active Agent for over a year. What are you, nineteen or twenty?"

I snorted. "The body is twenty, kid. I'm a touch older."

Derick looked at me with an odd expression. "You said your name is Matt?"

"Yep."

"There are rumors of a guy who's been around since the first imprint. His name is Mathew. He's supposed to be from up here."

"You don't say?"

He nodded, with a grunt.

"Oh, that guy's not real," Will said. "Everybody tells stories about him. You know how rumors go around this bunch. Sam even said the guy lives in the computer. You know that's gotta be a lie."

"Why's that?" Derick asked.

"Well, they say he remembers everything, even the time inside the computer. No one remembers time in the system."

"They certainly don't anymore," I said.

"See?" Will said. "He's one of those urban legends."

"Yeah, I guess so," Derick said, but he gave me a sidelong glance. He'd caught the last word of my statement.

"Oh, look," Will said. "Here comes the boss. I don't know how I drew this assignment, but damn."

I turned and saw the most beautiful woman I had ever laid eyes on.

"Best that money can buy," I muttered.

Derick glanced at me again. Will was staring at the gorgeous Corporate Head.

"Eyes out, Leroy," Derick said.

"Right." Will shook his head and took his eyes off the redhead.

Her hand slid across my back as she passed to get into the car.

"So pretty," she said in a soft voice.

I shot a questioning glance at Derick who shook his head minutely in warning.

I slipped around the car and entered the driver's door.

"Derick, join me. The new toy can sit in the front with the pretty one."

The passenger door opened, and Will got in with a frown.

As Derick sat in the backseat alongside the redhead, the panel went up between the front and back. Even with the enhanced hearing of an Agent, I couldn't hear the voices through the panel.

"Soundproof," I said.

"Yeah, Rosalyn doesn't like anyone to hear her conversations. I never get to ride in the back."

"Consider yourself lucky, kid," I said. "The last thing you want is to be in that inner circle."

"I don't know about that. You should hear some of the things she likes to do with her guards. You saw her. She likes to use all that."

"Of course, she does," I said. "She paid a lot of money for it. Trust me, kid. You're better off in the front seat."

"Whatever, man."

I grinned and shook my head. Then I pushed a button on the dash.

"Where to, ma'am?"

"Six eighty three Dumont Drive."

Her voice was soft and would send shivers down the back of most men. I guarantee it had been purchased.

Will had a forlorn look on his face. I shook my head again and pulled out. Thumbing the button, I said, "Yes, ma'am."

He punched the address into the dashboard computer.

"A nightclub." He was grinning.

I sighed. "What's your last name, Will?"

"Dickson," he said.

"How did you get into the program?"

"They recruited me right out of high school. I was a football player. I guess they needed a lot of body donors at the time. I started doing that, but after five years, they loaded a bunch of skill packs and started me in the field. They still upload more experienced Agents when they need to, but not since I got this gig about two months ago."

I nodded and weaved through traffic. This part of the city was always an adventure to navigate.

* * *

The music in the club pounded in my ears. It wasn't my preferred style of music. The flashing lights could easily distract someone, much like our boy, Dickson. I shook my head at the kid. I liked jazz and a little blues, not the electric pounding that seemed popular among the younger generation.

"Who am I kidding?" I asked under my breath. "Everyone is a younger generation."

Rosalyn was gyrating amid a group of men. She liked to toy with them. I'd seen women like her before. I let my eyes scan the crowd, returning to her every so often. She ground herself against a guy for a moment, then she whispered something and walked away from him, laughing.

An angry look crossed his face, but it was fleeting. He stopped dancing and followed, at a distance, as Rosalyn worked her way to the back. She entered the restroom, and he stood outside for a moment before following her in.

I went through the door a second behind him and slipped in front of him faster than his eyes could follow. My hand settled at his throat and lifted him easily from the floor. I held him against the wall and looked back toward the third stall that was opening.

Rosalyn stepped out of the stall in nothing but her smile. She had a sex toy strapped around her waist.

"Down, boy," she said, with a crooked smile. "He's harmless. I told him I would take his if he would take mine. Equitable trade. Please let him down. I have something for him."

I chuckled and dropped the guy. "Good luck, pal."

I turned toward the door and paused. Looking back at the gasping clubber, I said, "She's Management. She comes out of here with a scratch, I'll tear you apart, piece by piece."

She looked at me with a raised eyebrow. She wasn't worried about her nakedness. I could see how Will was so smitten. The woman was as close to perfect as they could make her.

I stepped out the door and stood guard.

"Glad this is a short job," I said.

"She playing with a new toy?" Derick asked as he leaned against the wall beside me.

"Yep. Kind of feel sorry for the guy after seeing what she was going to do to him. I don't even want to know where she was carrying that."

He laughed. "You really are that guy I was talking about, aren't you?"

I shrugged.

"I knew it. No one has as little reaction as you did when they see Ros. That takes age and experience."

"You don't seem to have an issue," I said.

"Been stuck working for her for close to five years."

"She as bad as I think she is?"

"Worse."

"Tell me."

"I can't. Orders."

"I see," I said.

"It's gonna be a hard one tonight. She always starts with one of these guys."

"Starts?"

"That's about all I can say."

I nodded and glanced back toward the door. I heard the guy in the restroom scream as Rosalyn did what she had told him she would do.

I let out a long breath. "Management. What are you gonna do?"

He just nodded.

* * *

The trip from the club to the hotel was much the same as the trip to the club. The divider was up, and Will kept looking into the mirrors.

"Keep your eyes on our surroundings, kid," I said. "She's Management. You don't want what she'll do to you."

"What?"

"Never mind, kid."

He shook his head and looked out the window of the limo. If he'd been in my squad back in the day, I would have slapped the back of his head. He'd been doing this for months. Derick needed to set the kid straight. I could tell he hadn't been out on any missions. You lose that innocence pretty quickly when they drop you into a mob of enemy combatants. I could tell this kid hadn't come out of one of those places covered in blood. Or, maybe, I had just come out of those places so many times, I had forgotten what it was like to be new.

I chuckled.

"What is it?" Will asked.

"Just trying to remember when I was as green as you," I said. "It was a very long time ago, and I probably wouldn't have listened to me either."

"So which imprint are you anyway, Matt?"

"Mathew Kade, of course."

He snorted. "Sure, you are, Mister Urban Legend. I asked for that one, I guess."

I shrugged and grinned at him. I couldn't help liking the kid.

"How'd you end up in that guy? If I looked like that, she'd be all over me."

"Jeez, kid."

"I know, she's Management."

"God, I don't miss my twenties." I turned on the cruise control as we merged onto the Interstate. "I miss Elena, but I don't miss the twenties."

"Who's Elena?"

"She was my wife," I said. "Lost her before I joined the Agent Program."

"That's rough," he said. "I'm never getting married. Too many gorgeous women out there to settle for one."

"You meet the right one, kid, and the others are just shadows."

"She must have been pretty spectacular, then."

"She was."

"Never saw one I would give up the single life for, well, may-be..."

"Don't even say it, kid."

"I know, I know. She's—"

"Management," we said in unison.

He laughed, and I couldn't help laughing along with him.

I turned the manual control back on as we took the off ramp leading to the Westgate. I pulled the car up in front of the building and stepped out. Will was already opening the door for Rosalyn.

"Hmph," I grunted.

Derick stepped out on my side and shook his head.

"Kid's got it bad," I said, with a grin.

Derick didn't answer, and he didn't smile either. He turned toward me as we followed Will and Rosalyn into the lobby.

"You're rear guard till we reach the room. Then, you're done. Our other guys will be here in less than an hour."

"Gotcha."

I fell back and followed the trio to the elevator. I was the last to step inside, and I felt her run her hand along my back.

"Such a pity," she said, just before the door opened, and I stepped out.

I sidestepped to let them proceed toward the double doors of the penthouse suite.

They reached the doors, and she turned to Will. "You, follow me. I think I want to play some more tonight."

She walked into the room after brushing her fingertips across the kid's chest.

He glanced back at me, with the goofiest grin I had ever seen, and shot me a thumbs up sign. Then he followed Rosalyn inside.

I chuckled until I saw Derick. He wouldn't meet my eyes as he said, "You're done, Matt. Enjoy the time off."

I nodded. "Good working with you, Derick. Maybe we'll meet again."

He shrugged. "If orders allow."

I got back on the elevator and took it to the lobby. At least, the kid would have fun tonight. I wasn't sure how much fun, considering what she had done to the guy in the club.

I got off the elevator and left the hotel. There was a bar around the back that several Agents frequented when they were off duty. They were close by if needed, but out of the way of the Heads staying in the Westgate. It's not like many of us had homes we could go to. There were some, but a lot of us were just imprints in donor bodies. I'd run into many of the imprints I was familiar with from the database, but none of them remembered their time inside the computer. It used to be different, but they had found that people went crazy if they remembered. For some reason, I was okay. At least, I thought I was okay. Maybe I was crazy and didn't know it.

I sat there wondering what I would do for five days. I could follow Will's lead and look for company, but all my friends were inside the world I had built inside the database. Everybody thought I missed the time inside my body, but I didn't care about that anymore. Sure, it was fun to feel physical sensation, but, usually, the sensation I felt when outside was pain.

Most of my time outside was on mission, and I was in the center of the war the majority of that time. Imprints specialized in their tasks. When they needed versatility, they called me. A hundred and sixty years of life experience, combined with the years of skill packages, meant I could do almost any mission they wanted. And they used me a lot.

So, I figured I would wander the streets and watch things from the shadows for a few days. I ate a decent meal at the bar and wandered outside and around the corner, where I leaned against a wall for several hours. I was just watching the bar patrons coming and going. It was pure chance I saw the van as it pulled up behind the Westgate.

I was immediately curious, so I stepped a little closer for a better view.

"Take him to medical," Derick said. I saw someone lying on a stretcher. "Make sure they know to override this imprint with his last update."

I moved to the side just a fraction to see who was on the stretcher. My left eye began to twitch. Will Dickson was unconscious, and I guess he was better off that way. He was unclothed and covered in blood.

Derick looked toward the dark area where I stood and lowered his head in shame.

I heard her voice behind Derick in the hallway. "I'm not sure if he's getting better or worse. Perhaps, I'm just bored. Derick, be a doll and bring me a new one tomorrow. Perhaps, a woman. I know, bring me that new one…Chu, I think her name is. Be sure to back up her imprint beforehand. I might like her quite well. Women handle pain much better than men."

I started to step forward, but Derick shook his head just a fraction.

He was right, this was not the time. I had to get back to HQ. I needed to warn Gloria.

* * *

She's Management, Mathew."

"I don't give a shit who she is. There are things that need to be stopped."

Gloria sighed. "But we can't do anything. She is very close to the top. The only thing I can guarantee is that Chu will have that update before she goes. It's too late to stop it."

My eyes narrowed. "Just put me back in the damned computer, Major Dans."

She didn't miss the fact that I didn't use her first name. I had been working with her for years and had been calling her Gloria for the last four.

I walked out of her office and down the ramp to the imprinter.

I sat in the cylinder, then laid back. I said, "Put me back into the machine, Gina."

"I thought you had a few days," she said.

"Not anymore," I said. "Nothing out here for me."

She looked troubled but did as I asked and started the machine.

My virtual eye began to twitch as I sat across the chess board from Doc Bern. It was autumn in the park in the construct, and the trees were brilliant red, yellow, and orange. It was a beautiful scene, but I couldn't enjoy it. The latest upload had been a doozy. And it had come with a plan.

"How much can the Admin codes you installed in me do?"

"That doesn't sound good. What happened?"

"Hypothetically, could I interfere with an upload/download situation?"

"Yes. What happened?"

"I'll fill you in in a minute," I said and called up the virtual console.

They had just placed Chu into the imprinter for her update. No way was that girl going to the Westgate. As soon as they initiated the upload, I initiated a download. I pulled from Chu's file and absorbed all her history. As I watched it play out in my mind, I knew I had done the right thing. I added the newfound understanding to the download and closed the console.

"What did you just do, Mathew?"

"Doc, there's some shady shit going on out there."

"Mathew, I just saw you override a download. I'm going to need a little more than 'shady shit' here."

"I don't think you really want to know, Doc. It's bad."

"Tell me everything."

As I gave Bern the rundown of my last mission, I watched him become increasingly agitated. Finally, he had to stand up and walk away.

"This isn't what my life's work is supposed to be used for, Mathew."

I watched him slowly walk across the park, and I said, "I feel you, Doc."

I spent the next six hours stewing about what I could do, and I came up with very little.

My virtual body lurched as the upload hit.

"Wasn't...supposed...to..."

* * *

I opened my eyes and glanced down and saw Chu's body.

"At least, that worked," I said, under my breath.

I accessed my memories of Chu and smiled at Gina. "I don't know why I needed an update. I had one about three weeks ago."

"Orders from above."

"So be it," I said. "Why am I back this soon?"

"I'm not sure. You're supposed to meet with Major Dans, and she will tell you what's up."

"Thanks, R…Gina." I had almost called her Red. Hopefully she hadn't caught it.

I sat up in the imprinter. Chu was short, her feet dangled six inches from the floor. I jumped down, waved at Gina, and walked up the ramp to the locker room where I retrieved the clothes Chu had worn. Clothes can be worn in the imprinter, but it slowed the machine. For the fastest results, nothing but the body should be in the cylinder.

After dressing, I strode up the ramp where Dans waited with a familiar figure.

Dans gestured toward the man. "Chu, this is Derick Jacobi. He will escort you to meet with a VIP. Miss Danforth is visiting and wishes for someone to join her for dinner."

"Really?" I asked. "That's different."

"Rosalyn doesn't like imprints," Derick said. "She prefers talking to someone with a little less programming."

Gloria shrugged. "Take it for what it is, honey. Fine dining with the elite."

"Sure. I've never met any of the Management before."

I followed Derick out the door, and he opened the door to the limo. I slid into the seat across from Rosalyn Danforth and acted suitably impressed with her beauty.

"It's a pleasure to meet you, ma'am."

"Perhaps," she said. "Alpha romeo eight six four gamechanger."

I felt my body slip into a relaxed state. I overrode it with my Admin codes, but I stayed relaxed.

"Do you affirm that I am Rosalyn Danforth?"

"Yes." I answered as she expected.

She smiled a crooked smile that reminded me of a predator looking at a piece of meat.

"Good," she said and repeated the phrase to release me.

I shook my head as if to clear it. "That was weird."

"You have no idea, honey," she said and patted the seat beside her. "Come here, my pet."

I felt the compulsion to do as she said, and I let it proceed without my override.

I could go into sordid detail about what Rosalyn Danforth did to me, but I would rather not. I will say that I asked for more of everything she did. She wanted innocence, and I gave her just the opposite. I've been wounded in battle in just about every way a person can be injured, and none were any worse than what she did to me. And, every time, I asked for more. By the end of the evening, she was furious and reduced to pummeling me with whatever she could find.

The most infuriating thing I said was in response to one of her questions. I think it was the one right before she unscrewed the bedpost. "Why do you think I wanted to be a donor? I can heal from almost everything."

That evening, Derick pushed the stretcher out of the room and looked down at my bloody grin.

When the elevator doors closed, he said, "You're not Chu."

I spit blood. "How many times?"

"What?"

"How many times…has Dickson been through that?"

"Ten, before she got bored."

"You just…kept bringing him back."

"You *are* that guy we talked about," he said. "You heard that code. You know we don't have any choice. She won't request Chu again. She said you enjoyed it too much. But she'll find another, and it'll happen all over again."

"When…did it come…to this?"

"Been like this for years," he said, his voice filled with bitterness. "Where have you been?"

"I've been out killing…" I coughed. "A bunch of people for these bastards."

I shut up as the elevator doors opened. He pushed the stretcher to the waiting van. The trip to HQ was silent.

I was wheeled through the door, and Gina ran to the stretcher. "Oh, my God! What happened to her?"

Another voice spoke up. "This one seems to have been through one hell of a fight, Major."

"She has, sir."

"Well, what are you waiting for? Get this Agent uploaded and get a SitRep. Then she needs to go to the infirmary."

"So much for not reliving that," I mumbled.

"What did she say?"

"I don't know, sir."

"Get her patched up and, maybe, we'll find out."

"Yes, sir."

I cracked an eye open and saw General Kilroy facing Major Dans. Kilroy was the head of the Philadelphia division. I glanced toward Gloria. What were the odds he would be here at this moment?

Perhaps Gloria was craftier than I had thought.

They wheeled me down to the imprinter and placed me inside. Gina reached across me to attach a lead.

"Seen better...days, Red," I gasped.

"Mathew?"

I gave her a bloody grin.

She said no more and pushed the upload button.

* * *

"Well, that sucked," I said as I staggered and sat down on the bench.

Doc Bern hurried across the park when he saw my reaction.

"I thought they were going to overwrite that."

"Too many people trying to do a good deed, Doc."

"What do you mean?"

"The major had General Kilroy there when the body was brought back in. My guess is they're discussing what just happened. I put a recording of the whole thing in a folder for Gina to deliver to them. That's about all I can do without revealing too much about the workings inside the construct."

"That's still pretty dangerous."

"Can't sit back and do nothing." I shrugged. "Tell me, Doc, how much can you do with your access from in here?"

"I can do a lot. Why?"

I smiled. "I got an idea."

"Is it a better idea than taking Chu's place as a torture victim?"

"I gotta say, Doc. Any plan is better than that one."

He nodded. "Let's hear it."

"It all comes down to you, Doc."

I outlined my plan, and he nodded. "Yes, I can arrange that. I will have to be careful. Can't let it be traced back to us."

"It's a worthy cause, Doc."

"It certainly is," he said. "I'll get on it immediately."

As Bern hurried away to his own virtual terminal, I sat and thought about the latest upload. I had no idea what was going on at the upper levels of Management. Was this widespread, or was Rosalyn just one of a few?

* * *

I was downloaded another twenty times before any of them were uploaded back into the computer. Over a period of a month, twelve of them had returned, and it was understood that the rest wouldn't be returning. I'd spent years of my life dying for Obsidian so they could do any twisted thing they wanted to their own people.

On the outside, it had been a month, but I had absorbed a year of life memories as twelve of me had gone on different missions around the world. What they had discovered troubled me. The war with Teledyne was hot in almost every country. It had been bloody. The bigger population centers were suffering. I remembered the Food Riots while the JalCom war was going on, and it looked like they would happen again, but on a larger scale this time.

This was going to be a tougher war than the last one, and *it* had been a rough one. Not as bloody as the DU, perhaps. But Teledyne was looking to be even worse. Agents and Specialists against regular soldiers tended to be one-sided affairs, and the common soldiers on both sides of the conflict suffered for it. I had done my share of hitting JalCom forces and was no stranger to it, but lately? Lately, I was having trouble with it.

Then an upload came that surprised me. It wasn't from one of my downloads, and I thought it was a mistake until I watched this young man's life as it occurred. And where it stopped. Next came the download that went out.

"That's going to be interesting," I said and entered the huge town square I had created for all of us.

Standing in the center of the square, near the park benches I had placed around the giant oak tree, was a twenty year old with slightly Asian features. He was looking around in wonder.

"Welcome, Lee. As far as POW camps go, this is one of the nicer ones."

"I'm not dreaming, then." His voice was filled with disappointment.

"No, kid. You're not dreaming. And the last thing you remember *did* happen."

He sat, heavily, on the bench behind him.

"They grabbed me from my car," he said.

"I know, kid. You're not the first. You are the first that was uploaded like this, though."

"Like what?"

"It doesn't matter," I said. "You're here, and you, the you that's standing right there, are never leaving. The one in the data bank? I'm not sure, but I think they'll delete it before too long. That's why I pulled you out. It's not the life you deserve, but it's the life I can provide for…"

"What?"

"Yeah, they just deleted the one they uploaded."

"What do you mean?"

"I guess I can tell you a story about the guy who became immortal. Then I can introduce you to some of the others I pulled before they were deleted. You'll like Lucy. She's always in the gardens." I motioned for him to join me. "Walk with me."

Whatever they had in mind for my latest download involved this kid who was in the wrong place at the wrong time.

* * *

I opened my eyes; my head hurt.

"That's different," I said as I sat up. It was much more difficult than usual. "No nanites."

"Just take a minute, sir."

I looked around for Gina, but she wasn't at her console. "Where's Gina?"

"She was reassigned, sir," the young man who greeted me said.

He was small framed with blond hair and blue eyes. His voice was soft and had a northeast accent. I hated him already.

"She's been here for over a decade," I said. "Reassigned?"

"I actually think she is retiring, sir. She was moved down to Charlotte for debriefing before her retirement."

"I see," I said and rose from the imprinter. It felt so strange being in a body with no nanites. I had spent decades in the Agent program and had never been downloaded into a regular body. At least, not that I knew of.

"I am Simon, Simon Gravely."

"Well, hi, Simon. Any idea why I'm in a regular body this time?"

"None, sir. If you'll hold on a minute, I'll escort you to the locker room. I just have one more thing to do…" He punched a code into the console. "Just deleting a file."

I was glad I had initiated the construct to pull the kid out. I had a feeling I knew what file he was deleting. I knew it wasn't mine. It would take much longer than the time he spent on this one. They would have to burn out the whole damn system to get rid of me.

He joined me and offered support as I walked unsteadily up the ramp. "It will take you a little time to get used to the body, but you will be fine."

I grunted as we entered the locker room.

"Once you are dressed, report to the major, sir."

"Will do."

I watched the new imprinter tech leave and opened the locker marked Lee Yen.

"Poor kid," I said under my breath. "Hope he can find some solace in the Construct."

When I was done, I walked a little steadier. At the top of the ramp that circled the facility, I entered Gloria's office.

"Mathew," she said. "Have a seat."

I sat across from her and looked around at the boxes in the office.

She shrugged when my gaze returned to her. "No good deed goes unpunished."

"I'm sorry."

"You didn't do this," she said. "You told me what was going to happen, and I did what I could. Not enough for that poor girl, but at least we had that update to put into her body so she wouldn't have to live it."

I looked at her with my eyebrows raised.

"We all did what we thought was right, Mathew. I know what you did, and I saw the price you paid. No one else realizes Chu is still an innocent after that performance. Mysteriously, she was retired shortly after the incident. I don't know how you do half the things you do, but you need to be very careful after the replacement arrives. They're cleaning house, and I don't want this to come down on you."

"I reckon they are," I said, with a nod. "I covered myself. If I'd known what you had planned, I could have done things a little different."

"And I know you would have stuck your neck out even further than you did, Mathew. But you'll need to tread lightly from here on out."

"You too, Gloria. It's been a pleasure working with you." I looked around the office again. "So, what's the deal with this new job?"

"We've lost a lot of Agents to Teledyne's Specialists. We need to know how they do what they do. We need an inside man."

"This guy?"

"He's just been accepted into the Specialist program. He thinks it's an—"

"Intern job with Invicta Securities," I said.

"That is why you're the man for this job," she said. "None of the other imprints can take that file and incorporate it into itself. You're unique."

"That's why I'm still here," I said. "They'd have purged me a long time ago if I wasn't useful."

She nodded.

"Frankly, I'm surprised they trust me after what I've seen."

"No one knows what you've seen, Mathew. The only ones who've seen the footage are transferring out. Kilroy's investigation has been halted, and the sharks are circling. Even Bern was sent south. They're cleaning house. If you keep your head down, you'll just be another imprint to them."

"And Red?" I asked.

"She accepted early retirement."

"What's to keep me from disappearing while I'm on the west coast? Why would you put that sort of opportunity in front of me?"

"Choices, Mathew. We all deserve our choices."

I nodded. "It *has* been a pleasure, Gloria."

"We made some history here, Mathew Kade."

"We may not be finished yet," I said. "Time will tell."

"I fear we have some dark days ahead of us," she said. "It's been an honor to work with you, sir."

"None of that sir crap; I work for a living."

"You should outrank any officer in the OAS on seniority alone. No one has served Obsidian as long as you. I'll sir you if I want." She tapped the insignia on her uniform. "These say I can."

I chuckled. "Officers."

"Good luck, Mathew. If you make it back, I wish you the best. If you don't, I still wish you the best. Your transport is waiting on the roof. It will deposit you back at your...or more accurately...*his* home in Oakland. The car is already there, and Agents have been sent to keep the illusion he's been home over the weekend. You report to Invicta Tuesday morning."

I stood and nodded to Gloria. It was probably the last time I would see her. I was uncertain whether her transfer involved disappearing, and I worried that Gina was retired in a more permanent fashion than the new tech had mentioned. Now, I had found out that Bern was on his way south, too? Just who was Rosalyn Danforth? And how did she wield that much power?

* * *

I could see why they had accepted Yen into the Specialist program. Unlike Agents, they couldn't be loaded with imprints. Yen was a patriot of sorts. A nation hadn't earned that patriotism. He believed in Teledyne. He believed Obsidian was the Devil on Earth, and he believed Agents were the demons. I wasn't sure he was wrong.

I had been disillusioned before I met Danforth. What she had done was a travesty. I knew Gloria had sent me here as a way out if I wanted to disappear, and I wasn't sure it wouldn't happen. Whatever I decided, I would proceed with the mission until I was sure. The *me* in the machine was still there, and I wasn't sure how I felt about deserting him/me.

I drove Lee's car onto the freeway and initiated the cruise control. It left me free to do some thinking. The sun shone through the smog in several places. The last ten years, and the advancements in electric motors, had been good for the environment. At least, good in the smog-covered west coast. Some of the places where that technology had been used weren't doing as well. But there was always a cost. The east coast was making advancements in electric motors too, but there were a lot more gasoline-powered vehicles there.

The fuel-powered vehicles were here, but the regulations had become pretty harsh, even before the Corporate takeover. You'd find more gas burners in the rural areas than you would in the urban sprawl.

I took a deep breath as I stopped the car in front of a skyscraper three hours later. I'm pretty sure traffic would always suck in the city.

"Last chance to walk away and disappear," I said. "Nobody would come looking."

If I chose to leave after joining the Specialists, I figured *they* would come looking.

I shook my head. "Not yet. I need to know if I was fighting on the right side."

I had a feeling the answer would be painful. If Obsidian was run by people like Rosalyn…

I let the thought drift away and walked into the building.

There was an information desk just across the lobby. Or, more accurately, a security desk. The pretty brunette behind the desk could have snapped my body into pieces. If you knew what to look for, you could always pick out the enhanced. They were like coiled springs. They were stiller than most people because they had to consciously make sure their moves were slower. So, they actually moved less than a normal person.

"May I help you?" she asked as I approached.

I handed her the letter I carried. "I'm supposed to have an interview today."

"Name?"

"Yen, Lee Yen."

She nodded. "I have you down for an interview with Mister Galley. Take a seat over there, and I'll tell him you're here."

I sat and watched the Specialist get up and exit the lobby. She wouldn't leave me there alone without surveillance of some sort, so I played the part of the anxious young man waiting for an interview. The papers in my hand bounced as I fidgeted. I had almost forgotten a time when I fidgeted. You train yourself to be still. The movements of the enhanced could be much more dangerous than those of a regular person.

She was suddenly right there. "He'll see you now."

I jumped. Everything was swimming as though it were covered in molasses. My body was not as fast as I was used to. This was what it was like to face one of us. I had gotten so used to being Superman, I had forgotten what it was like to be Jimmy Olsen. It was a little intimidating.

She chuckled as I stood up.

"Surprised me," I said. "Guess I was lost in my head." I snorted. "Maybe you're just really fast."

"You have no idea, kid." She grinned and headed back to her desk.

"Really? Kid?" I said under my breath. "You're, maybe, a biscuit older than me."

"Aren't you sweet? I'm touched you think so." She pointed to a door on the left side of the lobby. "Galley's in there."

I let my hands shake a little with nervousness, much like a normal person would if someone heard them mutter something from twenty feet away.

"Don't worry, honey, you'll do just fine. Welcome to Invicta Securities."

"Thank you," I said as I passed her desk on my way to the door.

The office I entered was sparse. A man in his sixties sat behind a desk. He was obviously not a Specialist, but Lee wouldn't know what a Specialist was.

"Take a seat, Mister Yen."

The man's voice was gruff, and his huge mustache waved as he spoke. He reminded me of an actor from a long time ago, one who did commercials about diabetes.

"Something amusing, Mister Yen?"

"No, sir." I sat down in the chair opposite him.

"I'm Jerrod Galley. I'll be the one deciding whether you are Invicta material."

"Yes, sir."

"As you know, entry into any of the major branches of our military is through the various security firms. We're what people used to consider basic training. Some of our people never move up into the TAF. And we do need people right here. My first question is, what are your intentions? Are you looking for a security job, or are you looking for a service job?"

"I'm looking for a service job, sir."

"Good, good. We need soldiers as bad as ever."

"I'm ready to serve, sir."

With his next questions, he probed the history of Lee Yen. All were facts known to them, but they were ascertaining whether any of those facts were incorrect. Most involved his lack of family or friends. I understood the probing. Bern had recruited me for the same reasons. There was no one who would miss me if I disappeared.

Three hours after I sat in the chair, he asked, "Have you heard of the Specialists?"

Rumors had been floating around, and Lee had heard them, just like everyone else.

"Rumors. Not sure if I believe some of the claims."

"The program is very real, and we would like to have you. Before we go into specifics, you'll need to sign the nondisclosure agreement. To sign the NDA, you'll have to sign these."

He pulled a stack of papers and a tablet from the desk. "First, you'll sign the paperwork, then you'll sign again on the tablet. Welcome to Invicta Securities, Mister Yen."

"Thank you, sir."

* * *

I wasn't prepared for the pain. I'd never actually gone through the nanite process.

"I warned you," said Doctor Li. "It hurts. The nanites' first task is to replicate themselves until they saturate the body. That is the painful part. Eat the rations."

I chewed a dried fruit bar that tasted like shit.

"Once they achieve saturation, the pain will lessen. Then they will begin to build. You must eat. The more you eat, the faster the nanites work. Your next few days will be spent…" She paused and shrugged. "…eating."

I groaned as another wave of pain washed over me.

"Eat faster, Mister Yen. If the nanites don't have fuel, they *will* use you as their fuel. That's the pain you feel. If you eat enough, it will be minimal."

I could deal with the pain; Rosalyn had done far worse. But Lee Yen had never felt that level of pain before, and I was him.

I ate the fruit bar and opened another.

"Good," Li said as she rose from the stool across from me. "Continue. I will be observing from the office. Eat."

I spent three hours eating the shitty ration bars, but they staved off the worst of the pain as the nanites Li had injected into me did their job.

"You may stop eating, Mister Yen. The nanites have reached saturation, and they will now begin to build. For this part, we will periodically hook you up to an IV, and we will supply you with the supplements they will need to do the structuring. Every six hours, you will report here for an IV. Anytime you feel hungry, you will need to eat. The pills you are receiving will need to be taken every two hours for the next twenty-four."

"Well, this is going to be interesting," I said, under my breath.

"Indeed, it will," Li said over the intercom.

I hadn't expected her to hear me. Perhaps my thoughts needed to remain thoughts. The next day was interesting as Lee's body kept changing. I stumbled and staggered all over the building as the changes occurred.

Twenty-four hours later, I felt much more like an Agent. It seemed a lot faster than I expected. Some of the imprints inside the construct had told me it took weeks for the nanites to finish. It seemed Teledyne's nanites worked faster than Obsidian's.

Li pulled the IV out of my arm with some difficulty. "This is the last of the IVs. You will need to eat often for the next twenty-four hours and take all the supplements provided. Each has its own interval, and you will need to make sure you are fairly accurate. The nanites will be searching for particular elements, and they will need to be present."

"Yes, ma'am."

I took the four bottles that felt heavier than supplements should. They were putting metal inside of me for the nanites to use.

"Go to your quarters, Mister Yen. Keep your movements to a minimum and take the supplements when they instruct. After the next twenty-four hours, the nanites will be finished, and you will need to begin training."

I nodded and slipped the four bottles in my pocket.

"The first pills need to be taken in approximately thirty minutes. Report to your quarters."

I stood, jerkily, and staggered out the door. The woman from the security desk was waiting outside for me.

"After you finish the procedures, you'll need to report to me in the training room. Then we can get down to business." She leaned in close and whispered in my ear, "Believe me, you'll enjoy this part."

She grinned and walked past me to enter the door I had exited.

I knew Lee would be flustered, so I let it happen as if he were still inside his head. In a way, he was. There was just a Kade filter on him. The longer I was inside Yen, the more I missed the days when I was young and dumb. It was a time of innocence I had a hard time remembering. Reliving it was a lot more fun than I would have expected.

* * *

"Jump!"

I leapt across the open space between the two balconies and overshot on purpose. I hit the wall on the other side, but I had brought my arms forward to push myself back out and away. I tumbled past the balcony and dropped the twenty feet to the floor in an uncoordinated landing.

Yelena Jaris, the first person I had seen when I entered Invicta, dropped from the balcony and landed with a leg on each side of my prone form. She landed lightly and sank down to sit on my chest.

"What, exactly, was that?"

"That was painful," I said. "And a lesson learned."

She snickered and rolled quickly to the side.

"Get up, dumbass. Now, you can try again."

I chuckled and stood up. "That was still pretty epic."

"Epic dumbassery."

"I don't think that's a word," I said.

She planted the palm of her hand against my chest with enough force to send me sprawling. "Until you can block that, you don't correct my English. Until then, dumbassery is a word, and the image alongside of it is you…falling from a balcony…and landing on your dumb ass."

I grinned and got back to my feet. I had seen the punch coming from a mile away, but I needed to be Lee Yen.

"Now, get your dumbass back up there and jump again."

"Yes, ma'am."

"Don't you ma'am me," she said, with a scowl. "I'm not that old."

I grinned again and climbed the ladder to the balcony in two short jumps.

I made the jump again and barely crossed the space between the two. I looked down at her with a goofy grin that wasn't all Lee's. She was shaking her head, but I could see the effort she was making to keep from smiling.

"Adequate," she said, looking down at her watch. "Training's done for the day. Hit the showers. We'll continue tomorrow."

I nodded and jumped down to the floor below, tripping slightly as I landed. It was fun keeping enough clumsiness in my movements to disguise my experience. Every lesson, I got a little better at the tasks she assigned me.

I stripped off my exercise clothing and stepped into the shower room. There were eight shower nozzles on each side of the room, and I walked to the nearest. The tiles were gleaming white, and I could see my reflection in the metal of the shower handles. There was movement behind me, and I turned with enhanced speed to find Yelena right in front of me.

She slipped in close. "Perhaps training isn't quite over."

She let her lips touch mine, and her body pressed against me. She bit my lip, and the sharp pain I would have ignored caused me to push back. Lee would not have ignored it.

She tumbled backward, and I sprang forward. "Oh God...I'm sorry."

"This is part of the training," she said. "You're going to have to know how to disguise every facet of what you can do when you're in the field."

She was once again close to me in a flash. "But first, you need to know what you are capable of."

She slammed me against the wall and kissed me forcefully. I didn't resist.

"Don't hold back, Lee," she whispered in my ear. "This is the fun part."

She threw me to the floor, and I rolled to my feet and caught her. I lifted her from the floor and slammed her into the wall as she had done to me. Her legs wrapped around my waist.

"That's what I'm talking about!"

Several hours later, I sat in my quarters in a daze. I've had sex many times since becoming an Agent. But never with another Agent. I had never been able to enjoy the moment as we had done. She wouldn't break if I let the passion out. It had been one hell of an experience, and I had thought nothing could surprise me after a hundred and sixty accumulated years.

* * *

I think they crammed six months of training into the next three weeks. I didn't ask about the training's furious pace. I already knew why it was so, and Lee wouldn't realize the pace was unusual. Regular soldiers got more time in training than Lee was receiving. Teledyne was desperate. They couldn't match Obsidian's numbers. After the nanites were through, Obsidian could put a seasoned Agent in the field in less than a week. Teledyne had to train their own.

"Hey, Sanford," I said to the newest trainer to come through as I passed him in the hall. "You heard from Yelena?"

He looked down. "Sorry, kid."

I took a deep breath. "When?"

She had left the previous week for a short mission to Vegas. She had said she would be back in less than a week.

"We got word this morning," he said, with a shake of his head. "One of those damnable Agents."

I remembered a pretty redhead on a rooftop. It could very well have been me who did it. They send copies of me out all the time. I stood there for a few minutes, and Sanford squeezed my shoulder as he walked past. Another Specialist walked down the hall. He looked older than some of the others. It could have been how he carried himself. Physically, he was about the same as the rest of them.

"I heard that," he said. "Yelena Jaris?"

"You know her?"

"I know most of the Specs down here. She was good."

"She *was*, umm…" I paused.

"Shey," he said and shook my hand. "Seems she meant something to you. I'm sorry. It's rough losing people."

I nodded. I really hoped it hadn't been me.

"I've heard that name," I said. "Spec Shey."

"Been doing this awhile," he said.

"They're talking about giving me my first assignment next week."

"Be careful," he said. "You go up against the big O, don't fight fair. Shoot that bastard from a distance, if possible. And aim for the head; it's the only way to be sure."

"Yes, sir."

He grunted and nodded. I'm not sure he knew what else to say, other than that I was a dead man walking, so he walked past me, toward Li's office.

* * *

"First time on the job?"

I looked at the squad leader, Jackson, as he pushed the button for the garage level. "Yes, sir."

"We're just doing security here. Stay out of the way and keep your eyes on the crowd. If anyone looks like they're planning to interrupt the boss, we intervene. Since this is your first mission, you'll hold back unless I give you an order. Watch how we work so you know what to expect the next time. You're an observer. If it gets so bad I need you active, we're already screwed. Got that?"

"Yes, sir."

"You don't need to sir me." He shook his head. "They don't even polish the new off you guys before they send you out."

"Sorry, si...Boss."

He chuckled. "At least you learn fairly quick."

"I try."

"You'll do, kid."

"Not sure if I'll ever get used to being called kid by people who look the same age as me."

"May as well get used to that," he said. "Almost every Spec is older than you, and we age fast. You ever run into the big O, you'll see just how fast."

I nodded, thinking of Yelena. She had been the first to greet me, and I would miss our time together for many reasons. There had been a lot of evenings in the shower room. And many more in my quarters or hers. It had been more than that, though. We had spent a couple evenings talking about our pasts. Specs didn't need much rest, just like Agents.

"Putting you behind the wheel in the car so we have hands free. Rookie always gets to drive."

"Sure thing, Boss."

"Then let's get to it."

I followed him from the elevator into a brightly lit garage. Jackson reached out and lifted a key from a peg. He threw it to me.

"Fetch the car, kid," he said, with a grin. "Director Shepherd will be down in five minutes."

I strode forward and pressed the button on the key fob. I saw the lights flicker on the second limo in the line. I slipped into the driver's seat and hit the button to start the large car. The hum from the electric power plant was loud. With the shielding the car had, it weighed a lot more than a regular car, and it took a hell of a motor to move it at speed. I missed the old gas-powered cars. I still remembered the car Ring and I had taken for a joy ride all those years ago.

I pulled the limo up in front of Jackson, just as the elevator opened and a large man exited, with two Specs alongside. One was a tall blonde woman and the other was a man who resembled her enough for me to peg them as siblings. I'd heard of the "Twins" several times. They were almost as famous as Spec Shey. They always worked together, and they had taken out a lot of Agents.

The big man in the middle wasn't enhanced like an Agent, but he had other enhancements. He was sculpted, much like Rosalyn Danforth. It seemed to be a thing with Management.

I stayed in the car while Jackson opened the door for Shepherd. He slipped into the backseat, and the twins sat on either side of him. He looked at me and then at Jackson.

"I don't like surprises, Jackson," he said. "New people on my detail are surprises."

"Training mission, sir. He'll stay quietly in the background."

He looked back at me in the mirror. "He better."

I turned my eyes ahead and put the car in drive. "Destination, sir?"

"Four two two Florence," he said.

I punched the numbers into the navigation system. After pulling out into traffic, I pushed the cruise control button and sat back in the seat while the car navigated the streets of Oakland.

Even with the navigator, it took nearly two hours to reach the Palace. It was a high end restaurant for the rich and shameless. I waited until they exited the car, then I passed the key to the valet and followed the others inside. The place was enormous, with gilded columns and arches. It was an extravagant show of wealth, the likes of which I had never seen. The servers, both male and female, were all wearing skimpy attire. All were beautiful. There were several genetically modified servers with fine coats of fur and different traits that were appealing to the eyes. My eye may have twitched a few times as I took in the surroundings. The Geno programs had been shut down years earlier when they discovered the cost of the modifications.

"You're over there, kid." Jackson pointed at a corner room that was separated from the main lounge. "Stand to the left of the door and keep your mouth shut."

"Gotcha, Boss."

I took my position beside the door, and the twins escorted Shepherd inside. In less than ten minutes, I saw another Director crossing the lobby. My eyes narrowed for a split second. This one was known to me, although only from the various files I had been privy to in the computer. Director Reynard was a small man, and he dressed like a peacock. His flamboyant colors drew the eyes of most of the patrons. What was causing the small twitch in my left eye was that Reynard was an Obsidian Director. What the hell was he doing here?

Two of his escorts entered the room with him, and I looked toward Jackson, who shook his head. Two other escorts parked themselves across from us on the right side of the door.

I stilled my body and listened to the conversation inside the room.

"Lawrence! It is so wonderful to see you again."

"Douglas." The voice was Shepherd's. "What have you been up to?"

"I'd say we're kicking your backside, Lawrence. And a nice backside it is. Would you care to take me up on my previous offer?"

"Not today," Shepherd said. "And don't be so sure about that claim. Wait until you see what Riddle has in store for your people."

I swallowed as a hollowness filled me.

"Oh, do tell."

"Can't ruin the surprise," Shepherd said.

"You keep your secrets, Lawrence, and I'll hold on to mine. We have something new for you too. I hope you're not afraid of clowns."

Shepherd chuckled. "Nope."

"Give it time," Reynard said. "What do you think? Shall we share one of the beasts tonight? Or would you like to have some of the other staff?"

"You're the guest, Douglas. You choose."

"I saw a pair of nice ones when I came in. Perhaps the little white one for you, and for obvious reasons, the pretty buckskin horsey for me. Did you see his…"

I tuned them out for my own sanity's sake. I sat there, stewing in a rage I couldn't shake. They were the same. I had seen what Obsidian was like at its upper levels and thought that, just maybe, I was fighting for the wrong side. But that rot was here, too. We were pawns in these monsters' huge game of chess. I could kill them all now, but I needed to get back to the computer and let the me in there know what I had found out here. He was disillusioned, and he might send other versions to escape to the west. It wasn't an escape at all.

The only way I would ever escape was to disappear into the world. I wouldn't be able to do that until I brought this information back to the computer. Then I could begin to plan something. I wasn't sure what that would be, but it needed to be done. I couldn't let them keep using me for their plans, and I couldn't let more of me come to work for these monsters either.

People like the Twins were plucked from the criminal justice system, and they didn't care who they served. But Lee Yen cared. He would have been devastated by what I had just heard. I don't know what the kid would have done, but I knew what I would do. I'd be disappearing into the night very soon, another casualty of the war with the big O. I wondered if Spec Shey knew who his keepers really were. Had Yelena known? Or Sanford? These were people I could have liked as soldiers in the same war as I.

What would *they* think of what I had just learned? Judging by the non-reactions of those around me, I doubted any of them would care. And I felt even more alone in this world than I had felt before. The only place I could go, where that loneliness could fade, was the computer. In there, I had friends. Perhaps, I couldn't reveal to them what was happening inside the machine, but I could meet them outside and let each of them know who they were serving.

But I would have to go back. If I didn't, none of them would learn the truth.

* * *

I watched the cameras as Gloria told my other self he could disappear and wondered if I would come back. I figured there was a fifty-fifty chance at best. As I watched her pack up her things, I wondered if she would make it to Charlotte. I wondered about Gina. Bern was too important to just disappear. Or, at least, I thought he was.

"This doesn't bode well, Mathew."

I glanced to my right where Bern stood watching the same virtual monitor I was.

"Looks bad, Doc," I said.

I watched her sit at her console one last time and press a few buttons. I followed what she did on my own virtual console. She deleted one link inside her files.

"Was that what I think it was?" Bern asked.

"It was her link to me, Doc." I cocked my head to the side a little. "If she doesn't inform her replacement about me or the construct, then my link will never come up when he or she searches for imprints to send on missions."

"She's trying to protect you the only way she can, Mathew."

"She's not going to reach Charlotte," I said. "She knows it."

"I'm afraid you're right, my friend," he said.

"Can you hack into her personal communicator?" I asked. "I think we should try to give her the same thing she gave me, a choice."

He called up his console. "I can."

"We need an emergency diversion of her transport to, say, Jackson, Missouri."

"I can do that. There's a man with a heart condition that needs immediate pickup and transport to Charlotte. I will set the plane she is on to divert and pick him up."

I nodded. "Next question. Can you do some of that magic and give her an ID?"

"It won't hold up long."

"It just needs to hold up long enough for her to get some distance. It's the best we can do from here."

"If they trace it back to this system, they may find us."

"More than likely, they'll think she did it before leaving. I wish we could have done the same for Gina."

He nodded, and his fingers twitched as he began his dive into the computers.

I was following Gloria's progress as she was escorted to a transport at one of the many public airports.

"Done."

I put the information in a file with a single name, Choices, and sent it through her console in her former office.

"That's all we can do," I said. "I guess we can start enjoying our retirement."

"You can slip out whenever you want to," he said. "You've shown that already."

"Doc, there's not anyone out there I want to see. As my downloads are uploaded, we'll be retired. Who would have thought any of this was possible? Besides you, anyway."

"I worry about the physical me outside the machine," he said. "He...I could ruin everything."

"But would you?"

"I wouldn't. But he's not exactly me anymore, is he?"

"Yeah, he'll probably spill his guts, and they'll delete us all."

"Really?"

"It's my new motto, Doc. Expect the worst, and you'll never be disappointed. I'm really tired of being disappointed."

"That's not a healthy outlook, Mathew."

I shrugged. "Then we may as well enjoy whatever time we have before then. Let's throw a deletion party for the Construct!"

I hadn't realized I had pulled quite so many people into the Construct. The town square I had constructed was full of people and imprints. Some of them had been formed from my own patterns, and others had been added after they stopped using my imprint as a template. Others were actual people who had been uploaded into the machine for unknown reasons.

Those reasons seemed more sinister after I had been out there with one of the Directors. I could only hope they were not all like Rosalyn. I didn't have a great deal of faith they were any better than her. If they were, she wouldn't have been able to do what she did with such impunity.

Sometimes, time seemed to move a little differently in the Construct, and it was a complete surprise when the upload of Lee Yen hit my digital consciousness. I dropped to my knees as I lived those days of rediscovered youth and the awful discovery that had sent me back.

I sat down in a corner, away from those still reveling in the square, and tears flowed down my cheeks as I found Yelena Jaris and learned to be young again. The tears were for the other memory of watching the life drain from those same eyes as we struggled in an alley and I killed her, a memory which had just been uploaded from one of my other copies. It wasn't the girl from atop the hotel in Las Vegas....but I'd killed her just the same.

I wasn't sure I would ever be able to forgive myself for what I had done.

* * *

Alarms were going off across the Construct, and I was jolted from my reverie. I had been thinking of Colonel Reggis' reaction when Dans' transfer and ID was traced to his console. It had gone no further, since it was assumed Gloria had done it before she left. Reggis had been furious about her escape.

The alarms quieted when I opened my virtual console.

"Oh, my God," I muttered as I saw Bern race across the square.

I began cycling through the consoles to find what I was looking for. There were two bodies in the imprinters. One was being loaded with Stephen Gaunt. The other was unassigned. The tech who had replaced Gina had fled up the ramp.

Bern looked at the first console I had pulled up. "Oh no."

"They've done it," I said.

"Nukes," Bern said.

"Doc, I need some help here. The EMP is gonna fry this place like cannoli. What happens to all of us?"

"Gone," he said. "Like we never existed."

"Okay, I have a plan. I want to put us all in that unassigned body. The other is a body donor, and I would like to put him back in his own body. Guy named Pratt."

"That will never work," he said. "We'll all be scattered through that brain like confetti."

"I think I can create a program that will keep me as Admin," I said, "but we have to start the download right now. I'll get the program together before I drop."

"It's the only chance you have of pulling it off," he said. "Without that program, we're lost in an ocean of voices."

"I have to try."

"Why not just drop yourself into it and run?"

"The rest of them have the same right to survive that I do."

"Not really. You are a legal individual. None of them are."

"Not arguing; I won't go without taking them with me."

I began shifting numbers in the machine.

"Mathew," he said.

"See ya on the other side, Doc."

He disappeared. I was sending them all from the Construct. Not from the database, but the Construct itself. I worked furiously to fix the program that would give me Admin access in the body.

I watched the time count down, and I knew I wasn't fast enough. Seconds before the machines sparked and died, I dropped into the body without finishing the program.

* * *

I woke, screaming. Screaming amid an ocean of screaming souls. What had I done?

Tiny bits of lucidity flashed across my consciousness. I remembered a face as a man held me down and forced something down my throat. It was some sort of ration bar, and I consumed it. Then I was lost in the maelstrom once again.

Multiple times, I saw the same face. Then it changed. In my tiny moments of clarity, there were others, but I didn't see the man again.

Then there was the pain. Pain that brought forth images of a beautiful woman holding a straight razor. A rage rose from the depths of the maelstrom. After that, all I saw was blood. Then an alley. Then a pale face and a colorful tunic.

* * *

To my utter surprise, I awoke in darkness. The darkness was familiar to me, and I made light. Standing in that darkness was a crowd of people, looking lost and forlorn. They had all been through the same thing I had, and it was terrifying.

One was screaming in fury and trying to hurt another. I looped chains around him and tore him away. Bars formed around him, and I sealed him in a cage for the moment. I recognized his rage, and I remembered what he had done when he came forth from the depths.

"Luca," I said. "You can't do that. You'll stay in the cage until we sort this out."

Doc Bern walked forward. "It didn't work, Mathew."

"I didn't get to finish the program, Doc. Somebody has put us back inside a database, though. I may have time to do it now."

"I'll access the outside and see what's happened. You finish the program in case we need it."

I called up a console and entered my codes. As the system opened for me, I grinned. "Now, let's see what this does."

The program took half an hour to complete, and Bern waited patiently for me to finish.

"Mathew, there is something you need to see."

I followed him to his console to access cameras that showed the streets of a city. It looked like Philly, but it was different. It was dirtier, and there were no cars. I recognized the area.

"These cameras belong to the Mint and the Federal Building. But the Fed is a mess."

"We're in an underground facility under the Mint. And we aren't alone."

He pulled up another console that contained another database with its own imprints.

"There's another database in Philly?"

"You're not going to like the next part," he said.

The camera pointed at a room with a familiar form standing over someone who knelt before her.

"How did that psycho survive? Of all the people who needed to die, why didn't she?"

"I don't know, but she is up to her old tricks. That, my friend, is one of her guards."

"I know exactly who that is," I said. "She's back to torturing her favorite. That's Will Dickson. Even after the world falls, he can't catch a break."

"That's the one you told me about?"

"Yeah, poor kid had such a crush on that psycho bitch."

"It appears to be close to a year after the nukes fell. This place must have been shielded."

"Well, they've screwed up now."

"What?"

"They let us inside."

I began calling up consoles and pulling the imprints into my rudimentary Construct. There were fifty-eight of them in the database and a single file I couldn't access.

The imprints were looking around in wonder. They'd never seen the inside of the machine.

"Welcome," I said. "I am Mathew Kade, and I think you might want to see a few things before I tell you what I have in mind."

"The guy in the machine," I heard someone say.

"Dickson. You, in particular, need to see what's been happening."

After we viewed a string of recordings, we realized very few of those in the database had been spared from the Director.

"Now, I want you to think about what comes next. We're leaving, and I'm offering you the chance to go with us."

"How, exactly, are you planning to do that?"

After I explained the plan to them, and the dangers, I was surprised they all chose to come. Perhaps the will to live was stronger when given a choice.

I waited until they brought in the body we had come in with, at least I think it was.

They were about to add one of the guards into the body, but I switched the program a bit.

"I won't be going, Mathew," Bern said and grasped my hand. "I intend to destroy every system connected to this place, and I'll need to be here for that."

"I can help," I said.

"You're the Admin for the mess you're dropping into that brain. They're what we just went through without *you*. I can't leave people like Rosalyn Danforth with this facility."

I knew he was right.

"Mathew, what you're doing is unprecedented, and I don't know how much of you will end up sacrificed to this gestalt you created. You may lose memories, and you may lose more."

"Doc, I got enough memories to spare and some I'd love to lose. More than likely, I'm coming out the other side as a gibbering idiot, anyway."

"Expect the worst," he said.

"Never disappointed, Doc." I shook his hand. "It's been an honor."

"The honor was mine, Mathew Kade. Now, go save what you can out there."

"I'll do my best, Doc."

I dropped into the body in the imprinter.

* * *

I stood up.

"Alright, Tommy," the tech said. "Report up top."

I nodded, not sure where I was. I knew I needed to get away from this place. I wasn't sure why. I picked up a tan coat from a table as I headed toward the exit and put it on. Then I reached down and picked up a straight razor from the same table.

I left the underground facility and walked out the door of the US Mint in Philly. I wasn't sure what the hell I was doing in there. There was a loud explosion from deep underground, and I paused for a moment. Something was niggling at me. I felt like I had been expecting the sound.

I knew I needed to get far away from this place. I walked into the night, flipping the straight razor open and closed.

I jerked as someone spoke to me.

Hello, Mathew.

"What?" I gasped.

It seems to have been a little harder on your memories than expected, my friend. My name is Stephen Gaunt.

And I am William Childers.

Lee Yen...

Lucy Padapolis...

Will Dickson...

Timmy Bolgeo...

The names continued as I walked down the dark streets that used to teem with life.

I turned east toward the coast. I figured I would need to find a place for all of us in this Fallen World.

# # # # #

About the Author

Christopher Woods, teller of tales, writer of fiction, and professional liar is the author of multiple series. His popular Soulguard series, the Legend series in the Four Horsemen Universe, The Fallen World, and Traitor's Moon in Kevin Steverson's Salvage Universe. He has written ten novels and been featured in several anthologies. As a carpenter of thirty years, he spends his time building, whether it be homes or worlds. He lives in Woodbury, TN with his wonderful wife and daughter. To see what he is doing just go to www.theprofessionalliar.com.

* * * * *

Other Books by Christopher Woods:

This Fallen World
Farmer's Creed
The Island of Doctor Laroue (with Chris Kennedy)
Legend
Daskada, The Legend

Anthologies:

Fistful of Credits
Luck is not a Factor
From the Ashes
We Dare
We Dare: Semper Paratus
When Valor Must Hold
Salvage Conquest
Through the Gate
The Dogs of God
Give Me LibertyCon

* * * * *

The following is an
Excerpt from Book One of The Devil's Gunman:

The Devil's Gunman

Philip Bolger

Available Now from Blood Moon Press

eBook, Audio, and Paperback

Excerpt from "The Devil's Gunman:"

I eased the door open and braced for gunfire or a fireball.

I got neither. I swept the entryway with my rifle's sights. Nothing more offensive than some high school photos glared back at me, and I didn't hear anything running down the hallway or readying a weapon. There were no shouts from police or federal agents, either.

What I did hear, from the living room, was incessant chatter underscored by the occasional interjection of a laugh track. The chatter was accompanied by the soft peripheral glow of my television. Whoever had broken into my house was watching a sitcom.

"I'm unarmed," a man's voice rang out. "So put down the rifle, and let's have a talk."

"The fuck we will," I shouted back. "You broke into my home!"

I moved down the hallway, keeping my rifle on the opening to the living room.

"That's part of what we have to talk about," the voice said. I peered around the corner and saw a young Caucasian man. His pale features and dyed blue hair did little to mask the malicious smirk on his face. He was dressed in an oxford shirt and slacks with a skinny tie, as though he couldn't figure out if he wanted to look like he'd just joined a band or an investment firm. He wore a silver tie clip with a red blood drop on it.

I stood there with my rifle sights on his head.

"I'm here as a messenger," he said and flashed his teeth. I saw pointed incisors. That was enough for me. "This is peaceful, Nicholas. No need to be violent."

I lowered the rifle. I didn't like the prick's condescending tone; he sounded like he enjoyed the sound of his own voice. Those types were always eager to give up information.

445

"Okay, let's talk. Who's the message from?" I asked.

"I hold the honored post of Emissary of the Lyndale Coven," he said politely, examining his nails. "We've taken a professional interest in   you,   and   Coven   leadership   sent   me."

"Oh yeah?" I asked. "What for?"

"To dictate the terms of your surrender," he said, locking eyes with me. His hands twitched, then curled slightly. I imagined him leaping off the couch and knocking me down. I fought the urge to bring the rifle to bear, keeping it at the low ready.

"Thought your kind needed an invite," I said.

The man snarled.

"We both know who built this house. I have a standing invite. The coven master says that the Duke no longer wants you, so you're fair game. Our agreement, which I have right here, has the details."

He pulled a no-shit scroll out of his suit jacket and put it down on my coffee table. I glanced at it. The Lyndale Coven seemed to be under the impression that I belonged to them. I read the word "slave" once, and that was enough for me to decide I wasn't interested.

"No dice," I said.

"These terms are much more charitable than those the Coven Master wanted," he said, warning in his voice. "Oath breakers aren't normally given this kind of clemency."

I didn't have much idea what he meant about oath breakers, but I wasn't going to play ball with this pompous fuck.

"Not charitable enough," I said. "Why do you guys want me? Running out of blood from young clubgoers and runaways?"

The young vampire smiled again, flashing his teeth with what I'm sure he thought was menace.

"It'll certainly improve our coven's standings with the Duke if we prove we can clean up his loose ends. I'm sure you'll make an excellent blood thrall. We'll be taking a pint of blood every month, as—"

I raised the rifle and sighted in on his head. He sighed, and rolled his eyes.

"Look, you primitive ape, guns won't—"

I fired three times, the rounds earth-shatteringly loud in such a tight place. He screamed in pain and terror as the holy rifle's bullets tore through him, the wounds leaving bright blue caverns of light.

His screaming echoed in my head, so I kept shooting. I fired the rest of the magazine until there was nothing left but a corpse, riddled with holes and glowing softly, and me, standing there in my gunpowder-fueled catharsis.

I dropped the mag and slapped in a fresh one, savoring the sound of the bolt sliding forward and knowing that if the emissary had any friends, they too, would be introduced to the kinetic light of St. Joseph.

"Anyone else here? I got more."

* * * * *

Get "The Devil's Gunman" now at: https://www.amazon.com/dp/B07N1QF4MD.

Find out more about Philip S. Bolger and "The Devil's Gunman" at: https://chriskennedypublishing.com/philip-s-bolger/.

* * * * *

The following is an

Excerpt from Book One of The Shadow Lands:

Shadow Lands

Lloyd Behm, II

Available Now from Blood Moon Press

eBook and Paperback

Excerpt from "Shadow Lands:"

The combatants, for lack of a better term, were both resting at the edges of the dance floor. To the left was a very butch-looking blonde in what looked to be purple leather, along with her entourage, while to the right, a petite, dark-skinned Hispanic in a princess outfit stood, surrounded by meat popsicles wrapped in leather. Vampire fashions make no damn sense to me, for what it's worth. There were a few 'normals' huddled against the far wall, which showed signs of someone's face being run along it, repeatedly. Sure enough, the London 'Special' was in the DJ booth. He killed the sound as soon as he realized we were standing there.

"Ladies and gentlemen, may I introduce the final players in our little drama, the Reinhumation Specialists of the Quinton Morris Group!" the Special said into the mike.

"Fuck me running," I said.

"With a rusty chainsaw," Jed finished.

The two groups of vampires turned to face us.

"Remind me to kick Michael in his balls when we get back to the office," I said.

"You're going to have to get in line behind me to do it," Jed replied.

"You can leave now, mortals," the blonde said with a slight German accent. She had occult patterns tattooed around her eyes, which had to be a bitch, because she would have had to have them redone every six months or so. Vampires heal.

"Like, fershure, this totally doesn't involve you," the Hispanic said, her accent pure San Fernando Valley.

"Jed, did I ever tell you how I feel about Valley Girls?" I asked, raising my voice.

"No..."

451

"Can't live with 'em, can't kill 'em," I replied, swinging my UMP up and cratering the Valley vampire's chest with three rounds into the fragile set of blood vessels above the heart. Sure, the pump still works, but there's nothing connected to it for what passes as blood in a vampire to spread. On top of that, company-issue bullets are frangible silver, to which vampires have an adverse reaction.

With that, the dance was on. The damn Special in the DJ booth at least had the good sense to put on Rammstein. *Mien Teil* came thundering out of the speakers as we started killing vampires. Gunny ran his M1897 Trench Gun dry in five shots, dropped it to hang by a patrol sling, and switched to his ancient, family 1911. I ran my UMP dry on Valley Vamp's minions, then dropped the magazine and reloaded in time to dump the second full magazine into the Butch Vampire as she leaped toward the ceiling to clear the tables between us and the dance floor. As soon as Butch Vamp went down, the remaining vampires froze.

"Glamour," the Special called, stepping out of the booth. "I can control a lot of lesser vampires, but not until you got those two randy cunts thinking about how much they hurt."

"You. Fucking. Asshole," I panted.

Combat is cardio, I don't care what anyone else says.

"Yes?" he replied.

I looked him over. He was wearing a red zoot suit—red-pegged trousers and a long red jacket with wide shoulders over the ubiquitous white peasant shirt, topped with a red, wide-brimmed hat. He even had on red-tinted glacier glasses.

I felt his mind try to probe mine, then beamed as he bounced off.

"My that hurt," he replied.

"You know, we don't work with Michelangelo for nothing," Jed replied. Apparently the mind probe had been general, not specific.

I went through the messy side of the business—staking and be-heading—assisted by Capdepon. Crash helped Jed sort out the normal survivors, followed by prepping the live lesser vampires for transport. The Special leaned against a wall, maintaining control of the lesser vampires until we could move them out. Once all the work was done so the cleaners could move in, and the lesser vampires were moved out of Eyelash, I stepped wearily to the Special.

"What's your name?" I asked.

"You can call me," he paused dramatically, "Tim."

I kicked him in the nuts with a steel-toed boot. Even in the undead, it's a sensitive spot.

* * * * *

Get "Shadow Lands" now at:
https://www.amazon.com/dp/B07KX8GHYX/.

Find out more about Lloyd Behm, II and "Shadow Lands" at:
https://chriskennedypublishing.com/imprints-authors/lloyd-behm-ii/.

* * * *

Made in the USA
Columbia, SC
14 March 2023

13784575R00248